Books by Mel Arrighi

DELPHINE   1978

TURKISH WHITE   1977

NAVONA 1000   1976

THE HATCHET MAN   1975

THE DEATH COLLECTION   1975

DADDY PIG   1974

AN ORDINARY MAN   1970

FREAK-OUT   1968

DELPHINE

DELPHINE

Mel Arrighi

NEW YORK   1978   *Atheneum*

Library of Congress Cataloging in Publication Data
Arrighi, Mel.
  Delphine.
  I. Title.
PZ4.A775De [PS3551.R7]   813'.5'4   77-15828
ISBN 0-689-10862-

DEDICATION

Freud says somewhere that the two most important things in life are love and meaningful work. This is for the person who has given me one and has thereby made the other possible, my wife, Patricia Bosworth.

PART ONE

It HAD turned ugly. Eric, when he thought back on it later, couldn't remember the exact moment it started to happen. The dinner party had just seemed to shade into unpleasantness, by degrees.

The conversation was civilized enough. The comments, while sometimes pointed, were never anything that couldn't be undone with a shrug and a smile.

But then Ward Kennan was staring at Christopher Greene and, in his most insultingly amiable tone, was asking, "What can *you* tell us about it? You're not really a man, are you?"

And there was a shocked silence. For there could be no backtracking onto safer ground now. There could no longer be any pretense that everyone liked each other.

When they had gathered in the Hubers' living room for coffee and brandy, there had been no warning signals of trouble ahead. There was the usual small talk, some gossip about friends, a brief discussion of the next season's fashions—Huber Casuals was looking forward to a big year, Jeff told them; Mandy was designing a knockout line.

Then the conversation turned, rather inevitably, to Delphine Heywood. She was the common bond that joined three of them, Mandy, Vivian and Chris, their mutual psychoanalyst. Eric was about to make it a fourth; he was starting with her the very next day.

"When is your appointment?" Mandy Huber asked.

"At two," Eric replied.

"I envy you."

"Envy me? Why?"

"Your first visit." Mandy smiled blissfully at the thought of it. "It's a once-in-a-lifetime experience."

"Maybe so," Eric said. "But I'm scared stiff."

"No need to be scared. Delphine will put you right at ease. I remember my first visit, when I went out of there, I was sailing. It was like I'd found a home, at last."

"What do you call *this* little pad?" Jeff asked, in a good-humored, slightly miffed tone.

"Oh, you know what I mean, Jeff," Mandy murmured. She didn't seem to appreciate this interruption. "You're going to love Delphine," she told Eric. "She's a very warm, very wise woman."

"So I understand," Eric said. "I feel like I know Dr. Heywood already. Vivian has been talking about her for years."

Chris looked over at Vivian Loring curiously. He had been lounging in the armchair, caressing a small, ridged sphere of heavy glass he had picked up from the coffee table—it was the kind one strikes matches on—not entering into the conversation. But now he asked Vivian, "How long have you been going to Delphine?"

"Eight years," Vivian answered.

Beside her, on the couch, Ward snorted. "That long?" He was her lover, but he acted thunderstruck by this bit of information, as if he had never even suspected it. "You've got to be joking!"

"Eight years," Vivian repeated.

"Do you ever graduate?"

"Do you ever know enough about yourself?" she responded sweetly.

It was a reasonable reply, but the pink of Ward's beefy face deepened. Ward Kennan, Eric knew, was very high up at a television network—the East Coast head of programming. He suspected that Kennan wasn't used to being corrected by anybody in the same room with him.

Eric swiftly changed the direction of the conversation. "How did you meet Mandy?" he asked Chris. "At Dr. Heywood's?"

Chris nodded. "I have the hour after hers. Our paths kept crossing. Finally, we got past 'hello.' " He cocked his head with charming, overplayed perplexity. "I don't remember which one of us made the plunge."

"I did," Mandy said. "I'd just seen Chris in his show. I thought he was the most gorgeous man I'd ever seen on a stage."

"Some people think I can act, too," Chris pointed out mildly.

The understatement of it could have been taken for conceit, since Christopher Greene was one of the more highly praised young actors in the theater. But he had a boyish, unassuming quality that kept the comment from sounding smug.

"Your play is about to close, isn't it?" Ward asked.

"It closes a week from Saturday," Chris said. "But we've had a good run. The investors might even turn a small profit." With a slight laugh, he added, "And that's saying a lot these days."

"We must see it before it closes," Vivian said to Ward.

"Why?" Ward asked.

"Because of Chris," she said. "He's supposed to be marvelous in it."

"I hate the theater," Ward said.

He finished his brandy in one swallow. It occurred to Eric

that, besides being a naturally ungracious man, Ward might, also, have a poor tolerance for alcohol. He had seemed to have only a little more to drink than the others, but already he was acting the part of a mean drunk. His upper-crust speech pattern was slurring into an arrogant drawl, and his eyes were dull and hostile. It didn't help, of course, that he obviously didn't want to be there, that he was dining with Vivian's friends only as a grudging concession to her.

Jeff, confronted with a moment of group silence, quickly offered his guests more cognac. Only Ward accepted. Jeff re-filled his snifter from a quaint, cut-glass decanter that looked as if it went back to the Victorian era; it was the sole anachronism in the starkly modern living room.

Chris waited until Ward's snifter was full again. Then he continued the conversation as if it had never stopped. "If you let me know what night you want to come," he said to Vivian, "I'll set aside some house seats for you."

"Oh, would you?" Vivian's voice was eager. With a sidewise glance at her lover, she said, "I don't have to go with Ward. I can take someone else."

"I see you *do* like the theater."

"I love it."

"Let me guess." Chris threw back his head and squinted thoughtfully at Vivian through his thick lashes. Eric realized then that he was somewhat nearsighted, but too vain to wear glasses, and too much the performer to restrict the play of his eyes with contact lenses. "You were an actress once."

Vivian laughed. "No."

"You were never in show business at all?"

Chris's assumption was understandable. Vivian, with her heavily shadowed, exotic eyes, creamy skin, and near-black, curly hair, had a rather theatrical beauty.

"Well," she admitted, "I was a dancer. Ages ago."

"A show dancer?"

"Modern dance. I toured with a company." She shrugged. "I didn't stay with it very long."

"You lost interest?"

"I got married."

Chris went on gazing at her, the charming smile lingering on his lips. It was starting to seem a little strange; not simply because she was a dozen years older than he, but because there was no real intent in his seductiveness. It seemed, rather, to be an exercise in narcissism. He was innocently enjoying his impact on her.

Whatever the reason, it was rash. Ward was staring at him resentfully. It didn't matter that he was a man with power, and that this was a mere actor he could hire and fire. In that moment, with Vivian smiling at Chris, flattered and fascinated, Ward was reduced to something more elemental, the unlucky half of a physical contrast, the coarse-faced, stout, middle-aged man with spiky gray hair, versus the lean, young god, with chestnut curls and perfect features.

"I bet you could still dance, if you wanted to," Chris said to Vivian. "You look in terrific shape."

"Thank you," she said. "I've tried not to go completely to pieces."

Chris fell silent again, but he didn't take his eyes off her. He was still holding the glass sphere in his lap, delicately stroking the rough surface of it with his fingertips. It struck Eric now that Chris had gotten himself trapped, as sometimes happens to very shy people who venture into conversations without knowing how to get out of them.

"Why don't you put that thing down?" Ward snapped. "You're getting me nervous."

Chris looked confused. It took him a moment before he realized what Ward was talking about. Then he glanced down at the glass sphere cradled in his hands, remembering it was there. He put it down on the coffee table. "I didn't mean to upset you," he said. "I like to pick up things and touch them. It's just a habit I have."

"A tic, you mean. Have you talked to Delphine about it?" With a show of falsely genial interest, Ward asked, "Why *are* you going to this shrink?"

Chris's face hardened. "I'd say that was none of your business."

"We all have our secrets, Ward," Eric intervened in a light tone, trying to take the pressure off Chris. "I'm not saying why *I'm* going, either."

Ward wasn't to be diverted. "Right now," he said, "I'm interested in his problem, not yours."

"Why do you care?" Mandy asked. It was clear that she was disturbed, almost panicked, by this turn in the conversation, but she kept up her bright hostess smile. "You met Chris for the first time this evening."

"That's true," Ward said. "But, in a way, I'm getting to know *all* of you for the first time. I mean, I've seen you and Jeff a few times—and I've met Eric before—but we've never really sat around and talked, have we? So, all right, now we're talking."

"Ward, please!" Vivian muttered under her breath.

"We're talking," he repeated, unheeding, "and what do I discover? You all go to the same shrink!"

Jeff raised a finger. "Not me, Captain."

"Except for Jeff," Ward amended. "But I think that's *fascinating*," he went on, in his snarling drawl, "that you all go to this Delphine woman. And, naturally, what I'm curious about is"—he looked around at them with his broad, unfriendly smile—"why are you all sick?"

Perhaps he meant it to be taken as a joke, but nobody smiled.

"The real question is," Eric said, after a moment, "what makes *you* so healthy?"

"He isn't," Vivian said quietly.

"I beg your pardon!" Ward said, giving her a mock-indignant look.

"You drink too much," she said, taking the brandy snifter from his hand and putting it down.

"A very human failing," Ward said. "I drink in my leisure time. But never on the job. I need a clear mind—and a healthy one," he added, with a nod toward Eric "—in my line of work."

"Choosing junk television series?" Chris asked. He was gazing at Ward challengingly.

"It may be junk to you, kid," Ward said, in a tone of amused condescension, "but there's a whole country that prefers it to arty-farty stage plays."

"How can you know that?" Chris wasn't backing off in the slightest. "It's free, so the people take whatever you pour through the tube. But it doesn't mean they *like* it."

"The numbers say they do."

"Yeah, but you're catering to the worst in people. You give them some murderous moron who shoots ten guys every program. Or a fourteen-year-old girl who gets raped with a broomstick. All you're doing is feeding them a sick fantasy!"

"Sure, it's a fantasy. But *I* didn't put it in their heads. It's the way people are. A man wants to beat down his enemies and screw beautiful women."

"I don't believe it!" Chris said emphatically. "A man wants more than that. He wants some beauty—" He was starting to stammer in his intensity. "—some—some *meaning* in his life. He wants—"

Ward cut him off. "What can *you* tell us about it? You're not really a man, are you?"

At last, it had happened. The danger point had been reached and exceeded. If there was any doubt that Ward had gone too far, one had only to look at Chris's face, at the open-mouthed, sick expression on it. It was as if he had just been kicked in the stomach.

It was Mandy who finally broke the silence. "Ward," she began hesitantly, not quite looking at him, "Vivian is one of my dearest friends. For her sake, I arranged this dinner for you." She paused and bit her lip. Then, her eyes downcast, she went on, in a small, timid voice: "I planned the courses carefully—I chose one of the best wines—I invited a couple of people I thought you'd enjoy. And all I can say is "—she looked up at him now, her eyes bright with tears—"you can go fuck yourself!"

Jeff stared at her in astonishment. But Ward rose deliberately, his expression calm, as if she had said exactly what he had expected her to say.

"We must be going," he said. He reached down, took Vivian's arm, and drew her to her feet.

"Won't you stay for another drink?" Jeff blurted out, with the automatic courtesy of the good host.

"I'm afraid we can't. I have to catch one of the opposition's shows. It was a lovely dinner," he said, turning to Mandy, with a bland smile. "Thank you."

Mandy didn't reply.

"Nice seeing you all," Ward said. His sweeping glance included everyone but Chris. "Let's go," he said to Vivian.

Vivian seemed in a daze. But now she looked at Mandy and tried to smile. "Thanks, darling. I'll call you tomorrow."

"Yes," Mandy said, "we'll talk."

"Let's go," Ward repeated. He grabbed Vivian's arm again and all but dragged her away. They disappeared through the archway.

Mandy stared at the half-empty snifters and demitasse cups, the aftermath rubble of her dinner party. "Oh, God," she said softly.

"Mandy, I'm sorry," Chris said. "I should never get into arguments. I—"

"Don't apologize!" Mandy said firmly. "You have *nothing* to apologize for."

Jeff looked at Eric. "Would you mind going down for a moment? To make sure everything's all right?"

"I don't understand," Eric said. "Why?"

Jeff shrugged vaguely. "Ward can get violent."

"Yes, Eric," Mandy said, "I think you'd better."

Eric thought the Hubers were being a little melodramatic. They had mentioned Ward Kennan's supposed "brutal streak" before. But Vivian, who was one of his oldest friends, had never said a word to him about it.

Still, if they insisted, he would humor them. "All right," he said.

Chris rose quickly. "I'll go with you."

"You don't have to."

"You may need help."

Eric was about to say it wasn't likely. Then he realized that Chris might want some excuse to get out of the apartment, for a few minutes' respite from the situation.

"Okay," Eric said. "Come on."

They left the living room, passed through the foyer, and went out into the hall, by the elevator. The OCCUPIED light was on, but, as they came up to it, it went dark. Ward and Vivian had just reached the ground floor. Eric pushed the DOWN button.

"What a mess!" Chris said softly, as they waited.

"Yeah," Eric replied.

Chris said nothing further. His face was somber, and he still seemed a little shaken.

The elevator arrived and they descended to the lobby. It was empty, except for a somnolent doorman. With Eric leading the way, they went out to the street.

As soon as they came out onto the sidewalk, Eric stopped. Ward and Vivian were standing by the curb, twenty yards away, arguing. Eric pushed Chris back and retreated into the doorway.

He peeked out carefully. Behind him, Chris pressed up against him, looking out also. Eric couldn't make out the words of the quarrel, but Ward clearly was the more angry of the two. He gripped Vivian's arms, raising his hand once to signal to a cab coming down Central Park West, but without releasing her, and without interrupting whatever it was he was saying.

Then Vivian was the one who was talking. Eric could hear the desperately reasoning tone in her voice. But Ward wouldn't hear her out. His voice swelled in volume as he cried out, in rage, "Why didn't you defend me?"

Vivian's reply was sharp, and Ward slapped her across the face.

Eric heard Chris take in his breath. "The son of a bitch!" Chris started out from the doorway.

Eric grabbed him by the arm. "Don't be a fool!" he whispered. "Stay out of it!"

Chris tried to pull free of him.

"She doesn't *mind*," Eric whispered insistently.

Chris stared at him uncomprehendingly. Then he looked at Ward and Vivian again.

Vivian had one hand to her cheek, but she was still talking, still trying to reason with Ward.

A taxi swung over to the curb. Ward opened the door, pushed Vivian into the rear seat, and got in after her. The cab pulled away.

Chris gazed after the departing taxi. His handsome face was dark with anger and perplexity.

When Mandy came out of the bathroom, she saw her nightie laid out on the bed. Jeff had arranged it with care, puffing up the filmy fabric at the bosom, pinching it in at the waist, flaring it at the hips. It was like a little person lying there. It was Jeff's usual signal that he wanted to make love.

Mandy pulled her bathrobe a little tighter around her, looked over at Jeff sitting in his pajamas by the window, and wondered how he could even consider it. The evening had been a total disaster, and all she wanted to do now was put an end to it by going to sleep. And yet here Jeff was, ready for sex, as if nothing at all had happened. But, then, being around Vivian always seemed to turn him on. He would probably be fantasizing Vivian's full breasts rather than her flat ones, Vivian's round ass rather than her bony one.

Well, she didn't owe it to him. Delphine had made that much clear. Sex was something for her to give, when *she* was in the mood. It wasn't to be taken as his due.

Anyway, he was far from seeming a desirable specimen at that moment. He was studying the sketch she had left on the bedside table that afternoon, and the downward tilt of his head brought out his second chin. His hair was sticking out at angles and his bushy mustache needed clipping. The stripes of his pajamas made his pot belly look twice its real, considerable size.

Jeff rose and put the sketch back on the bedside table. He looked at her, taking in her expression, then asked, "What are you thinking?"

"About this evening," she said. "Are you ashamed of me?"

"Ashamed? Hell, no!" He laughed. "Intimidated, maybe."

"Intimidated?"

"I didn't know you were such a tigress."

"I'm not."

"I didn't think so. I mean," the joking tone vanished and he reverted to his essential straight-arrow self, "you never even use that kind of language."

"The occasion called for it," Mandy said. She sat on the edge of the bed and patted her neck hair, which was still damp from the bathwater. "Delphine says that if I feel like telling a man to go fuck himself, I should tell him to go fuck himself."

Jeff's eyebrows lifted. "Delphine uses those words?"

"She said it indirectly."

"Well, that's interesting advice." He joined her on the bed. "Just don't try it on any of the big buyers, huh?"

Mandy smiled briefly. It was a preposterous idea, particularly since she never had much of anything to say to the buyers. Jeff always took care of the business side and Mandy restricted herself to the creative area. That was the way Jeff had said it would be when he had picked her out of the graduating class of the Parsons School of Design, finding a designer and a wife in one swoop. It had remained that way through ten years of childless marriage and thirty million dollars of sales volume.

She lay back and rested her head on the pillow. On his side of the bed, Jeff stretched out, turning on his side to look at her. The untouched nightie lay between them, like a sword.

Mandy glanced over at the sketch on the bedside table. "Did you like it?" she asked.

"Like what?"

"My sketch."

"No," Jeff answered. "What were you doing? Fooling around?"

"I was trying out an idea."

"It was no big breakthrough," he said. "There are a hundred other designers trying out that same idea."

Mandy clenched her teeth with annoyance. She had sketched a man-tailored four-part outfit, with a plaid blazer top, solid vest and pants, and a long-sleeved, open-collared shirt. The blazer was unbuttoned and floppy and the whole outfit had the free-flowing look she thought of as distinctively her own.

"It wouldn't hurt if we had a few man-tailored outfits in our line," she said.

"It wouldn't help, either," he said.

"We're getting awfully stodgy," she persisted. "We should try to be a little more with it."

"Let Halston worry about being with it. The bulk of our business comes from those few standard bodies we do every year. The rest is window dressing, and you know it."

"Window dressing can be fun."

"Fun? Where would we be if I let you have fun? Who kept us out of evening pajamas? Me! Some of the other houses took a bath, but we weren't hurt. Trust me."

"Man-tailored suits aren't the same thing as evening pajamas."

"Look, we're not going to have our models coming out looking like George Sand."

He said it with a crisp finality that put an end to the discussion. Jeff always had the last word when it came to the business. He had put in years as a salesman before starting Huber Casuals. He had been out in the field; he knew what people wanted to buy. He could say, as he often did, that it was his marketing sense that had taken the firm from a modest, shoestring beginning to a respectable status as one of the solid houses on Seventh Avenue. But they had leveled off, Mandy thought now, they were in a rut. They had settled in as a nice, medium-sized firm that never did anything exciting, that never forged into the front rank.

"Let's not talk about the business now," Jeff said. He reached over, slipped his hand under her bathrobe, and fondled her breast. He chafed her nipple with his palm. Mandy lay perfectly still for a couple of moments. Then she took his hand by the wrist and put it aside.

"What's the matter?" he asked.

"I'm depressed."

"About what?"

She wondered why he had to ask. His scornful treatment of her sketch was certainly reason enough. But she didn't want to talk about it any more. So, instead, she replied, "About what happened tonight."

"Don't worry about it. It could happen at any dinner party. Ward had too much to drink, that's all."

It wasn't that simple, she knew. It was too pat an explanation for what had been a very ugly scene. She remembered Ward's gloating smile, when he realized he had drawn blood, and the stricken, almost fearful look in Chris's eyes. "Is Chris gay?" she asked.

"I suppose he must be."

"Funny, it never occurred to me."

"He isn't obvious about it. But Ward is in show business. He can smell them out, I guess."

After a moment, Mandy said, "I feel sorry for Vivian."

"There's no need to feel sorry for her."

"Ward is such a pig, and she's so hung up on him."

"Oh, come on!" Jeff said. "She isn't some dewy-eyed kid. She knows exactly what she's doing."

"Does she? She's been obsessed with him for over a year now."

"There's obsession and there's obsession. Don't you think Ward's money has something to do with it?"

"It's got nothing to do with it."

"No? You mean, if Ward was a truck driver, with that terrific personality of his, she'd still be hot to marry him?"

"I guess not," Mandy admitted.

"Let's face it," Jeff said, "Vivian is—well, she's a courtesan."

"That's not true!" she insisted loyally.

"I'm not saying she's a whore," he added quickly.

"What's the difference?"

"A whore sells her body to strangers. A courtesan," he went on, phrasing it carefully, "can be a nice, sophisticated lady like Vivian who depends on her men friends to cover her living costs."

Mandy felt uncomfortable. It wasn't that she hadn't had this thought about Vivian, herself. But she didn't like hearing it from Jeff. "She gets alimony," she pointed out.

"It's not enough. You know it isn't."

"In that case," she said, after a moment, "a lot of the women I know are courtesans."

"I'm not disagreeing," he said.

Mandy looked at him searchingly. Delphine had told her that many men felt compelled to think of all women as whores, as a way of degrading them. It hadn't occurred to her to suspect Jeff of this, but now she was starting to wonder.

"Would *I* make a good courtesan?" she asked.

Jeff was instantly aroused. "You'd be the best," he said. "A champ." His hand went inside her bathrobe again.

This time she didn't resist. She lay still as Jeff pulled open her bathrobe, slipped out of his pajama bottoms, and heaved himself onto her. Only at the last moment did she put her hands up against his shoulders and hold him off. "I don't have big breasts like Vivian."

"Breasts?" He was slightly wild-eyed. "Who cares about breasts? They're vastly overrated."

"If you say so," she murmured. She said nothing more. He was arousing her with his fingertip and she was focusing on the sensation.

Mandy felt herself giving in to it, falling away into desire. But, still, she felt the need to salvage some small shred of self-assertion. Clutching at the mattress beside her, her fingers dug into the smooth nylon that had been laid out for her.

With her first convulsion, as he entered her, she flung the nightie up and away from them.

2

DR. HEYWOOD'S OFFICE was in her apartment, which took up
the bottom floor of a converted townhouse on East Seventy-
fifth Street. The apartment was a little below street level and it
had its own private entrance behind an iron gate. Eric went
down the three steps from the sidewalk, pushed open the gate,
and peered at the name beneath the doorbell to make sure he
had come to the right place. It was printed out in full:
DELPHINE HEYWOOD, M.D.

Eric rang the bell. After a few moments, the door opened
and a rather plump woman in a green print dress smiled out at
him. "You're Eric Bayliss," she said.

"Yes. And you're Dr. Heywood?"

"Delphine," she said, shaking his hand firmly. "Come on in,
Eric."

Eric stepped inside and glanced around. He was at the end of a narrow hall. Through the nearest doorway, a bit of the living room was visible. But the curtains were drawn, there was only a subdued electric light, and, in a brief look, he could see little; he was left simply with an impression of mauve fabric and floral patterns. At the other end of the hallway, the door to an office was ajar.

"Let's go into my office," Delphine said and started down the hallway. As Eric followed her, he noticed that she walked with a slight limp. One of her legs seemed to be shorter than the other.

At the door, she stepped aside and let Eric go into the office first. She followed him in and closed the door.

The curtains were drawn in the office too. But the indirect lighting gave it a warm, homey glow. There was a desk near a book-lined wall. A leather couch was against the opposite wall. Toward the center of the room, two leather armchairs faced each other. Delphine gestured to the armchair that had its back to the door and sat in the other one.

Eric sat. There was a box of Kleenex, near at hand, on a little table beside his chair. He wondered if he was expected to cry on the first visit. He settled back and met Delphine's gaze.

She was, he realized now, less ordinary-looking than he had first thought. She was of an indeterminate age, neither young nor old; in her early forties, perhaps. Her dark-brown hair, which was drawn back along the sides of her head, had threads of gray in it. But her face was without lines; the skin seemed very smooth and quite pale, as if the sunlight never touched it. Her pallor struck Eric as rather odd, since he could hear, from the other side of the curtains, the twittering of birds in a garden that was attached to the apartment.

Delphine's one extraordinary feature—it was what kept her from seeming merely a somewhat matronly, benign medical lady—was her eyes, which were large, gray and remarkably luminescent, as if they had a property of reflecting light in a way that human eyes rarely do. They held on him fixedly now, without blinking.

"You said on the phone that you were a friend of Vivian's," Delphine began. Her voice was low-pitched, soft, and musical. "Have you known her long?"

"Yes, for quite a while. Thirteen or fourteen years. Has she ever mentioned me?"

Delphine smiled slightly. "No, I don't think so."

"Oh." Eric was a bit chastened that Vivian, in her eight years of therapy, had never had reason to bring up his name. "Well, we've had one of these New York friendships. We've gone months without seeing each other at all. I first got to know her in the days she was married to David Loring."

"Yes." She conveyed, somehow, that there was nothing Eric could tell her about Vivian's ex-husband.

"They're both a little older than I am, of course," he went on. "I met them when I got out of college. We had mutual friends. They were practically the first people I looked up when I came to New York."

"But you're from New York, yourself, aren't you?"

"I was born here." With faint astonishment, he asked, "How could you tell?"

"I'm fairly good at placing people by their speech. You speak like a well-educated native of Manhattan."

"I'm a native, I guess, but I don't really feel like one. I lived all over the place when I was growing up. My mother liked to take houses in different parts of the world."

"Why was that?"

"Well, she didn't have to stay in one place, so she didn't. She was a writer."

Eric waited to see if Delphine would make the connection. Right on cue, the realization dawned in her eyes. "Bayliss," she repeated. "Margaret Dare Bayliss?"

"Yes."

He braced himself for the usual gush. But Delphine merely commented, "She was a very famous lady."

"You've read some of her books, I suppose."

"No," Delphine said. "I never read novels."

"Sometimes I wish *I* could say that," Eric said, with a little laugh. "But I have to."

"Why? What do you do?"

"I'm a book editor. With Galton and Hill."

She looked impressed. "That's a very good publisher. Then you must be successful in your field."

"I'd feel more successful if I was doing what I wanted to do." He paused. "I suppose that's why I've come to see you."

"Yes, why *did* you want to see me, Eric?" Her manner, almost imperceptibly, became more professional, and she asked the age-old examining doctor's question. "What seems to be bothering you?"

"Well, nothing is *bothering* me as such," he replied. "I mean, I'm not greatly troubled. I'm not particularly neurotic. I function—I'm in good spirits, most of the time—I'm not subject to fits of depression. From our point of view," he said cheerfully, "that's just as well. As I understand it, if I were deeply neurotic, there wouldn't be much psychiatry could do for me."

"Everyone can be helped," she said.

"Helped, yes. But neurosis can't be cured, right? However," he went on, "if you have a symptom—like insomnia, or a psychosomatic rash—therapy can alleviate it, get rid of it, maybe. Isn't that so?"

"Why don't you just tell me your problem, Eric?" Delphine said gently.

Eric suddenly felt foolish. It occurred to him that he probably wasn't the first disturbed person to come into her office insisting he was basically healthy.

"I can't write," he said.

She looked perplexed. "You don't have the talent for it?"

"I have the talent, all right. But I can't finish anything. Sometimes I can't get past page three."

"Oh," she said, comprehending. "Writer's block."

"That's it, writer's block," he said. "Have you ever treated anyone for it?"

"I've had patients who were writers," she said, after a moment. "Sometimes they have had that problem. But it's never the major problem."

"With me, it is," Eric said.

She regarded him with a faint smile. "Why is it so important to you that you write?"

"It's what I set out to be. A writer. I had some stories published in my college literary magazine. Pretty damned good ones, too. After I graduated, I went to work at *The New Yorker* as a checker. You know, checking out all the facts in the pieces. After a while, they let me do a couple of things for 'Talk of the Town' and a few book reviews. Then they assigned a long profile to me—" He broke off.

"What happened?"

"I never finished it," he said more softly. "I quit the magazine and knocked around Europe for about a year. When I came back, I went to work at Galton and Hill. I've been there ever since."

"Did you keep up your writing?"

"No, I stopped. I didn't try again for a long time."

Delphine thought for a few moments. She had an almost Zen relaxation about her as she sat, very straight, her back not quite touching the leather of the chair, her hands folded gracefully in her lap.

"When did your mother die?" she asked finally.

"Five years ago."

"When did you try writing again?"

Eric hesitated, then answered, "About five years ago."

Delphine's eyes seemed very bright now as they held on him.

"There's no connection," Eric said. "My mother always encouraged me to write."

"I'm sure she did. But isn't it possible that she also wanted you to fail?"

"That's not true!" But, even as he said it, the resentment sprang up in him, his childhood sense of having been wronged incomprehensibly. He had thought he had buried it, had done with it. And yet, one simple question from this woman, and the miserable feeling was alive in him again, getting him sick to the stomach as in the old days.

"My mother loved me," Eric insisted, reaching blindly for a sheet of Kleenex. "She wanted me to succeed at everything I did." He crumpled the tissue and started to raise it to his suddenly moist eyes, caught himself, and wiped his nose instead.

Delphine waited until he had collected himself. "We can say nothing now," she said at length. "We have a great deal of ground to cover, much to talk about, before we can come to any conclusions. But, in answer to your question, Eric, yes—I think we can get rid of your writer's block." She leaned toward him, with something like maternal yearning in her posture, as if she wanted to draw him to her. "I know already," she went on, in her low, soothing voice, "that you're an intelligent, sensitive, talented man. I'm sure I can help you release what's in you."

With that bright, compelling gaze on him, Eric believed her, believed it was really going to happen, for the first time in years, believed in himself.

He hadn't been back in his office a minute when the editor-in-chief, Abel Suderman, stuck his head in. "Where have you been? I was looking for you."

"I was at the doctor's," Eric replied.

Abel looked appropriately concerned. "Feeling all right?"

"Terrific. I'm healthier than I knew. Hope I didn't keep you waiting long."

"No, not really," Abel said, coming into the office. "I just got back a half hour ago myself."

"Long lunch with someone?"

"I took in a flick." He eased into the chair beside Eric's desk.

"What was this one about?"

"A housewife who sells herself into slavery."

"That was the plot of the last one, wasn't it?"

"Who notices the plot? You go to see the star do her thing. This one was called Felicity Bang or something like that. Big bush and plump thighs." Abel's round face glowed and his eyes seemed to sparkle behind his rimless glasses. "I'm an old-fashioned man, Eric. I get turned on by plump thighs."

Eric smiled politely. Abel Suderman, Rilke scholar and father of three, was, as just about everyone at Galton and Hill knew, a late-blooming voyeur. He had taken to wandering off, during the business day, to see porno movies on Times Square. It was harmless enough, a bookish, middle-aged man's aberration. It didn't interfere with his work, he left for his suburban home punctually every evening, and the secretaries around the office didn't seem in any particular danger from him.

"You ought to come along with me some time," Abel said. "Every civilized man owes it to himself. Hard-core porn is the art form of our age."

"I'll stick to the soft-core stuff," Eric said. "The books we publish." He tapped the ream box that was on the desk before him.

"Oh yeah," Abel said, glancing at the box. "Naomi Lamb's new book. That's what I wanted to talk to you about. What do you think is wrong with it?"

"Maybe I shouldn't come to a conclusion on just one half of a book," Eric said carefully. "But it seems to me that Naomi is suffering from the same bug that's afflicting most women writers these days. A morbid desire to be Erica Jong."

"I kind of like the sex parts," Abel said, mildly demurring.

"So do I—up to a point. But a heroine who rises to the top through her skill at blow jobs isn't going to play in Peoria. Not without some redeeming social value."

Abel thought for a moment. "No, I didn't see much redeeming social value. Not in one reading."

"I've read it twice, and there ain't none," Eric said. "I think the kid may be the answer."

"What kid?"

"The illegitimate daughter. The little girl the heroine leaves behind in that small town. The way it is now, Naomi doesn't make her any part of the story. I think she should bring her into it—have the heroine miss her daughter terribly, have the kid come to New York to stay with her. She should show the heroine's anguish—her knowledge that she's a bad mother—her longing to be a good one. It would give the housewives something to relate to."

"It would mean a heavy rewrite," Abel said.

"There's time," Eric said. "We're in no hurry. We've got *Bitter Victory* to push for a long time yet." This was Naomi Lamb's current novel; it was being published that day, and he was reminded now that he had the book party to go to later on. "Can you make it to the party, Abel?" he asked.

"Afraid not," the editor-in-chief said. "We're having people over for dinner." The excuse, Eric knew, was only for form's sake. Abel rarely went to book parties, other than those for the books he had personally edited. "Give Naomi my love."

"I'll do that."

"As for this new book of hers, I'll trust you to put her on the right track. You always seem to be able to do that." Abel rose, then looked down at the ream box again quizzically. "Can't a heroine simply be an out-and-out bitch?"

"My mother used to say," Eric said, "that in a good woman's novel there is no such thing as a bitch. Only a woman who has had bad luck with men."

"Mother knew best," Abel said and left the office.

Eric stared at the empty doorway, vaguely upset by his boss's parting comment. Though, certainly, no flippancy had been intended. Abel, he knew, had a commercial publisher's healthy respect for Margaret Dare Bayliss, an author whose titles, years after her death, were still in print and selling nicely.

It had, in fact, been simply a statement of the obvious, a reference to the basis of Eric's expertise, of his position as the house specialist in popular women's fiction. He knew all the right ingredients, the formulas that worked. He had learned these secrets, quite literally, at his mother's knee.

"Mother knew best." No, it wasn't the comment as such that struck him unpleasantly. It was the fact that now he was thinking of it in conjunction with Delphine's question—"Isn't it possible that she wanted you to fail?"

He had always been a little ashamed of his mother, though it was only now that he could admit it to himself. He had loved the fitfully affectionate private woman, but had resented the blatant self-promoter, the celebrity author who was never happier than when she was on a television talk show, likening herself to Charles Dickens. He had endured his share of digs and put-downs on his mother's account. The digs had been motivated by envy, but hadn't lacked some element of truth; since, as he had realized even then, a Margaret Dare Bayliss bestseller, for all its flair and professionalism, usually had a certain tackiness to it.

He had kept such disloyal opinions to himself, of course, but his mother had sensed them anyway. Once, when he had ventured a mild criticism of her latest novel, she had said to him, in her dry voice, "Eric, if I had known you were going to turn into such a wretched little snob, I would have sent you to a trade school instead of Harvard."

Well, the fact was, he *had* been given a good education, he had associated with people of taste, and her kind of book was just not his cup of tea. When, while still an undergraduate, he set out to write a novel, he emulated the authors on his college reading list—D. H. Lawrence, Virginia Woolf and company, not Margaret Dare Bayliss.

He gave his mother the first hundred pages to read. She curled up in the love seat in their living room, put another custom-made cigarette into her holder—the holder had a filter in it, but it didn't keep her from getting lung cancer, in the long run—and read straight through the manuscript.

He watched her anxiously. She never looked up from the pages. She had the same nervous habit he had of tugging at a lock of her reddish hair—the hair, too, was identical to his—as she read. He found the mirror-image unsettling.

When she finished, she said a few complimentary things that seemed less than heartfelt. Then she got to the point. "But, darling," she asked, "what are you trying to do in this? What this whole book seems to be saying is that you—or your hero—are a terribly intelligent, terribly sensitive, terribly anguished young man who is living in a cruel, obtuse world that doesn't deserve you. I mean, you can't expect people to *pay* for that information."

Eric listened in silence. Then he took the manuscript from her, went to his room, and tore it up, savagely, in many little pieces, mixing them up in the wastebasket so he wouldn't be tempted to put the thing back together.

He had written a few short stories after that, but it was a long time before he tried a novel again. Not until his mother was dead, as Delphine had pointed out. Even now, his only contribution to book-length fiction was his tidying up of the vulgar outpourings of semiliterates like Naomi Lamb, a pushy young woman with all of Margaret Dare Bayliss's greed and ambition, but not even one-tenth of her craftsmanship and grace of style.

It didn't have to be that way. He could have done good work. He was thirty-five, and at that age he should already have had the beginnings of his own shelf at the public library.

"Isn't it possible that she wanted you to fail?"

Damn it, his mother wanted *everyone* to fail. He remembered how she would sink into a foul, snarling mood if some critic had the temerity to give one of her rivals a favorable review.

Yes, for all of her talk of her great dreams for him, her unfailingly expressed disappointment whenever he came off second best, she did—she wanted him to fall on his ass.

The cold-hearted, competitive bitch!

The book party was being given in a suite at the Plaza. As Eric entered, he sized up the crowd, fifty or so people drifting back and forth between two large, elegant rooms. In the first room, there was a perfunctory spread of hors d'oeuvres and a basic supply of hard liquor, augmented by chablis and burgundy. Naomi Lamb had made a big fuss about having champagne for her party, so, reluctantly, the firm had also provided four magnums of a New York State vintage.

Half the guests were cheerful and lively, which meant they were friends of the author. The other half were the faintly bored veterans of these occasions: a fair-sized contingent from Galton and Hill, a few paperback executives, a couple of editors from *Publishers' Weekly*, and a half-dozen very familiar faces who seemed to be at almost all book parties given by all publishers, with no particular reason for being at any of them. Naomi's agent was there too, with a worried look on her elfin face. Eric couldn't imagine why she should be anxious, since, just a few days before, they had sold the reprint rights to *Bitter Victory* for a hundred and fifty thousand dollars.

He saw Naomi in a far corner of the room. She was talking animatedly to a man and a woman, a pretty brunette in a belted gray tunic and pants, and a large Madison Avenue type in a pinstripe suit. Eric went over to her.

Naomi, when she caught sight of him approaching, broke off whatever it was she was saying and took two or three quick steps to meet him. Now that she was turned toward him, Eric saw that she was really done up for the event. She was wearing a shimmering sheath dress that was stretched taut on her heavy hips. Her bleached blond hair was teased in a pile on her head, her close-set eyes were blue-shadowed, her lips were painted a blood-red.

"How are you feeling?" he asked.

"Anhh," Naomi nasalized, meaning she wasn't sure. She sometimes punctuated her sentences with inarticulate sounds. This habit came through in her prose too. "I'm depressed," she said finally.

"I know how you feel," he said sympathetically. He assumed that she was reacting to the pan her book had just received in the *Times Book Review*. "Tawdry" and "simple-minded" were but two of the uncomplimentary adjectives the reviewer had used. "But don't pay any attention to it. That guy didn't know what the hell he was talking about."

"Who?" Naomi looked briefly confused. "You mean, that *Times* review? Anhh," she whined, signifying that she couldn't care less, "I expect that kind of shit from a male reviewer." With a tight, grim smile, she said, "They should have had a woman review it."

She wasn't just putting up a brave front, Eric realized. She actually believed it, that her bad review had simply been an expression of male chauvinism. It was a rationalization that would serve her in good stead for the critical knocks that still lay ahead. "Then why *are* you depressed?" he asked.

"Anhh—" Naomi lowered her eyes, as if she were hesitant now about bringing up what was on her mind. "I'm depressed about the paperback sale."

"What's depressing about a hundred and fifty grand? That's pretty damned good, I'd say."

She looked up at him, her expression distressed and uncomprehending. "I was expecting a million. I was *sure* I was going to get a million."

"A million! That hardly *ever* happens."

"But I just knew *Bitter Victory* would go for that," she said, with the hushed earnestness of one who has had faith in a vision. "I was going to be a million-dollar writer." Her eyes narrowed and a touch of accusation came into her voice. "What went wrong?"

Eric was too taken aback to give an immediate answer. He was tempted to point out that her manuscript, when it had come to him, had been barely publishable, that he and the copy department had slaved long hours over it, that the copy editor had said, only half jokingly, that she should demand a translator's fee. Instead, with an editor's tact, he replied, "Well, you know, Naomi, it *is* a first novel. Maybe we'll do better next time."

Suddenly, her shattered hopes were forgotten and she was the eager author again, as she asked, "Have you read my new book?"

"I've looked at it," he said cautiously. He was annoyed at himself for blundering into referring to the manuscript, even obliquely. This was not the time or place for a serious conference.

"What did you think?" she asked.

Eric, looking away for a moment, noticed that the brunette in the belted tunic was still there, just a few feet from them, standing where Naomi had left her. Her companion in the pinstripe suit had disappeared, but she had remained and was watching them, and listening, perhaps, with a faintly amused smile.

"We'll talk soon," Eric said to Naomi. "There are a few points I want to discuss with you."

"Did you like it?" she persisted.

"I don't want to say too much now. But I'll tell you this, by the time we're through with it, we'll have a blockbuster."

Naomi's homely face broke into a joyful smile.

"Now, let me get a drink," he said and headed for the bar.

He asked for a glass of soda, with ice in it—he had long ago learned to forego alcohol at book parties; a couple of stiff drinks and he was likely to give an honest opinion. As he watched the bartender pour, he continued to marvel over his weird interchange with Naomi. A million dollars! He was used to authors' grandiose dreams of fame and fortune. But, with Naomi, it was a little more startling than most, since, until this book, she had done nothing but a few erotic self-help pieces for women's magazines.

"She's always been that way," a woman's voice said behind him.

Eric turned. The brunette in the tunic was smiling at him. "Who has?" he asked.

"Naomi. I heard what she said about expecting a million dollars." She laughed. "It didn't surprise me. Naomi has never been modest about her own value. Back in high school, she used to announce to us regularly that she was the finest mind in Nutley."

"Nutley?"

"It's in New Jersey," she said helpfully.

"Oh yeah. That's where she's from, originally?"

"Yes. Me, too. Originally."

"And you're—?"

"Lucy. Lucy Castelli."

"I'm Eric Bay—" he began.

"I know who you are," she said, cutting him off amiably. "Every time I see Naomi, she talks about you. At first, I thought she must have some kind of crush on you. Then I realized it's just that she depends on you so. She calls you her Maxwell Evarts Perkins."

"That's sweet. Actually, I just make a few suggestions," he said modestly. "She does all the work. She's a talented girl."

"Yes, isn't she?" Her response was quick and uninflected, as if to underscore that she was being a loyal friend rather than a critic.

He took her in for a moment. He assumed she was around

Naomi's age—which was thirty-one—but she looked younger. Her hair was short and curly, her face was thin, with high cheekbones, her smile started slowly and a bit crookedly, then flashed bright. She wasn't his type at all—her look was a little sharp for his taste, her manner a trifle too aggressive—and yet already he was slightly aroused by her.

"Are you connected with writing in some way?" he asked.

"Not directly," Lucy replied. "I'm an art director at an advertising agency."

"Nonverbal. Bless you for that."

Lucy laughed. "That's more than the copywriters do." She eyed him askance. "And don't tell me you don't like writers?"

"This side of rapture, let's say."

"But aren't you a writer yourself?"

"Of course not. Editors don't write."

"Sure," she said skeptically. "Like art directors don't paint."

"Well, I've written a few things," he admitted, with a shrug. Then, to change the subject, he asked, "Are you enjoying the party?"

"It's all kind of new to me. I've never been to a book party before. Are they usually like this?"

"This one is fairly standard. No better, no worse."

"Standard or not, I'm having a good time. But *you* sound pretty blasé about it. I suppose you grew up going to these."

"What do you mean?"

"Because of your mother." As she went on gazing at him, her smile faded. "I shouldn't have said that, I guess."

"I didn't mind."

"Yes, you did. You clenched your teeth."

Eric laughed uncomfortably. "Do I still do that? I thought I'd outgrown it. Anyway, I'm a lot less self-conscious about my mother than I used to be. When I was young, I'd introduce myself to people"—he thrust out his hand to an imaginary person and forced a nervous smile—"'Hi, I'm Eric, Margaret Dare Bayliss's son.'"

"You must have been *very* young."

"I was. And, yes," he went on, "my mother did bring me to a few book parties when I was a kid—usually for her own books. She was very effective at those occasions. My mother could read a publishing party like a map. In a matter of moments, she could locate all the 'A list' people and the 'B list' people, even when they were surrounded by a barren waste of people who didn't count."

Lucy was looking at him a little perplexedly now, as if she couldn't figure out what he was trying to say.

"Forgive me," Eric said. "I don't usually rattle on like this about my mother. I started with a shrink today," he explained. "I guess I'm rehearsing."

"Your shrink has a treat in store," she said. "It's fascinating."

The man in the pinstripe suit reappeared, coming back in from the other room. Eric looked over at him and said, "There's your friend."

"Who?"

"The big bozo in the pinstripe suit."

Lucy turned her head and exchanged a smile with the man. He didn't cross to them, but stayed where he was, eyeing Eric uneasily.

"Do you know him well?" Eric asked under his breath.

"I'll know him less well in a couple of weeks, I think," Lucy replied softly.

"The end of the affair?"

"It's turning out that way."

"Let me know when you're free."

Lucy looked at him quickly. Her smile began, hesitated, then broadened.

"I'm afraid I'm going to have to circulate now," Eric said. "This is business for me, not pleasure. I've got some paperback moguls and media giants to chat with."

And Eric, hot trade book editor, and his mother's son, set out to work the party.

3

Vivian carefully stroked the moisturizing lotion onto her face. As she stared at herself in the dressing-table mirror, she remembered something she once had read in Vogue—"After twenty, every third cell of the skin is a poor one." In a couple of weeks, she would be forty-one. By now, she thought, it had to be two out of three. Her skin looked it—in the strong light, at least—played-out, two out of three of the cells stale, dried-up, old.

It could be said for her days as well—two out of three were a total loss. That day, for instance. In the morning, she had put on her makeup, as always, even though she had no place to go. Now, at ten in the evening, ready to turn in early, she had taken it off. In between, she could remember little of what she had done, if anything. It had been a blank, gray void; a day notable only for the fact that Ward hadn't phoned.

She assumed it was still on for tomorrow evening. She had bought the groceries, had already planned the dinner she would prepare for Ward. But she couldn't be sure; this silence was ominous. In the normal course of things, he called most days of the week; and certainly after that ghastly scene at the Hubers' a phone call was in order, if only to reassure her that there was no lingering bad feeling, that the incident was forgotten. But a whole day had gone by. Not a word.

With a twinge of anxiety, she remembered the harsh expression on Ward's face when he had dropped her off at her door, without coming in. He blamed her, she knew; not simply, as he had said, because she hadn't stuck up for him, but also, as he had avoided saying, because she had been the provocation for the argument in the first place.

All right, she had flirted—just a little. But why should he have cared so? The boy was a fag, he had pointed it out to her himself. Surely Ward didn't feel threatened by him!

She conjured up Christopher Greene's face in her mind. An absolutely gorgeous young man. His eyes were beautiful, but it was his skin that had struck her most of all. It was smooth, translucent, delicately textured. She had wanted to stroke it, the way one strokes marble.

He had looked at her so intensely, so admiringly!

Vivian dipped her fingertips into her jar of skin cream and spread the cool, white substance around her eyes. Georgette, her cosmetician, had promised her years before that if she used this special cream faithfully she wouldn't get bags or crow's feet. But the lines had appeared anyway, lengthening and deepening at the corner of each eye. Perhaps the cream had slowed down the process, who could know? One had to have faith.

Even so, she thought, as she looked at her reflection, it was still a good face. It was slightly lopsided, the left side was bigger than the right, but she had learned to conceal it by shading that side more. The eyes were clear, the jawline was holding firm. When she was rested, and the lighting was soft, it was the face she had had when she was nineteen. Christopher Greene, with his flattering gaze, hadn't necessarily been insincere.

She wondered if he was *really* gay? Ward was quick to accuse any too good-looking, too gentle young man of that. Anyway, as Delphine had once told her, few men were completely homosexual. More often, they were bisexual, which meant that they could love women as well as men. Chris had certainly looked at her the way a normal man looks at a woman.

Vivian caught herself short in her reverie. She had to watch it, she warned herself. She had started to be attracted to gay young men, even before this. She hadn't realized it was happening, that she was doing anything differently. But for her party at Christmastime, she had unthinkingly invited more than the usual number of charming, stylish, feminine young men. Her daughter, Jane, had called her attention to it. "Mother," she had said, "be careful. You're turning into a fag hag."

She was reminded now that she hadn't sent Jane her monthly allowance, and, as she thought it, she saw the worry lines deepen in her face. It was just one more nagging money problem; not a very big one, in this case, since Jane's tuition, room, and board at Radcliffe were provided for and all she needed from her was something every month to cover her day-to-day expenses. But it was frustrating, nevertheless, when Vivian at that moment had less than two hundred in the bank.

She wouldn't have been in this pinch, of course, if David's check had come in. But, once again, he had fallen behind in his alimony and child-support payments. There was little hope of anything from him soon; his latest business venture, in Montreal, was, as usual, going to pieces. David was turning out to be as much of a loser in his new life in Canada as he had been in his old one. Vivian felt a little sorry for him these days and she didn't have the heart to pressure him. As she had so often, when they were married, she would give David some time to get his act together. Now, *there* was someone who would jump for joy if she married again.

If she married again.

Ward. Why didn't he phone? A terror crept through her as the thought formed in her mind that she might have lost him.

She fought off the urge to call Delphine She had phoned her too many times already, early in the morning and late at night. Not that Delphine had ever complained; she was wonderful about it, always sympathetic, always warm and wise. She longed to hear Delphine reassuring her that everything would work out, that in the end Ward would realize Vivian was right for him. For all his bluster and worldliness, Delphine had explained, Ward was basically a little boy who needed a woman to pamper him, comfort him, make him feel worthwhile.

But, no, she mustn't bother her. She would have to sweat this out by herself—or, at least, until she saw Delphine in the morning. She was entitled to three hours of therapy a week. For the rest of the time, she had to learn to cope with her anxieties alone.

Alone. She had thirty years or so more of this, and it wasn't going to get any better. As she stared at herself in the mirror, she felt a chill of desolation.

She drew in her breath sharply. The reflection had changed abruptly. For one instant, she had seen her old-lady face, the face she soon would wear, had seen it as if it were there in the glass already.

The phone rang.

Vivian quickly wiped her hands with a tissue, rose, and hurried across to the phone beside the bed. She took a deep breath to calm herself, then picked up the receiver. "Hello?"

"Hi, Vivian. It's Russell."

The disappointment hit her hard and it took a moment before she could speak. Then she forced a squeal of delight. "Russell! It's been a long time. How are you?"

"The same as always. Working hard." He said it with virtuous self-satisfaction. Russell was one of the three or four biggest insurance agents in the East, and he always seemed fully aware of it. "How are things going with you?"

"It's a little tight for me right now," she said. "I'm late on my life insurance, I know."

"Don't worry about it, kid. That's not why I'm calling."

His tone had shifted to a seductive purr. Russell, apart from being her insurance man, had also in the past been her occasional lover.

"Just wanted to hear the sound of my voice, huh?" she asked with automatic coquettishness.

"Yeah. And more than that. I want to see you. I've been thinking about you a lot."

"I've been thinking about you too, darling," she lied. At that moment, she had no vivid memory of him. She recalled that his body smelled vinegary, and that was about it. "We should have lunch sometime."

"I've got a better idea. I'm going to Bermuda this weekend. Why don't you come along with me?"

For a moment, she was at a loss for what to say. "I don't know if I told you, Russell," she said carefully, "but I've been seeing a man pretty regularly."

"Yeah?" He sounded unimpressed, as if she had raised a trivial objection. "Does he have you taken up for this weekend?"

"Well—" She hesitated, then admitted, "I don't know. It's not definite yet."

"Then forget about him. Come with *me*. A friend is lending me his house. It has its own private beach. We'll have a great time." He waited for her to say something. "The usual arrangement," he added quietly.

"Look, Russell," she said, "I can't think now. I've got something else on my mind. Can I get back to you?"

"Sure. Call me tomorrow."

"I'll do that. Nice hearing from you, darling."

Vivian hung up, sat on the edge of the bed, and stared before her. Then, belatedly, it dawned on her that she hadn't said no.

It would mean a thousand dollars. Her unconscious, more practical than she was, had kept the possibility alive.

But she wasn't going to do that any more. She was going to marry Ward. She had committed herself.

She looked around at her bedroom, which suddenly seemed vast and cold as a tomb, and understood that her commitment was futile, meant nothing, when it was thrown out into the silent, uncaring dark.

And that this bedroom, with its past, with its ghosts, could for all she knew be the future too—*her* future, with all its spidery terrors.

"Is he seeing another woman, do you think?" Delphine asked.

"I don't know," Vivian replied helplessly. "I just don't know. Ward is like three people walking around in one. There's the person he lets me know—and the network executive, who's kind of scary, I don't *want* to know *him*. Then I get the feeling there's a third person I can't see at all, who's living some totally different life. And maybe, in that other life, that other person is laughing at me, thinking what a fool I am."

"You realize that this is a very common paranoid delusion, don't you?"

"Well, isn't paranoia ever justified?"

"You mean, do people ever laugh at other people behind their backs? Quite often," Delphine said. "But it isn't meaningful." Her face shaded into a weary sadness, as if she were disappointed with Vivian for being so slow to comprehend. "As I've told you many times," she said patiently, "people interpret life only in terms of themselves. If Ward laughs at you, it relates only to himself. If you laugh at Ward, it relates only to you. You are each a self-contained whole, your own theater, your own stage, your own audience."

"But everything Ward does affects me," Vivian protested. "If he's nice to me, I'm high as a kite. If he's mean to me, I'm miserable."

"It affects you, yes. But what it affects is *your* feeling about yourself."

Vivian shifted her position in her chair, tucking her legs tighter under her, and craned her neck. The muscles at the top of her spine were tensing again. They always seemed to do so whenever Delphine, in any of her various ways, told her that she must learn to feel good about herself. After all these years, it still wasn't easy.

Delphine was gazing at her steadily. She was wearing black today—a black blouse, black pants. It made her seem paler than ever, and the black-and-white effect, against the creamy brown leather of her chair, was rather stark. Vivian felt a little frightened of her now, since she knew that that fixed, pensive look meant Delphine was pursuing some fresh thought, fastening onto some possibility that she herself had overlooked. Vivian was hurting this morning, as vulnerable as an open wound. She didn't think she was ready for it.

At length Delphine said, "Let's get back to practical reality. Is there a chance that Ward is seeing another woman?"

"Of course, there's a very good chance. Ward isn't the faithful kind." Vivian hesitated, then said, "I'm almost sure of it."

"Why are you sure?"

"Well, a couple of weeks ago, I went to his place in the morning. We had a date to go to the country." She paused, a little sorry she had brought it up. She had almost forced it out of her mind, and now it was an uncomfortable thing to remember. "In the bathroom, balled up in the corner, there was a pair of pantyhose. Dirty," she added, wrinkling her nose. "I checked."

Delphine's eyebrows raised slightly. "You mean, you think someone else spent the night?"

"It certainly looked like it. *I* wouldn't have known the difference. I hadn't seen him for a few days. He'd been putting me off." She thought of the pantyhose, wrinkled and soiled, but with a scent of bath powder still clinging to them. "The bitch probably left her undies there deliberately."

Delphine smiled, amused by the thought. "Perhaps she did."

"So, okay," Vivian said, "Ward is having affairs with other women. What can *I* do about it?"

"Does it make you feel jealous?"

"Yes, I suppose it does. That's only natural."

"*Why* are you jealous? You don't have any legal claim on him, after all."

"I know that, but—" She concentrated, trying to pinpoint the exact nature of the pain. "I guess it hurts me that, for a day or two at least, he preferred being with someone else."

"And you're afraid that he might have found this someone else more desirable, more satisfying?"

"Yes," Vivian replied softly.

Delphine leaned forward. "Don't you think Ward could feel that way? Don't you think he could be afraid, too, that you might find someone else more desirable?"

"No, I don't think so. He has no reason to be afraid. He can be confident of me."

"But does *Ward* know that?" Delphine persisted.

Vivian looked at her uncertainly. She hadn't intended to bring up the incident at the Hubers' until later in the hour. But now she wondered if Delphine had been told about it already. "As a matter of fact," she said, "something did happen, just the other night."

"Oh? Where?"

"At Mandy Huber's. Ward and I had dinner there Sunday evening. Eric Bayliss was there—and Christopher Greene."

"Oh, yes," Delphine said, nodding. "Christopher."

"I suppose Mandy told you about it?"

"She mentioned she was having the dinner. And that she was inviting Christopher. But I haven't spoken with her since. Her first session of the week is tomorrow. Christopher's too."

So Delphine *didn't* know about it yet. Vivian decided to keep it brief. Mandy and Chris would be telling their own versions soon enough. "It didn't work out too well," she said. "They had a fight."

"Who did?"

"Ward and Christopher Greene. It was a silly argument. Something about television programming. But that wasn't the *real* reason they were at each other."

"What was?"

"Chris was flirting with me, and—I guess this is what you were asking about—Ward seemed to get jealous."

"Ah!" Delphine smiled with satisfaction, her supposition vindicated. "Does that astonish you? Christopher is extremely handsome."

"But he's just a boy," Vivian said. "How old *is* he?"

"Twenty-nine."

"Oh." Vivian was a bit surprised. She had been thinking of Chris as little more than a post-adolescent. "But it doesn't make any difference," she went on, "I'm still a lot older than he is." With a wry shrug, she added, "I suppose he was just being kind to a middle-aged lady."

"I doubt that very much." Delphine's eyes hooded slightly as they held on her. "You're a beautiful woman, Vivian," she said, her low, musical voice dropping almost to a murmur. "You're beautiful to anyone, of any age. Christopher was simply paying you your due."

"All right, I feel complimented. But, the fact remains, it led to a very ugly scene." It all came back to her now—Ward yelling at her on the street, the stinging slap on her face. Her cheek tingled, as she remembered it, and the muscles at the bottom of her neck tensed painfully. She reached back with her hand and rubbed them.

"Is your neck stiff?" Delphine asked.

"Yes, a little."

"Here," Delphine said, rising, "let me relax you." She gestured toward the couch.

Vivian obediently got up, crossed to the couch, and lay flat on her stomach. She waited, without moving, as her therapist positioned herself on top of her, straddling her just below her buttocks. The sensations came in the by-now familiar sequence: first, the lemony scent of the soap Delphine used, then the warmth of the flabby inner thighs as they closed on her, then the strong, practiced hands gripping her where her neck sloped into her shoulders, kneading the tautened flesh with the attentive steadiness of a repeated caress.

"You *are* tense," Delphine commented. "As soon as I loosen them, the muscles knot up all over again."

"I'm so afraid!" Vivian whispered. Her pent-up anguish welled up now, and the tears streamed down her cheeks, wetting the leather of the couch. "I'm going to lose Ward, I just feel it! I don't know what I'll do if I don't marry him!'

"It will all work out," Delphine soothed her, her hands continuing in their sure, compelling rhythm. "Believe me, it will work out."

Vivian felt her body easing, from her neck down through her legs, as the tension seeped out. She was no longer thinking of anything in particular; she was aware only of Delphine, heavy on her, but without weight, a warm, engulfing presence with a faintly sour, soapy scent that reminded her of the way her mother had smelled, long ago, when she had taken the little girl she was into her arms. Her eyes closed as a drowsiness came over her.

"Feeling better?" Delphine asked.

"Yes. Much."

"I've been thinking," Delphine said after a moment, her hands working on, "about that insurance man—what's his name—?"

"Russell." Vivian's eyes opened and she was alert again. She had mentioned her conversation with Russell at the beginning of the hour, but her therapist hadn't followed up on it. Evidently, it hadn't been forgotten.

"I think you should tell Ward about him," Delphine said.

"Tell him what?"

"That he wants you to go away with him for the weekend."

"But Ward would get angry!"

"Jealous, you mean. I think Ward has been taking you too much for granted." The hands paused. "This man, Russell—is he as rich as Ward?"

"Richer, I think."

"Good. Then Ward would see him as a real threat. Maybe it would be a good idea to let Ward know that *you* have choices, too. It might bring him a little closer to making a choice himself."

"I don't know," Vivian murmured uncertainly.

"It's worth a try, don't you think?"

As Ward sat to take off his shoes, he glanced at the framed photograph of Vivian's daughter on the bedside table. "How's Jane?" he asked.

"Studying hard for her finals," Vivian replied, stepping free of her slacks.

"Is she worried about them?"

"Jane? Hardly. She's never gotten less than a B in her life." She held up the slacks, letting them hang straight, then folded them neatly over the back of a chair. "I'm the one who's worried."

"Why?"

"I can't send her any money this month. I'm strapped."

"Is money such a problem with her? I've paid for her room and board."

"Yes, but there's more to life than sleeping and eating. She needs walking around money too."

Ward started to unbutton his shirt. "How much walking around does a freshman at Radcliffe do?"

"I usually send her two hundred."

Ward paused on a middle button as if he were astonished.

"It's not the same as when you were in school," Vivian said, slipping off her blouse and tossing it aside. "Inflation."

She turned and faced him. Ward's gaze fixed on her bare breasts appreciatively.

"I'd appreciate it if you'd help me out, darling," Vivian said casually. "Could you lend it to me? Two hundred?" She always said "lend" when she asked Ward for money. They had an intimate relationship, and, on principle, she never took cash from him as a stated gift.

"Let's not talk about money now," Ward said. He stood up and started to take off his trousers.

Vivian said nothing more. Naked, except for her panties—Ward liked to pull them off himself—she went to the bed, sat on the edge of it, and waited. She felt slightly chilled. Ward had never put her off that way before, not with such curtness.

She watched him as he stripped down to his ridiculous-looking jockey shorts. The older men she knew usually wore boxer-style underpants, but Ward persisted in wearing the scant white-cotton briefs, as if he had no middle-aged spread, no gray-pelted pot belly hanging over the elastic band.

He removed his shorts and came toward her, already half erect. He sank down beside her and began mouthing her breasts, nipping at them with controlled but hurting bites. As always, he concentrated on arousing himself, not bothering to give her pleasure. Vivian sat completely still, unresponding, unexcited. She was thinking about what Delphine had said. She was right, Ward *did* take her too much for granted.

"I may not be seeing you this weekend," she said.

He raised his head and looked at her. "What do you mean? You're coming to the country with me."

"Oh? That's the first *I*'ve heard of it."

"I hadn't gotten around to telling you."

"Well, I may not be able to make it. A friend has invited me to go to Bermuda with him."

His face darkened. "What friend?"

"You wouldn't know him. An old friend."

"What's his name?"

"I said you wouldn't know him." Ward went on staring at her. "His name is Russell, okay?"

"Is he fucking you?"

"He hasn't in a long time." She gave him her slow, wicked smile. "But he wants to again."

Ward's expression had been frozen with anger. But now it gradually transformed into a knowing, almost leering look. "Is he generous?"

"Very generous." She sensed that already it had gone wrong, and inside her there was a growing panic. But she managed a calm, reasonable tone, as she said, "That's not why I'm thinking of seeing him. It's just that—well, you know, the way our relationship is, with no real commitment—I feel I have to keep my options open. I mean, I'm not being fair to myself if I only see *you*."

"Is Russell a nice man?" His voice was gentle and benign.

"Yes, he's quite nice."

"Do you enjoy being with him?"

She shrugged. "So-so."

"Is he demanding?"

"I don't know what you mean."

"You know what I mean." A steely insistence came into his tone. "Is he demanding?"

Ward was getting flushed, and she realized that he was hungry for every detail. The thought of her selling her body to another man was turning him on. "Normal for a weekend," she said. "A couple of times a day."

He put his hand on her thigh and moved it slowly toward her

crotch. "What do you do that makes him so generous?"

"I don't want to talk about this," she said, trying to push his hand away.

He sank his fingers into her thigh. "Do you blow him?"

She met his gaze and smiled. "Yes."

Ward rose to his feet and faced her. His hardened penis stood out before him. He leaned in toward her, bringing the head of it to within a few inches of her face. "Do to me what you do to Russell."

A shiver passed through her. She put her lips around the head of his penis and darted the tip of her tongue along the crack. Then she started the back-and-forth movement, taking it into her mouth bit by bit. She felt it swelling. A premature drop trickled onto the back of her tongue.

Just as she thought he was about to come, he pulled free of her. He reached down, grabbed her left arm, and yanked it up behind her back. Her body tilted away from him and, for one moment, she saw his face. It was hate-filled, contorted with rage. Keeping her arm twisted, he turned her around on the bed and forced her, face down, onto the mattress. His fingernails scraped her as he swiftly pulled down her panties, and only then did she understand what he was about to do. Her pleading cry was turned into a scream of pain as he pierced her anus.

He was wild, unsparing. In less than a minute, it was over. She felt him rising from her, leaving the bed. She lay still, her face buried in the pillow, humiliated by the ache of the torn tissue and the twitching desire in her.

She heard him moving about the room, dressing. Then she felt his presence near her again, bending over the night table. There was the faint, scratching sound of a pen on paper.

She waited until he had left before she raised her head from the pillow. Then she took the curling paper from the night table and looked at it. It was a check for two hundred dollars.

4

"TERRYCLOTH!" Mandy, shocked, looked around at all three of the men.

"Terrycloth," Jeff repeated, studying the sketch in his hand. It was a design for a belted mini-smock, and it was the last of the several croquis that Mandy had brought to this meeting, the *pièce de résistance* of the batch. "I see it as beachwear," he said. He passed the sketch over to the sales manager. "What do you think, Harry? Nothing we can push on the better dress buyers, huh?"

Harry looked at the sketch and shook his head. "Afraid not. Not this year."

"This *is* the year," Mandy insisted. "In Paris, the mini is coming back strong."

"That is Paris, France," Jeff said. "In the United States of America, all the ladies don't have such great legs."

"Mandy does," Dan, the production manager, said genially. "That's why she likes minis."

"What is this, schmuck?" Jeff turned on Dan in mock-indignation. "You shouldn't even *notice* my wife's legs."

The men laughed with the suggestive heartiness that always left Mandy feeling embarrassed, as if she had found herself, by accident, in the Executive Club locker room of the Mc-Burney Y.

"If you're through looking at these," she said grimly, gathering up the croquis, "I'll go back to work."

"It's a good design, Mandy," Jeff said more gently. "It will look very nice on the beach."

"It could be very big," Harry said.

Mandy glared at them wordlessly and walked quickly out of Jeff's office.

When she got back to her own office, Phyllis, her assistant, looked up from her desk inquiringly. Mandy turned the stack of croquis around, with the mini-smock design face out to her, and spat out one word. "Beachwear!"

Phyllis shrugged resignedly.

Mandy went to her desk and sat behind it disconsolately. It was a broad slab of black formica, her ideal working surface. She loved the cool feel of it as she sketched, just as she loved the other particular features of the office, the busy side wall, with its tacked-up textile swatches, sketches, photographers' proofs, and fashion magazine tear sheets, the slanting sunlight through the windows, the river view. Ordinarily, she was never happier than when she was in this, her office, the creative heart of Huber Casuals. But now, suddenly, it struck her as nothing more than a barren shell; all of her work seemed pointless.

She glanced at the mini-smock design again. The flowing, graceful line of it called for Dacron or Orlon. "For crying out loud, *terrycloth!*" she moaned.

Phyllis looked over at her, attentively waiting in case she said something further. She was a tall, gawky girl, talented and shy, with a gift for filling in the spaces in Mandy's thinking.

"Phyllis," Mandy asked, "who knows more about what women like to wear? Us—or those macho morons out there?"

"Do I even need to give an opinion?" Phyllis replied quietly.

The phone rang. Phyllis answered it. "Mrs. Huber's office," she said crisply. Then her voice warmed. "Oh, hi. Just a moment." She put her hand over the mouthpiece. "It's Vivian Loring."

Mandy debated whether or not to take the call. She was hardly in the mood to hear Vivian's troubles at that moment. Still, a friend was a friend. She picked up the receiver. "Hi, Vivian. How are you?"

"Not too good," she heard Vivian say.

"Why? What's wrong?"

"I think I've screwed up everything with Ward."

Her words were slightly slurred, as if, this early in the day, she was already doped up with her tranquilizers. It was even worse than Mandy had feared; Vivian was in one of her super-depressions.

"What happened?" Mandy asked.

"Well, you know me, ready to try anything." Her bright, careless tone didn't quite come off. "Last night, I tried something new on Ward."

"What?"

"I told him I was going away for the weekend with another man."

"Are you?"

"Not necessarily. But I let it sound that way."

"Whatever made you do a thing like that?"

"I thought Ward was taking me too much for granted." Vivian said it with a peculiar flatness, almost as if she were reciting by rote. "I thought it would be a good idea to let him know that I have choices, too."

"So you told him you were going to shack up with another

man?" Mandy was openly incredulous. "Did Ward have plans for you this weekend?"

"Of course."

"So how did he take it? You had a big fight, I suppose."

"No, but—it wasn't pleasant. I don't want to talk about it," she said, with sudden curtness. "The main thing is that he walked out on me. And now I don't know where I stand. What am I going to do, Mandy?" she asked, a desperation coming into her voice. "What am I going to do?"

"What can I tell you? You know the way *I* feel about Ward."

"We've been over that before. You don't understand him the way I do. Ward can be such a sweet, dear man."

"Yes, I realize that," Mandy said, to avoid an argument. They *had* been over it before, the morning after the disastrous dinner party, and she didn't want to hear that nonsense again. "Well, if you really want to keep the guy, then call him right away."

"But what do I say to him?"

"Tell him what you told me. That you didn't really mean it, you were just trying to make him jealous. Tell him that you're looking forward to spending a whole, wonderful weekend with him."

"I guess I *should* do that," Vivian said after a moment. She laughed softly. "You're so sensible, Mandy."

"Of course, I'm sensible. But anyone else would have told you this. Why didn't you call Delphine? She would have said the same thing."

There was a brief silence. "I didn't want to talk to Delphine about this," Vivian said quietly. "I wanted *your* advice."

"Okay, if you want another piece of advice, after you talk to Ward and straighten it out with him, put it out of your mind. Don't stay in tonight. Go out somewhere. Do something."

"Yeah, that's a good idea. Maybe I'll go to a movie. Or a play."

"And, no matter what happens, remember, life must go on."

"So they tell me," Vivian said wryly. "Thanks, darling. Talk to you soon." She hung up.

"I can't help it," Mandy said, "sometimes I think she's imposing upon me. I mean, I'm younger than Vivian, I could be her kid sister. I feel a little foolish when I have to come on with her like a mother-figure."

"Age has nothing to do with it," Delphine said. "Vivian will always have to lean on other people. She'll never be able to stand on her own."

"Is that why she needs Ward? I couldn't let that man even touch me."

"Ward could be very good for her. If nothing else, he's a strong man. And that's what Vivian needs."

"Well, maybe," Mandy said dubiously.

She reflected on it for a moment. This discussion of Vivian had taken them off on a tangent, but she knew that, sooner or later, it would lead back to her own problem. And she rather enjoyed this aspect of her therapy. Delphine was willing to talk about her patients, the ones that Mandy knew anyway. Her first therapist, a stone-faced male Freudian, had been so reticent she couldn't even get an opinion on the weather from him.

"Do all women need a strong man?" Mandy asked.

"Not if a woman is strong in herself," Delphine replied. "Some women don't need men at all."

"Well, I wouldn't ever go *that* far," Mandy said with a laugh.

Delphine smiled. Mandy couldn't tell whether she was agreeing with her thought or was simply amused by it. Probably the latter. She had often wondered if Delphine had any sex life at all. Vivian and she had speculated on the matter, and, since there was no evidence of Delphine's having any kind of romantic involvement, they had come to the conclusion that she was asexual, like a nun. Certainly in the outfit she was wearing at that moment, a shapeless gray tweed suit and a ruffled white blouse, she seemed like nothing so much as one of those modern sisters who have given up the habit without quite managing the transition to contemporary dress.

"There's no hard-and-fast rule," Delphine went on. "We're raised to believe that a woman is happiest when she is mated with one man to the exclusion of all others. That's a convention of society, not a natural law, and it's true only in some cases. For Vivian, yes—but for other women, not necessarily."

"And for me?" Mandy asked.

"What do *you* think?"

"Well, I can't remember what it was like *not* to be married. I got married at twenty-two."

"Presumably, you had *some* life before the age of twenty-two," Delphine said dryly.

"Oh, sure. But it was nothing out of the ordinary. Just growing up in Baltimore. Dating boys now and then. Being mad about clothes and wanting to design them some day. I was sort of a formless blob. I really wasn't a person yet."

"You feel you became a person when you married Jeff?"

"Yes. In a way."

"You mean, because you took on an identity then? *His* identity?"

"Well—yes and no. I knew I couldn't become *him*. Jeff was already established. And he was much older—or he seemed much older then, anyway."

"The age difference was an issue?"

"Not to me. But to other people."

"Your parents?"

"Yes. At first."

They were going back over old ground, and Mandy couldn't quite understand why. Whatever misgivings her parents may have had originally, they doted on Jeff now. When they would come up to visit, they would pay even more attention to Jeff than to her. Her mother would flirt with him girlishly. And, sooner or later, her father and Jeff would get off by themselves and talk about their respective businesses—Jeff about the garment business, which didn't interest her father at all, and her father about Baltimore real estate, which didn't interest Jeff at all—and somehow seem to have a thoroughly good time with each other.

"But that's all in the past," Mandy said. "Once we were husband and wife, our ages didn't mean anything any more."

"You feel your marriage has been a good thing for you?" Delphine asked.

"Of course it's been a good thing. Jeff is a strong man. And I need him."

"Do you need him the way Vivian needs a man?"

"No," Mandy said after a moment, "Vivian is a different kind of person. I can't remember a time she hasn't been with some man or the other. If I were alone, men wouldn't be the biggest thing in my life. My work is what matters to me."

"Your work," Delphine repeated thoughtfully and fell into silence.

Mandy waited, a bit nervous now. She sensed that each one of Delphine's questions had a purpose, that she was preparing her for something—another breakthrough, perhaps. In the course of her therapy, a breakthrough happened every two or three months, and Mandy was overdue for one.

"What about your work?" Delphine asked. "It seems to me, Mandy, that every time you come in here in a state of depression it's immediately after something has gone wrong in your work."

"That could be," Mandy admitted.

"Today, for instance, you're upset about what happened this morning. The way Jeff downgraded your design. What was it—something about terrycloth?"

"Yes. It's a design that should be one of our leading sportswear numbers and Jeff wants to do it as beachwear."

"And you didn't put up a fight? You're accepting his judgment?"

"Well, yes. He's—" Mandy's voice trailed off.

"He's the man. He's your husband."

"He's my partner too."

"What about this partnership?" Delphine asked. "It's been a constructive one, I suppose?"

"Very constructive."

"You've reinforced each other? Neither one of you could have done it alone?"

"I couldn't have, anyway. When I started out, I was a kid fresh out of school. I didn't know anything about business. The rag trade is a jungle. I would have been cut to pieces if I hadn't been teamed up with Jeff."

"But now? You've learned something about the rag trade. Quite a lot, I should imagine." Her glowing eyes were holding on her. Very gently, she asked, "Do you still need him?"

Mandy didn't answer right away. "I don't know," she said finally.

Delphine smiled slightly, with a hint of approval, as if Mandy's answer, uncertain though it was, had satisfied her. "Tell me," she went on, "Jeff's sound business sense, is it something that's unique to him?"

"No, not really. He makes pretty much the same decisions any experienced, conservative garment manufacturer would make."

"Is your designing talent unique?"

"Yes, I think it is. I mean, there are other talented designers, and a couple of them are better than I'll ever be. But I have my own style, my touch."

"I know you do." Delphine looked away for a moment and pursed her lips, as if a thought was disturbing her. Then she fixed her gaze on Mandy again. "Has it ever occurred to you, Mandy, that Jeff might need you more than you need him?"

"Well, I—" Mandy was suddenly apprehensive. "I don't think of it that way."

Delphine leaned toward her. "You've *never* thought that? You feel you just can't function without him?"

"Oh—" Mandy paused, then, a bit guiltily, said, "I've sometimes thought that, if Phyllis and I could get together with some good people, we could put out a line of our own. All our own concepts," she went on, warming to the idea, "some really terrific stuff." She caught herself. "I've thought it, but I've never been *serious* about it."

"Why not? Why can't you go out on your own?"

Mandy stared at her. "Jeff's my husband. I couldn't do that!"

Delphine sat back. "Let's analyze that for a moment," she said. "You feel obligated to your husband. Therefore you're not free to be as good a designer as you want to be. That doesn't sound like a free and equal partnership to me. That sounds like oppression."

"Well, isn't that the way it usually is? Between a husband and wife?"

"Too often, yes. Marriage, in many cases, is nothing more than that—institutionalized oppression. A woman may be naturally talented, but she is raised to believe that a man is superior to her. In marriage, she assumes that her gifts can't possibly match her husband's gifts. So she defers to him, diminishes her own worth, for the sake of a fallacy." She paused. "Take your case, for instance."

"Jeff and I are good at different things," Mandy said quickly.

"But good to the same degree?" Delphine asked pointedly. "This is an interesting example of what I'm talking about, how our conditioning distorts our perception of reality. You sincerely believe that you owe everything to Jeff. But I, an objective outside observer, see the situation quite differently. I see a clever businessman," she went on, her words measured, her voice steely, "in no way remarkable, who has exploited his highly talented wife to build a successful business for himself."

Mandy could no longer meet Delphine's insistent gaze. She looked down at her lap; her fists were clenched, the knuckles were white. "I don't want to talk about this any more," she said.

"That's all right," Delphine said. "The hour is almost over."

But Mandy knew she couldn't back off from it now. The question in her mind couldn't be left just hanging, unvoiced, unanswered, until the next session. In a small, timid voice, she asked it. "Are you telling me I should leave him?"

"I'm not telling you to do anything," Delphine said in a calm, reasonable tone. "I'm simply helping you to gain insight into your problem."

Mandy felt only confused and vaguely frightened. "My work matters to me. But it isn't everything." She put her hand over her eyes. "I don't want to be alone," she said softly.

"But, Mandy"—her therapist's voice was suddenly warm and soothing—"*you* would never be alone." Mandy lowered her hand and looked at her. Delphine's pale face had relaxed into a tender smile. "Don't you know how attractive you are?"

"I've never thought of myself as attractive, somehow."

"Maybe Jeff hasn't wanted you to think it."

"But I—well, I'm not like Vivian. She's beautiful."

"You're as attractive as she is, in your own way. You're young, you're slender, you have that lovely, long, blond hair."

Mandy brightened a little, in spite of herself. "Do you really think men could desire me—the way they desire Vivian?"

"There's no doubt of it."

"Well, I don't know," she said with a laugh.

Delphine shook her head sympathetically. "Poor dear, you're so unformed! You married too young, you went into business too young. You've never been free to be yourself—as a talent, as a woman. I can't decide for you, of course, but—" She paused, then, with a shrug, concluded, "Who knows? Perhaps you owe it to yourself."

Mandy remained silent for a few moments. Then, hesitantly,

she said, "I think maybe I do."

As soon as she uttered the words, she began to feel a sense of release. It was nothing sudden, nothing explosive; it was more like a gradual opening within her. But by the time she left the office it had built to a giddying excitement. When she stepped out onto Seventy-fifth Street, the sunniness of the afternoon dazzled her, the colors of the painted brownstones seemed startling and new.

Christopher Greene was coming toward her on the sidewalk, arriving for his hour. He stared at her curiously as he neared her. "Hi, Mandy. Is something wrong?"

"Why do you ask?"

"You've got the funniest look on your face."

"Nothing's wrong," she said, smiling happily. "I feel wonderful! See you, Chris."

And she walked on, forgetting Chris, forgetting the street, focusing entirely on the pure inner light of her breakthrough.

I don't need him! she cried out within herself, exultantly. *I don't need him!* Her step quickened as she hurried toward the delicious, unpredictable future.

5

"I SHOULD have done something about it," Chris said. "Instead, I just sat there. That was my mistake, I guess." He laughed shortly. "I've been having fantasies ever since. Punching him in the mouth—kicking the shit out of him—"

"Is that something you might actually do?" Delphine asked.

"No," he admitted. "I'm not the violent type."

"But it's the macho thing, isn't it? The male thing. Does it make you feel better to fantasize doing it?"

"Sure. I've been raised on the same movies as everyone else. If a guy insults you, shames you in front of other people, a swift right to the jaw and everything is solved, right?"

"In movies, perhaps. But in life it works differently. Even if you'd hit Ward, it would have had no effect on the real issue—the way you feel about yourself." She paused. "What was it he said again?"

Chris felt perplexed and a little resentful. Delphine had had him repeat the statement twice already. It was almost as if she were forcing him to say the words, again and again, to torture him. His voice was sullen now as he repeated them still once more. "He said—'You're not really a man, are you?'"

"*Why* did he say that?"

"You know what he meant."

"But I don't know why he thought it. There's nothing effeminate about you. You're as masculine as any other young man."

He shrugged. "I suppose he must have heard something."

"Heard something about what?"

"About Noah and me. We've been lovers for a long time, after all."

"Have you been openly lovers?"

"No, not openly. It's never been open. But show business is a very small world. It's no secret, either."

"How long has this relationship been going on? Eight years, is it?"

"Nine years."

"Nine years." Delphine looked thoughtful. "You have had a sexual relationship with an older man for nine years. And yet you're upset when a relative stranger makes an insulting reference to it? You see what I mean, Christopher," she went on, in her low, soothing voice. "The real issue is not some casual insult. It's the fact that, even after nine years, you still react with such shame to it."

He started to reply, then caught himself. He had wanted to say that there was more to his anger at Ward Kennan than just shame. But there was no point arguing; basically, he realized, she was right. His shame *was* the issue. It was why he was paying her sixty dollars an hour.

"Okay," Chris said curtly. "That's why I came to you."

"You came to me because you want to change?"

"Change? I don't know. I just want to stop feeling lousy about myself every day of my life." He gazed at her challengingly. "I'm not a queer," he said. "I don't like feeling like one."

"I believe you, Christopher," she said, smiling gently. "You don't have to prove anything to *me*." Her smile faded. "But, if you want me to help you, I'm afraid you're going to have to cooperate more than you have so far."

"I've cooperated. I've told you everything."

"Only up to a point. Then you block."

He knew what she was getting at—lately, in their sessions, she had kept returning to this same area, poking at it tentatively—and, as always, he stiffened with apprehension.

"We've discussed your work," Delphine went on, "we've covered your childhood, and we've touched on some of your affairs with both men and women. We've also talked about your relationship with Noah—but not completely." She paused significantly. "Every time I ask you about the way it began, you cut me off. You don't seem to want to talk about it."

"No, I guess I don't," he said.

"But then, if you're not open with me, there's no point in going on with our therapy. You understand that, don't you?"

"Yeah." He waited, but Delphine didn't continue. She seemed to want more of an answer from him. "I haven't tried to hide anything," he said. "I intend to tell you all of it—but gradually, in my own good time. There are some things I just haven't been ready to go into." With a vague gesture, he added, "Like what you're referring to."

"Are you ready now?"

"No. But you're right, I can't keep putting it off." He ran his hand through his hair nervously, then mustered up a smile. "What's the question again?"

"How did you first meet Noah?"

"Yeah, well, you see," Chris began, "we didn't become friends the usual way." His mouth was dry and he felt his voice weakening. "We met on Third—" He broke off. The words wouldn't come.

After a moment, Delphine asked gently, "Would you like to lie down, Christopher?"

He glanced at the leather couch against the wall, imagined himself stretched out on it, and almost laughed at the cliché image. "I don't think I need *that*."

"It might be easier for you. It would relax you—and help you to focus."

"All right," he said, rising. "I'm game."

He crossed to the couch and lay down on it. He heard a light scraping noise as Delphine pulled over a chair and sat a few feet from him but beyond his range of vision. He didn't turn his head to look. He stared up at the ceiling and concentrated on the yellowish streaks in the plaster.

He would think of it as an acting exercise, he decided. He would take an adjustment and become that other Chris—Chris Gustafsen, from Racine, Wisconsin, the first-string halfback at Park High who used to neck with his girl out by the lighthouse on Wind Point. He would let that Chris tell it, as just a role he was playing.

"I was a hustler," he said. "I peddled my ass."

There was silence. Then he heard Delphine say quietly: "Go on."

"I was working Third Avenue. One night, Noah picked me up. I was trade. Get the picture?"

"Trade?" she echoed uncertainly. "That means a male prostitute?"

"More than that. When you're trade," he explained, "you're straight, but you sell yourself to gay men. You don't have to do anything, just let the man have his fun. You don't even have to pretend to like it. Or like him."

"Why were you doing this?"

"Why do you think? Because I was broke."

"Couldn't you get a job?"

"I was twenty, I didn't know anybody in New York. I'd dropped out of college after one year—I didn't have any job skills—I was just a kid bumming around. It was about the only thing that presented itself."

"What do you mean, 'presented itself'?"

"First, you get propositions. After a while, if you're broke enough and hungry enough, you say, 'What the hell?' "

"Wasn't it a difficult step to take—with your background?"

"What background? Where I grew up, you end up working at either the Johnson's Wax factory or the Horlick's factory—or you work at Trantum Lumber, like my old man does." He laughed. "Turning hustler didn't seem such a come-down." He paused, then added: "Anyway, I knew it was only temporary. Until I got on my feet."

"And it was Noah Porterfield who put you on your feet?"

"Yeah. After that first night, he wanted to see me again, so it became a regular thing between us. He started treating me like a person, like I was someone who might have a mind. He'd give me books to read, and he'd have me read out loud from plays—Shakespeare—Chekhov—Tennessee Williams—I was flattered that he took such an interest in me. I was just a hayseed, after all, and he was a big Broadway producer."

"But, of course, you wanted to be an actor."

"Not then. Not yet." Chris thought for a moment, then qualified it. "Oh, it *had* crossed my mind. In school, girls would make a fuss about the way I looked—tell me I should be in the movies, that kind of thing. But I didn't take it seriously. The only people who acted in Racine were the fags at the little theater, and I didn't want to be one of *them*," he said, affecting a horrified tone. "It was Noah who made me get serious about it."

"He encouraged you?"

"He made it all possible. He paid for my acting classes, my professional photographs, bought me a wardrobe. He even picked out my stage name—'Greene' with an 'e' at the end; he said the 'e' gave it class. Then, when I was ready, he set up my first auditions and helped me get my first jobs."

"But he was helping you for his own purposes, wasn't he?"

"What do you mean?"

"Well, for instance, was he developing you to act in his productions?"

"No. Noah has made a point of never using me. He didn't want to seem like he was playing favorites. We're talking about my doing the lead in his next show," he added. "But that would be the first time."

"Has he profited from your success in any way?"

"No, not at all."

"Then why did he do it? Why did he help you so much?"

Chris was a bit perplexed; it seemed a strange question to ask. "Because he loves me," he said.

Though he couldn't see her, he sensed her disapproval; it was an almost palpable chill in the silence. He felt as if he were back at grammar school and he had just given a disastrously wrong answer to the teacher's question.

"And what do you feel?" Delphine asked at length. "Do you love him, too?"

"I don't know," Chris said. "I care for him. I care for him a lot."

"You care for him," she repeated slowly, laying out the phrase, as if she were trying to get a hold on it. "You care for him as a father."

"No, I don't think of him as a father."

"He's old enough, isn't he?"

"Sure, he's old enough. But he's not my father. I have a father already."

"But Noah is everything that your biological father isn't—cultured, sophisticated, tender. Don't you see, Christopher? Noah is a substitution." Her voice was warm and insistent. "He is the father that you wanted, that you needed."

Chris thought it over, tried to see Noah in this new light, but it only confused him. "I don't know. My feelings for him are—heavier somehow."

"Yes, of course. Your feelings are complicated, tangled, so that sometimes you feel you love Noah and—sometimes you hate him, don't you?" She paused. "Haven't you ever hated him? Wanted to be free of him?"

"Yes," he whispered.

"Why do you hate him, Christopher?"

He hesitated, though he knew he would have to answer. In the silence, he could hear himself breathing, more rapidly, agitatedly. "Because I think he's destroying me."

"Destroying you?"

"Yes!" he cried out, the anguish surging up in him. "He's fucking up my whole life!" He put his hand to his eyes, a second too late to hold back the unmanly tears.

Delphine was stroking his hair gently, with maternal tenderness. "It's all right, Christopher," she murmured. "It's all right."

Her touch was healing. The pain faded and he breathed evenly again. "Well," he said, trying to smile, "you see why I'm coming to you."

"Because you're afraid you're being destroyed?" Her hand withdrew and her voice was quietly authoritative once more. "That's not neurotic. That's a healthy recognition of a dangerous situation. Noah *will* destroy you," she said, "if you continue in this relationship. He won't do it consciously, he'll think of it as love, but it *will* happen."

She paused, as if she were waiting for him to reply, but he kept silent. She had never said it directly before, and he was fascinated. He sensed the great importance of this moment and his whole being focused on whatever her next words might be.

"Think of yourself as sixteen years old," Delphine went on. "Because, emotionally, that's what you are now—a very sensitive boy, still unformed, highly impressionable." She spoke carefully, in the patient tone of a concerned teacher, as if he were, indeed, a teenager, her most cherished pupil. "From this point, you can develop in one of two directions. You can become an avowed homosexual like Noah, with all of the loneliness and unhappiness that involves. Or you can become a normal, self-sufficient man, with a woman to love you, a man who is totally accepted by everyone." She waited a moment, allowing time for it to sink in, then asked, "Which would you rather be?"

"I want to be a normal man," Chris said.

"Good," she said.

The approval in her voice soothed Chris, eased him. He had given her a right answer, at last, and he felt a warm glow from having pleased her with it.

"Then," she went on, more briskly, "we can start taking the first steps toward that goal now. When are you seeing Noah next?"

"Tonight. After the show."

"Don't see him. Make an excuse."

"I can't do that," he protested mildly. "He'd be disappointed."

"Well, of course. But you have to be prepared to disappoint Noah from now on."

"Yeah, I know, but—" She was missing the point, and he searched for the words now to express it. "Aside from everything else, Noah is my *friend*. He's just about the only real friend I've got."

"All right," Delphine said, "then you can go on having him as a friend—for now. But that is all." She stressed the words meaningfully. "A friend, nothing more. Tonight, when you see him, don't have sexual relations with him."

"I won't."

He felt the touch of her hand again. It rested on his shoulder and patted him reassuringly. "Some day, Christopher," she said, "you will meet a woman that you'll love very much. Then all this unhappiness, these growing pains, will seem childish and unimportant. Do you believe that?"

"Yes," he said after a moment.

*   *   *

Chris took off his makeup. He applied the Albolene cream with his fingertips, spreading it around on his cheeks and neck until it swirled orange, then wiped it off with Kleenex tissues. His paler street face looked back at him from the mirror now, damp and glistening, with dark smudges still around his eyes and bits of base remaining at the bridge of his nose and near his scalp line. He dipped his fingers into the cream jar and repeated the process.

He was in no hurry. He was expecting visitors, but even when no one came back to see him after a performance he was still one of the last to leave the theater. He liked the special feel of the place, not only the excitement when the performance was on but the stillness when the house was empty, and he tended to spend more time there than the other actors did. Usually, he would get to the theater an hour early, before the rest of the company had arrived, and settle into his dressing room to go over the script. He would pick out a scene and try to find something new in it. Or he would just think, but as his character, not himself, getting himself in a frame of mind for the performance.

The performance was everything. Each moment of the day, from the time he woke up in the morning, pointed toward it, prepared him for it.

But when the curtain went down, the performance ceased to exist for him. It was as if it had never happened. He would feel keyed up, fatigued, but seemingly for no real reason—because of something that was past, gone beyond recall, leaving only the barest memory.

And so now, as he removed the last of his makeup, he wasn't thinking back on the previous two or three hours, the latest dead fragment of his on-stage existence. He was remembering what Delphine had said to him that afternoon. He was wondering if, in fact, he would some day meet a woman that he could love.

Outside in the corridor, the ingenue was calling out a cheery "good night" to the stage manager. She was already dressed and was hastening to meet her boyfriend. Chris glanced at his wristwatch, which was lying beside the tubes and jars on the dressing table. It was about five minutes later than he had thought.

Could Vivian Loring have changed her mind? When she had called him that morning to ask for house seats, she had specifically said that she would come back to see him after the show. Perhaps her escort, whoever he was—she had casually mentioned that it wouldn't be Ward Kennan—had other plans. Or perhaps, Chris couldn't help thinking, with an actor's insecurity, they hadn't thought he was any good.

He would be disappointed if Vivian didn't turn up. He liked her, as he liked all stylish, attractive women. That was a good point—he should have brought it up with Delphine—that, as a general rule, he liked women more readily than men.

But love? That was something else.

Then again, he reflected, some women could touch off emotions in him; not real love, perhaps, but actual, honest-to-God emotions, often with no logic to them. As in Vivian's case, for instance. He barely knew her, and yet he had been ready to fight a man for her sake, and would have, if her friend Eric hadn't restrained him. Something about her had gotten to him.

The stage manager poked his head in the doorway of the dressing room. "People to see you, Chris," he said. "Is it all right?"

"Sure," Chris replied. "Send them on in."

The stage manager disappeared. A few moments later, Vivian was standing in the doorway, stunning in a low-cut black dress. A slight, red-haired man wearing a bow tie appeared behind her. It was Eric Bayliss.

"Hi," Chris said to them. "I was wondering if you'd made it."

"Well," Eric said, "sophisticated New Yorkers that we are, we couldn't find the stage door."

Chris laughed and said, "Come in."

Vivian and Eric stepped into the dressing room, but hesitated by the door shyly. They both were eyeing him with rapt, uneasy smiles on their faces. Chris knew that look; it was the typical member-of-the-audience-seeing-him-after-the-show expression. He may have seemed an ordinary fellow-citizen when he had dined with them at the Hubers', but now, with the spell of the performance not yet faded, they were looking at him as if he were something other than human, an artifice that might disintegrate before their eyes.

"You were wonderful," Vivian said fervently.

"Terrific," Eric said.

"Thanks," he said. He wiped the cream from his hands and watched Vivian out of the corner of his eye as she sat in the chair nearest him. She was gazing at him rather hungrily. He glanced in the mirror, at his bare, lean torso and well-muscled shoulders, dispassionately taking in what she was seeing.

He tossed the tissue aside, swung around in the chair and faced them. "How did you like the show?"

Vivian looked uncertain. Eric, standing beside her, supplied the answer. "It was fun," he said brightly but guardedly.

Chris needed to ask nothing further. He knew that the play was no great shakes, a stock family comedy that was being produced only because it provided a meaty part for the star, a modestly talented but greatly exposed television comic. Chris didn't like the man, didn't like acting with him, and he had never been comfortable playing his loving son. He hadn't minded it at all when, after Chris got the reviews, the star stopped talking to him completely. But he didn't kid himself; the star was the reason they had all picked up a full season's employment from the show.

"It's a good vehicle for Alan," Chris commented.

"Maybe," Eric said. "But he's never been my favorite

comedian. You're a much better actor."

Chris shrugged. "The people don't pay to see *me*. They flock in to see Alan. The power of television." He said it unthinkingly. But then, remembering his argument with Vivian's lover, he smiled at her and added, "I guess I don't have to tell *you* about it."

Vivian seemed embarrassed by the reminder. "Please," she said, "don't confuse my opinions with anybody else's. What Ward thinks is one thing, what I think is another."

"I don't doubt it."

"I love the theater more than anything," Vivian went on earnestly. "There's nothing so exciting as watching a talented actor work on stage. Tonight, you made me laugh, you made me cry, and, for a little while, you made me glad to be alive. Pictures on a box can't do any of that for me."

It was a pretty speech, with sentiments he had heard many times before, but he recognized that it was more than the usual fan gush. As Vivian leaned forward in the chair, her dark eyes large and intense, she seemed to be trying to communicate with him and, at the same time, to draw something from him, to ingest some essence of him.

Chris looked at her, momentarily mesmerized. Now, as at the Hubers', he felt oddly moved by her, though he couldn't tell exactly why. It wasn't simply because she was beautiful, or because she was so clearly in desperate need. Somehow, in some obscure way, it was the combination of both.

Eric broke the silence. "Are you free now, Chris?" he asked. "We'd love to have you come along with us to get a bite to eat."

"Thanks," Chris said, "but I have a date."

"A date?" Vivian echoed.

"Well, it's not really a date. I'm dropping by to see an old friend of mine." Vivian continued to look curious, and Chris wondered if he should clarify the sex of his friend. Instead, he told her, "We'll get together soon."

"I hope we do. We all have something in common, after all," she said lightly. "Delphine."

"We may have even more in common than that," Chris murmured, meeting her gaze. It was automatic matinee-idol flirtatiousness, he could turn it on in an instant, but now the impulse felt halfway real.

He remembered Delphine's prediction. Give it a chance, he thought.

"I'll tell you what," he said suddenly. "I'm usually free in the afternoons. I know Eric is working, but would it be all right if I came by *your* place, sometime in the next few days, to have a drink with you?"

Vivian's smile was quick and radiant. "Yes," she said. "Yes, I'd like that."

Noah had made a particularly good supper for him; steak béarnaise and artichokes vinaigrette, accompanied by a fine, vintage Médoc. Now, as they sat on the terrace of the penthouse apartment, sipping brandy and looking out over the moonlit park, Chris felt settled in and relaxed, drowsy with a sense of well-being. It was the kind of mood that phases naturally into lovemaking and sleep. He had to remind himself that, this time, he wasn't staying. Soon he would have to cut it short and leave.

Noah hadn't said anything for a while. He was savoring his brandy and enjoying his view. His bald, Roman emperor's head was turned away from Chris as Noah gazed down and to the left at the moving lights flowing uptown on Central Park West.

At length, Noah looked at him and asked, "How did the show go tonight?" Sooner or later he always asked it, and it was never an idle question. Noah had a keen interest in the workings of every performance in every theater in town.

"It was a little down, I thought," Chris replied. "But we had a good audience. We didn't have to force at all."

"Is Alan still stepping on your laughs?"

Chris snorted. "He's starting to grind them in with his heel."

"There are ways of fighting back, you know."

"Yeah, but I'm too disciplined, I guess. Anyway, what difference does it make? We're closing next week." After a moment, he said, "A couple of people I know were there tonight."

"In the business?"

"No. Fellow patients. They go to Delphine too."

"Oh yes," Noah purred. He had never met Delphine, but he seemed to dislike her anyway. Whenever Chris mentioned her name, the dangerous purr would come into Noah's voice and a tight smile would compress his mouth.

"How did they like the show?" he asked.

"They thought it was junk."

Noah's eyebrows went up. "They said that?"

"They didn't have to say it. Oh, I don't know about the woman," Chris qualified. "But I could tell that's what the man was thinking. He's a publishing type," he added.

"Publishing!" Noah drawled scornfully. "What do *those* people know? I suppose this man expects Beckett every time he goes to the theater. You can't raise a quarter of a million on Beckett."

"It doesn't have to be Beckett," Chris said. "But it doesn't have to be the crap I'm doing now, either. Why can't I ever be in a good play? *You* do them."

"That's because of my misguided attitude, baby."

Noah said it ruefully, as if it were the cross he bore. In fact, he was one of the most successful producers on Broadway. He had earned a solid reputation and a considerable fortune in a field where only a handful of entrepreneurs could even survive.

Noah, who came from an old-money Maine family, had started off his adult years with a Yale degree, a modest but sufficient inherited income, and a passion for the theater. He had served a lengthy apprenticeship in the business as an actor, a stage manager, a stock company director—"I was equally lousy at all of them," he would cheerfully tell Chris—and then, finally, had tried his hand at producing and had found his true calling.

He operated on one simple rule: he would only do a play that he, personally, thought was good. Otherwise, he disregarded trends, agents' packages, and the economic wisdom of any given season. As a result, almost fifty percent of his shows had been hits.

"How's the new one going?" Chris asked. "Has the rewrite come in yet?"

"I got it this morning."

Chris's interest perked up. Noah had discovered a play at a staged reading in an Off-Off-Broadway loft. Chris had read it and had been impressed with it as it was. But Noah had set the playwright to work on a major revision.

"So?" Chris asked. "Is it better?"

"Aren't we eager?" Noah regarded him with a teasing smile. "Yes, it's better." He paused. "The lead role is juicier than ever."

"I was asking about the play."

"Of course you were, baby. Actors *never* worry about their own parts."

Chris smiled and tried to look indifferent. Underneath, he felt elated. Noah had half promised him the part already. But this was the first time he had implied it was an accomplished fact.

"I had a copy xeroxed specially for you," Noah said. "You want to see it?"

"Sure," Chris said.

They rose and went back into the apartment. Chris followed Noah down the hallway that was lined with framed posters for the biggest Noah Porterfield successes, as well as a few for the beloved failures. He thought that they were going to Noah's office-den. But they passed by it and went on into his bedroom.

The script was lying on a table beside the king-sized bed.

Noah picked it up and held it out to him. "Here it is," he said, with an upward lilt in his voice, as if he were presenting a gift to an insistent child.

Chris took the script and looked down at it. It was a plain xerox copy, bound with a rubber band. It seemed a bit heavier than the first version he had read. "Thanks. I'll read this when I go home tonight."

The smile vanished from Noah's face. "Tonight?"

"Yeah. I don't feel so hot." He felt a little foolish making the excuse, claiming an ailment as if he were a reluctant wife. "Maybe I've got a bug."

"You look fine to me."

"I want to go home," Chris said shortly. "All right?"

He sensed the tremor of anger in Noah. He could never see it; it came and went invisibly. But, for one moment, he would get a distinct impression of the power in Noah's short, barrel-chested body, the lethal violence latent in his thick, muscular arms. Chris registered the tremor, a severe one; then it passed and Noah was once again a benign, middle-aged man in sandals and a half-unbuttoned sports shirt, his eyes twinkly, his smile serene.

"Did you see your shrink today?" Noah inquired pleasantly.

"Yes." Chris knew what he was thinking, and quickly he said, "We didn't talk about you."

It was a futile lie, and Noah's skeptical expression let him know it. "No? You never talk about me?"

"Oh, I've mentioned you. But mainly I talk about my career, my hang-ups."

"And Delphine—she talks too? She's not like a Freudian who just hums in his beard?"

"She talks, all right. She's got a lot to say."

"I can imagine," Noah purred. "The way you describe her, she sounds more like a guru than an analyst."

"Well, she's *not* an analyst."

"Then what is she?"

"The one time I asked her, she said she was a—" Chris paused, to make sure he had it right: "—a growth therapist."

"A growth therapist," Noah repeated. Quietly he said, "You've grown from nothing, baby, in the time I've known you."

"I can grow more," Chris said.

Suddenly Noah looked tired, defeated. "All right," he said. "Go home, if you want."

Chris gazed at him helplessly, all of his determination gone. A powerful, threatening Noah he could resist. A weak, wounded Noah he couldn't bear.

Nine years with a man, he realized, couldn't just be undone, so coldly, so swiftly. He would have to go about it more gently, over a longer period of time. He owed it to Noah. He owed it to himself.

Chris sat on the edge of the bed and slipped off his shoes.

Noah looked at him uncertainly for a moment, then his smile slowly reappeared. He came over to Chris and ruffled his hair tenderly. Chris put his arms around him and rested his head against his chest.

"Feeling better already?" Noah asked.

"I feel fine now," Chris said.

And, in fact, for the first time that day, he felt at ease, secure. He closed his eyes and drew in Noah's warmth.

6

"IF VIVIAN wasn't such a dear friend," Mandy said, "I would have tried to forget about it. And then, I suppose, I would have gone on feeling guilty for God knows how long."

Ward shrugged lightly and poked his fork into his coquilles St. Jacques.

"But she does matter to me," Mandy went on, "and I know she matters to you. So, I've made the first move, and here we are, and"—she took a deep breath before she said it—"I want to apologize."

"For what? For telling me to go fuck myself?" Ward laughed. "My dear lady, you're not the first person in this town to have made that request."

"But it was wrong of me. You were my guest."

"Don't be silly. I would have said the same thing in your place. Anyway," he added, "you're stealing my lines. *I* was going to apologize to *you*."

"Okay, I've beaten you to it."

"On second thought, let's neither of us apologize. Let's just enjoy our lunch."

"Yes, but—" Mandy began, then stopped. She had been about to pursue it further. Instead, she sat back and relaxed. Perhaps she had made too big a thing of this, she realized. Now that she was alone with Ward Kennan in one of his more natural habitats, the "21" Club, seeing him as he was during his business day, civilized and sober, she had a very different impresson of him. He was a long way from seeming the drunken lout who had disrupted her dinner party. She was beginning to have some idea of what Vivian saw in him.

"We can look at the bright side of it," Ward said, with his most charming smile. "If nothing else, it's been an excuse for us to have this lunch and get to know each other better."

"Well, yes," she said, with a little laugh, "this *is* nice."

Was he coming on with her? she wondered. She assumed that Ward was simply being gallant. Then again, Delphine *had* said that she could be as attractive to men as Vivian, if she gave herself the chance. She found herself speculating, for a brief moment, as to what kind of lover Ward might be. Experienced, certainly, skillful, and yet, she guessed, very tender.

But, no, she chided herself, she musn't think that way. Ward belonged to Vivian. Anyway, it wasn't the reason she had proposed this lunch.

"When I called you," Mandy went on, "I wanted to straighten things out between us. But also I wanted to talk to you about something else. I have an idea, and I'd like to know what you think of it."

"An idea? About what?"

"About Vivian," she said. "You know she's been in a blue funk lately."

It was an understatement. She hadn't seen her in a week and a half, since the night of the unfortunate dinner, but Vivian had been phoning her almost daily. Her calls were becoming progressively more despondent.

"Yes, she *has* been down," Ward commented. "What's your idea?"

"I thought it would be nice if we got together to make some kind of gesture—you know, to cheer her up."

"What do you have in mind?"

Ward's expression was noncommittal, and Mandy paused, suddenly uncertain. She had checked out the idea with Delphine, and her therapist had given it her blessing. "It could only have a positive result," Delphine had said. But now, with Ward's cautiously curious gaze on her, Mandy was starting to feel uneasy.

"You know that Vivian's birthday is next week?" she asked.

"Yes, I'm aware of it." There was a touch of vagueness to Ward's tone; it was clear that it hadn't been too much on his mind. "Thursday, isn't it?"

"Wednesday," she replied. "I think it would be nice if we gave Vivian a dinner party."

"That's a *terrific* idea," Ward said, with polite enthusiasm and a perceptible loss of interest. He went back to his coquilles.

"When I say 'we,' I mean 'you.' "

He looked up, a bit startled. "Me?"

"The invitation should come from you, and the dinner should be at your place."

He laughed uncomfortably. "Well, you know, I'm just a bumbling divorced man. I don't even know how to cook."

This seemed a little disingenuous to Mandy, since she knew that Ward had two in-help, a chauffeur-valet and a maid.

"You don't have to worry about it," she said. "I'll order the food, I'll do the cooking. But it all has to seem as if it's coming from you, as if the whole thing is your idea. That way, it will mean something to Vivian."

Ward was still looking dubious. "I don't know—"

"She's feeling so insecure these days," Mandy said more intensely. "You have to show her you care for her."

"I *do* care for her. But it's been so long since I've done this kind of thing. Were you envisioning something big?"

"No," she assured him, "we'll keep it very small." She quickly revised the plan in her head scaling it down to the bare minimum. "Jeff and myself—Eric Bayliss and a date—Vivian—you."

Ward thought for a moment, then shrugged. "All right, I'm game."

"Then we're on?"

"We're on. Another dinner party." His smile was easy and charming again. "This time, we'll see if we can behave."

"Vivian is so excited about this birthday dinner," Mandy said. "You know what she did today? She went out and bought a new dress."

Jeff glanced up from his copy of *Women's Wear Daily*. "Doesn't she have enough dresses already?"

"She wanted to wear something new. For luck."

"I thought you said she was broke," Jeff said returning to his paper.

"She is. But she has credit cards."

"What about the shrink?" he asked. "Does Delphine take American Express, too?"

Mandy stared at him for a long moment. "What do you mean by *that* crack?" she asked icily.

Jeff looked up at her now, saw her expression, and almost quailed. "Just making a joke," he explained weakly.

"Don't make jokes about what you don't understand."

"What don't I understand? Not paying bills I understand."

"Vivian and Delphine have a very close, very special relationship. Money doesn't enter into it. Anyway," she added, "if Vivian marries Ward, the bill won't be a problem any more."

"No, I suppose it won't," Jeff agreed.

He waited for her to say something further. She didn't and he went back to reading his paper.

Mandy sat still in the straight-backed chair. She had intended to sit for only a few moments, just long enough for a swift chat before dinner, but now she lingered and studied her husband with cool distaste. She noticed that he was continuing to put on weight. Already he had reached the point where he seemed to be not so much sitting in the armchair as deposited in it, a bulging mass sinking into the upholstery. He had unbuttoned the top button of his pants, a relatively new step in his evening ritual.

Otherwise, the rest of it was the same; he hadn't deviated from the ritual in ten years. He was about two thirds of the way through now; the *Post* was done with, *Women's Wear Daily* was in progress, the martini beside him was all but consumed. Soon she would ask "Are you ready for dinner now?" and he would grunt an amiable "Yeah." It could go on like this for another thirty years and nothing would change, except that Jeff would grow fatter, and he might start drinking a second martini, perhaps.

There had to be something else.

She remembered Delphine's words: *You've never been free to be yourself—as a talent, as a woman.* She had that thought often now, a thought she hadn't dared think before—or only rarely, and not early in her marriage, certainly. Then she had delighted in this cocktail hour with Jeff, reveled in the company of her strong, tender, all-knowing husband. She had seen him differently in those days. She hadn't had her breakthrough yet.

A clever businessman, in no way remarkable, who has exploited his highly talented wife to build a successful business for himself.

No, she could never see him in that dumb, loving way again.

"Well, what do you know!" Jeff said suddenly. "Looks like Vivian may need some luck after all."

"What are you talking about?"

"Take a gander at this." He folded the copy of *Women's Wear Daily* and turned it toward her, with the "Eye" page, the gossip section, facing out.

Mandy rose and went over to look at it. The page was covered with photographs of guests at some glittering party. At first, the pictures meant nothing to her. Then she saw the one at the lower right-hand corner and snatched the paper out of Jeff's hands.

It was a photograph of Ward Kennan, in a dinner jacket, and a blond girl in a long dress. She was prom-queen pretty, with a snub nose and a petulant mouth, and she was hanging rather clingingly on Ward's arm. The caption simply said: *Ward Kennan and Suzy Beswick.*

"Who's Suzy Beswick?" Mandy asked.

"You're asking me?" Jeff responded. "*I'm* not one of the beautiful people."

Mandy studied the photograph for another moment, then handed the paper back to Jeff. "It doesn't mean a thing," she said. "Ward dates other women. We all know that."

"But this one is so young," Jeff said, looking at the picture again.

Mandy sniffed. "She's as old as I am."

"No, she isn't. You're young, but she's *really* young. No more than twenty-three or twenty-four." He gazed at the photograph appreciatively. "She's a good-looking piece."

"Are you trying to upset me?" she snapped.

Jeff looked up quickly, as if her tone had startled him. "Just making a comment."

"You're doing it deliberately, aren't you?" she said, flaring up. "You're glad about it!"

"Why would I be glad?"

"Because you think it's making a fool out of me! You *know* all the trouble I'm going to for this dinner."

Jeff's eyes were wide. "Why do you look at me that way?" he asked softly.

The question stopped her short. "How am I looking at you?"

"Like you hate me."

She avoided his eyes now. "Oh, I'm worried about Vivian, I guess."

"It's got nothing to do with Vivian. You look at me that way, sometimes, when we're talking about other things. I don't get it," he said perplexedly. "Have I done something wrong?"

She looked at him and tried to smile. "No."

"Then, be nice, hon," he said, gently pleading. "Please, be nice. I can't stand it when you're like this."

A wave of tender concern went through her. When Jeff dropped his wise-guy manner and let her see him like this, helpless and vulnerable, a chubby, middle-aged boy, he could always melt her. Her impulse was to go to him, sit on his lap and stroke his hair.

But she caught herself. It was what she would have done before, when she didn't yet understand. She couldn't be taken in so easily now.

"Are you ready for dinner?" she asked.

Phyllis answered the phone. "Mrs. Huber's office . . . Just a moment, please." She looked back at Mandy. "Ward Kennan."

Mandy turned away from the sketch she was working on and picked up her receiver. "Hi, Ward. How are you?"

"Fine, thanks, Mandy. And you?"

"Getting ready for Vivian's birthday," she said brightly. "I've got the most delicious menu planned."

"Yeah, well—" He paused. "Maybe you'd better hold up on that."

"What do you mean—hold up?"

"I'm having second thoughts about it, Mandy." Ward sounded uncharacteristically awkward; the self-confidence was gone from his tone. "It might be a better idea if I just took Vivian out to a restaurant somewhere."

"After all this build-up?" For a moment, Mandy was too shocked to go on. Then, very emphatically, she said, "We've told Vivian we're giving her a party, we'll *give* her a party. What's got into you, Ward? You agreed to it!"

"It's making such a big thing of it. It's only her birthday."

"It has nothing to do with her birthday. It means *more* than that to her."

There was a silence.

"I just don't feel right about it, Mandy."

"Why not?"

"Private reasons."

"Can you tell me?"

"No, I can't."

There was something disturbingly ominous in his tone, but Mandy didn't question him further. She was in no mood to play guessing games with him. "Look, Ward," she said, "I don't know what your problem is. But it would break Vivian's heart if you canceled now. We're going through with this."

After a moment, he said resignedly, "All right, if you insist."

"Is it such a difficult thing to do? It's just a dinner."

"That's right, it's just a dinner." There was another brief pause. "Remember, Mandy, this was *your* idea."

"What do you mean by that?"

"Just clarifying it. See you Wednesday night." He hung up.

Mandy held the receiver in midair, frozen with apprehension. For the first time it occurred to her that, with the best intentions in the world, in the purest spirit of friendship, she might have arranged another disaster.

7

THERE WAS a small pink envelope in Eric's morning mail. No return address was on it; only his name, the firm, and the firm's address, written in a round, flowing hand. Curious, he opened this envelope first.

It contained a square white card, with a black border drawn along its edges. The words on it were meticulously and ornately printed in ink:

> *Ms. Lucille Castelli wishes to announce*
> *the demise of her relationship with*
> *the big bozo in the pinstripe suit.*
> *(No flowers. All contributions*
> *should be sent to the Fresh Air Fund.)*

Eric smiled as he remembered the brunette at the book party, Naomi Lamb's friend. He had thought back on her once or twice, but he had assumed that their brief party flirtation had been the beginning and end of it. Evidently, Lucy had other ideas.

She had printed two phone numbers at the lower left-hand corner of the card, with "business" and "home" after them. Eric dialed the business number now.

It was a direct line and a woman's voice answered. "Hello?"

"Lucy Castelli?"

"Yes."

"This is Eric Bayliss."

"Oh, *hi*." Her voice hit a little grace note of delight.

"I got the sad news this morning," Eric said solemnly. He decided he might as well go along with her joke. "About your relationship. Did it suffer much near the end?"

"It never knew what hit it."

"I don't know what to say. Is there anything I can do?"

"Yes," she replied instantly. "You can take me out."

This was going a little fast, even for Eric's rhythm. "If you had given me a couple of seconds," he pointed out mildly, "I would have suggested it myself."

"A girl never can be sure."

"But you're going to have to let me think about it. I'm not sure where to take you. I don't know much about you, after all. Just that you're cute, you're an art director, and you're from Nutley, New Jersey."

"That's all there *is* to know. I have no mystery. Do you mind?"

"I don't mind. But it still doesn't tell me what kind of food you like."

"I can eat anything, in any surroundings, at any price range. And we can go Dutch, if you want," she added helpfully.

"That won't be necessary. But—" A sudden thought occurred to him. "I've got an idea. A friend of mine is having a birthday Wednesday. Her gentleman friend is giving her a little dinner party. Would you like to come along with me?"

"I'd love to."

For the first time, there was a touch of hesitancy in Lucy's tone. She, of course, didn't know what to expect. Eric, for that matter, didn't either.

"Fine," he said. "I'll pick you up at seven. Where do you live, by the way?"

"One twenty-four Waverly Place. Do you know where that is?"

"Sure. I live in the Village too. Bank Street."

"That simplifies things, doesn't it?" she said with a laugh.

"Yeah." He hesitated, not wanting to be too transparent, then asked, "Is it your name by the doorbell?"

"My name." As if she were reading his thought, she assured him, "No roommates. It's just me and my cat."

"Terrific," Eric said. "See you Wednesday evening, then."

The three of them found themselves alone in a corner of the maisonette's living room. Lucy had drifted into the room by herself. Eric, a little concerned about her, had followed her, and, a moment later, Vivian had joined them.

"How's it going?" Eric asked Lucy. He kept his voice subdued. Ward and the Hubers were only a short distance away, in the library-den that was on the other side of the arch.

"Fine," Lucy replied. "Why do you ask?"

"You haven't said much."

"Oh, I'm a slow starter. Anyway, this isn't quite what I expected." She laughed nervously. "I'm so embarrassed!"

"Why are you embarrassed?" Vivian asked.

"Well, look at me—" Lucy tugged at the wool of her plain brown sweater. "And look at *you*." Her gesture took in Vivian's pale-blue satin gown. It flowed from her neck to her ankles along classic Grecian lines, but was completely open at the sides, baring the outer halves of her breasts almost to the nipples.

"Just a little something I threw on," Vivian said negligently.

"I think you almost missed."

The comment might have sounded bitchy in the mouth of another woman. But Lucy said it with a good-natured smile, and Vivian simply laughed.

"No," Lucy went on, "you look sensational. I'm the drab mouse in this crowd. Eric didn't warn me this was going to be so posh."

"I'm not dressed," Eric pointed out.

"A man in a dark-blue suit is always dressed."

"Well, what were you expecting?"

"You told me a little dinner party. I thought we'd be sitting on the floor, drinking Gallo wine. A Village-type party, you know?"

"I guess I should have said uptown."

"Uptown! You should have said Versailles."

Lucy glanced around with an appropriately awestruck expression at the exquisite furniture in the cavernous living room. The pieces were consistent in style; all of them seemed to come from the same long-ago period, and Eric, who knew nothing about antiques, guessed that they might indeed be Louis Quatorze, or Louis Quinze, or some slightly later French king. At any rate, the room reminded him of nothing so much as one of those roped-off interiors in the Metropolitan Museum.

"Does Ward really *live* in this room?" Lucy asked.

"He hardly ever comes in here," Vivian said. "Oh, maybe he did when he had his family with him—his wife, his children. But since the divorce, it's just been he and the servants."

Lucy looked dismayed at the thought. "I wouldn't want to knock around in a place this big. Would you?"

"It could grow on me," Vivian said with a quiet smile.

Eric glanced at Vivian curiously. He had thought he had detected a note of confidence in her tone. If so, it was something new. It had been a long time since Vivian had shown any optimism at all about her relationship with Ward.

"I think we'd better join the others," Lucy said, turning to go back into the other room.

Eric didn't follow immediately. With a smile, he asked Vivian, "Things looking up?"

"I don't know," Vivian replied. "What do you think? Ward has never done anything like this for me before. Last time I had a birthday, I don't think he even noticed." With a little laugh, she said, "This must mean *something*."

"Let's hope it does," Eric said, holding out his arm to her.

She took his arm, squeezed his hand excitedly, and they went on into the library-den.

The white-coated manservant was passing around fresh drinks, another ginger ale for Mandy, a second martini for Jeff, and, for Ward, what was probably his fourth Scotch on the rocks. Lucy was standing by the archway, shyly hesitating before she sat again. The other three looked properly civilized and companionable as they sat at facing angles to each other, Ward and Jeff in dinner jackets, Mandy in a frilly beige gown. But the Hubers seemed a bit stiff, and Ward's fixed smile was cold, almost baleful. There was a silence as Eric and Vivian re-entered, and Eric had the impression that the conversation had not gone well in their absence.

Someone had to get the conversation rolling again, and it was Lucy, finally, who made the effort. "We've been looking around," she said to Ward. "And I don't think I've ever seen such a beautiful place."

"Yes, it's gorgeous, isn't it?" Mandy chimed in brightly.

"It's like a French chateau on Sutton Place," Jeff said helpfully.

"But done with taste," Mandy said.

"*I* like it," Ward said tersely, his set smile not even flickering.

There was another silence.

Lucy tried again. She crossed to the oversized chess set that was resting on a low table in front of the sofa and, tentatively, picked up the white king. It was the tallest of the ivory pieces, about six inches high. "What a magnificent chess set!" she said. "Where did you get it?"

"It's been in the family for a while," Ward said. "My grandfather bought it."

"It must be a joy playing with it."

Ward's interest seemed to perk up slightly. "You play chess?" he asked.

"No," Lucy admitted. "Actually, I don't."

"*I* used to," Eric offered.

Ward's gaze fixed on him. "Are you any good?"

"Not very. If you're serious about the game, I'd be no match for you."

"You used to play with David all the time," Vivian said.

"That was years ago," Eric said. "I haven't played since."

"Let's play a game," Ward said suddenly.

For a moment, Eric didn't know what to say. It was hardly the time or place for a game of chess. But Ward didn't seem to want to talk to his guests anyway; he had said very little to them, in fact, from the time they had arrived. Eric guessed he was seizing upon this as an excuse to be quit of his host's responsibility entirely.

"All right," Eric said.

Ward rose, pulled over a chair, and sat at one side of the board—the white side, Eric noticed. Eric sat opposite him on the sofa. Vivian stood beside Ward, one hand resting lightly on his shoulder, and looked down at the chessmen. Years before, Eric remembered, she had stood in that same way beside her husband, David, during those youthful evenings of chess, wine, and talk at the Lorings' old apartment.

Wasting no time, Ward played pawn to king four. Eric replied with pawn to queen's bishop four.

"Ah, the Sicilian Defense!" Vivian said softly.

"Is that what it's called?" Eric asked innocently. "Then maybe you can give me the next ten moves."

"You may not last ten moves," Vivian said. "Ward's got a killer gleam in his eyes."

And Ward, indeed, did have a demonic look of concentration on his flushed face, as he brought out his king's knight, then pushed his queen's pawn, the standard moves of the opening.

Eric made his moves quickly, going through the motions rather than playing with any great thought. Nevertheless, after a dozen moves, he could see that the game was turning out to be something other than he had expected. Ward had made a couple of pointless pawn moves in the center of the board, losing tempo. He was ignoring the build-up of power on the black queen's side. He was setting up an obvious doubled-rook attack, without the forces to back it up. Ward, Eric realized now, was quite a weak player.

After several more moves, Ward was a piece and a pawn down, and Vivian, beside him, was looking distressed. Her hand tightened on his shoulder as he moved his queen onto a square where it could be caught in a knight fork. A checking move by the black knight and the white queen was lost, the game was all but over.

Eric, responding by reflex, reached out to move his knight, then stopped his hand in midair. He glanced up at Vivian. There was a pleading look in her eyes.

He withdrew his hand and pretended to study the board for a moment. Then he moved his queen into the path of Ward's bishop.

Ward's lips parted excitedly. He slashed his bishop along the diagonal, took Eric's queen, then sat back and smiled at him triumphantly.

Eric shook his head. "You've got me beat, Ward." He tipped over his king. "I resign."

Ward clapped his hands together. "Good game," he said, rising. He turned to his manservant, who had just reappeared. "Is dinner ready?"

"Yes, Mr. Kennan."

"Okay, kiddies," Ward said genially. "Let's adjourn to the dining room." He now seemed in immensely good spirits.

Ward started out, with the Hubers close behind. Vivian lingered for just a moment before following. "Thank you, Eric," she said quietly.

After Vivian had gone on, Lucy asked, "What was she thanking you for?"

"I went into the tank," Eric said.

"You mean, you lost the game deliberately?" Lucy looked at him perplexed. "Why?"

"I've had more experience at losing than Ward."

They went down the hallway and into the dining room. The first course, avocado, was already served, and Ward and his guests were standing by their chairs, ready to sit. Candles burned in silver candelabra, casting a soft, flickering light onto the faces around the table.

Ward and Vivian were at either end of the table. Eric's place card put him on Vivian's left; Lucy took her place on Ward's left. When they were all in position, the men drew out the ladies' chairs and everyone sat.

It was only then that Vivian noticed the little square package beside her plate. "Is this for me?" she asked, picking it up.

"What do you think?" Ward said cheerfully. His victory elation hadn't quite worn off yet. "It's your birthday, isn't it?"

"A present?" Vivian put on a pretty little show of delighted surprise. Then, feebly, she protested, "I *told* you no presents."

"Open it up, Vivian!" Mandy said eagerly.

"Yeah, go on!" Jeff urged her.

While Vivian fumbled with the string and the wrapping, the maid went around the table pouring a red wine—a Margaux, Eric noticed, glancing at the label, a Château Lascombes 1967.

Vivian finally got the box unwrapped. She removed its lid and took out a diamond bracelet.

"My God!" she whispered. This time her astonishment was quite genuine. The diamonds were far from small. They gleamed impressively in the candlelight.

"It's beautiful!" Mandy exclaimed softly.

Jeff was staring at it, with an almost sick look on his face—thinking, perhaps, of the ornament's likely cost. "That's a hell of a good-looking bracelet, Ward," he said lamely.

"Oh, Ward," Vivian said, "I don't know what to say. It's—" She broke off, overcome.

"Put it on," Ward said.

Vivian carefully clasped the bracelet on her wrist and, extending her arm gracefully, admired it for a moment. Then she rose to her feet, tears streaming down her face. "Oh, Ward!" she murmured. "Ward!"

She started around the table to embrace him. But Ward quickly put up his hand, stopping her where she was. A bit puzzled, though with her happiness undampened, she took her seat again.

"I'd like to propose a toast," Mandy said, raising her glass.

"Hear, hear!" Jeff cried out, raising his glass also.

"To Vivian and Ward," Mandy said. She added, "Let's hope we'll be celebrating something for the *two* of them very soon."

They all raised their glasses and drank. All except Ward. He held his glass in midair, unmoving. His smile was tight and cold again.

"You're not drinking, Ward?" Jeff asked.

"I'd like to rephrase that toast," Ward said. He paused, as if he wasn't sure what to say next. "Mandy knows I was uncertain about this dinner party."

Mandy's smile shaded into uneasiness. "Why talk about it now, Ward?"

"Then I decided it might be a good idea after all," Ward went on. "It would give me a chance to tell all of you nice people a bit of good news."

He looked around at them. Eric found his hard, genial expression unsettling now. The gleam in his eyes was unfriendly, he had never looked meaner, and yet Ward was clearly enjoying himself, more than he had all evening. He seemed to be savoring each moment.

"I've made a big decision, folks," Ward announced. "I've decided I don't want to live alone any more." He raised his glass. "So, let's drink to *that*."

They all raised their glasses again. Vivian froze for a moment before remembering to raise hers. There was a dazed but excited look in her eyes.

Ward gazed directly at her. "I'd like to propose a toast to the woman I plan to marry."

Vivian smiled tremulously, as if she didn't dare yet believe, but was teetering on the brink of joy.

"Miss Suzanne Beswick."

The glass broke in Vivian's hand. The wine streamed down her wrist and over the bracelet, a red blur dulling the diamonds.

PART TWO

8

Dr. Sergius Winter went into the little social room at the end of the corridor. It was empty, as he knew it would be. He sank into an armchair and concentrated on getting his breath back. The ache in his chest was fading, the pain in his left arm had gone. This time, he felt sure, it was only fatigue, not the beginning of a coronary episode. He had spent a long day at the clinic and he was tired; it was as simple as that. He should have gone home and gotten into bed, instead of coming here to the Institute.

It wasn't too late to correct the mistake. As soon as he was up to it, he would leave. It wouldn't matter if he missed this seminar. He had been appearing regularly at these meetings, every other Tuesday night, for many years; not for any pleasure he derived from them—he was long past that point—but because he knew, though it was something unspoken, that his presence was required. He had been with the Institute almost from the time of its founding; he had worked personally with Harry Stack Sullivan. To the younger psychiatrists, he was the sacred relic that sanctified these occasions.

Well, soon they would have to learn to do without him. He would start appearing more infrequently now; after a while, he would stop coming at all. The demands of his work, he would tell them, his health.

His real feelings he would keep to himself. There was no diplomatic way he could make them understand that, while it could be touching, even sweet, to be venerated, it was a bitter thing to be venerated without respect. And Winter had no illusions about the opinion his colleagues had of him. They thought that, like a plaster saint that has been paraded in all weathers a few too many times, he had gone soft in the head.

A couple of years before, at retirement age and with an already deteriorating heart, Winter had given up his lucrative private practice to open a clinic on the Lower East Side. There, he and his handful of assistants took only the most desperate cases and worked only for nominal fees. It was something that no other current member of the Institute had done or was likely to attempt, and he knew how his more practical-minded colleagues interpreted it. "Pathological altruism"—"a compensatory mechanism"—"an avoidance compromise"—these were but a few of the descriptive phrases, gently dropped, that were meant to give him insight into his aberration. What they never actually said, but certainly thought, was that he was an old fool who was trying to earn his passport into Heaven.

The truth would have shocked them. Quite simply, in his heart he had disowned them. He had turned against them, as, a generation before he and the others had turned against orthodox Freudianism.

He still believed in the original Sullivanian principles. Sullivan's system had brought about a necessary revolution in psychotherapy. It had liberated a whole new generation of American psychiatrists, had rid them of the rigid structure of classic psychoanalysis, had loosened the grip of Freud's pessimistic theories, of his concept of the human animal as a creature driven by dark libidinal compulsions. They had concentrated instead on interpersonal relationships, interpersonal events; they had focused on people dealing with people. They had shown that a man or a woman, through most of a lifetime, was capable of growth and change.

But, once they were freed, a free-for-all had resulted, one that was going on still, and Winter could not accept the distortions that had taken place. Growth therapy had taken strange forms, some of its practitioners had adopted strange roles. Winter could not feel himself to be a spiritual forefather to those mutants who, at that moment, were chatting in the lounge, waiting for the seminar to begin.

Oh, there were good people in the bunch still, honest doctors, responsible therapists. But Coleman, with his Playboy philosophy and swinging sex therapy practice, was not his descendant. Taussig, with his gold earring and his fascistic commune of brainwashed votaries, was not his descendant. Lisa Gorman, with her cat therapy—a cat for each patient, as something to learn to love—was definitely not his descendant.

And then there was Delphine Heywood.

The ache sharpened in his chest. As dispassionately as if he were diagnosing someone else's pain, Winter made the connection; the thought—the psychosomatic reaction. It wasn't merely fatigue, he realized now, that had provoked this mild seizure. Seeing Delphine had also been a factor. As always, she had made him feel anxious.

Her appearance had been unexpected. Delphine was well-known for her reclusive ways, and she almost never came to the Institute. But, then, suddenly, there she was, limping into the lounge, with that mysterious smile on her face, greeting the members easily, as if it hadn't been a year or more since she had seen most of them.

Delphine was special to Winter; she was his particular responsibility. He had been her training analyst. He had guided her through long years of analysis, the rigorous, complete psychoanalysis that was required before one could be certified by the Institute. He knew Delphine, knew her as no one else in the profession did.

In the course of his career, Winter, unavoidably, had made a certain number of questionable decisions. But none of them, in retrospect, disturbed him more than the decision he had made concerning Delphine. He had gone before the committee and had declared that she had been successfully analyzed. He had approved her to practice psychotherapy.

He had meant well. He had hoped that by working to help others she would clear up her own problem. It had been a fine, optimistic, Sullivanian assumption. But, since then, more than once, he had been given reason to believe that he had been misguided.

This evening was one of those times. Again he had cause to feel deeply troubled by her.

When he had arrived at the Institute, Kupperman had mentioned it to him. Delphine had "lost" a patient, he had said, putting it the usual way—psychotherapists rarely uttered the word "suicide" in this context. The patient, a young woman, a manic-depressive photographer's model, had thrown herself out of her window.

Winter had said nothing, but underneath he had been shocked. Not that it was such an unusual thing. It could happen to any of them. Every psychotherapist was haunted by this fear, that he would lose a patient through suicide.

But it wasn't the first time, he remembered; it wasn't the first time something had gone tragically wrong with one of Delphine's patients.

Well, there was no point in brooding about it now. It was simply losing time, and he had less time than ever to spare. His pain had eased, he was feeling a little better, so he took out his pen and notebook and flipped to a blank page. At the top of

the page, he wrote: *Roberta Foehr*. She was the last patient he
had seen at the clinic that day.

He thought back on their hour. Roberta was a nursing student, with a facial melanoma at an advanced stage. She had
only a few months left, a year at the most, but she was determined to get her diploma. She was determined to live out her
life with her husband as if nothing unusual was happening. She
was in great anguish.

Winter wrote in his notebook: "Has created a fantasy that
her husband is having an affair with one of her friends. Don't
discourage it at this point. It alleviates the guilt she feels for
putting him through this ordeal."

He had even more desperate cases, but Roberta was the patient who moved him beyond his usual clinical concern. She
would have seemed like any ordinary, reasonably pretty girl of
twenty-four, if it hadn't been for her disfiguring facial cancer.
She laughed frequently as she talked to him, a self-deprecating,
apologetic laugh, as if she thought it was probably silly to take
up his time with such an unimportant problem. Her problem
was that she was sure that she had become horrifying to her
husband, repugnant to the man she loved.

During this last session, she had made several references to
her sleeping pills. Offhand references; but they had occurred
repeatedly, sometimes for no clear reason.

Winter wrote: *I am almost certain she is contemplating
suicide. Deal with it the next few times, bring it out into the
open. Have her consider it as a plausible option, but a less
desirable one than her other options.*

He paused and considered the last sentence, with its conventional therapist's wisdom. Suicide was never permissible. But
could there be any "desirable" option for someone with a malig-
nant melanoma? In over forty years as a doctor, he hadn't
found an answer.

"Oh, here you are, Sergius."

Winter looked up. Delphine had entered the room.

"Are you running away from me?" She asked it teasingly, but her eyes held on him intently.

"No, of course not," he replied. "I wasn't feeling too well. I came in here for a moment."

"Are you all right now?"

"Yes, I'm fine, thank you."

Delphine sat near him, on the little sofa that was next to the armchair, and studied him. She was checking his color, he knew, his respiration, his eye movements. Delphine was, he remembered, a talented diagnostician with an intuitive gift, and he began to feel uneasy. He pretended to go back to his notes.

"Am I interrupting you?" she asked.

"Not really. I was just writing down a few comments on the last patient I saw. Someone you know," he added.

"Oh? Who?"

"Roberta Foehr."

"Roberta Foehr?" she echoed, puzzled.

"A nursing student with a melanoma," Winter said. "You sent her to me."

"Oh yes. How is she?"

"What do you expect? She's a terminal case."

He had said it with irritation, he realized. He hadn't intended to make anything of it, but Delphine was looking at him questioningly now, and he couldn't just let it drop.

He put away his notebook. "Tell me, Delphine, why wouldn't you accept her as a patient? Was it because she couldn't pay your fee? Or because her case was too unpleasant?"

"Because of the fee, of course," she answered calmly. "I don't shy away from unpleasant things. You know that, Sergius."

If he had meant to put her on the defensive, he had failed. It was as if she hadn't even noticed the mild rebuke in his question.

"She was in need," he said. "She went to you because she wanted a woman as her therapist."

"She's better off with you," she said indifferently. "Thanatology isn't one of my interests."

"So I gather," he said dryly. "Particularly if a dying person can't pay more than ten dollars an hour."

She looked at him for a moment, then gave him her most charming smile. "You did very well, Sergius, in your long and successful career. You can afford these gestures. I can't."

"I have doctors younger than you working with me at the clinic."

"I know that. And I understand why those people are there."

"What is it that you understand?"

"They're afraid to compete."

There was a complacent certainty in her tone. She was unshakable, he realized, as unshakable in her view of the young idealists who worked with him as she had been in her distorted perception of her own childhood world.

Winter changed the subject, changed it to what was really on his mind.

"By the way," he said, "I heard the news. I'm sorry."

"What did you hear?"

"That you lost a patient."

"Were they talking about it?"

Delphine asked it casually. Even so, he sensed the paranoia. It was carefully hidden these days; but, finely attuned to her as he was, he could still detect it. And it occurred to him now why she was there that night. She had come to the Institute to brave the gossips, to silence them with her presence.

He was sure that was the way *she* saw it, anyway. In fact, only Kupperman seemed to have known about the incident.

"Someone mentioned it," he answered finally.

"She was beyond help. I did all I could." She paused, then said simply, "She was weak."

"And I suppose she was very sick." He shook his head. "It's such a tragedy when this happens! I know you must be upset by it."

"A little," she said. "It means I've lost a patient hour."

Winter stared at her for a moment. "That was a joke, wasn't it?"

Delphine smiled. "I was being realistic. *You* were the one who taught me to be realistic, Sergius."

"Yes," he admitted. "Yes, I guess I did."

Suddenly, she was looking at him in the old way, her head slightly tilted, her eyes wide; the uncertain, questioning way she would look at him during her analysis whenever, childlike, she would ask for his approval. "I've grown strong," she said. "That's good, isn't it?"

"It's good to be strong," he replied. "If you don't lose your humanity."

Her face relaxed into a smile again. He realized that she hadn't heard the last part of his answer. Only what she wanted to hear.

Winter reached out and took her hand. She responded instantly, gripping his hand with a hunger that surprised him. It was as if her transference had never converted, as if he were still her father figure, the only love object she had.

"Delphine," he asked gently, "how can you live so alone? Don't you ever feel the need for someone of your own? Someone to love?"

"I have my patients."

"Your patients aren't enough."

"They are," she insisted. "For now, they are."

"Do you feel that way always?" he asked.

Delphine was silent for a long moment. Her eyes looked past him and they seemed to go dull. "Sometimes," she said softly, "when I'm alone in my apartment—and it's getting late—I'm tempted to phone you."

"I wish you would."

She withdrew her hand and sat back. "No," she said, her voice firm and assured again. "I don't need you now."

Her eyes were fixed in that bright gaze that could seem so compelling, so all-comprehending, and that Winter knew to be the mask of her hostility. He had done nothing to provoke this veiled hatred; but he had witnessed her in one vulnerable moment, and that was enough.

"Perhaps you need *me*, Sergius," she said.

"Why would I need you?"

Delphine smiled cryptically. Then she rose and started out of the room. At the doorway, she turned and regarded him compassionately.

"It isn't so terrible," she said, in a warm kindly tone. "We all come to it, sooner or later. You musn't let it frighten you so."

Her glowing eyes held on him, then she passed through the doorway and was gone.

Winter stared at the empty doorway. A band of pain had suddenly tightened on his chest, and he felt chilled.

How had she guessed it? he wondered. How had she sensed that he was afraid to die?

9

THAT MORNING, a bird had brained itself against the picture window. It was still lying where it had landed, near the rose bushes. Russell hadn't wanted to touch it; he was waiting for the caretaker to come by and take it away.

Vivian thought of the dead bird now, as she manipulated Russell's penis. The curtain of the picture window was drawn, blocking out the sunlight, the view. But she imagined the brown, feathery body, lying on its back just on the other side of the glass, only a little way from where they were stretched out naked in front of the fireplace. She saw its parted beak, frozen in a startled cheep.

Russell raised his head and looked fondly at his member. "It's getting there," he said. It was half erect now.

"Don't worry about it, hon," Vivian murmured. "Just let it happen."

"Stay with it, Pierre," Russell urged his penis. He could take the humorous view of his sexual problems. "You know why I call it Pierre?"

" '*Pierre, attention,*' " she repeated wearily. " 'Prepare for dishonorable discharge.' "

"You know that joke, huh?"

"I heard it in grammar school. Enough of the jokes. Lie back and relax."

Russell sank back. But he was still looking at her, and Vivian kept her lips set in a faint, sexy smile to conceal her distaste. It had been a long while since she had seen him with his clothes off, and, in the interim, he had grown more corpulent than ever. At that moment, lying flat on his back, he reminded her of a beached whale, and his modishly long gray hair, already moist with sweat, looked lank as seaweed.

"I can't seem to get there," Russell said, showing his distress now.

"There's no hurry," Vivian said. "We've got time."

She repositioned herself and took his penis into her mouth. The vinegary smell filled her nostrils, that particular sour scent she always associated with Russell.

Almost immediately, she began to get results. As she moved her head up and down in a steady rhythm, the soft flesh in her mouth gradually hardened. But it was a touch-and-go thing, a delicate, imperiled virility that might vanish any second. She was getting a crick in her neck, but she didn't dare let up long enough to massage it.

At least, she thought, this should be it for the day. They would be going to a garden party in Amagansett when this was over—the first big one of the Hamptons' season, Russell had told her. That evening, they were supposed to have dinner with some people in Sag Harbor. She had brought along a book to read at bedtime, when, she hoped, she would at last be alone. There was a good chance of it, since, as she remembered, Russell was randy only in daytime. By nightfall, he had drunk too much.

Russell was workably stiff now. He sat up quickly, in a hurry to enter her before he lost the precious erection. She lay back and opened her thighs wide, to make room for his spreading, womanish hips. He flopped onto her, almost knocking the wind out of her in his eagerness.

It hurt with the first thrust. She wasn't lubricating. She whimpered slightly, anyway, and churned her hips, hoping to bring him to a climax quickly.

But, now that he was successfully consummating the act, Russell was curbing himself, setting a leisurely tempo. He seemed to want to play a control game. This was going to take some time, she realized. She stopped moving, closed her eyes, and her thoughts started to wander.

She wondered if she was ever going to have a chance to stroll through the grounds of this estate? Russell had rented one of the more lavish showplaces in East Hampton, and Vivian had looked forward to this weekend as an escape from the oppressive confines of her apartment, a cleansing of her brain with the beauty of nature. But she might as well have been in a beach bungalow on a rainy day for all of the sense of freedom she had. They had driven out early in the morning. She had made a late breakfast—the foolish bird had collided against the window while they were having their orange juice—they had unpacked, and since then she had been politely listening to Russell, whose small talk, on this day at least, consisted mainly of old dirty jokes and platitudes on the joys of country living.

The chafing was really getting painful now. She realized that she had better make some effort to become aroused, simply to moisten herself. She blotted out the image of Russell's bloated face and cast about for a fantasy of some attractive man.

The first one who came to mind was Christopher Greene. She imagined him as he had looked the afternoon he had dropped by to visit her, just after she had seen him in his play. He had worn a loose dark-green velvet jersey, and the breeze had mussed his hair so that the dark curls had fallen forward onto his forehead. She evoked the image of him, bending over her. She pulled up his jersey, stroked his ribs, ran her fingers along the swelling muscles of his smooth chest.

It was working. The honey pleasure was welling up in her.

Suddenly, Christopher was gone, and she saw Ward instead, his wine glass raised, his face suffused with smiling hate.

Russell had stopped. "Did I hurt you?" he asked.

She opened her eyes. "What?"

His expression was very concerned. "Did I hurt you? You cried out."

"Did I?"

Vivian turned her head to one side and stared at the drawn curtain. Russell waited a moment, then started up again, but a little less confidently than before, and a little more urgently.

She wondered if there were crawling things on the bird. It wasn't right to leave a dead creature out in the open like that, she thought. Even a dumb bird deserves a bit of dignity at the end.

"You should put tape on that window," she said.

"What?"

"The picture window. If you put tape on it, birds wouldn't fly into it."

He stopped again. "Why are you thinking about that *now?*"

She turned her head and looked up into his bewildered eyes. "Don't you care?"

"No, I don't care."

Vivian started crying. A keening sound came out of her and tears streamed down her cheeks.

She couldn't stop herself. Her head tossed from side to side as the uncontrollable anguish buffeted her. It was all-consuming, it obliterated everything. She was only vaguely aware of Russell's stunned expression, of the lessening of pressure as he went soft in her.

When she had calmed down a little, he said bleakly, "I can't go on."

But he remained on top of her, propped on his elbows indecisively, as if he were unsure as to what to do next.

Vivian felt spent now, dead, beyond feeling anything. "Russell," she said, "I want to go back to New York. Please, take me back."

Vivian picked up the scissors and cut into the pale-blue satin. They were large scissors that took a greedy bite, and in a few seconds she sundered the garment from hem to neckline. She remained as she was, kneeling on the living room floor, and looked down at what she had done. She hadn't changed anything. It still had its identity as an evening gown—as a humiliating reminder.

She snipped at the satin again, wildly at first, slashing it diagonally and crossways, rending the fabric with her free hand. Then becoming very methodical, she cut up what was left into neatly triangular pieces. When she was through, she gathered up all of the fragments, rose, crossed to the fireplace, and threw them into the grate.

Vivian gazed at the heap for a moment. Scraps, nothing to upset her now. Still, she couldn't leave them there, blue and shiny as they were.

She hurried to the kitchen, almost running. She was alone in her apartment, the door was locked, but she was vaguely fearful that she might be surprised before the whole thing was done. She snatched up the box of kitchen matches and an old newspaper and went back into the living room. She crumpled a few sheets of the newspaper into a ball and stuck it under the grate. She struck a match, hesitated—the fireplace hadn't been used since the winter—then lit the paper.

The satin didn't burn well. It smoldered more than it flamed, and it cast off an almost chemical stench. Vivian backed away from the fireplace, her hand over her nose. Her headache had been bad before, but now it was excruciating.

She glanced at the pill bottle on the side table. It was empty; she had taken the last two capsules of Placidyl in the morning. The electric clock next to the bottle said a quarter to three. She knew she shouldn't phone Delphine for another five minutes. She used to call her at any time, until Delphine had told her that, during the day, she would prefer it if Vivian phoned only in the last ten minutes of an hour, when she was between patients. Unless it was an emergency, of course.

Vivian went to the window, put her hands against the glass and looked down at Fifth Avenue. A little earlier she wouldn't have been able to go near any of her windows, much less touch one of them. When she came within ten feet of the glass, she would be seized by terror, the chilling terror she sometimes felt when she got too close to the edge of the platform in a subway station. But she had solved it. She had put tape on every window in the apartment, in large, conspicuous X's. It was all right now.

The smell of the smoking satin was filling the room. It was in her nostrils again, and she was reminded that she hadn't paid for the gown. How could she pay for it now? Without Ward, without anyone?

Russell hadn't given her a cent. She could hardly blame him, after what she had done to him. There were no other Russells she could turn to. That kind of thing was over for her.

What was she supposed to do now? Go to work at Macy's? Wait tables? She hadn't held any kind of job in years. Who would want her?

Eight stories below, on the park side of the avenue, an old scavenger lady, her shopping bags bulging, was inching along the curb. Vivian turned away from the window quickly.

She went over to the electric clock. It was thirteen minutes to the hour. She stared at the second hand, which was turning so slowly it almost seemed to be standing still. "Move, you fucker!" she snarled at it. "*Move!*"

The minute hand eased on to the next line—twelve minutes

to. She couldn't bear it any longer. This *was* an emergency. She rushed to the phone and dialed.

There was one ring, then Delphine answered. "Hello?"

"Delphine, I need you."

"I'm in session, darling."

"I know, but—" She hesitated, then blurted it out. "I think I'm going out of my mind."

"Now, it may not be that bad, darling," Delphine said soothingly. "Have you been taking your pills?"

"They're all gone."

"I wrote you that prescription just two weeks ago," Delphine said with mild reproof.

"I've been bugged. You *know* how I've been bugged."

"All right," Delphine said after a moment, "when you come in tomorrow, I'll give you another prescription."

"I can't wait that long!" Vivian cried out desperately. "You have to come over now!"

"*Why* can't you wait?" Delphine's tone was suddenly careful. "What are you thinking, Vivian?"

Vivian guessed what was in her mind, and she hastily assured her, "Oh, don't worry, I won't do anything like *that*. I've taped the windows."

There was a brief silence at the other end of the line. "You've taped the windows?"

"Yes, they're all taped now. Nothing can happen to me."

"Vivian, listen to me." Delphine was speaking slowly and precisely, as if she wanted to make sure that Vivian understood every word. "Lie down and take a nap, if you can. Or, if you're too tense, then get into a warm bath. I can't come over right away," she went on. "I'm expecting a patient in a few minutes. But I'll be there in an hour."

"An *hour!*" Vivian wailed. "Not an hour! That's too long!"

"Hold the line a moment."

Vivian heard nothing at all now. Delphine probably had her

hand over the mouthpiece as she talked to whoever was in the office with her.

Vivian waited, staring at the electric clock, at the second hand dragging itself around the dial. She began to feel a crushing sense of abandonment.

Finally, Delphine's voice came back on the line. "Vivian, are you there?"

"Yes."

"Christopher's here."

"Christopher Greene?" She felt her cheeks tingle with sudden embarrassment.

"Yes. We've just finished our session. Christopher is coming to see you right now."

"No!" she said instantly, panicked. "He doesn't have to do that!"

"He *wants* to see you," Delphine insisted in a warm, reassuring voice. "So, then," she went on, going over it patiently, "Christopher will be there in a few minutes. And, in a little over an hour, *I'll* be there. Is that all right, darling?"

"Yes," Vivian whispered and hung up.

Now that it was done, and there was no undoing it, Vivian wondered why she had made such a fuss. She wasn't really going crazy, after all. She was just having a bad few hours. She could have sweated it out on her own.

Certainly, she hadn't counted on Christopher Greene being in Delphine's office. The last thing she wanted was to have him see her in this state.

She drifted into the bedroom and stared at herself in the dressing-table mirror. Her eyes were puffy, her hair was stringy, and she had never looked so haggard and old. She was hardly an enticing dish for a beautiful young man like Chris.

What *would* be his type? A Suzanne Beswick? Of course. One perfect specimen matching another.

She had seen her photograph in the newspaper just that

morning, next to the item that announced her engagement to Ward. A mass of blond hair, great bone structure, a blaze of white teeth, and young, young, young.

Vivian conjured up the face in the photograph and tried to fix it in the mirror. She caught it in the glass for one moment and clawed at it with her fingernails. "Bitch!" she growled. "BITCH!"

She sank into the chair by her dressing table and buried her head in her arms.

She remained in that position for some time, unmoving, trying to still her brain, to will the distressing images away. When the doorbell rang, she sat up, startled. Already? she thought. She glanced at the clock beside the bed. It was five minutes past three.

Vivian rose, passed through the living room and into the foyer. She stroked back her hair and opened the door. Christopher Greene was standing there, smiling at her engagingly. He was wearing a striped, open-collar shirt, no jacket, and his forehead was moist. Evidently, it was warm outside.

"Hello," Chris said. "Is it all right if I come in?"

"Yes, of course." She stepped back to let him enter. As she closed the door after him, she said, "This isn't necessary, you know."

"I know it isn't. I just wanted to see how you were," he said casually. "I've been thinking about you."

"I'm glad," she said. "I'm glad you've been thinking about me."

Chris went on into the living room and she followed. He stopped as soon as he saw the fireplace. The blackened remnants of the satin gown were still glowing and smoking in the grate. "Are you cold?" he asked.

"No. I'm just burning some old rags."

Chris looked at her perplexed but made no comment. He turned and studied the windows with their sprawling, taped X's. Still, he kept silent.

"I know what you're thinking," she said. "You think I'm flipping out."

He turned back to her. "You're a little upset, that's all."

"Did Delphine tell you why?"

"It's none of my business."

"Did she tell you why?" she asked again, more insistently.

"Yes." He shrugged. "You know what I thought of that guy. You're well out of it."

"Oh, I'm out of it, all right." She tried to say it gaily, with a laugh, but she heard the choking sound she made in place of a laugh. After a moment, she said, "I'm not being very mature about it, am I?"

"You're upset. It's understandable."

His gaze was clear-eyed and sympathetic, and suddenly she couldn't bear it any longer. She ducked her head and took a couple of steps to one side. Still, she felt that unwavering gaze on her. She turned and went several steps in the opposite direction. But she couldn't get free of it; she was transfixed.

She whirled on him abruptly. "Why are you looking at me that way?" she asked sharply. "Am I such a freak? We *all* have problems."

"Yes, we do," he agreed.

"That's why we're going to Delphine, right? Because we're disturbed?"

"Yes, I guess we are."

"It could be the other way around," she said, her voice rising edgily. "It could just as easily be *me* patronizing *you*."

"I'm not patronizing you," Chris said quietly.

Vivian looked at him now and saw him as he was, kind and gentle, meaning well, and she felt sick with shame. Why was she screaming at him? He really did want to help her.

But *he* needed help too; that was the point. She was overcome with sorrow as she thought of it, that this beautiful, strong creature might need help even more than she did.

She raised her hands to her mouth, half wanting to stop the

question even as she asked it. "Chris, are you gay?"

He seemed to wince slightly. "Why do you ask?"

"I want to know." She took a step toward him and held out her hands, tentatively imploring. "Please, tell me. Don't be afraid. I just *have* to know!"

"I've had experience with both sexes," he answered slowly. "But I'm straight."

She looked at him uncertainly for a moment. His expression was serious, almost pained, and there was no mistaking the sincerity in his level gaze.

"Oh, I'm so glad to hear that!" she whispered. Suddenly, she was in his arms, and she was crying uncontrollably. "You don't know how glad I am!"

Chris was holding her firmly, with both of his arms encircling her. His body was throwing off a great warmth that passed through her in a healing wave. Very soon, her tears stopped and she rested her head on his shoulder drowsily.

"I think you should take a nap now," he said gently.

Vivian didn't resist as he led her into the bedroom. Her eyes were half closed and she was barely aware of what she was doing or where she was.

Then, she was aware of nothing at all. She was sleeping, she had some glimmering sense of that, and she was starting to come awake.

A hand clutched at her wrist. She screamed and sat upright. She was staring into Delphine's face.

"It's all right, darling," Delphine cooed. She pressed her back down onto the bed.

Delphine finished taking her pulse. Then she unzipped Vivian's slacks and started to pull them down around her hips. Vivian wasn't awake enough yet to comprehend. Frightened, she asked, "What are you doing?"

"I want to give you something to relax you," Delphine said. "Thorazine." She held up the syringe so Vivian could see it.

Vivian started to feel better. Delphine was taking care of her, and that was all that mattered.

She raised her head to see what was happening. She was an ungainly sight, with her slacks bunched around her knees, and her exposed thighs looking a sickly white, almost as white as her panties. Delphine was prodding the flesh below her hip, searching for a suitable vein.

"Has Chris gone?" Vivian asked.

"No, he's still here."

"Where?"

Delphine glanced up and to one side. Vivian quickly turned her head in that direction. Chris was standing in a corner of the bedroom, watching them uncomfortably.

Her first thought was that she should be embarrassed that he was seeing her at half-mast like this. But he was looking so distressed, so obviously concerned about her, that she had to smile. A tenderness welled up in her and she held out her hand to him.

Chris hesitated, then came over, sat on the bed and took her hand. She lay her head back and closed her eyes.

She barely felt it when the needle plunged in. She was only aware that Chris and Delphine were both with her now, and she was going to be all right.

10

"I GUESS what I want," Eric said, "is to have you tell me I'm making the right choice."

"You can only decide that for yourself," Delphine replied.

"Yes, I know. But you're the one who's encouraged me to write. Hell, you've made it possible. You must have some opinion on *this*. Quitting my job is no small thing."

"I realize that." She thought for a moment. "The question is, I suppose, is it necessary?"

"I think so," Eric said. "I don't see how else I can write my novel. I've finally got going on it, but I can't make any real progress. A page here—two pages there—in the evenings and on the weekends. I envision this as a big book, and I'll *never* get it done at this rate. And I feel torn," he went on. "I mean, it's a schizoid thing—to spend all day editing junk, and then come home, try to clear my head of all the garbage and do my own work."

"Which, of course, isn't junk."

"You're damned right it isn't," he said firmly.

"Have you shown it to anyone yet?"

"Well—" He hesitated. "I let Lucy read the first chapter the other night."

"What did she say?"

"Oh, she liked it—but she didn't make any particular comment." The truth was Lucy hadn't seemed too enthusiastic. "She isn't a literary type," he explained. "The point is I know it's good. This book may sell only three copies, but I don't care. It will express the best that's in me."

"Well, then," Delphine said, "if this is really what you want to do—"

"Of course it is." But he paused now. He thought he had detected a dubious note in her voice. "It's what you've been telling me all along, right? I should be what I want to be?"

"Yes, certainly. But you should fully understand the consequences of such a sharp change in your life. You've been with Galton and Hill for quite a long time, after all." Carefully, she asked, "Do you plan to break off with the firm completely?"

"Not if I can help it. I'm hoping I can work out something as a consultant for them—you know, where my time would be my own. That way, I could develop book projects, put writers together with ideas, but not actually have to do the dog work myself."

"So, you're not burning *all* your bridges behind you."

"No, I guess I'm not," he admitted.

"I'm glad to hear that." After a moment, she added, "For selfish reasons."

"Selfish reasons? What do you mean?"

"Well, I haven't told you this, Eric—" She paused, then said almost shyly, "I'm writing a book too."

Suddenly, Delphine no longer seemed the omniscient doctor. She was like any fledgling author, eyeing him timidly after hopefully throwing out the bait. And, weary, seasoned editor that he was, he backed off from the hook a little and murmured politely, "Oh, really?"

"And it *had* crossed my mind," she went on, with unconvincing casualness, "that I could show it to you—when it's finished, of course. I don't know much about publishing, but it might be something Galton and Hill would be interested in."

"Is it nonfiction?"

"Oh yes. As you'd expect, the subject is psychotherapy. But it's not a technical work. I'm writing it for the average reader. I suppose it's what you'd call a self-help book."

Eric's professional instincts responded now. "Abel has been looking for something like that," he said thoughtfully. "Self-help books can do very well. When you're ready to show it, let me know."

"I will," she said.

He glanced at his watch. He had only twenty minutes left of his session. "Now, if you don't mind, Delphine, we were discussing my problem," he reminded her. "In about an hour, I'm going into Abel's office and drop the bomb."

She seemed a bit surprised. "You're doing it this afternoon?"

"I thought I'd better. Before I lose my nerve."

"If you've decided to do it—" She shrugged lightly and said nothing more.

There was still that touch of dubiousness in her tone, and it was starting to unsettle him. "I have and I haven't," Eric said with an upsurge of nervousness. "It's not too late to change my mind."

"Let us go over what we've learned." Delphine's manner was totally professional again. In her calm, authoritative voice, she said, "Your mother had complex and ambiguous feelings toward you. In one part of her, she wanted you to do well in the world. In another, deeper part of her, she—" Delphine broke off and waited, as a teacher waits for a class to supply an answer.

"—she wanted me to fail," Eric said, completing the sentence obediently.

"She loved you, of course," she went on. "You were closer, in fact, than most mothers and sons. But along with her positive feelings for you, she had negative ones, too. And why was this?" she asked, pausing expectantly again.

"Because of my father," he answered, continuing the catechism. "When he died, Mother shifted—" He paused uncertainly. "That's not the word—what was that verb you once used?"

"Displaced?"

"Displaced. Mother displaced the whole bag of feelings she felt toward my father onto me."

Delphine nodded, satisfied with his reply. "And one of those feelings was resentment," she said, "because she felt that your father had discouraged her in her work. He was a prominent lawyer, much older than she was, and he hadn't wanted her success to overshadow his own. Or so she thought. Actually, *she* was the competitive one. It was she who wanted to outshine her mate. She had to be the star in the family. She went on feeling that way, even when you were the only one left."

"She was afraid that *I* would outshine her?" Eric asked, a bit incredulous now. "I was only eight when my father died."

"But she could foresee the man you would be," Delphine clarified. "And I'm not saying she didn't want you to succeed in general. She would have been delighted if you had excelled as a book editor—or a lawyer—or a stockbroker. But you showed an inclination to follow her in her own line of work. In effect, you were setting out to beat her at her own game. On the surface, she pretended to encourage you—it was her maternal duty, after all. But underneath, she was quite disturbed—because of the threat you presented—because of her sense of her own inadequacies as a writer."

"Mother was damned good," Eric insisted loyally.

"In her own way." Delphine paused reflectively. "You know, Eric, while I've never read much fiction, I've always kept up with book reviews. And I seem to remember that Margaret

Dare Bayliss was not always dealt with kindly." Delicately she commented, "Some of those cruel reviews must have hurt."

"They did," he said. "They hurt her more than she ever let on."

"So, do you see?" Delphine spoke very slowly now, and emphatically, a sign that she was about to make a crucial point. "When your mother criticized your work so harshly, what she was really doing was projecting her own insecurity onto you— her insecurity about her writing. And this insecurity could only have been more intensified by the fact that she recognized you were more gifted."

"More gifted?" He brightened. Delphine had never actually said it before, and it had a gratifying sound in his ear. But then his sense of logic came into play, tempering the moment. "How can you know that?" he asked. "You've never read a word I've written."

"I don't have to read your writing to know it," she said almost negligently. "I can perceive it in the situation that existed." With a warm smile, she added, "And I can perceive it from knowing *you*."

"I wish I could believe it," he murmured.

"But you do believe it, don't you, Eric? You're writing again? Your writer's block has gone?"

"Yes. Yes, it has."

"Then, if nothing else, you have confidence in yourself now. Still," she said, looking serious again, "we have a long way to go. We've made enormous progress in—how many sessions?— twenty or twenty-one? You've gained intellectual insights, but your core problem remains untouched."

Eric looked at her perplexed. She had never used that phrase before. "What's my core problem?"

"Your mother dominates you," she said. "Long after her death, she continues to."

After a moment, he said quietly, "Yeah, I guess that's true."

"But already we've gotten rid of one of your repressions," she went on. "And, for the time being, while we explore this deeper level, you'll be functioning as a more fulfilled human being—a creative writer." She paused, as if struck by a mildly troubling thought. "One thing concerns me, though. I've been thinking about what you're planning to do this afternoon. I understand why you want to quit your job. But tell me, Eric," she said, leaning forward solicitously, "will it create any financial difficulties for you?"

"Oh no, of course not," he replied quickly. "I haven't really needed to work at all. I was my mother's only heir. And her books keep selling, year after year."

"Oh. I didn't realize that." There was a pensive purr in her voice. "Then you can do what you want." Relaxing, she sat back in her chair and regarded him benignly.

Eric had noticed her pleased little smile when he had enlightened her on his financial circumstances, and he felt briefly uneasy. It crossed his mind now that Delphine might have been dubious about his decision simply because she had been afraid he would no longer be able to pay for his psychotherapy sessions.

It was an ungracious thought, he realized, and he banished it immediately. She was a wise, objective doctor, and he owed her everything. She had given him faith in himself. No one had even tried to do that before.

"Financially, I've always been free to do what I want," Eric said. "But emotionally, I wasn't ready until now."

"And now you *are* ready?"

"Yes, I am," he said eagerly. "I can hardly wait to get started. I'm looking forward to it—working totally on my own—not needing anyone's approval." He broke off and considered the proposition. "But that isn't possible, is it? You always need *someone*'s approval."

"Yes, you do."

"My mother isn't around any more. And there's no one else I feel I have to impress." He laughed uneasily. "You think I can do it? Can I stick it out—trying just to please myself?"

"You mean, without an authority figure to approve? I wouldn't worry about that, Eric," Delphine said quietly. "After all, you have *me*."

Fanelli's, as usual, was packed. All of the tables and barstools were taken and the standees filled up the remaining space. Eric fought his way through the crowd by the door, glanced around, and caught sight of Lucy standing in a corner holding a wine glass. When she saw him, her face brightened with a glad but uncertain smile. He went over to her.

"So, what happened?" she asked. "Did you do it?"

"I did it," Eric said cheerfully. "I went into Abel's office and let him have it—pow!—one month's notice."

Lucy looked a bit aghast. "You didn't tell him why?"

"Sure, I told him. Rather movingly, I thought."

"And what did he say?"

"He said I should have my head examined."

"But you *are* having your head examined."

"Yeah. I told him that too."

"Then what did he say?"

"Nothing. Abel just gave me one of his sad 'Now I understand' looks. Then he wished me good luck in my new life. And, of course," he added, "he said he wants to see my book when it's ready."

"Are you going to show it to him?"

"I don't think so," he replied. "It sounds incestuous. Anyway, I'd rather have one of the classy houses do it."

Lucy looked at him askance. "Suddenly you're snobbish about your own company?"

"But it *isn't* my company. Or it won't be after next month. I belong to *no* company now," he said happily.

"Well, terrific," Lucy said with restrained enthusiasm. She raised her glass. "Let's drink to that."

"Let me get a beer and I will."

Eric went over to the bar, found a crack in the wall of flesh, leaned in, and ordered the beer. While he waited, he took in the faces around him. Fanelli's, a sleepy neighborhood tavern during the day, metamorphosed into an artists' hangout after six. Now, instead of the afternoon's handful of unemployed workingmen staring blankly at the TV, the place was crowded with painters, filmmakers, self-styled poets, part-time academics, and a few characters who defied any classification. Eric as he looked about saw some of the same people, now grayer and thicker, that he had observed back in the fifties, when, as a prep-school kid, he had hovered, timid and wide-eyed, on the fringes of bohemia. He had seen them first at the White Horse, then at the Cedar, at several Village waystations after that, and now, with the southward drift of the artists' community into SoHo, he found them at Fanelli's.

Eric had always felt himself an outsider in this crowd. He knew that these free spirits saw him as a super-straight, a representative of the commercial establishment, with a necktie cinching his collar and a blank contract in his briefcase, a buyer rather than a seller. But now he felt a sense of camaraderie with the scruffy types around him. Soon he would be one of them, an artist, a free-agent creator, living by his wits and his talent. The thought gave him a warm, good feeling. It was like being twenty-one all over again.

The bartender returned with his bottle of beer. Eric paid for it and rejoined Lucy.

He filled his glass and raised it. "Here's to freedom," he said.

Lucy smiled and clinked her wine glass against his beer glass. She started to take a sip of her wine, then stopped. "I feel funny drinking to this," she said with a little laugh. "It's like I'm betraying Naomi."

"Naomi Lamb? What does she have to do with it?"

"It's just that she's going to be very upset. I had lunch with her the other day. She raved on and on about you—about how much she owed to you—how much you were helping her with her new book—how she was looking forward to working with you some more on it. I didn't have the heart to tell her what you were planning to do."

"You're not going to make me feel guilty," Eric said pleasantly. "Your friend Naomi will just have to learn to do without me. The poor dear is capable only of writing schlock. And I'm putting schlock behind me. Forever."

"I never thought of you as schlocky," Lucy demurred.

"Well, whatever I was, I'm different now. Don't I *seem* different?"

She shrugged. "You seem happier."

"And more attractive, maybe?" Eric asked, preening a little. "Sexier?"

"I thought you were divine before. But, yes," she said, "now that you mention it, you've become crushingly irresistible."

He laughed. "Bless you, mum." He kissed her lightly on the lips.

"You *have* changed," she said. "You've never kissed me in public before."

"Wait till we get back to your apartment. Then the *real* surprises will start."

Lucy rubbed her hip against his playfully, acknowledging his boastful promise. Actually, his words had been meaningless. The sex part of their relationship was fine as it was. Or, at least, he lacked the imagination to think of any improvements.

Lucy grew pensive again. "Now that it's almost over, Eric, may I ask you something about your job?"

"What?"

"Why were you always so down on it? You didn't just work with schlock. You had some good writers too, didn't you?"

"A couple of terrific ones."

"Like who?"

"Cassie Prine and Tom Halvorson."

Lucy frowned uncertainly. "Who are they?"

"You see? That's the problem. Cassie Prine happens to be one of the three or four best writers of American fiction under the age of thirty-five. And Tom Halvorson writes nature books that will be read long after we're dead. But you didn't know who they were, did you?"

"Does it matter whether I know them—as long as they write good books?"

"But you don't understand, Lucy. In contemporary publishing, a 'good book' is not what you and I think it is. To a smart commercial publisher, a 'good book' is, purely and simply, a profitable book, one that makes a pile of money, a winner. All other books are just books. Cassie Prine's novels sell fewer than five thousand copies. Tom Halvorson's books never go into paperback. In short, they don't matter. Prine and Halvorson boil no pots at Galton and Hill. And I scored no points for being their editor."

"I see," Lucy said after a moment.

Eric said nothing further. It depressed him to talk about this. And it had saddened him to be reminded of Cassie and Tom. He would miss working with them. He lingered fondly on his images of them—wild-eyed Cassie, clutching her manuscript to her breast possessively, so that it had to be all but pried from her; pipe-smoking Tom, regarding the people in the Galton and Hill offices with amused fascination, as if he were seeing them as delightful additions to his bestiary. Fine writers, both of them. And they did matter to *him*.

At length Lucy said, "But these are the people you admire, right? And now you're going to be their kind of writer?"

"I'll try. But I may not have what makes them so special."

"You mean, their talent?"

"No, it's something more than talent," he replied. "Lonely courage."

He thought of the fragment of manuscript waiting for him on his desk at home, and of the blank plaster walls of his tiny workroom, and, for the first time since he gave his notice, he felt a pang of fear.

Eric raised his glass again. "Here's to courage," he said.

11

"Is THERE another room?" Liz asked.

"A lovely one," Chris replied, taking her by the arm, "and quite dark."

"I'd rather stay here," she said.

Chris picked her up in his arms suddenly and carried her across the room.

"Oh, God, what are you doing to me?" Liz cried out. "Alfred!"

Chris threw her down on the bed and knelt over her. "Emma, I worship you!" He unzipped her skirt and started to pull it off.

Liz grabbed at her skirt. "Wait, please, at least wait. Go," she said, weakly attempting an imperious tone, "I'll call for you."

"Let me help you," Chris said, persisting.

"But you're tearing everything!"

"Don't you wear a corset?"

"I never wear a corset. Neither does Duse, incidentally. You can unbutton my boots."

Chris sat back and picked up her foot, which was actually in a ballet slipper. He pantomimed unbuttoning a boot, removed the slipper, raised her foot to his lips and kissed the arch tenderly.

"That tickles!" she squealed.

Chris let go of her foot. "That's not in the script," he said.

"I don't care," Liz drawled, in her own Alabama accent. "It *does* tickle." She sat up and rubbed her foot. "Anyway, I'm tired of rehearsing."

"Okay." But he remained in position, kneeling on the bed. "Maybe we *should* work on it some more," he said, after a moment. "We're doing this scene in class tomorrow."

"It's good enough," she said indifferently. "We don't have to sell it. It's only about the fiftieth time *La Ronde* has been done at the Actors' Studio."

"You chose the scene," he reminded her.

"I know. Lee says I should stretch myself. So I'm stretching myself." She lounged back on the bed, threw a lazy arm up beside the pillow, and fingered a strand of her long blond hair. "How am I doing?" she asked.

"It's not bad," he said. "We've got a relationship going. And your reactions are truthful."

Liz simply smiled at him—her broad, openly suggestive smile—and he realized that her mind was no longer on acting technique. He noticed, also, that she hadn't pulled up her skirt. It was still down around the bottom of her panties, and her full hips were enticingly on display.

Chris had no reason to be surprised. It had been building up to this through the couple of weeks they had worked on the scene, and this was the last rehearsal. Still, he felt vaguely embarrassed. He sat back against the wall and pretended to study the Salvation Army furniture in her bedroom.

"What about what *I'm* doing?" he asked without looking at her.

"You're great," she said, "as usual."

"I'm not great," he muttered modestly.

"Sure you are. You're the big star of tomorrow. Everybody at the Studio says it. I guess I'm lucky you agreed to do this scene with me."

"I like to work," he said, turning to her again. "An actor should always keep working. Even if it's class work." He noticed that a button of her blouse had come undone since he had last looked. "I think we should go through the scene once more."

"I won't get any better," Liz said amiably.

"But maybe *I* will," Chris said with a touch of annoyance. Her attitude was starting to irritate him. He understood now why she didn't get too many jobs. "Anything can be improved."

"Well, we're not going to improve if we just keep on saying this dumb dialogue."

"There are some people who *like* Schnitzler," he pointed out.

"Oh, he's all right," Liz drawled, grudgingly conceding it. "What I mean is we're not really getting the feel of the scene."

"How so?"

"This boy is supposed to be horny for this girl, right? I mean, he's creaming-in-his-pants hot for her?" She paused and looked unhappy. "Well, I just don't get that from you."

"I'm playing the action," he said.

"You're playing it, but you're not feeling it. Look, Chris, why don't we try something?" She smiled up at him reasonably from the pillow. "Why don't you kiss me? Not like this Schnitzler person—but the way *you'd* kiss me."

He gave her his slow, dangerous smile. "I don't think that would be a good idea."

"Why not? We might find something we could use."

"Yeah, but if we got started we wouldn't stop with just a kiss. And I don't believe in mixing sex with work."

"I think we can control ourselves," she purred. "Let's try it."

It would be more of an issue if he refused, he realized, than if he went along with it. "If you insist," he said.

He carefully extended himself on top of her, propping himself securely on his elbows, and kissed her. Her arms tightened around him, forcing him to sustain the kiss. Her tongue darted in between his lips and her belly pressed up against his penis.

When, finally, their mouths parted, Liz murmured, "Now, *that* feels right."

Chris disentangled himself and lay back beside her. He had half an erection, and it confused him; he hadn't expected to be aroused.

He stared at the burlap drapes that were drawn over the bedroom window and tried to get his bearings in this situation. The bright midday sunlight was seeping through the brown fabric, and he was reminded that he had an appointment with Delphine in less than an hour. He musn't be late for it.

Still, this girl had turned him on, and he vaguely sensed an imperative to do something about it. *Don't negate it,* Delphine had told him. *Whenever it happens, don't negate it.*

Liz's hand was resting lightly on his thigh. Her fingertips were stirring, teasing him.

"Noah Porterfield is a friend of yours, isn't he?" she asked suddenly.

The question startled him, and he felt instantly apprehensive. "Yes," he answered after a moment. "I've known him a long time."

"You know him *real* well, don't you?"

He turned his head to look at her. Her eyes were just a few inches away from his, unblinking and intent. What had she heard?

"I know him," he said. "Why do you ask?"

"Well, people have been telling me"—she gazed up at the ceiling and her words came hesitantly now—"that there's a part in his new show that's just perfect for me. They say you're going to be doing the lead, and I was wondering—" She looked at him again and smiled hopefully. "Could you put in a good word for me, Chris? Could you ask him to read me?"

Chris almost burst out laughing. Here he had been thinking that this poor kid was dying to have him just for his beautiful self, and it turned out that she was trying to lay him to get a job with Noah. It brought him back to reality, and immediately he felt better.

"Sure," he said, unfastening his belt. "I'll do what I can."

Confident now, he pulled her skirt completely off and threw it onto the floor. He took note of the look of fear that fleeted across her face—it seemed to be in response to something in his own expression—then he pulled down her panties. The lips of her vagina were already glistening wet, and he felt briefly repelled. But he didn't hesitate. He lowered his pants and shorts and threw himself between her thighs.

Slut! he thought, as he drove his hips against her, fueling his desire with the word. *Cheap slut!* He hammered at her, in a punishing rhythm.

But something was wrong. The tip of his penis was just inside her and would go no further. With each of his heaving motions, it bent futilely, soft and uninvolved, no part of his frenzy.

Beneath him, Liz lay totally still, her eyes closed, her lips parted in expectation of pleasure. *Help me!* he thought pleadingly. *Why don't you help me?* But she did nothing. She seemed divorced of responsibility, of even the need to acknowledge that it was going well or badly.

He faltered, slowed, and then stopped entirely. He felt paralyzed, gutted with humiliation. He lay helpless and heavy on her, lacking the strength to roll free of her.

The silence seemed endless. Then he heard her say, in a kindly tone, "That's all right. I didn't really want to anyway."

He rose to his hands and knees and looked down at her. Her

expression was cheerfully understanding; she was trying to be nice about it. Even so, he thought he could detect a sensual woman's contempt behind her good-natured smile.

Chris hurriedly pulled up his pants and zipped his fly. "I have to get going," he said.

"Where are you off to?"

"I'm seeing my shrink."

"I thought I could do it," Chris said. "When she asked about Noah's show, I felt *sure* I could."

"I don't understand," Delphine said. "What did Noah's show have to do with it?"

"Because then it meant nothing. She wasn't asking anything of *me*. All I was to her was Noah's friend. And this was just part of the game. You know, an actress sleeping around—trying to get jobs."

"You mean, nothing was at stake? You didn't have to prove yourself to her?"

"I guess you could say that." He paused and remembered the embarrassing anticlimax of it. "But I was a bust anyway," he said unhappily.

"Now, you musn't be too hard on yourself, Christopher," Delphine said with a smile. "This girl has to take her share of the blame too. Did she do anything to arouse you?" she asked delicately. "To help—make it possible?"

"Not a damned thing. She just lay there. She may have slept with half the guys at the Actors' Studio," he commented sourly, "but she's sure no great shakes in bed."

"So we can attribute this mishap to the particular individual. In which case, it's meaningless. You've been successful with other women, after all."

"Not in a long time. I haven't been trying. You know that." A bit sulkily, he added, "I only tried this time because you keep saying I should."

She eyed him quizzically. "There was no natural process in you that also said you should?"

"Oh, sure," he replied, with a shrug. "I got hot. For a little while anyway."

"But you couldn't sustain the mood." She thought for a moment. "Obviously, ambitious young actresses aren't for you. Perhaps what you need is an older, more giving, more sophisticated woman."

"Terrific. But where can I find one?"

"Oh, they're around. It could be someone like—Vivian, let's say."

"Vivian?" Chris looked at her uncertainly. Delphine had tossed off the name indifferently, as if she had come up with it on the spur of the moment. But he sensed that the choice hadn't been accidental.

"Do you find her attractive?" Delphine asked.

"Very."

"Just hypothetically speaking, Christopher, do you think you could have an affair with her?"

He remembered Vivian as she had looked the last time he had seen her, when he had dropped by, a few days after her crack-up, to find out how she was feeling. She had seemed wan, almost frail, and the skin of her partly exposed bosom had had a creamy, deathlike whiteness to it. She had reminded him of a poetic, pining lady in a Victorian painting, and she had never looked more beautiful. Her eyes had lingered on him, following him wherever he moved.

"Yes, I think I could," he said.

Delphine smiled quietly to herself, and Chris, even more than he usually did, longed to know what was going on in her head. But she simply said, "Enough of the hypothetical. Let's get back to your experience today. When you told me about it, I was struck by something." She paused reflectively. "Let me see if I have the sequence right," she went on, more briskly. "You kissed her. You were aroused. She asked you if you were a friend of Noah Porterfield. You stopped being aroused. It was only when you realized that she wasn't bringing up your homosexual relationship that you were able to go on. Is that correct?"

"Yes."

"Now, what I'm wondering, Christopher," she asked gently, "is how you could have expected to continue at all, just moments after being reminded of your relationship with Noah? Your sense of shame was awakened. It could only have had the result of making you impotent."

Chris, avoiding her eyes, looked down. He saw that his hands were clenched together. "Yeah, maybe that's what happened," he muttered.

"And it will always be that way, Christopher," he heard her say. "It will *always* be that way."

When he looked up again, she was gazing at him sorrowfully. "When did you last have sexual relations with Noah?" she asked. "Last night?"

"No."

"The night before?"

"Yes."

"You promised you would stop. Do you remember? You promised."

"I'm not ready yet."

"You were ready a long time ago."

"I'm not ready to hurt Noah yet," he said, more intensely.

Delphine shook her head and let out her breath wearily, as if she despaired of ever making any progress with him. "Do you want to get better, Christopher?" she asked. "Do you want to be a normal man?"

"Yes. Yes, I do."

"Then it should be evident to you that you can't continue your homosexual activity and, at the same time, hope to have any kind of meaningful relationship with a woman."

"Well, aren't there people who do that? You know, who swing both ways?"

"They're only deluding themselves. Every person has a basic sexual orientation, in one direction or the other—though it can change at different times in a person's life."

"If it can change, then people aren't just one thing or the other."

'No. But they *are* either arrested or mature. Let me explain it this way," she went on. "A person goes through several stages in his early development. First, there's infancy. Then childhood begins as he learns language. Then there's the juvenile era, when he begins dealing with other children of his own age. After that, there's preadolescence, when he starts to create relationships of trust, and even love, with persons of his own sex. Do you follow me so far?"

"I think so," Chris said. He concentrated and recited, "Infancy—childhood—juvenile era—preadolescence."

Delphine nodded approvingly. "In early adolescence," she continued, "the transition in sexual orientation begins. He transfers his trust to a biological stranger, someone of the opposite sex—though hesitantly, at first, incompletely. When he crosses the threshold into late adolescence, he finally and fully adopts the heterosexual pattern." Her lecturer's manner vanished and she looked at him directly again, with a faint smile. "Do you remember, Christopher, when I told you that you should think of yourself as being sixteen? That's what I meant. You haven't crossed that last threshold yet." She paused, then said quietly, "I think the time has come for you to do so."

Chris looked at her apprehensively. "What do you want me to do?"

"At this point, there are two alternatives. One is that we cease our therapy right now and admit that it's been a failure. Do you want that?"

"No!" It was a quick, fearful whisper. An unexpected terror overcame him at the thought.

"The other alternative is that you stop seeing Noah entirely.

If you don't have the strength to resist him, then you can't risk seeing him even as a friend."

He had known she was going to say it. A heaviness spread through him, a leaden apathy. He gazed at her blankly and said nothing.

"You understand why you have to do it, don't you, Christopher?"

"Yes," he said finally. "I understand."

Noah didn't get angry, as he had feared he might; he didn't even seem particularly perturbed. He simply looked at Chris with patient disdain, as he would at a production assistant who has committed a stupidity, and said, "You're going to have to come up with something better than that, baby. It doesn't make sense."

"I can't help it, Noah," Chris said. "It's the way I feel." He lounged back on the couch, with his arm resting on the top of it, and tried to seem relaxed, as if this were nothing more than a casual chat between friends. "If I'm going to be working in your show, then we can't be seeing each other. Later on, after the show has been running for a while, it will be all right. Then everything can be the same between us again." He wasn't leveling with Noah, but he felt he had to soften it. He was breaking off with him, that was the main thing. There was no hurry to let him know that it was, in fact, permanent. "Until then," he went on, "I should be just another actor to you. I don't want you to be playing favorites when we're in rehearsal. It wouldn't be fair to the director. It wouldn't be fair to the other actors. And, anyway, how can you have any objectivity on my work if we're balling every night?"

"I can manage that," Noah said.

"Okay, maybe you can, but *I* can't. It would be too much of a strain. I don't believe in mixing sex with work."

"Well, listen to Miss Integrity!" Noah's tone was mockingly

effeminate. "What were you doing when I picked you up on Third Avenue?"

"Don't pull that on me, Noah," Chris said grimly. "That was a long time ago. I'm different now."

"That's right, you're an artist. An actor!" Noah tugged at the knot of his necktie, as if the silk were too tight around his collar—he was just back from his office and hadn't changed yet—then, impatiently, he clawed at it and got it half undone. Noah *was* angry, Chris realized now. It was his most dangerous kind of anger, an invisible, seething rage. "Let me tell you something," Noah said, leaning forward in his armchair. "You're not nearly a good enough actor yet. You can't act *this* scene worth shit!"

"I'm not acting."

"Sure you are. I don't believe a word you're saying." He glared at him coldly, then picked up his glass, rose, and crossed to the bar. He poured the Scotch straight this time, refilling the glass almost to the brim. Without turning, he asked, "Is there someone else?"

"No."

Noah faced him again, pleasantly smiling now. "Don't try to bullshit me, baby."

Chris was silent. He was beginning to realize how pointless it was to keep up this pretense. Maybe it *would* be better to tell him the truth. Or something close to the truth, anyway.

"Yes," he said at length. "There's someone else." He paused. "A woman."

"A woman!" Noah echoed in an impressed tone. "Anyone I know?"

"No."

"Someone I might have heard of?"

"I doubt it."

"Good," Noah said genially. "Then you can tell me her name. Names make it more human, you know?" He waited. "Just her first name, if you want."

"Vivian."

Chris had said it unthinkingly, and he was startled now. He hadn't intended to mention any name at all.

"Vivian," Noah repeated. "That's a nice name." He took a swallow of his Scotch, then regarded Chris balefully. "Have you fucked her yet?"

Chris rose. "That's none of your business, Noah."

"I don't think you have," Noah said slowly, studying him. He laughed suddenly. "That's wild! You're throwing me over for some cunt you're not even screwing!"

"If you want to think that, go ahead. I'm leaving," he said, turning toward the door.

"Wait a minute!"

Chris turned back, very deliberately, making it clear that it was of his own choice and not in response to Noah's sharp command.

"Why are you doing this, Chris?" Noah asked.

"I want to be straight."

"Straight! What the hell for?"

"Because it might make life easier for me."

"Who says? Your shrink?"

"I've decided this on my own."

"No, you haven't. Your goddamned shrink is behind this!" Noah said bitterly. "She's gotten you all confused."

"I *was* confused," Chris said, "but no longer. I was confused when I thought I couldn't change. When I thought I'd have to go on being what you want me to be."

"Don't lay it on *me*, baby. We're not that different."

"We *are* different. Because you can't help yourself. I can."

"You're kidding yourself, Chris." Noah spoke calmly now, with pointed certainty. "It won't work. You're gay. You're gay today. You'll be gay next year. You'll die gay."

Chris met his gaze uneasily for a moment. "You don't know me," he said.

"I don't know you?" Noah stared at him incredulously. "I don't know you?"

"After nine years, you still don't really know me."

There was an expression of pain in Noah's eyes. But then the anger rose, surfacing quickly and obliterating it. "Ah, fuck it!" he muttered and took a large swallow of his Scotch.

When he lowered his glass, he gazed at Chris again, broodingly, with disgust. "Get out of here!" he said. "Get out of here, you poor, self-deluded faggot!"

12

As SOON as she saw Mandy, Vivian knew this wasn't going to be the usual relaxed, gossipy chat. Mandy was sitting alone at a corner table, leaning forward at a tight, self-absorbed angle, her eyes unseeing, as if she were in a deserted hall rather than in the Algonquin lounge at the height of the cocktail hour.

When Vivian greeted her, she snapped out of her reverie, smiled, rose, and kissed her on the cheek. "I'm so glad to see you," Mandy said rather fervently. "This is on such short notice," she added apologetically. "I hope I haven't inconvenienced you."

"Not at all, darling," Vivian said. "This happens to be on my way. After this, I'm going on to Chris's apartment."

"Christopher Greene?" Mandy showed a bare flicker of curiosity.

"Yes. We're having dinner together."

Mandy didn't react to this. She sat again and seemed to sink back into her own thoughts.

Vivian sat opposite her, ordered a vodka and tonic, and waited, without forcing a conversation. Mandy had sounded tense on the phone and had been somewhat cryptic, saying little more than had been necessary to arrange this meeting. Vivian had thought it was probably some business worry, a Huber Casuals crisis. But now that she was with her, she was beginning to wonder. She had never seen her friend so solemn-faced and preoccupied.

Finally, Mandy raised her eyes and gazed at Vivian intensely. "Tell me something, Vivian. When you broke up with your husband, how did you do it?"

"Why do you ask?"

"I just want to know. Did you do it all at once, in one stroke? Or did it drag on?"

"It dragged on. It was kind of messy, in fact."

This was ancient history, going back to the time before she knew Mandy—just before, actually, since Mandy had been one of the first of the new friends she had made after her marriage ended. Vivian had started seeing a stockbroker who had grown up with Jeff Huber in Brooklyn. One night her beau and she had gotten together for dinner with Jeff and Mandy. The two women had hit it off instantly. Her fling with the stockbroker had fizzled out shortly thereafter, but her friendship with Mandy had lasted through all the years since.

Now she wondered why Mandy, at this late date, was so curious about her breakup with David. It occurred to her that she might need help in advising someone else, one of her employees, perhaps, who was having marital problems.

"I told David on a Monday that he should move out," Vivian continued. "It took him until Thursday of the next week to agree."

"*He* was the one who moved out?"

"Of course. The man usually does in these cases."

Mandy toyed with the stem of her martini glass and thought for a moment. "Jeff loves his home too much," she murmured, half to herself. "I couldn't ask him to do that."

"Jeff?" Vivian was startled. "What's this about Jeff?"

Mandy looked up at her again. "I've decided to leave him."

Vivian stared at her. "When?"

"Tonight."

"But isn't he out of town on business?"

"He's coming back this evening. That's when I'll tell him."

At that point, the waiter arrived with Vivian's drink. Vivian was grateful for the interruption; it gave her some time to get over her shock and to choose an attitude. She expected that Mandy wanted her moral support. She wasn't sure she could give it.

She took a sip of her vodka and tonic, then asked, "Does Jeff have any inkling of this?"

"No," Mandy replied softly. She managed a wan smile. "This is going to come as quite a surprise to him, I'm afraid."

"I can imagine," Vivian said. "How are you going about it? Are *you* moving out?"

Mandy nodded. "I'm already packed."

"Where will you stay?"

"Phyllis, my assistant, will put me up for a while. She has an extra room."

Vivian visualized it for a moment, the wretched, cramped existence, the dazed sense of dislocation. It would be a nightmare. And yet Mandy was stepping into it, clear-eyed and determined. For no visible reason. There had been no sign of friction between the Hubers that Vivian had noticed, or that anyone else had commented on.

At length, Vivian said, "The inevitable question is—why do you feel you have to do this?"

"I just can't go on with it," Mandy said with a helpless gesture. "I've been married since I was twenty-two. My twenties are gone. My thirties are passing by. I've given all those years to Jeff. And—" She paused, then concluded sadly, "He doesn't give me enough in return."

"He loves you very much," Vivian said.

"Oh, I know he does," Mandy conceded, "in his own way. But I'm not happy. I don't know who I really am. I don't know who I would have been if I had never met Jeff."

"Every married woman feels that way, at some time or the other."

"I suppose so. But most married women have children to give them a reason for their existence. We don't have children. So, I'm not a mother—and I'm not even a wife, in the usual sense. All I am is one half of a business partnership."

"What *will* you do about the business?" Vivian asked. "Do you intend to give up your work?"

"Oh no, I couldn't do that. Designing is my whole life." After a moment, she said, "I'm thinking of going out on my own."

"You mean, start your own business?"

"Yes. Phyllis and I have already worked out the preliminary plans."

Vivian shook her head wonderingly. "It seems like you're taking on an awful lot."

"I know. It's scary. I wouldn't be able to go through all this if I weren't in therapy. Delphine has been so wonderful!" Mandy said, her voice warming with gratitude. "She's helped me to see things clearly." She looked away and, in a low, earnest tone, ticked off the insights she had gained. "How Jeff has used me, exploited my talent—how he has held me back in my work—how he has kept me from fulfilling myself as a woman—"

Vivian felt a little intimidated by this itemized indictment, and she was humbled into silence. If Delphine had come to these conclusions, she had no business contradicting them. She was a friend of the Hubers', but she had never really understood the inner workings of their marriage. Delphine had probed it. Delphine had analyzed it. As always, she knew best.

Finally, simply as something to say, Vivian commented, "You have a rough scene ahead of you this evening."

Mandy nodded glumly. "I'm dreading it."

"And you've made it harder for yourself. I mean, if you're packed, why haven't you moved out already?"

"And not be there when Jeff comes home?" Mandy seemed shocked by the idea. "He's so tired when he comes back from a business trip. If I weren't there, who would cook his dinner?"

She had been talking about it too long already and she was afraid Chris might be getting bored, but Vivian felt compelled to clarify it, if only to explain away her lingering sense of shock. "You know how some people seem meant to be married?" she said. "You can't imagine them ever having been single? Well, Mandy and Jeff have always seemed that way. Every other marriage might break up, but you thought they'd go on forever."

"Some people do," Chris said. "My folks have been married thirty-one years. But that's Wisconsin."

"Even in New York it can happen. But you need one stable marriage, as a constant, a point of reference, to show that a man and woman really *can* be happy with each other. For me, the Hubers were that constant. So of course," Vivian said, with a shrug, "I'm shaken up." She paused, as she remembered Mandy's condemnation of Jeff, her rather startling references to his "using" her and "exploiting" her. "I guess it hasn't helped they've been in business together."

"You mean, the tensions?"

"The tensions. The ego clashes. Maybe that kind of arrangement can never work out." She looked at him questioningly. "Would you want to be married to someone who acted in your plays with you—or who produced them?"

Chris didn't say anything for a few moments. He didn't

actually seem to be pondering the question; it was just a peculiar suspension in the conversation. He was sitting on his studio bed, leaning back against the wall, holding a book of matches in the fingertips of his hands—matches that someone had left; or so she assumed, since he didn't smoke. He was tearing the matches out of the book, one every ten seconds or so, tossing them into the unused candy plate that was on the night table. He seemed to have little awareness of what he was doing, and Vivian was reminded of the abstracted, compulsive way he had fondled the glass sphere at the Hubers' dinner party.

"I've never thought about it," he answered finally. "I suppose if I loved the person it wouldn't make any difference." He looked at her glass. "May I get you some more wine?"

"No, thanks." It was cheap white wine, some mass-produced California brand, and on top of the vodka it was a little sour in her stomach. But it was all he had, and she had politely accepted a glass of it. "It's very nice, though," she said, with a good guest's insincerity.

She put down her wine glass, rose, glanced around at what was on the walls, then went over to look more closely at a large poster of a Japanese print. It depicted a samurai, with a top knot and a flowing kimono. The poster had been stuck onto the dingy plaster with masking tape, and Scotch tape had been added to the curling upper corners. It was the kind of thing that could be picked up at Marboro's for two dollars, and the reproductions of Degas ballet dancers on the other walls had clearly been cut out of an art book. This makeshift decor gave Vivian a rather charming impression of dewy, newborn culture. It was as if she were in the dormitory room of a college freshman rather than the apartment of a sophisticated Broadway leading man.

Actually, this main room was the only one in which Chris had made any effort at all. The kitchen–dining room was totally bare, and the tiny room beyond it was nothing more than a cluttered catch-all. The window in the kitchen looked into a grimy air shaft. In the main room, roll-down shades blocked out what would have been a view of Hell's Kitchen tenements.

She turned back to him. "How long have you lived here?"

"Years," he replied. "Longer than I'd care to admit."

"Rent-controlled?"

"Of course. It's a hundred and twenty-one. That kind of rent can trap you. You don't dare move out."

"But you can afford a little more than that now, can't you? You've been doing well lately."

"For an actor, it's feast or famine. Maybe the feast is over for a while," he said with a philosophic shrug. "Anyway, I'm always ready for the famine."

"I don't think you have anything to worry about," Vivian said.

She went over to the studio bed and sat beside him. Chris smiled at her vaguely and went on tearing at the matchbook. He was near the end of it, and the candy plate was almost filled with discarded, unburned matches.

"Why are you doing that?" she asked.

"Doing what?"

"Tearing up that matchbook."

Chris looked down at the matchbook, which had only two matches left in it now, then tossed it aside. "Just something to do with my hands," he said, a bit sheepishly.

"I thought actors knew what to do with their hands."

"*I* don't. It's been a problem. Directors are always giving me props to carry. If it's a living room comedy, I pour myself a drink and hold the glass. If I'm a studious type, I carry a book or some papers. Once I shined shoes through a scene, another time I ate peanuts. If I play any kind of guy with a horse—a farmer or a period aristocrat—it seems I'm always carrying a broken harness." He laughed ruefully, then said, "Offstage, I don't have a director. So I just grab anything."

"All the time?"

"When I'm nervous."

"Are you nervous now?"

"No." He reconsidered it. "Yes, I guess I must be."

"Why?"

"Because I can't entertain very well. And I know you think this place is tacky."

"I don't think that, Chris."

"I don't know why you shouldn't," he said amiably. "It's the honest-to-God truth."

"I like it." She sat back and looked around the room approvingly. "It reminds me of the place I had when I first came to New York."

"It was like this?" he asked, a bit dubiously.

"Worse. It was down on the Lower East Side, and it had a bathtub in the kitchen—you know?—with a metal lid over it? And the john was out in the hall. When my mother came down to see me, she didn't say a word. She just sat and cried."

He smiled. Then he shifted around on the bed, faced her and looked at her curiously. "Where are you from?" he asked.

"Upstate," she replied. "Rochester."

"Then you haven't always lived on Fifth Avenue?"

"Did you think so?"

"Oh, I didn't know. I sort of thought you came from the lap of luxury."

She laughed. "Hardly. We weren't poor, exactly, but we were always struggling. My father had a little hardware store. For him, I don't think the Depression ever ended."

"And that's why you lived that way when you came to New York? You didn't have any money?"

"I lived that way because that's the way I had to live. I was trying to make it in the arts. I was a dancer, remember?"

"That's right," he said, nodding. "Modern dance."

"You can make a living at that now. But not then. Anyway," she went on, "I got married, and I've been middle class ever since."

"I don't think of you as middle class." He regarded her appreciatively. "You're very stylish."

"So are you, Chris," she said. "That's why you shouldn't worry about what I, or anyone, thinks of this place. You have great natural style—and elegance."

His smile was rather shy, but pleased. He had a quite genuine modesty, she realized—considering who he was, a slightly incredible one—and he had never seemed more appealing to her than he did at that moment, this handsome, godlike male, flushing boyishly at being told the obvious about himself.

Vivian met his gaze, said nothing for a few moments, and waited. She was starting to get aroused. His leg was drawn up on the bed and his knee was only a couple of inches from her hip. It was tantalizing her; she longed to have some part of him touching her. She was ready for him; she had put in her diaphragm before coming over, so that, if it happened, it could happen spontaneously, without interruption.

But Chris was simply looking at her, mildly and uncertainly, as if he were trying to think of what to say next.

At length, Vivian said, "What you *do* need is someone to create an environment for you. A woman. Hasn't that ever occurred to you?"

"I hadn't thought much about it before. I was too busy with my career." He paused, then said gravely, "But I've started thinking about it lately."

"Oh? Is there some woman in your life?" she asked, a little too casually.

"I don't know." He cocked his head seductively and, suddenly, he seemed very self-assured. He fixed her with a charismatic actor's piercing look and murmured, "Maybe there is. Now."

He inclined toward her slowly, then took her in his arms and kissed her, a long but delicate kiss. She gave herself up to it. She felt his hand touching her breast, cupping it hesitantly for a second or two. Then it withdrew.

When they separated, Chris sat back, looking happy and excited. The kiss had gone well, they both knew it, and they were warmed in the afterglow of it.

Vivian's whole being was yearning for him now and she reached out to caress his thigh. But, even as she touched him, stroked the hard muscles that swelled against the cotton, she felt vaguely disturbed, aware that something was wrong. She sensed that he was still remote from her; the distance had not been narrowed.

Chris took her hand from his leg and squeezed it affectionately. "Let's think about where we should go for dinner," he said.

There was a glazed look in Jeff's eyes, as if she had literally stunned him with a blow, shocking his system beyond all responding. "I understand," he said tonelessly. "It's all right, I understand."

"No, you don't," Mandy said. "Let me explain."

"I *understand*, I tell you. You don't have to go on."

"What *can* you understand?"

"That you don't want to be with me any more. What else is there to know?"

She was doing it all wrong, Mandy realized. She had prepared her arguments, rehearsed them aloud. But now she was at a loss to contradict his logic. "Nothing else, I guess," she said.

Jeff stood where he was, in the center of the living room, looking awkward and rumpled in the suit he had traveled in, clutching his glass, his welcome-home martini. Uncertainly, he ventured, "There's a guy, right?"

"No, there's no one."

"No one at all?"

"I swear to you, Jeff."

"It's just me?"

"You and me. The way things have worked out."

"It's just me," he muttered dismally. "Jesus!" He looked over at his suitcase, which was where he had left it, by the archway. "Well, there's no point in my unpacking. I'll just go on to a hotel."

"You don't have to go," she said. "This is your home."

"I can't stay *now*."

"Yes, you can. I'm all packed. I'll leave."

"Don't be silly," Jeff said testily. "A marriage breaks up, the man moves out."

"But why should you? You haven't done anything wrong."

"I must have done *something* wrong," he said despairingly, "if you don't want to stay with me."

"Oh, Jeff, please, don't blame yourself," she said, going to him impulsively. He looked so pathetic that she came close to taking him into her arms. Instead, she put her hand on his shoulder gently. "You've been a wonderful husband—" She paused, then qualified it: "—in your own way."

Jeff looked at her. "Then I don't get it."

Mandy dropped her hand and glanced away. "It has nothing to do with you, really. I have to do it for myself."

"Well, I want you to be happy," he said mildly. "I've always wanted you to be happy." He pondered the situation for a moment, screwing up his face as he tried to make sense of it. "Where are you going?" he asked.

"I'm moving in with Phyllis for a while."

"Phyllis? She lives over by Needle Park!"

"So what?"

"It's not safe over there!" he said. "*Anything* could happen to you!"

"I'll be fine."

"I can't let you do this, honey!"

"Jeff," she said patiently, "you don't have to worry about me any more."

"Oh, I'll worry about you, all right." Jeff looked down at his glass. Then, stricken, he whispered, "Jesus, this is really happening!" He took a quick, convulsive swallow of his drink.

"Look, why don't you sit down?" Mandy suggested soothingly. She saw that the martini on the rocks was down to its last watery inch and she took the glass from his hand. "I'll get you another drink," she said, leading him over to an armchair. He sat, dazed.

Mandy went to the bar to fix another martini. Her hands were shaking and, when she filled the bottle cap with vermouth, she spilled it and had to do it a second time.

She heard Jeff's voice, muted and timid, behind her. "Mandy?"

"Yes?"

"I thought your silk bloomers design was very nice. I didn't mean to make fun of it last week. I was just teasing."

She turned, glass in hand, and looked at him. He was leaning forward in the chair, in an almost supplicant posture, gazing at her hopefully.

"And your picture skirt was terrific," he said. "The best thing you've ever done."

"It doesn't matter now," she said.

Jeff started crying. He put his face in his hands and sobbed.

Mandy stared at him bleakly. She hadn't expected it would be like this. She had such good, solid reasons, and he was killing her with the way he was taking it.

She would be strong, she wouldn't waver. And yet she couldn't help wondering, as she watched her forty-six-year-old baby blubbering desolately—who would take care of him?

13

It was the best idea she had had in ages—this picnic in Central Park. As Vivian unwrapped the sandwiches, she listened to Chris and Jane going at each other in friendly argument, testing each other like two wily young animals. In the blazing sunshine, they looked gloriously vital and beautiful. It was a secluded little meadow; there was only one other group of picnickers, with a frisky, yellow cocker spaniel that kept coming over to check them out. This expanse of grass, the surrounding trees, the Fifth Avenue skyline beyond—it was the proper setting for the first meeting of the two people in the world she cared for the most.

"It's interpretive, sure," Jane was saying, "but I don't see how you can call acting an *intellectual* art. Oh, maybe those people who work with Grotowski and Peter Brook are into something pretty cerebral. But actors in Broadway shows are—well, they're performers—like rock singers are performers."

A year at Radcliffe had changed Jane in more ways than one. She hadn't simply been physically transformed from an awkward girl into a gracefully maturing young woman. She had also come back, Vivian noted, with mingled amusement and dismay, a full-blown intellectual snob.

But Chris didn't seem the least bit bothered by Jane's earnest pedantry. Good-naturedly, he asked, "So, what do you think an actor is doing up on that stage? Wandering around in a daze? Shaking to the beat? If he's a good actor, he's making a hundred choices every minute. And don't you think that takes brains?"

"It depends on the play," Jane said. "If it's a Neil Simon comedy, I shouldn't think he'd make a hundred intellectual choices in a *year*."

Chris looked at Vivian with mock horror. "Great Scott, Vivian, you've spawned a critic!"

"Don't blame *me*," Vivian said. "I raised her to be a pompom girl."

"Oh, don't say that, Mother," Jane murmured, a bit disgusted. "You know you didn't."

"Well, then, maybe I should have. I mean, you're arguing with Chris about something he does as well as anyone in the country. A year of freshman English doesn't make you Walter Kerr, you know," she chided gently.

Jane blushed. It was one childhood characteristic she hadn't lost, the swift crimsoning of her cheeks when she was embarrassed. It was a pretty effect, since she had Vivian's own coloring, the creamy complexion and the near-black hair. But it was the only real resemblance, Vivian thought, as she studied her. Jane was three inches taller than she, and Jane had inherited her father's tough wiriness. It was clear, now that she was full-grown, that there would always be a suggestion of hard angles to her.

Jane could be bullheaded, too—one of her father's less endearing traits—and she displayed this stubbornness now.

"But you don't understand what I'm trying to *say*," she burst out suddenly, refusing to abandon the argument. "I've never seen Chris act, but I don't doubt he's marvelous. And I can tell he's bright."

"Thanks, kid," Chris said.

"But a Stradivarius violin is marvelous, too," Jane said.

"What you're trying to say is that an actor is an instrument?" Chris asked.

"Yes. A sensitive instrument," she said slowly, painstakingly composing her definition, "that is guided by the director to express the playwright's thoughts."

"There's some truth to that," he said. "But we're something more than inanimate objects."

"You're highly trained. But what you train is your body, right?—and your voice? You don't go around thinking abstract thoughts all the time, do you?"

"Maybe not," Chris said indifferently. He was perceptibly losing interest in the discussion.

"Which doesn't mean you're any less of an artist," Jane hastily added. She seemed a little uneasy, as if she sensed that she might be antagonizing him. "I mean," she went on, trying to flatter him now, "you're so wonderfully expressive. It's beautiful just the way you're sitting on the grass."

"All that body training," Chris murmured dryly.

"Do you take dance classes? Or do you work out at a gym?"

"I work out. Every day."

"What do you do? Calisthenics?"

"Calisthenics. Acrobatics."

"Oh, come on, Chris!" Vivian chimed in skeptically. "You're not really an acrobat, are you?"

"You don't believe me? Watch!"

Chris quickly emptied his pockets, kicked off his loafers, and sprang to his feet. He was smiling and eager, obviously happy to have a chance to show off for them. He took a gymnast's poised-at-attention position, looked sideways to make sure they were watching, then plunged forward and executed a perfect series of handsprings, three in a row.

"Bravo!" Vivian cried out, clapping her hands.

The yellow cocker spaniel seemed to be applauding him too. It was cavorting around Chris, barking excitedly.

"For my next feat," he declaimed dramatically, "I will perform a daring, death-defying forward flip."

He sprinted a few steps, soared upward, did a complete somersault in the air, and came down on his feet. An almost perfect landing. But, possibly because the ground was irregular, he held his balance for only a second, then sprawled onto the grass.

"Terrific!" Vivian clapped enthusiastically. "Oh, you're fabulous, Chris!"

The cocker spaniel rushed over to Chris and nipped at him in a frenzy. Chris jumped to his feet, with comic alarm, and ran around in a circle, taking a clown's grotesquely high steps. The dog pursued him, leaping up futilely, never quite catching him.

Vivian was laughing wildly, delighted by his silliness and lithe grace. She turned her head to see if Jane was enjoying his performance as much as she was.

But her daughter wasn't watching Chris at all. She was gazing at Vivian intently, as if she were assessing the way she was responding. Her face was hard with thought.

Chris came back to them, holding the panting little dog in his arms. He sat down and affectionately stroked its yellow fur. "I should make him part of the act. We're a good team." He glanced up at Jane. "Just two trained animals, right, Jane?"

Jane smiled faintly but said nothing. Whatever she was thinking she kept to herself, and she remained uncharacteristically reserved for the rest of the afternoon.

It wasn't until early that evening, after Chris had gone home, that she gave Vivian any clue as to what was on her mind.

Vivian was lying on her bed, with the drapes closed; not napping, but simply resting in the cool dark after the afternoon of bright sun. Jane came into the room silently and sat on the edge of the bed, not quite facing her. "Is Chris coming back this evening?" she asked.

"You know he is, darling. At seven-thirty. He's taking us out to dinner."

"Oh."

She couldn't have forgotten it, Vivian knew. It was as if she hoped there had been a change in plans.

"You like Chris, don't you?" Vivian asked.

"He seems nice enough," Jane said. With a shrug, she added, "I've got nothing against him."

"Why would you have anything against him?"

Jane swung around on the bed and looked at her probingly. "He's more than just a friend, isn't he, Mother?"

"I care for him a lot. He was very kind to me when I was ill."

Jane started to ask something else, then hesitated, as if she were afraid to voice it. Finally, grave-faced, she asked the question. "Is he straight?"

"Of course, he's straight!" Vivian answered, in a surprised tone.

"How do you know?"

"Because he told me."

"He *told* you?" Jane seemed a bit taken aback. "Then you felt you had to ask?"

"We've talked about a lot of things," Vivian said impatiently, trying to dismiss it. "Look, Jane, what are you getting at? Chris seems queer to you? Is that it?"

"No, he doesn't. He's sexy, in his own way. But there's something not right about him. I just sense it."

"Since when do you know so much about it? Does a year of college make you an expert on people's sexual proclivities?"

"You don't have to be that smart to know *some* things. For instance, he's a lot younger than you. If he really were straight, why would he be spending so much time with you?"

"Why the hell do you think?" Vivian was getting angry now. "Because he *likes* me. And he's not *that* young."

"He's closer to my age than yours."

"Halfway in between," Vivian snapped. "And I don't want to talk about this any more!"

"All right, Mother," Jane said calmly. She rose from the bed. "All right, we won't talk about it." Her troubled eyes held on her for a moment. "But, please, don't make a fool of yourself."

Chris was moving his hand slowly, in a delicate, circular motion, chafing her bare nipple with his palm, maddening her. When she could stand it no longer, Vivian growled loudly, with playful ferocity, and rose up from the mattress to bite his shoulder. But then she caught herself, put her hand over her mouth, and lay back.

"What's the matter?" Chris asked.

"I don't want Jane to hear us."

"Are we going to have to worry about that?" He eased back onto his elbow and looked faintly annoyed.

"No," Vivian said after a moment, "let's not worry."

It was a ridiculous thing to be anxious about, she realized. Jane's room was on the other side of the hallway, and the walls were thick. But she could imagine Jane as she probably was at that moment, propped up on her pillows, not quite concentrating on her book, looking in their direction every so often, willing her disapproval through the cracks in the doors.

There had been a time when Jane's presence in the apartment had not oppressed her, when she had felt free to let a man stay over occasionally. But Jane was no longer a child, and she had changed toward her; their tense conversation, earlier in the evening, had left no doubt of it. Vivian couldn't feel completely comfortable now with a man in her bed and her daughter just across the hall from her.

"Next time, we should go to your place," she said.

"All right," Chris said. "Next time, we will."

It occurred to Vivian that she was talking about their relationship as if it were an ongoing affair. In fact, nothing had really happened yet. A couple of sessions of delicious kissing, some tentative petting, but nothing more.

Now, though, after a wonderful day and evening together, they were lying naked beside each other. Her skin was tingling with excitement. She sensed the building anticipation in him. But what did she find herself thinking about, as they approached the moment when they would connect? That wretched girl!

Well, if she couldn't get her out of her mind, she might as well talk about her. "What do you think of Jane?" she asked.

"I like her," Chris replied. "She's a bright girl."

"Bright?" With maternal pride, she corrected him. "She's brilliant."

"Yeah, she has a good mind. And I enjoy talking with her. But I don't know—" He hesitated. "I'm not sure she really cares for *me*."

"You mean, because of that argument you had this afternoon? Don't worry about it. Jane was just being pompous. The way eighteen-year-olds can be pompous."

"Oh, I understand. And I didn't mind. I'm used to being condescended to. It hasn't changed that much for actors. A lot of places, we still have to go in the servants' entrance. But, with Jane," he went on, looking thoughtful, "I got the feeling it was more than just that."

"You're right," she said after a moment. "It *was* more. Delphine warned me about it a long time ago."

"Warned you? What about ?"

"She said the time would come when Jane would try to compete with me."

Chris laughed. "You mean, Jane wants me? She has a funny way of showing it!"

"I don't know if she wants you or not. But she doesn't want *me* to have you. After all," she said, uncomfortably echoing Jane's words, "you're a little closer to her age than mine."

"But she's a *kid*."

"Some men like kids."

It was a mistake to say it. It opened up a door in her memory that, until then, she had managed to keep shut. With a stab of anguish, she thought of the two of them now . . . Jane and Ward . . .

Vivian suddenly reached out for him, pulled him to her, and embraced him fiercely. "Let's not talk about her!" she whispered. "Let's not even think about her!"

Her intensity touched off a quick urgency in him. He kissed her, very hard, grinding his mouth down against hers, his teeth nicking the soft underflesh and hurting it. Vivian whimpered expectantly and spread her thighs, opening herself to him. His hips drove against her insistently. But she could sense the fear that was tensing the lean, strong body on top of her. She realized he wasn't ready.

She remembered what Delphine had said: *Don't forget that Christopher, in many ways, is still a child, a very high-strung child. When the time comes, you must be very patient with him, as patient as if you were his mother teaching him how to walk.*

"Wait, darling," Vivian murmured, gripping his arms to restrain him. "Just wait a moment."

Chris bucked rebelliously, trying to continue. But she stroked him soothingly, and, at length, he relaxed and lay motionless on her. She eased him onto his side, swung around, and took his penis into her mouth. It still had a softness to it, but, almost instantly, it swelled and hardened.

She felt his head burrowing between her thighs. His tongue explored her, searching for the precise spot, then finding it. The pleasure surged up through her, surprising her with its suddenness, with its keen edge of ecstasy that she had almost forgotten could exist. She went still now, with the warm, throbbing member in her mouth, the sweet smell of his loins in her nostrils, and gave herself up to the consuming orgasm.

14

"DELPHINE," Chris asked, "how would you define love?"

"I know the way Harry Stack Sullivan defined it," his therapist replied. "Having a greater concern for someone else's well-being than for your own."

Chris pondered it for a moment. "Then maybe I'm in love with Vivian."

"The definition fits?"

"Well, she was bugged the other day. She'd had another fight with Jane, and—" He stopped, as he remembered who he was talking to. "I suppose you know that."

Delphine nodded. "Yes."

"I had this tennis date I'd been looking forward to," he went on. "A guy who's just a little bit better than I am—you know?—so the matches are always exciting? I canceled it to spend the afternoon with Vivian. I entertained her, did all my shticks, until she was happy and laughing again. And that made me happy—happier even than if I'd played tennis." He looked at her questioningly. "Love?"

"It could be something like it, I think," Delphine said, smiling.

"So, okay, you said it would happen some day, and it looks like it's happened." He shrugged helplessly. "What do I do now?"

"What do you mean?"

"Should I ask her to marry me?" He watched her face closely. Her expression didn't change in the slightest. "That shocks you, doesn't it?"

"No," she said calmly, "it doesn't shock me at all." She paused, then asked, "Is this a sudden idea? Or have you been considering it for a while?"

"Not for very long. I've had to adjust my thinking first. I mean, I've always expected I'd get married some day. But I would imagine it as, well, you know, like in the commercials—a young guy and young girl, cute little apartment, cute little kids." A bit wryly, he said, "I just can't think of Vivian in those terms."

"Life isn't always like the commercials, is it?"

"No, it isn't. But—well, would it make sense? If we got married?"

"Would it make sense?" she echoed. "Make sense to whom? Are you worried about what other people would think?"

"I couldn't care less what—" he began, then broke off. "Yeah," he admitted, after a moment, "I guess that's a factor. She *is* older than I am."

"Yes, she is."

Chris looked at her expectantly, waiting for her to say something further. When she didn't, he asked, "So, how does the idea strike you?"

"What can I tell you?" It was one of those rare times when Delphine actually seemed to be at a loss for an answer. She meditated for a few moments, then said, "I think the very fact that you're opening your mind to this possibility is a positive thing. Very positive." Her bright gaze held on him and her expression softened with tenderness. "You have made remarkable progress, Christopher, and I'm proud of you."

Chris felt warmed by her approval; he basked in it happily for a moment. Then, trying to be casual about the whole thing, he said, "It doesn't seem like such a big deal."

"But it is. We both know the terrible problems you've had to overcome. Now you're no longer confused about your sexual role. You're thinking like a normal, healthy male choosing his mate. It isn't easy finding a compatible mate," she went on, in a careful, judicious tone. "You seem to have achieved a love relationship with Vivian, and that's a precious thing; it's nothing to be taken for granted. In which case," she concluded, "in considering this question, I don't think we should worry about the world's opinion. The slight difference in ages doesn't really matter."

"It does matter in some ways, doesn't it?" he asked uncertainly. "Could we have children?"

"It's biologically possible," she said. "But I don't imagine it's too likely. Is it important to you to have children?"

"I don't know. I always sort of thought I'd have a family."

"Of course, you *would* have a family," she pointed out. "A family structure, at any rate. Jane would be your stepdaughter."

"Terrific." Chris laughed uncomfortably. "That's all I need! Jane as a stepdaughter. Do you know her?"

"I know her very well," Delphine said quietly.

There was something in her tone that conveyed that her knowledge of Jane went beyond the simple familiarity she might have with a patient's relative. Chris paused to figure it out, then took a guess. "Has Jane come here, too?"

"Yes," Delphine replied. "She was my patient, up until a couple of years ago." With a cool, tight smile, she added, "I wasn't able to help her much, I'm afraid. She's a very neurotic girl."

"Yeah." Chris was puzzled by the faint emanation of hostility he was getting from her; he hadn't realized that his therapist even had it in her makeup. This hostility had been awakened, evidently, by their brief discussion of Jane, and now he hastened to dismiss the girl from their conversation. "Well, she's away at school most of the time. I wouldn't be seeing much of her anyway."

"That's true."

"But you haven't answered my original question," Chris reminded her, a bit impatiently.

"You mean, should you marry Vivian?"

"Well, should I ask her? I don't know if she'd say yes, after all."

"She would be favorably disposed to the idea, I think," Delphine murmured, almost offhandedly.

"Has she said so?" he asked quickly.

"I can't tell you that." She was the cautious doctor now. But, after a moment, her expression relaxed and a rather teasing smile appeared. "I'll say this. Vivian cares for you at least as much as you care for her."

"Oh." Chris sat back, pleased.

"As for your question," she went on, "it's something you'll have to decide for yourself."

"You *always* say that, Delphine!" he burst out, with sudden exasperation. "You *always* say that!" He leaned forward intensely. "Delphine, I owe you everything. You've helped me get my head together. You've helped me clear some bad things out of my life. You've given me a whole new direction. But this choice now may be the most important one I'll ever make. Just this once," he pleaded, "tell me what I should do. Should I go ahead with it? Is it the right thing? Would it make me happy?"

"Would it make you happy?"

Delphine looked pensive, as she paused to shape some answer for him. Chris waited for it hungrily. He had spent so many crucial hours over the past year concentrating his whole being on this mysterious, pale face, with its radiant but unsettling eyes, its delicate, enigmatic mouth that could express an infinite range of subtle and sometimes unreadable moods. Now, more than ever, he craved a sign from her, something clear and un-equivocal; a benediction, perhaps.

Finally, Delphine spoke. "If Vivian and you got together," she said, with a warm smile, "if you created a good life with each other, it would make *me* very happy."

After he left Delphine's, Chris took a cab and went directly to the Plymouth Theater, where he was due for an audition. As the cab cut across the park, he opened the script and glanced through it, only now giving some thought to the upcoming reading. Ordinarily, on the day of an important audition, Chris would have canceled all appointments, his therapy session in-cluded, and would have prepared intensively. But this was no usual audition. It was for the play Noah Porterfield was pro-ducing, a play Chris knew backward and forward. And he was reading for the male lead, a part he had thought he had been penciled in for long ago. It didn't make sense.

Ira, his agent, was as perplexed about it as he was. "Your guess is as good as mine," Ira had said over the phone. "All I can tell you is they called to set up this reading. It's kind of crazy."

Ira Sherwin was the only agent he had ever had—by now, he was his friend as well as his representative—and Chris's close relationship with Noah had been no secret to him. But Ira, a good family man and mildly puritanical in his outlook, had never commented on it. The closest he had come was when he had said, at a time when Chris had been keeping some flagrantly queenish company, "I don't care what a client wants to be in his private life—just as long as he doesn't put it in neon." Chris had taken the hint and had dropped his new acquaintances.

This time, too, Ira had let it go with a bit of understatement. "It isn't as if Noah doesn't know your work."

"Maybe he's doing it for the director's sake," Chris suggested.

"Could be. But this director has been around for a while. You would think he'd know you're perfect for the part."

"Some directors don't take anything for granted. They have to be shown."

"You think that's the case here?"

"No," Chris said after a moment. "I don't know what the fuck is going on."

"Well, okay, all you can do is go ahead and read."

"Do I really have to, Ira? I'm not some kid fresh out of acting school. And Noah promised me this part a long time ago."

"Did you sign a contract?"

"You know I didn't."

"So, there you are," Ira said quietly.

They had ended up agreeing he should turn up for the audition. Just a formality, probably. But why take chances?

Now, as the cab came out of the park and plunged into the midtown traffic, Chris began to get nervous. His stomach was acting up, just as it used to when he was starting out in the business and each audition seemed a survive-or-fail challenge. He had to remind himself that he was no longer a green beginner, that, since those days, he had won an Obie award, a Derwent award, and had been nominated for a Tony. People treated him with respect now. He might have to go through the same old motions, sometimes, but it wasn't the same thing.

Even so, he realized that he hadn't spoken with Noah since the night he had broken up with him. He didn't know what to expect. For all he knew, Noah had turned against him. He might even have changed his mind about giving him the part.

But Chris couldn't bring himself to believe this, that Noah would let personal considerations keep him from casting the best actor available for a crucial lead role. Noah hadn't reached the top in the theater, hadn't won a reputation for having the highest standards of any producer, by settling for second or third best when he was piqued. There was just too much at stake in a Broadway production, in money, in reputations, in the futures of everyone involved.

Still, when the cab came to a stop in front of the theater, Chris was edgy with apprehension.

He went in through the stage door entrance. In the hallway inside, a half-dozen young men were sitting in wooden chairs along both walls, clutching opened scripts, poring over them. Chris didn't recognize any of these actors. They were unknowns, he was sure; but all of them, he noted uneasily, were good-looking, of his general physical type, about his age or a few years younger.

The door that led to the stage area opened and Kevin, Noah's assistant, came out, carrying a clipboard. He was followed by the young actor who had just auditioned. The actor had the frozen smile of a performer who knows he has bombed out. He handed his script to Kevin with a mumbled "thanks" and walked out dazedly.

Kevin came over to Chris. "Hi, Chris," he said with a friendly smile.

"What the hell is this, Kevin?" Chris asked under his breath. "A cattle call?"

Without replying, Kevin looked down at his clipboard and put a check beside the name of the actor who had just read. Chris saw his own name farther down on the list, with a half-dozen unchecked names before it.

Kevin turned and called out the next name. An actor rose from his chair abruptly.

Kevin started away, but Chris put a restraining hand on the assistant's arm and leaned forward to whisper into his ear. "Tell Noah I'm here."

"You'll have to wait your turn, Chris," Kevin said without looking at him. He stood still until Chris's hand dropped, then walked on to lead the actor through the doorway and out onto the stage.

Chris sat in a chair and opened his script. He sensed that the other actors were sneaking looks at him, but, when he glanced up, all eyes turned away. Ignoring them, he did a brief breathing exercise, breathing deeply and evenly, trying to relax himself, trying to free his mind of all extraneous thoughts so he could concentrate. But he couldn't focus on the page before him. His eyes were hurting and the stenciled print was blurring. He debated whether or not to put on his glasses, then decided against it. There was no need, of course, to worry about his appearance with Noah and his staff; but, whenever he felt most insecure, it was the compulsive thought that would come into his head—he had to look terrific.

The next actor in his turn was led out to the stage, then another actor after him. All the while, Chris was trying to figure out what was going on. Perhaps what they really were doing, it occurred to him, was casting his understudy. At the same time, in the same call, they were getting his token reading for the director and playwright out of the way.

He tried to convince himself of it, but it just didn't seem very plausible. For that matter, he thought with growing anger, it wasn't plausible either that he was sitting there preparing to audition for a role that he practically knew by heart, that he had discussed endlessly with Noah, that he had actually helped revise with his suggestions.

What the hell was Noah trying to do?

Chris got up suddenly, went to the end of the hallway, opened the door and walked out into the backstage area.

The actor on stage had just finished his audition, and now Chris heard Noah's voice, clear and echoing in the empty theater, call out, "Thank you." It was the goodbye-and-sorry thank you that ended most auditions, a singsong incantation that hit the first word hard and lingered on the nasalization—"Th*annn*k you."

Kevin was standing in the wings. Chris went over to him and said in a half-whisper, "I can't wait any longer."

"It will just be a few minutes, Chris."

"I'm not waiting one minute longer!" His voice rose to full volume. "Tell Noah I'm reading *now*."

Kevin just stood there, seemingly paralyzed by indecision. He didn't even look at the departing actor drifting by them on his way out.

"Announce me, Kevin," Chris said.

Kevin sighed resignedly, then stepped out onto the stage. "Christopher Greene," he said loudly.

Chris walked out to center stage. He nodded to the stage manager, who was standing downstage right, script in hand, then turned and looked out into the house. Noah, the director, and the playwright were sitting halfway back in the orchestra, too far away for him to make out their faces. They were simply three blurred figures in three adjoining seats near the center aisle. The one right on the aisle was Noah; even without his glasses, Chris could discern the bald head that crowned the blur.

Chris waited for a few moments, but no one said a word. He started his reading.

Almost from the outset, he knew it was no good. The stage manager was feeding him the lines in a passionless monotone, but Chris was used to that problem. He, himself, was blocking; he could get nothing into his delivery. His throat felt constricted, his voice was coming out thin and strained. When he tried to move around the stage in an attempt to free himself, he felt his knee joints tightening, and he found himself walking stiff-legged, like a frightened summer stock apprentice.

He read the scene through, to its very end, and no one spoke up to stop him. When he had said the last line, he looked up and squinted uncertainly at the three blurred figures.

"Th*annn*k you," Noah called out.

Chris turned slowly and started off the stage, his head down.

He was in a stupor of humiliation, was barely thinking at all; but, dimly, he was aware he was making a bad exit. He stopped, turned, drew himself up, and stared resentfully at the indistinct, bald-headed figure on the aisle.

"Fuck you, Noah," he said.

"I'm so happy, darling," Vivian murmured, cuddling up to him.

Chris put his arm around her and leaned back on his studio bed. The piled-up throw pillows—the multicolored pillows that she had picked out for him at Bloomingdale's and had insisted that he buy—were poking their corners into his back; but he scarcely noticed. He felt protective, comfortably settled, a man joined with his woman.

"There's just one thing that puzzles me," she said.

"What?"

"Will I be Vivian Greene? Or Vivian whatever-it-is?"

"Gustafsen?" He thought for a moment. "I really don't know. I'll have to check it out."

"Well, it doesn't matter. Gus-taf-sen"—she labored over the syllables a bit—"is beautiful, too. If ever I learn to pronounce it."

"It will be the least of our problems."

"There are no other problems," she said, emphatically confident. "When you're in love and about to be married, there are no problems at all."

"What about Jane?" he asked after a moment. "She isn't exactly my biggest fan."

"Why should we care what Jane thinks? I'm of the age of consent." She smiled up at him. "Is that the best you can do for problems?"

"It's all I can come up with now."

Her expression clouded slightly, as if something mildly distressing had just occurred to her. "I can think of one. You say we should get married in the next couple of weeks. But, after that, you're going into rehearsal. What about our honeymoon?"

"Don't worry," he said. "We'll have a honeymoon."

"How?"

"I'm not doing the play."

She sat back and stared at him, astonished. "Since when?"

"My agent and I were talking it over this afternoon. We decided against it."

"Why?"

He shrugged vaguely. He had no intention of telling Vivian—or anyone—the truth. But he hadn't worked out an alternate explanation yet. At length he said, "It just isn't the right situation at this point in my career."

"The part isn't good enough?"

"The part is all right, I guess. But it would mean doing another play. And how many plays have I done already? Maybe it's time I started thinking about movies."

She brightened instantly. "I've thought that all along. Have you been offered a movie?"

"I've been offered a few things in the past. Nothing that's tempted me. I've been hard to please."

"So, lower your standards a little, huh?" she said eagerly.

Vivian, he realized now, wasn't that different from any typical member of the American public. To her, as to almost everyone else, movies represented the ultimate in success.

"Maybe I will," he said. "It's time I made some real bread. I'm going to be a married man, after all. With responsibilities."

"And you'll be *terrific* in movies. You're so beautiful, you can't miss! You'll be a superstar!" She threw herself back on the studio bed, overcome with delight. "Oh, I'm *glad* you've decided this!"

Chris looked down at her, amused by this suddenly revealed aspect of her—the ecstatic movie fan. Then, as he studied her face, illuminated now by the bright light of the bedside lamp just a couple of feet above her, his amusement faded and he felt vaguely disturbed. He had never really noticed how deep the lines were around her eyes, on either side of her nose, slashing down from the corners of her mouth. The harsh light gave her a face that contradicted her girlish exuberance.

He stretched himself full length over her, resting on his elbows, blocking the light with his head. Her face became soft and beautiful again.

"This means a big change in my life," he said, still uneasy.

"For both of us, darling," she murmured. "For both of us."

Her lips found his, and, with the warm touch of her mouth, his chill vanished, was forgotten.

15

THIRTY LINES by noon. He had vowed he would do that much if it killed him. Eric counted the manuscript lines, summing up the morning's total so far, the three last lines on the previous page, fifteen lines on the page that was in his typewriter. He had twelve more lines to go. They could be *any* twelve lines, he told himself. What the hell, it was only a first draft.

The phone rang. Eric rose, went out of his workroom and into the living room, and picked up the receiver. "Hello?"

"Hello, Eric?" It was a feminine voice, young and faintly familiar. "Am I disturbing you?"

"No, it's all right. Who's this?"

"It's Jane. Jane Loring."

"Oh, hi, Jane. I thought I recognized your voice." He felt he had to say it. While he hadn't seen much of Jane in the past year, he had talked with her only a couple of weeks before at her mother's apartment. "How are you?"

"I'm not feeling too good, I'm afraid."

He hadn't expected such a literal answer to the meaningless question. But dutifully he asked, "What's the matter? Are you sick?"

"No. Worried." After a moment Jane said, rather ominously, "You know my mother is getting married next week."

"Yes. Vivian called to tell me."

"I want to talk to you about it, Eric."

"Talk to *me*?"

"You're our oldest friend. Who else can I talk to?"

Eric was a bit touched. He knew Vivian felt close to him, but he hadn't realized he had any special place in Jane's scheme of things. "All right," he said, "we can talk, if you want."

"Not on the phone. May I come to see you?"

"Sure. When?"

"Now?"

He glanced toward his workroom uncertainly. "Now is fine," he said.

"I'll hop a cab." She hung up.

Eric toyed with the idea of going back to work, but only for a moment. There would be no point to it, he decided, now that Jane Loring was about to turn up at his door. He switched on the hi-fi, concentrated on the piece of music that was being played on WNCN, identified it finally—Vivaldi's *The Seasons* —settled into the armchair, picked up the *Times*, and resumed reading it from where he had left off at breakfast.

It was a pleasant way to pass a half-hour, and he was almost grateful to Jane for giving him the excuse for it. But he was a little *too* ready for these distractions, he admitted to himself ruefully. Lucy on the phone just wanting to yak, the maid coming to clean, a commotion out on the street, anything served to draw him away from his typewriter. Jane, he was sure, simply wanted to complain about her mother's upcoming marriage to Christopher Greene. Her distress was understandable; Eric himself had a few misgivings about the match. But, for better or worse, it was a nearly accomplished fact, and there was nothing to be gained from hashing it over with Jane now. Still, when he was given a choice between that and going back to his workroom to sweat out a floundering interior monologue, it was no contest.

He glanced at the clock. Eleven-fifteen. If he were still at Galton and Hill, it would be the peak of his morning. The phone would be ringing and he might be juggling three crises at once. He would be confirming his lunch date—delicate veal and succulent publishing gossip at Le Perigord or the Brussels. Instead, here he was, in a maddeningly peaceful living room, looking forward to a tuna fish sandwich in the white solitude of his kitchen.

It had been fun, in its own way. There was no denying it, he missed it.

At half past eleven, the doorbell rang. Jane had lost little time in getting there. Eric buzzed her in and stood in the open doorway, listening to her light footfall as she hurried up the inner stairway of the brownstone.

"Hi," Jane said, as she appeared on the landing below.

"One more flight," Eric said.

"No problem." With an eighteen-year-old's energy, Jane took the last steps at a run. Her slim, long-legged body was clad in snug blue denims and a sleeveless blouse, and the sight of her ascending swiftly toward him inspired in Eric the hopeful, dirty-old-man thought that she might have come there to seduce him. But the fantasy lasted only a moment. Her grim expression as she came up level with him was enough to evaporate it.

He shook the hand that she held out gravely. "Would you like some coffee?" he asked.

"I wouldn't mind a cup, thanks."

Eric showed her into the apartment, then went to the kitchen to pour two cups of the brew he kept ready and warm in the Silex. When he returned with the coffee to the living room, Jane was standing, looking down at his Italian Renaissance desk, the most impressive of the several antiques in the room.

"This is beautiful," she said. "Did you buy it?"

"I could never afford that. It was my mother's. Anything good you see around here was my mother's."

Jane nodded comprehendingly, took a cup from him, and sat on the sofa.

Eric sat opposite her, in the armchair. "Speaking of mothers, how's yours?" he asked. "Looking forward happily to the great day?"

"Don't be sarcastic," Jane said.

"I'm not being sarcastic," he said mildly. "I mean it."

"You can't *really* mean it." Her eyes fixed intensely on him. "That 'great day' will be a disaster—if we let it happen."

"I don't see how we can keep it from happening, Jane. And why would it be such a disaster?"

"What else would you call it? My mother marrying a fag?"

"You don't know that Chris is a fag."

"I know it, all right. I suspected it when I first saw him. And I've been asking around since. Now I don't have a doubt in my mind."

"Well, okay, then, he's bisexual," Eric said reasonably. "He can go both ways. And now he's decided he wants to be straight."

"That's fine. More power to him. But if he's going to try the great experiment, why does it have to be with my mother?" Jane rose suddenly, leaving her coffee untouched, and moved away restlessly, as if she were too agitated to sit still. "Look," she said, turning back to him, "I like Chris well enough. He's a sensitive, decent man. I'm worried for *him* as much as I am for my mother. You know how neurotic and screwed up Mother is. If things go wrong in this marriage—and they're bound to— that poor guy is going to get wiped out!"

"Why don't we wait and see?"

"Wait and see!" She stared at him incredulously, as if the idea was unthinkable. "Eric, you have to stop it!"

"Me?"

"My mother respects your opinion. She might listen to *you*."

Eric let out his breath wearily. She was just a kid, he reminded himself, an only child who was resentful of her mother's remarriage. He had to be patient with her.

"Jane," he began, "I know you're upset about this. And it's understandable. I must admit this isn't exactly *my* idea of a marriage made in heaven. But Chris and your mother really do care for each other. They seem to need each other. They make each other happy. So, why not give it a chance?" He paused to take in her reaction. Her expression was set stubbornly; she was unyielding in her outrage. "Vivian," he went on, "no matter how screwed up you think she is, is a loving woman. And Chris, whatever he may have been in the past, is quite sincere about this. He's had time to consider it carefully and he's made up his mind."

"*He* hasn't made up his mind," Jane burst out. "Delphine has made it up for him!"

"Let's not exaggerate. Delphine has advised him, of course—"

"Oh, it's a lot more than advice," she broke in, her voice trembling with intensity. "She's invaded his head like a disease! That's the way she works." Almost fiercely, she added, "My mother, too. She's completely in Delphine's control!"

"You know, *I* go to Delphine too," he reminded her. "And I think I'm capable of making my own decisions."

"Maybe you are," she said impatiently. "I'm not saying it happens with everyone. But we aren't talking about you, are we?"

Eric glanced toward his workroom, suddenly uneasy. "No, let's not talk about me," he said quietly.

"It's happened with Chris," she went on, "and with my

mother—and with Mandy Huber too. Delphine is like God to them. They won't make a move unless Delphine tells them it's all right. And they do a lot of things only because *she* wants them to. It's like they don't have wills of their own any more. Delphine runs their lives for them. She manipulates them like puppets."

"Delphine has some power over them, yes," he said carefully, keeping his tone reasoned and calm. "But it's the doctor's power over his patients. It's power for the sake of healing."

"It's power for the sake of power," Jane retorted sharply. "Don't you see? Delphine is into control. Pure, naked control over people—anyone she can suck in. She doesn't care if she helps or hurts someone. All she really wants is to keep her control over a person. She feeds on it!" she said emphatically. "Her ego needs it to live."

"You're going a little overboard, don't you think?" he murmured coolly.

Jane caught herself now. The passion seemed to go out of her and she just stared at him helplessly. "You don't believe me, do you?"

"No, I don't," Eric said. "You're eighteen years old—you're a high-strung, emotional adolescent—and you're making a sane, well-intentioned psychotherapist sound like Countess Dracula." He saw Jane's cheeks turn pink. For all of her intensity, she could still blush at his rebuke. "Also," he went on, "as I remember, you had a bad relationship with her once. I suppose that colors your opinion."

"My mother made me go to her for a while," she said with a shrug, "if that's what you're referring to. Delphine did her whole number on me—but it didn't take."

"She didn't gain control over you?" he asked, pointedly using her word.

"No. Not then." She paused. "She got to me later."

"What do you mean by that?"

Jane regarded him thoughtfully for a moment, her expression

intent, as if she were weighing some decision. Finally, she said, very quietly, almost wearily, "Eric, Delphine Heywood is evil. The most evil human being I've ever known. You don't believe me—and I guess I shouldn't be too surprised. But if I can give you evidence, will you at least take what I'm saying seriously?"

"I *am* taking it seriously, Jane. But—"

"No, you're not," she said, cutting him off. "So, I'll tell you. I'll tell you something that no one knows, aside from my mother—and Delphine."

She returned to the sofa, sat, picked up her cup of coffee, and took a slow swallow of it. At length, she set down the cup and looked up at him. "Do you know that Ward Kennan has been paying for my education?"

"Oh?" It wasn't really news to him; he had been vaguely aware of it. "I think Vivian alluded to it once."

"Do you know *why* he has been doing it?"

"Well, he's a wealthy man. I imagine he's just being generous."

"Generous!' She whispered it to herself, with a tight, bitter smile. She looked down at her cup, seeming to withdraw from him for a moment. Then she met his gaze again. "He raped me."

He was simply startled, at first. The shock came a second or two later, a delayed reaction. "Go on," he said softly.

"When my mother first started going with Ward," she said in a matter-of-fact way, "he seemed to take a special interest in me. I saw a lot of him—he was staying over at our place most nights of the week. Sometimes he would get me alone, joke with me, kiss me on the cheek. I didn't think there was anything strange about it. I was only sixteen, and I figured he was trying to be a father to me." Her gaze fixed on some point just past him. Her voice became distant, almost toneless, as she relived it. "One night I woke up, and there was a man on top of me. There was a sharp pain—it was the pain that woke me— and the smell of whiskey, and a grunting noise in my ear. I was still half asleep, and it took me a while to realize what was happening—and who was doing it. I started crying. That seemed to excite him all the more—and he climaxed. My mother came rushing in—and there was a big, emotional scene." She looked at him and smiled wanly. "I had been a virgin until then."

"How could Vivian go on seeing that man?" Eric asked.

"That's a good question," Jane said. "Well, Ward *was* terribly apologetic. He said it was because he'd been drinking—he didn't know what he was doing. He offered to try to make it up to us any way he could. He pleaded with us both to forgive him. But Mother didn't know if she *could* forgive him—or if she could ever bear to see him again." She paused. "That's where Delphine came in."

"What did Delphine have to do with it?"

"She's the great oracle, isn't she? So, of course, my mother told her the whole story and asked her what she should do. Well, the answer is self-evident, right? A man rapes your young daughter, and maybe you call the police. At the very least, you cut him out of your life. That's what almost anyone would tell you. But not Delphine. Ward has money, Ward has power, and Delphine is fascinated by money and power. The last thing she wanted was to have my mother break up with Ward. He was the rich, mean bastard who was going to solve all of Mother's problems—or so Delphine kept telling her. Of course, his rape of her virginal daughter took a little explaining. But, knowing the way Delphine works, I can guess how she got around it." Bitterly mock-dramatic, she said, "I provoked Ward—I led him on—really I *wanted* to get raped." She paused, keeping the lie hanging, then dismissed it with a gesture. "You know how shrinks can twist the truth."

"Sometimes, I guess," he murmured. This last comment had sparked a twinge of uneasiness in him.

"As for what was to be done about it," Jane went on, "Delphine had the solution. Ward had offered to make it up to us, so she said—fine, he should pay for my college education. My mother jumped at the idea—she didn't have the money to send me to college otherwise. And so it all ended happily," she said, with acid brightness. Her expression serious again, she continued, "I was too dazed to do anything but go along with it. It took me a long time, almost until now, to realize what had happened—how Delphine finally got to me."

"Got to you?" he echoed. "What do you mean?"

"I was sent to Delphine because I was emotionally disturbed," she said in a flat, unemphatic voice. "I was disturbed because my mother was a whore. So, Delphine made a whore of me, too." With a faint smile, she asked, "Now do you see Delphine a little differently?"

Eric looked away. "I don't know what to say."

"You don't have to say anything. Just tell me one thing. Will you try to keep this marriage from taking place?"

He met her gaze. "I can't interfere."

"Okay. I tried." Jane rose. Almost as an afterthought, she said, "I'm not going back to college."

"You don't want to take Ward's money any more?"

"No, I don't. Anyway, I think I should be here in New York. My mother is going to need me."

It was an Anglican church in the West Forties, a rundown church that was an Off-Off-Broadway theater most of the week, but which served as the place for the weddings and funerals of actors, and of the handful of Episcopalians who still lived in Hell's Kitchen.

The first thing Eric noticed as he entered with Lucy was that almost no one was there, fewer than a dozen people. Then he became aware of how close and warm it was, and depressingly dark. The mugginess of the August day had permeated the place. The sun had gone behind the clouds again, and only a murky twilight was filtering through the stained-glass windows.

It was hardly a joyful ambience for Chris and Vivian's nuptials.

"Where should we sit?" Lucy asked in a whisper.

"We have our choice," Eric replied.

He glanced around at the people sitting in the rear pews. He recognized the five middle-aging types on his right as Vivian's friends. None of them was more than a bare acquaintance of his, and he merely nodded. The four fresh, youthful faces on his left were unfamiliar—Chris's show business friends, he assumed.

Eric and Lucy started down the aisle. Jane was sitting by herself, near the front. She looked back at them as they approached, her face solemn. Eric mouthed a silent hello. Jane acknowledged it with a brief wince of a smile, then faced forward again.

There was a woman sitting alone, across the aisle from Jane, wearing a fashionably floppy cap that hid her face from behind. It wasn't until they were abreast of her that Eric realized it was Mandy Huber. He was a little surprised to see her there among the spectators. He had expected that she would be part of the ceremony.

Mandy looked up at him and smiled. "Hi, Eric." Then she looked past him and greeted Lucy warmly. "Oh, *hi*, Lucy." She slid over in the pew and made room for them to sit beside her.

Eric let Lucy go in first and they sat. "When will it start?" he asked Mandy.

"Any moment now, I think."

"Who's the matron of honor?" Lucy asked. Evidently, she had had the same expectation Eric had about Mandy.

"Tina Nevins."

"Oh yeah," Eric said. "I know Tina. She used to dance with Vivian," he explained to Lucy, "years ago, when they were touring with that company. But I'm surprised," he said to Mandy, "I thought Vivian hadn't seen her in a long time."

"I don't know, maybe she hasn't," Mandy said. After a

moment, she asked, "Are you wondering why *I'm* not matron of honor?"

"Well," Eric said, "you seemed the logical choice."

"Vivian asked me. But I said no."

"You don't believe in this marriage?"

Mandy's suddenly guarded expression revealed clearly enough that, in fact, she didn't. But this wasn't the occasion to say it; so, instead, she shrugged lightly and answered, "These days, I'm not sure I believe in marriage in general."

"Oh, dear, don't say *that!*" Lucy exclaimed softly with a sidewise, smiling glance at Eric.

Now that Mandy had referred to her marital break-up, if only obliquely, Eric felt free to ask about it. "So, how's it going? Where are you living?"

"The same place," Mandy replied.

"I thought you moved out."

"I did. But Jeff insisted that I keep the apartment. He didn't want to deprive me of my home, he said. So, I moved back in."

"That was considerate of him."

"Yes. Jeff has been marvelous, really. About everything. The settlement he worked out to buy my half of the business was very generous. Enough to start two companies."

"And how's your new company coming along?"

"We're getting there. We should have our first collection ready by spring."

"What are you calling your line?"

"I'm calling it 'Mandy,' " she said, with a smile. "Why be modest?"

Behind him, Eric heard an uneven, limping footstep coming down the aisle. He turned to look. It was Delphine, wearing a black dress, and with a little white hat perched on her head, an old-fashioned, demure hat that might have been worn in an Easter parade twenty years before.

She nodded a greeting at Mandy and Eric and then turned

her attention to Jane, who had swung around in her pew and was gazing at her. Delphine approached her, bent forward, and, with her sweet, compassionate smile, said something to her in a voice pitched so low that only Jane would hear. But Eric, sitting on the aisle, could make out the words.

"Jane, darling, are you upset that your mother is going to be happy?"

Jane shuddered with revulsion and edged away, her wide eyes fixed on her.

Delphine turned back up the aisle and sat, two pews behind Jane. She folded her hands in her lap and gazed serenely at the altar.

At that moment, the minister appeared, a young fellow, poetically good-looking, with his hair thick around his ears. He positioned himself at the head of the aisle and looked toward the back of the church.

Eric turned to see what was happening. Chris and his best man, both in dark-blue suits, were walking slowly down the aisle. The best man was middle-aged, with thinning hair and an expression of mild anxiety etched indelibly on his homely, care-worn features. Eric knew that look, and he was almost sure this was Chris's agent. He marveled that Chris should be so isolated that he would have to call upon his agent to stand up with him at his wedding. Then it occurred to him that the agent might be one of the very few heterosexual men that Chris knew at all well.

Vivian and her matron-of-honor came down the aisle next. Vivian was wearing a violet dress, and her expression was set in a pensive, almost absent, smile. The matron-of-honor, her contemporary, looked much older than she, a dancer gone to fat. At the end of the aisle, they stopped beside Chris and his best man, then all four turned to face the minister. The little group looked strangely desolate in the murkiness of the near-empty church.

The minister began. "We are gathered together today to join in holy matrimony Christopher and Vivian."

At that point, the sunlight, suddenly released from its cloud cover, burst through the grimy stained-glass windows. Eric looked at Delphine and saw that a shaft of light was illuminating her pale face. Her bright eyes were kindled and her benign smile had turned exultant.

PART THREE

PART THREE

16

SHE's JUST a bitch, Mandy thought bitterly. She never *could* stand the woman. If Nan Powell weren't an editor on *Women's Wear*, she'd be the loneliest person in town.

Mandy hung up her coat, settled behind her work table, and picked up her sketch-in-progress, but she knew she was simply going through the motions. She wouldn't be able to concentrate now, not after Nan had let drop her poisonous little goodie.

She had saved it until they were almost through with the lunch, when they were sipping their coffee. Then Nan, oh so casually, said, "By the way, I saw Jeff last night at Sardi's. He's looking good these days, I must say." She paused—a very studied pause, as Mandy remembered—then asked, "Is Ellen Hanahan his steady girl?"

"Ellen? Why? Was she with him?" Mandy couldn't conceal her surprise. Ellen Hanahan was the lead model at Huber Casuals, and the only special notice Jeff had ever given her was to criticize her kooky hair styles now and then.

"Oh, you don't know about this?" Nan put on a show of consternation.

"Why *should* I know about it?" Mandy was openly irritated. Nan Powell was someone no ready-to-wear designer ever dared antagonize, but, at that moment, Mandy didn't care. "You expect *me* to tell you what they were doing at Sardi's together?"

"I *know* what they were doing, darling," Nan purred. "They'd been to the theater and they were having a bite to eat. But it probably doesn't mean a thing." Complacently, she concluded, "I guess I should have kept my big mouth shut."

Oh, Nan Powell had done her work, all right, slipped in the blade, gotten her jollies. And with her genius for cattiness, she had picked on exactly the right name to hurt her.

Ellen Hanahan! My God, *she* was the one who had insisted on hiring her! Jeff hadn't liked the way she looked. He had thought she was *too* thin.

Maybe it wasn't just Ellen Hanahan, she thought suddenly, anxiously. Maybe Jeff was knocking off the other models too, and the secretaries, and the receptionist. Anything was possible. She had lost touch with Jeff, she hadn't seen him in months. For all she knew, he could have turned into an insatiable Don Juan, a superswinger. God knows, he had had it in him.

Maybe—and this thought sent a chill through her—he was making it with that Mary Wintle, the woman who had replaced her as head designer at Huber Casuals. Jeff had chosen someone even younger than she—four years younger—and *that* had given her pause. She had seen this Wintle person's photograph in *Women's Wear*, but it hadn't told her much—or, perhaps, just enough. Plain face, big tits.

Well, Mandy reminded herself, she had to be fair. She had wanted her freedom; Jeff had a right to his. But the way it was working out, it didn't seem such an equal bargain, since she didn't know how really free *she* was. Staying home most nights to watch television hardly qualified as a life of abandon.

She was discovering that the double standard worked even more unfairly in her single state than it had in her marriage. There was an inequity in the situations, in people's attitudes. If a man called up a woman to ask her out, he was a charming, attentive gentleman. If a woman called up a man to ask him out, she was a hard-up nymphomaniac. So, Mandy had to wait for the phone to ring. When it did, it was almost never one of the handful of men she found genuinely attractive. It was usually some crude opportunist who was operating on the belief that a woman who has just separated from her husband has to be hot as a pipe. As it happened, Mandy wasn't. Not on the first date, anyway. And if she wasn't forthcoming the first time around, there generally wasn't a second time.

As a consequence, Mandy was watching a lot of television, catching up on her reading, and learning how depressingly cavernous a Central Park West apartment can seem when one is the only person in it.

There was still her work, of course, but Mandy had found out something rather unexpected about herself. If she went for a long time without sex, she missed it, missed it painfully. She would find herself thinking about sex, in all its forms and variations, when she should be concentrating on her work.

Phyllis came into the office, with three swatches of fabric. She laid them out on the work table before Mandy. "We have to order the material for the ruffled skirt outfit by tomorrow," Phyllis said. "Have you decided which color we're going with?"

Mandy glanced at the swatches, the beige, the tan, then looked at the third one more closely. "What's this?" she asked uncertainly. "It looks sort of like mustard."

"It *is* mustard. It's that new shade you asked to see. They just sent it over."

Mandy studied the lively interwoven mix. "It's not the mustard *I* know."

"It's jazzed up. Hot mustard, I guess." Phyllis wrinkled her nose. "I'm not wild about it."

Mandy rose, went to the side wall, took down her sketch for the ruffled skirt and T-shirt combination, returned to her work table, and placed the sketch beside the swatches. She sat again, leaned forward and concentrated, trying to envision the final product in each color. She had done her preliminary work on this design in beige, but she hadn't been excited by it.

But even now she couldn't focus on it. Jeff was still on her mind—and Ellen Hanahan—and her own situation. She looked up and took in Phyllis, skinny, flat-chested Phyllis, with her large, mournful eyes and her slightly weak chin. She was a grind too, just like herself. She wondered how *she* solved the problem.

"Phyllis," Mandy asked, "do you ever get horny?"

Phyllis seemed mildly startled. "What do you think? I'm not made of stone."

"What do you do about it?"

"Well—" Phyllis hesitated. "I see guys."

"There was Pete," Mandy said. "But you haven't seen him in weeks, have you?"

"No, I haven't." A bit sadly, Phyllis said, "I've stopped seeing Pete."

"So, what do you do?"

"Why are you asking?"

"I don't know, I guess it's because *I'm* running up the walls. I'm curious how you manage to find release—if you *do* find it."

Phyllis eyed her uncertainly. "You really want to know?"

"Sure."

"I have a vibrator."

Mandy stared at her, astonished. "A vibrator? You mean, one of those things they sell in drugstores?"

"Yeah."

"Does it work?"

"Very well. Better than most men."

Mandy felt embarrassed now. Ducking her head, she went

back to her work and the decision she had to make. "The mustard," she said suddenly. "Let's go with the mustard."

"Are you sure?" Phyllis looked dubious. "The tan would make more sense."

"The tan is for the birds. So's the beige. I like this mustard."

"But dull colors are in this year. You can't go against what they're doing on the Avenue."

"That's the kind of thing Jeff would say!" Mandy snapped. "Why do I have to do what everybody else does? This color is alive—it's exciting. I like it," she said firmly, "and we're using it."

Phyllis shrugged, obviously not convinced. "You're the boss," she murmured. She gathered up the swatches, rose, and left the office.

"Delphine, is it wrong that I don't masturbate?"

Delphine seemed a little taken aback by the question. Mandy had sprung it on her out of nowhere, in the midst of a placid discussion about her current loneliness. "It's not a matter of right or wrong," Delphine replied. Then she looked at her curiously. "You don't?"

"No, I don't," Mandy said. "I never have. I don't know *how* to masturbate."

"I should think the technique would be self-evident."

"Oh, I've tried. I've diddled myself with my finger. But nothing ever seems to happen."

"That's too bad." Her therapist seemed genuinely regretful. "Why did you bring this up?"

"Well, I was talking with Phyllis this morning. And I happened to ask her what she does for sexual release. She told me she uses a vibrator."

"A vibrator, yes," Delphine said approvingly. "That's very effective. Have you thought of trying it?"

"I couldn't!" Mandy exclaimed with horror. "It sounds so

awful! I mean, it's a *machine*. It just makes the whole thing too dehumanized."

"If that's the way you feel," Delphine murmured with a shrug. "Actually, I don't think you should feel too upset about this. There are still some women in this country—a minority, but a substantial minority—who have never masturbated. It's optional, I suppose."

"If I *had* the option, fine. But I read so much about it these days—you know, the things feminists write. And I feel it's some kind of lack in me that I can't even do it," she said unhappily.

Delphine smiled slightly. "It would help in your present circumstances, certainly."

"You mean, because then I wouldn't be yearning for Jeff so much?"

"You wouldn't be yearning for *any* man so much. That could be a desirable thing."

Mandy looked at her uncertainly, not quite knowing how to take this. They had always discussed her freedom in terms of its new opportunities—as an opening out to more, not less. She hadn't realized that permanent abstention might be part of the package. "What would be desirable?" she asked. "Not needing men?"

Delphine nodded. "Not needing men."

"Is that possible? Okay, I'm going through a period of transition, so, for the time being, I'm doing without. But, in the long run, could I live without a man?"

"Very easily, I would think," Delphine replied. "Provided you found sexual fulfillment otherwise. Nature has programmed you to need orgasms," she went on. "But it hasn't specified how you are to achieve them. It could be through a man—through a woman—or through yourself."

"I don't think I'm ready for a woman," Mandy said with a nervous little laugh.

"Then that leaves yourself. That is, if you don't want to be totally dependent on men, a captive to any sexually capable male who comes along." She reflected for a moment, then concluded, "Perhaps it *would* be a good idea if you learned how to masturbate."

Delphine was showing a somewhat livelier interest in the subject than Mandy had anticipated, and she was a little sorry now that she had brought it up. "Well," she said, "I don't seem to be able to learn."

"It can be taught you."

Mandy eyed her uneasily. "Who would teach me?"

"There's a woman who has a workshop for just this purpose—to teach women to know and enjoy their own bodies. Her name is Peggy Watson. If you want, I'll arrange to have you attend one of her classes."

"You mean, this is a class where women sit around—doing *that*?" Mandy asked, a trifle aghast.

"Yes. It can be very liberating."

"Maybe so. But I don't think I could do it."

"You'd be amazed at what you can do with serious-minded people to guide you. You're afraid of your own body—even a little ashamed of it. As long as you have these inhibitions, you can't really be free. I think this experience might help you, Mandy." Delphine's smile was warm and reassuring. "It wouldn't hurt to give it a try, would it?" She glanced toward the phone. "I can call Peggy right now."

Mandy simply stared at her, indecisive now, not knowing what she should say.

"Or we can let the matter drop," Delphine said.

And where would that leave her? Mandy felt that she could no longer tolerate herself as she was, up-tight, frustrated, tormented by her own fantasies.

"No," she said suddenly. "I'll try it."

They were all there for the first time, it turned out; it was an introductory class. They stood in the mirrored studio, saying little to each other, waiting for the session to start. Mandy took in the group—there were ten in all, including herself—and decided that they looked no freakier than any random selection of youngish New York women. They just as easily might have been housewives enrolling in a cooking course.

Peggy Watson entered the studio carrying a briefcase and a canvas overnight bag. She was a short, compact woman in a leotard, with cropped hair and a cheery smile. She put the briefcase and overnight bag down on a table, turned to the waiting group, introduced herself, then told them to take off their clothes. Down to the last stitch.

The initiates filed into the adjoining dressing room, with Mandy lagging in the rear, and silently began to strip. They avoided looking at each other as their variously imperfect bodies were gradually bared to view. All except for the woman standing next to Mandy. She was heavy-set, with a head of frizzy, coarse, dark hair, and armpits to match. She watched attentively as Mandy removed her blouse, dropped her skirt, and pulled down her pantyhose. She herself was peeling to the buff easily, without constraint, as if it were something she did in the same indifferent way on all occasions, public and private.

"Hi," the woman said finally. "I'm Sarah."

"Hello." Mandy was about to leave it at that, then she realized that the woman was waiting for a name. Reluctantly, she supplied it. "I'm Mandy."

"Getting divorced?" Sarah asked.

"Do I look it?" Mandy asked, shyly curious.

Sarah pursed her lips knowingly but didn't answer.

"I *am* separated from my husband, yes," Mandy said. "And you?"

Sarah seemed a bit startled. "Have *I* been married? Hell, no!"

"Then why are you here?"

It was a naïve question, Mandy knew, even as she asked it. There were other good reasons, of course, aside from having been a victim of male dominance, for a woman to want to know her own body. Still, Sarah didn't strike her as someone who was in particular need of this kind of education.

"I've heard a lot about the work Peggy Watson's been doing," Sarah replied as she stepped out of her slightly soiled panties. "They say she's helping to radicalize the Movement. Just thought I should check it out for myself." She poked an exploring finger into her vagina, then raised her hand and examined the fingertip. "Shit, my period's come! It wasn't due for another week. Must be some kind of sign, huh?" She held out her pink fingertip for Mandy to see.

Mandy, repelled, turned away. The women who were completely naked now were starting to leave the dressing room, their eyes forward, their faces solemn. Mandy followed them.

In the studio, Peggy Watson had finished installing her equipment and was putting the emptied overnight bag back on the table. She had taken off her leotard and was now as naked as they were. Her pubis was shaved, Mandy noticed, and the smooth hairlessness of her well-muscled crotch gave her a neuter, almost otherworldly look.

Electrical cords had been plugged into every fixture in the walls. They snaked along the floor, toward the center of the room, with a small, square vibrator at the end of each. The vibrators were the kind used for massage, not the battery-operated, phallic-shaped ones that Mandy had expected.

When all of the women had returned, Peggy instructed them to sit in a row on the floor. Mandy sat toward the middle of the row. Sarah settled down beside her, on her left. Peggy sat facing them and adopted the lotus position.

"All of our lives," Peggy began, "we've been taught to be feminine. Not female—feminine. 'Feminine' means being weak, passive, someone to be used as an object according to a man's will. I want to teach you to be women. I want each one of you to be, not feminine, but strong like a woman. Being strong means having a strong, functioning body—taking pride in that body—taking pride in all that that body can do, whether it be belching, farting, vomiting, or coming."

Mandy felt excited, almost in spite of herself. She found Peggy Watson's imagery somewhat revolting—farting and vomiting, for instance, were bodily functions she doubted she would ever cherish. Still, there was a compelling quality about the way Peggy spoke—she reminded Mandy of Delphine in that respect. But Peggy had something that her therapist lacked: a sense of urgency. She had the intensity that stems from total commitment to a belief.

Peggy went on to talk about breathing and the importance of cleansing one's respiratory system. She had them do breathing exercises for a few minutes, and then she led them through a series of yoga postures. As Mandy shifted easily from one posture to the next, the lotus, the plough, the lion, and so on, she began to feel at home. These exercises were nothing new to her; there had been a time when she had done them every morning, along with the yoga instructor on television.

After a half-hour of exercises, Peggy announced, "Our bodies are in tune. Now we're ready."

Peggy rose, opened her briefcase, and took out a stack of very large photographs. She placed the stack on the table, then picked up the top photograph and showed it to the group.

It took a moment for Mandy to realize what she was seeing, then she gasped with shock. It was a blow-up, in color, of a woman's genitals in extreme close-up.

There was an uneasy stirring around her, and Mandy guessed that she wasn't the only one in the group who, never having looked at herself so closely, was seeing it for the first time; not a diagram, not a painting, but a very clear, very detailed image of the real thing. She glanced out of the corner of her eye to see how Sarah was reacting. Sarah was leaning forward, gazing at the photograph intently, a faint, appreciative smile on her lips.

"Each of our genitals is unique," Peggy said, "as unique as one flower is when compared to all other flowers. These are photographs of the genitals of some of the women who've taken my classes. I want you to notice how each one has a particular personality, its own special beauty."

Peggy went through the stack of photographs, showing them one after the other, commenting on the characteristics of the pictured genitalia, the skin texture, the hair color, the individual and delightful forms of each clitoris, vagina, and anus. She had descriptive names for the first few photographs: "Gothic"—"Baroque"—"Mother Earth"—"Danish Modern." Then, as she neared the end of her exhibition, she reverted to her horticultural analogy, describing the pink, gleaming vaginas as roses, opening up to the sunlight.

Mandy watched, fascinated and slightly horrified. She couldn't help wondering about the real women who were attached to these abstracted genitals, walking about the city, at that moment, unaware that their most private parts were being minutely inspected. It occurred to her that, if she took Peggy's classes, her own genitals might some day be held up for display. She sneaked a look down at her sparse, mousy-brown pubis. It seemed nothing to make a fuss over. More of a shrub than a flower.

When she was through with the photographs, Peggy put them back on the table, stooped, and picked up the plugged-in vibrator that was on the floor near her. She stood straight again, vibrator in hand, and looked at them silently for a few moments, her expression grave, as if she were about to come to a matter of special importance.

At length, she continued: "The most intense physical experience a woman can have is orgasm. But, in our repressed society, all women aren't equal in this experience. Some women have orgasms easily, others have them only occasionally and with guilt, still others don't have them at all. That it is why it is so important for a woman to masturbate," she said with quiet emphasis. "Masturbation is important as a means of understanding your orgasmic pattern, gaining control over it—and, in some cases, as the only way to make an orgasm possible." She paused, letting this sink in; then, in a more conversational tone, went on, "Some of you may feel that you can't masturbate, you don't know how. Don't worry about it. With the help of a vibrator, anyone can do it. Here, let me show you," she said, swiftly sitting on the floor.

Peggy spread her legs wide, exposing her denuded cleft, and it dawned on Mandy that she was about to masturbate for them. Suddenly frantic at the thought, Mandy averted her eyes and fixed her gaze on a point on the floor before her. This is going too far, she thought. You just don't *do* that sort of thing in front of people.

Peggy was explaining why a massage-type vibrator was infinitely superior to a phallic-shaped one, discussing it as calmly as if she were describing the relative virtues of two kinds of coffeemaker. Mandy wasn't really listening now; she didn't want to. She tried to think of other things, and, inevitably, her thoughts turned to Jeff. She wondered where he was at that moment. Was he out with Ellen Hanahan, doing the town? Were they bouncing around the dance floor of some discotheque? Were they seeing a movie? Were they holding hands over dinner at some quiet, romantic restaurant? Whatever Jeff was up to, it was bound to be a lot healthier than what *she* was doing—sitting naked on a wooden floor to watch a woman play with herself.

Peggy had stopped talking now. Mandy, a bit fearfully, looked up at her. Peggy was tilted back slightly, with her eyes closed, holding the switched-on vibrator to her genitals. The whole thing didn't take her very long. She began breathing more rapidly, her lips parted, and she climaxed, neatly, unspectacularly, with an almost inaudible sigh.

Peggy lowered the vibrator, opened her eyes and smiled at the group. Mandy peered at her intently, trying to detect whatever change might have taken place in her. But Peggy seemed exactly the same after her orgasm as she had before, serene and rather asexual.

"Now, before you try it," Peggy said, "we should make sure you're perfectly relaxed."

Before *we* try it! Mandy thought, with a stab of apprehension. Uneasily, she glanced behind her. A vibrator was lying on the floor, just a couple of feet from her.

"I want you to turn to each other," Peggy said. She went down the line, pointing, "The two of you—the two of you—" until they were all paired off. The women swung around toward their indicated partners, and Mandy found herself facing Sarah.

"Women should never be afraid of touching other women," Peggy told them, "in friendship, in sisterhood, in love. Lay your hands on your partner's shoulders, just where the shoulders meet the neck. Massage the muscles gently, tenderly."

Sarah's hands were on her at once. Mandy reacted more slowly, but obediently, dazedly, as if she were carrying through an illogical action in a dream, fulfilling some pattern she didn't quite comprehend. She placed her hands on Sarah's shoulders and delicately kneaded the moist flesh at the base of her neck.

Sarah was massaging her with equal gentleness, but insistently. Her eyes were half closed and she seemed to be concentrating on the feel of her. Mandy sensed that her partner was becoming sexually aroused, and she started to withdraw from her. But Sarah's grip tightened and she leaned into her, almost to the proximity of an embrace. Her forearm grazed Mandy's breast.

"No!" Mandy cried out. She broke Sarah's grip and jumped to her feet. "I can't do this!" She ran out of the studio and into the dressing room.

Mandy collapsed onto a stool and waited, expecting someone to come after her. No one did. She heard Peggy's voice, faint now, her words inaudible, but calm as ever, continuing the class as if nothing had happened.

Mandy put her face in her hands and cried. She felt ashamed, as if she had betrayed all of the women in the studio, every woman in the world. She was weak, she knew, cowardly, unworthy to be joined with her sisters.

But this was all too strange, too difficult, for her. Just a few months before, she had been spending her evenings, not in a studio full of sweaty, naked, lonely women, but cuddled up on the couch with Jeff, small talking the hours away in the aimless, silly fashion of the long-married. Now fervently she wished she were with him again.

What was she doing to herself?

17

"I'M FINISHED," Lucy called out.

Eric went back into the living room and looked at Lucy apprehensively. She was sitting straight in the armchair, his manuscript was on her lap, and her face was stern with thought.

"Did you read it all?" he asked.

"Every word."

"Oh. It didn't take you long," he said, a bit unhappily. The manuscript was a hundred and eighty-two pages, half of his novel. She had gone through it in less than two hours. His achievement seemed somehow diminished by her swiftness. "So, what do you think?"

Lucy gazed at him, with what could be interpreted as an expression of faint distress, and didn't answer immediately. Instead, she asked, "Do you have a cigarette?"

Eric went to the coffee table, picked up the glass case containing cigarettes that he kept available for guests, and crossed to Lucy. "They're a little stale," he said, unlidding the case and holding it out to her.

"I don't mind," she said, taking a cigarette.

As he lit her cigarette, he braced himself for the worst. Lucy smoked only on rare occasions; usually, in the tense, more unpleasant moments of life. He watched her take a deep drag, then he moved away, instinctively putting a distance between them.

He remembered that time, years before, when he had waited, with this same anxiety, for his mother to pass judgment on his work. But this was different, he reminded himself. His mother had been a top professional writer; Lucy was just any member of the public, a nonverbal art director, not really knowledgeable about literature at all. He shouldn't care what she thought.

Still, a reader was a reader.

When he turned back to her, Lucy was on her feet moving about nervously. She had put down his manuscript on the table beside the armchair, and she was eyeing it uncertainly. Finally, she faced him and said, "Eric, if we're going to be married, we'll always have to be honest with each other."

"Agreed. But what does our getting married have to do with my book? All I'm asking for is a critical opinion."

"I just want you to understand. If you were simply a friend—like Naomi Lamb, let's say—I'd be polite. I might fake an enthusiasm I don't really feel. I can't do that with you."

"Okay," he asked quietly, "what's wrong with my book?"

"You don't *do* anything wrong." She spoke slowly, choosing her words carefully. "It's well thought out, you have a good command of language, the whole thing is very intelligent. But—" She paused, then said it: "It's dead."

"Dead?" he echoed numbly. "That's a strong word."

"Then I take it back," she said quickly. "It's not dead, exactly, but it lacks a certain kind of life—the life that almost any real novel has."

"It seems a real enough novel to *me*," he said sullenly.

"But you didn't have to write it, did you, Eric? I mean, you didn't need to?" Gently, she added, "It shows."

Eric said nothing now. Lucy took an agitated puff of her cigarette and watched him, with a miserable look on her face. Her expression was probably for his benefit, he thought bitterly. She wanted to show him that this was hurting her more than it was hurting him.

"You understand what I'm talking about, don't you?" she went on. "You ought to. You've worked with so many writers, I'm sure you know much more about it than I do. But it seems to me that every writer writes out of some kind of need. Take Naomi. She's a crappy writer and she wrote a dumb book—but it's alive. It's alive because she *had* to write it. She just *had* to work out her fantasies on paper, and there are lots of people out there who are ready to share them with her. For better or worse, Naomi is doing what she was meant to do. I don't feel that about you. Or, at least, I don't see it in this book. It doesn't seem to have any real reason for existence."

"Is what you're trying to tell me," he asked coolly, "that I'm not cut out for this work?"

"I don't think I should be the one to say that." She thought for a moment. "Let me ask you something. How good an editor were you—I mean, compared to other editors?"

"That's hard to say. Different editors are good at different things."

"But at what you did best—guiding writers, putting a book in shape—were there other editors in the business who were better?"

"A half dozen people were as good," he replied. "But there was no one who was better." After a moment, he asked, "What are you getting at?"

"Well, it's just that I believe that everyone has his special knack—something he can do better than most other people. Myself, I could never be a really good painter, or a first-rate graphics designer, but I have an eye for design, and I can put together a layout as well as anyone in the world. Sure, working at an ad agency can be a pain in the ass. And I suppose I might have more fun if I were down in a loft in SoHo painting canvases. But then I'd just be ordinary. And what's the kick in being ordinary? You tell me," she went on, "that you were one of the very best book editors. Didn't that count? Weren't you making a real contribution? Can't the editing of a book be as important—and as creative, in its own way—as the writing of one?"

"Sometimes it can. But why even talk about it? I've quit being an editor."

"Quit for good? Don't you still have the option?"

"Sure. Abel would give me my old job back in a minute. If I asked for it. But I'm not going to ask for it," he insisted. "My God," he burst out agitatedly, "I've been in therapy for months to find out what I really want to be. Now at last I know—and you're confusing me all over again!"

"I'm sorry, darling," Lucy said apologetically, "I don't mean to confuse you." She looked away for a moment, then, rather tentatively, she persisted. "I guess what I'm trying to say is that there can be a difference between what you want to be and what you *think* you want to be."

"I'm aware of that. Delphine happens to be an expert on that particular distinction. When I went to her, I was all screwed up in the way I thought about myself. She's helped me to see myself clearly."

"Maybe," Lucy said quietly. "And maybe she's told you what you've wanted to hear."

Eric looked at her sharply. Lucy had never criticized Delphine before—or, at least, not so directly. "What do you mean by that?"

She ground out her cigarette. "Let's talk about Delphine for a moment."

* * *

"And then what?" Delphine asked, in the patient, faintly amused tone of someone who is prepared to hear any nonsense. "She told you your book was no good and that you were wasting your time as a writer. What did she say after that?"

"Nothing more about the book," Eric replied. "We talked about you."

"Me?" Delphine sat back slightly. She, clearly, hadn't expected this. "Was this still in connection with your book?"

"In a way. But it was more than just that." Eric was standing by the bookshelves. He hadn't been able to sit still when talking about Lucy's reaction to his novel, and he pretended to take a sudden interest in one of the fat volumes on the eye-level shelf. Actually, he was trying to hide his consternation. He felt he might have gone too far; he hadn't intended to mention Lucy's criticism of his therapist at all. But he had let it slip, and now he was crawling with uneasiness, as if he were back in grammar school and he were about to tattle to the teacher.

"Well, then, what did Lucy have to say about me?" Delphine's tone was pleasant, almost jocular. "She's such a tough critic," she added, "perhaps I shouldn't dare ask."

He faced her again. "I don't know if I dare tell you. You might get angry."

"I'm a doctor, Eric," she reminded him. "I don't get angry."

Eric gazed at her silently, hesitating still. Jane Loring's words came back to him—*Delphine Heywood is evil. The most evil human being I've ever known.* At the time, it had sounded excessively melodramatic; and it seemed all the more preposterous now that he was looking at the subject of the statement, this plump, motherly woman with her benign smile. And yet, since talking to Lucy, he had found himself thinking about what Jane had said, remembering it again after having put it out of his mind for months.

At length, he said, "Lucy thinks you've been leading me down the garden path."

"I haven't been leading you at all," Delphine said. "You've

chosen your own direction."

"Lucy doesn't see it that way. She doesn't agree with what I've been doing with myself—and she blames you for it."

Delphine nodded thoughtfully. She seemed neither irate nor surprised, just mildly saddened. "Sit down, Eric," she said, pointing to the leather armchair he had abandoned. "Let's discuss this."

Eric obediently returned to the chair and sat opposite her again.

"We've come a long way, Eric," Delphine said. "We've made real progress. You're no longer the confused, blocked-up person you were when you first came to see me. You've grown tremendously. But your friend—Lucy"—she uttered the name with faint distaste now—"doesn't seem to believe that. She blames me, you say. What, exactly, does she think I've done wrong?"

"She thinks you've been encouraging me in my fantasies."

"I see."

"And she thinks I should go back to being a full-time book editor," he went on. "She says I was happier and more fulfilled when I was an editor. More so than I am now, anyway."

"She's entitled to her opinion, of course," Delphine said reasonably. "But don't you think that you and I know a little more about the situation?"

"Sure, *I* think so. I don't go along with her opinion at all. But she's making a big issue of it. In fact—" He paused nervously, then finally came to the crucial point, the real reason he had brought up this whole thing: "—she's decided that she can't marry me as long as I stay in therapy."

He had expected that Delphine would be, if not angry, at least annoyed, but she received this bit of news with an unruffled, good-natured smile. It was as if she found Lucy's absurdity rather entertaining. "This girl seems most unsympathetic to the idea of psychotherapy," she commented. "Has she never needed help herself?"

"Lucy doesn't believe in it. She says it reminds her too much of when she was a kid—when she was still a devout Catholic—and she would confess to a priest every week to keep from going to hell."

Delphine seemed slightly taken aback by this analogy. "Where was this?"

"In New Jersey. Nutley, New Jersey."

"Well," she said, with a little laugh, "this is the first time I've ever been likened to a priest in Nutley, New Jersey."

"That's the way she put it—when I asked her why she'd never gone to a shrink. She said she hadn't escaped one kind of mind control to give herself up to another kind."

"Mind control, yes," Delphine murmured coolly. He at last had said something that seemed to irk her, and her expression hardened. "We know about mind control, don't we, Eric? Haven't we been struggling with it in your case? Your mother's control over you? Her influence on all your thoughts about yourself?"

"Yes."

"And weren't you reminded of something when Lucy criticized your book?" Delphine leaned forward, as she did when she was on the scent of some half-concealed but significant truth. "Weren't you reminded of that time, long ago, when your mother destroyed your self-confidence in exactly the same way?"

"But that was different," Eric said. "My mother was an experienced writer criticizing a beginner."

"The motivation may have been different," she said. "But the pattern was the same then as it is now—a domineering female imposing her control over a vulnerable male by undercutting his belief in himself."

It took Eric a moment or two to grasp this. It wasn't easy, since it had never occurred to him to think of Lucy as a "domineering female." "Well, maybe," he said, not quite convinced. "But when we get back to motivation, it doesn't make sense. I can understand why my mother wanted to keep me from being a writer, but what does Lucy have to gain from it?"

"Let's examine that question," Delphine said quickly, like a professor pouncing on a fortuitously raised point. "Let's think about Lucy for a moment. Lucy"—she paused uncertainly—"Castellano, is it?"

"Castelli."

"Italian?"

"Italian descent."

"And what's her family like?"

"Simple, hard-working people. Her father has a small moving business."

"In Nutley, New Jersey?"

"In Nutley, yes."

"Immigrant stock—lower-middle-class values—" She pondered this data for a moment. "Don't you think a girl with that background wants security in a husband?"

"Well, yes, I suppose so. But I'm not going to be poor very soon."

"I mean she wants the *image* of security. That can be more important than the substance. She doesn't want a well-heeled bum for a husband. She wants a solid, respectable executive with a solid, respectable company."

"I don't know." He fidgeted uncomfortably, balking at this analysis of Lucy. "I don't think she's like that."

"You don't think so?" Delphine smiled. "But you're quick to accept her as an astute literary critic. What's her background in evaluating manuscripts?"

"She has none, of course. She's just like any reader of books."

"And you didn't question her judgment? You didn't question it, even though you are the sophisticated expert on the novel form and she really knows nothing about it at all? Why were you so sure she was right?"

"Well—it was an objective opinion."

"Objective?" she echoed incredulously. "When that book was standing there as the major threat to her dream of a comfortable, bourgeois married life? Of course she cut it down! What else did you expect her to do?" She paused, then asked, "Do *you* think your book is good?"

"I *thought* so," he murmured uncertainly. "But now I'm so confused."

"Don't be confused, Eric. Don't let Lucy confuse you. You're a prize catch and she's desperate to land you—but on her own terms." With a faint smile, she added, "This time I think she may have gone a little too far."

"Maybe she has," he said grimly.

The anger was building in him, his anger at Lucy for having played games with his work, his work that was so precious to him. She had almost persuaded him to abandon his book. He understood now, thanks to Delphine and her clear-eyed perception, he understood what Lucy had tried to do to him. But it had been a close call. He had almost let his life be ruined, all of his hopes.

"This girl says she won't marry you as long as you're in therapy," Delphine said. "You know, that could be a blessing in disguise. It wouldn't do any harm to wait, would it?"

"No," Eric said. "That might be a good idea."

Delphine regarded him with quiet satisfaction. Then, as a generous afterthought, she said, "We must be fair to her, though. There aren't many women who can sympathize with an artist's needs." With a soft, rueful laugh, she went on, "I'm only beginning to understand a writer's problems myself—now that I'm trying to be one."

"Oh yes," he said, remembering. "You've been writing a book."

"I've finished it." With a little gesture, she indicated a ream box that was resting on her desk.

Eric looked at it. He hadn't paid much attention to it before, but now he realized that it had been placed there especially for him.

"I'd like to read it," he said.

"I was hoping you would." Casually, she asked, "Are you still a consultant with Galton and Hill?"

"Yes. And it's my job to find books for them."

"Good. Then I'll give it to you now." She rose and went over to the desk.

Eric rose to his feet and waited as she picked up the ream box and came back to him with it. Eric took the box from her and glanced down at the title that was typed out on the glued-on label: *How to Get Well.*

"A nice, direct title," he commented.

"It's what the book is. I've put everything I've learned into it."

"I'm looking forward to reading it."

"Please, let me know what you think. And what I might do to improve it." Her smile was shy and she looked almost girlish as she said, "After all, we writers have to help each other."

18

CHRIS had noticed him first in the body-building room. The guy had been standing in front of the wall mirror, doing a series of undemanding barbell lifts. A couple of times, he had stopped to stare at Chris as he struggled through his fifty sit-ups on the inclined board. Chris hadn't bothered to look back at him.

But now the two of them were alone in the heat room and Chris couldn't very well ignore him. He was just a kid, he realized, six or seven years younger than himself. The boy stood, naked and still, by the opposite wall—which, in this tiny room, put him only eight feet away—watching Chris with a hopeful smile. Chris had his hands on his hips and he was doing a simple twisting exercise to make the sweat pour more readily. As he turned his torso to the left and then to the right, he took in the details of his admirer; blond, curly hair, angelic features, a slim V of a body, well-hung.

Finally, the boy spoke up. "This heat is a waste of time, you know." His voice was light and his accent was faintly Southern. "It only dehydrates you."

"I like to sweat," Chris said.

"The first long drink of water and it all comes back. So, what's the point?"

"If you don't believe in it, why are you in here?"

"Because *you*'re in here."

This kid doesn't fool around, Chris thought. But he went on twisting to the left and right and was careful not to look any more interested in him than he had before. At length, Chris asked, "What's your name?"

"Robbie."

"I'm Chris."

"I know. I'm one of your big fans."

"A theatergoer?"

"Well, I go whenever I can," Robbie said. "Any time I can scrounge up the money for a ticket. Or when someone takes me." He managed to make the "takes me" sound faintly suggestive. "Are you going to be in another show soon, Chris?"

"No. Not in any play. I think I'm going to do a movie next."

"Oh? Which one?"

"I'm not free to say." There wasn't any movie yet, but he wasn't about to admit this to a hustler in a YMCA heat room.

There was a silence, as Robbie, evidently, could think of nothing further to say. He turned away from Chris and began to do a series of quick, toe-touching waist bends. He had angled himself so that Chris could observe his smooth, lean buttocks. His rectum spread with every bend.

Chris stopped his own exercise and watched the boy for a few moments. Finally he said, "I haven't seen you here before."

Robbie straightened up quickly. "It's my first time. I've just moved to this neighborhood. I used to live on the East Side. I went to the Y over there."

"The Vanderbilt Y? That's not a very good one."

"I like this one better already."

Robbie's gaze was intent, his smile was eager, and Chris realized that he had encouraged him. Why am I doing this? he chided himself. I should know better.

Robbie made his move now. "Where are you going after this, Chris?"

"Home."

"Look, I live just down the block. Why don't you come up to my place and have a beer with me?"

"Sorry, I can't. I've got someone waiting for me."

Robbie's smile faded. "An old friend, I suppose?" he asked, bitchy with disappointment.

"My wife," Chris said.

Jane came by before dinner to return a couple of books she had borrowed from her mother. She stayed on for a few minutes, and the three of them sat in the living room talking.

Chris had long since gotten over feeling uncomfortable with Jane. In the early days of his marriage, when she would visit them he would be keenly aware of the strangeness of the situation. He was living as the head of the household in an apartment that had been Jane's home, the place where she had grown up, and he couldn't help but feel uneasy, as if he were an intruder who had invaded the nest and had driven her out.

This had been one reason he had tried to persuade Vivian to move into some new apartment with him. But, in the end, they hadn't. Money was a consideration, and there wasn't much likelihood they could find an apartment of similar space and elegance for anything near the rent they were now paying.

Anyway, as time had gone on, his feelings toward Jane had changed. He had developed a real affection for her, and he had started to enjoy her company. He even, on occasion, sought her out. Sometimes when he was wandering down Madison Avenue he would drop into the art gallery where Jane worked and while away a half-hour with her.

And now, as Vivian and he chatted with Jane about the events of her day, her monster of a boss, the boy she was dating that evening, he wished she could stay longer. The three of them together formed a warm family unit. When Jane was gone, Vivian and he would move to a distance from each other again, and they would be little more than tense roommates, maintaining an uneasy peace. It wasn't always that way, of course; they still had their good, happy times. But there had been ominous signs that day. He sensed an edginess in Vivian, one of her dark moods was forming, and he was in no hurry to be alone with her.

Jane was through filling them in on herself, and now she asked, "What about you, Chris? Anything in the works?"

"Maybe," he replied. "A TV movie—if I want to do it."

Vivian looked at him in surprise. "What TV movie?"

"The offer just came. Ira called me about it this morning."

"Is it starring?" Vivian asked.

"Co-starring."

"Are you going to do it?" Jane asked.

"I don't know. I'll have to read the script first. It's probably junk." With a shrug, he added, "And then there's the image thing."

"What image thing?" Jane asked.

"Well, if I'm going to get started in films, I'd rather go in the front door. Not through the tube."

"Maybe it's better to just keep working," Jane said.

It had been the tactful way to put it, he recognized ruefully. It wasn't a matter of *keeping* working. Chris hadn't worked at all for half a year.

"Yeah," he said, "maybe you're right."

A couple of minutes later, Jane excused herself and left. As soon as the door closed after her, Vivian turned on him. "Why didn't you tell me about that offer?"

"I was going to," he said. "But I wanted to think about it for a while before I talked to you."

"You didn't hesitate to tell Jane. Do you tell *her* things before you tell them to me?"

"No. It's just that she asked."

Her eyes held on him anxiously. "What *is* this with you and Jane? What do the two of you talk about when you go see her?"

"We don't talk about anything at all. And I haven't seen her that much—except right here." He laughed. "Darling, you're being very silly, you know that?"

She smiled now, acknowledging the absurdity of her jealousy. "It's just that Jane is so young," she said. "She gets more beautiful every day." Her face saddened. "And I'm losing my looks."

"Oh, come on!" he said, taking her into his arms. "You're more beautiful now than ever. And you look almost as young as Jane."

"You're just saying that," she murmured into his shoulder.

"It's true."

It wasn't. Vivian had aged visibly in the past few months. He assumed it was the acceleration that took place with some youthful-seeming people when they were past forty; not so much a deterioration as a sudden catching up to true time.

But Chris didn't mind. The chic of youth aside, she was, in fact, even more beautiful than before. And her soft womanliness and warmth, as he held her in his arms, was as comforting to him as ever.

He kissed her lightly and said, "Now, let's have dinner."

"Okay," she said, disengaging herself from him. "But I'll have to change first."

It took him a moment to realize what she meant. "We're not eating in?"

"No. We don't have any food in the house."

It was her usual answer. But he couldn't let it pass, not any longer. They were supposed to be living on a budget, and yet they had gone out to restaurants three times in the last five days. "We can't afford this, you know," he said.

"Well, I don't have time to shop and cook every night."

"Time?" The impatient, negligent way she had said it angered him. "You've got nothing *but* time! All you do is go around buying clothes."

Vivian stared at him icily. "*Your* life isn't exactly hectic and crammed. Why don't *you* cook?"

"I don't know how," he said.

"Then take lessons!" she snapped. "Or take that TV offer— so we won't have to argue about money any more!"

She left the room abruptly.

Chris felt a little sick, as he always did after these flare-ups; and, as always, he sensed that somehow he was in the wrong. He had known what he was getting into. Marriage was supposed to be expensive, particularly if one had a wife with fancy tastes. He had taken on the responsibility and now he had to be a man, grown-up about it. But it was hard not to get panicked when his savings account was dwindling rapidly to the zero point.

He waited until he had calmed down sufficiently, then went into the bedroom. Vivian was in her half-slip, holding up and inspecting the dress she would wear when they went out.

"I'm sorry," he said. "I didn't mean to yell at you."

"You didn't yell at me."

"I got angry. I raised my voice. I'm sorry."

Vivian looked at him now, rather thoughtfully. He couldn't tell whether she was accepting his apology or not. "What about that TV movie?" she asked. "Are you going to do it?"

"I don't know."

"I think you should do it. And not just because of the money. It would be good for you to get out in the world and start working again." With weariness in her voice, she said, "We're spending too much time here together."

"Do I get on your nerves?"

"I didn't say that. But you're a healthy young man, filled with energy. And all you do is pace around the apartment—like you're in a cage. You go into the kitchen and open the refrigerator," she went on, singsonging it to stress the monotony of it. "Then you come in here, throw yourself down on the bed, and watch TV for a few minutes. Then you go back into the kitchen and open the refrigerator again. You're not hungry, so why do you do that?"

"I don't know why I do it."

"I think you should take this job," she repeated.

"I'm not saying I won't." He paused. "But there's something about it I don't like. Someone who's involved with it."

"Who?"

"That guy."

Whenever he said "that guy" to her, he meant only one person. Vivian voiced his name now. "Ward?"

He nodded. "It's his movie."

"But he's too high up at the network. He wouldn't be *personally* involved in it."

"He approves the star casting, doesn't he?"

She thought for a moment. "All right, I guess he does. But you're being offered the job. So, he must have approved you."

"I don't like it."

"What's past is past," she said quietly. "Chris, you're being too sensitive. Also," she added, "you're being impractical."

"Yeah, maybe so," he admitted.

Chris lay in the bed, his head propped up on two pillows, watching Vivian put on her skin cream. She was sitting at her dressing table in her bathrobe, applying the stuff with rhythmic strokes, her nightly ritual. No amount of his teasing could make her skip it even once. Actually, his teasing was half in earnest, since he didn't much care for her precious cream. It was greasy on her face and stank like sewage.

She had been silent for some time. But now, bemused, she said, "Darling, I've been thinking—"

"Thinking what?"

"We've been fighting about money so much lately. It just makes things uglier. It would be nice if we had some money again."

"That's for sure."

"Well, something has occurred to me." She was still gazing into her mirror and she hadn't looked at him. "We have resources we haven't called on yet."

"Have I forgotten something?"

"My diamond bracelet."

"You're not selling it," he said curtly.

She swung around and faced him. "Why not?"

"We don't need that money."

"I never wear the bracelet. It's not doing me any good."

"I don't want that money!" he said sharply.

Vivian stared at him silently for a moment. "I should never have told you who gave it to me."

"No, you shouldn't have."

She hadn't told him much; she had simply mentioned once that Ward Kennan had given her the bracelet. But it was all he needed to know. She had earned it whoring and he wanted no benefit from it. He wished the damned diamonds would turn into dust.

Vivian was studying his expression worriedly now. She rose, came over to the bed, slipped off her bathrobe, and sat naked beside him. She put her hand on his. "Forgive me. I shouldn't have brought it up."

"You're forgiven."

"It was dumb of me."

"You were trying to be helpful, I guess."

"You know how much I love you, don't you?"

"Yes," he said.

She drew back the blanket and slipped into bed with him. He received her into his arms warily. Her nipples had hardened and were almost abrasive against the bare skin of his chest. She thrust her tongue boldly into his mouth, as she did when she wanted him urgently. It was a bit of foreplay that no longer turned him on. The sensation of her wet, rough tongue moving along his palate had started to disgust him.

But he was careful not to show it, his revulsion or his faint sense of apprehension. He flung the blanket away from them, leaving their naked bodies unencumbered, swung around on the bed and plunged his head between her thighs. His tongue found her clitoris instantly.

"No, darling, no," she said. He could hear the excitement in her voice and he went on, disregarding her protest. More insistently she repeated, "No!" and pulled free of him.

He propped himself on his elbow and looked at her.

She gazed at him with pleading in her eyes. "Penetrate me," she said. "This one time, penetrate me. Oh, baby," she whispered, reaching for him, "I want you inside me so much!"

Chris obediently climbed on top of her. But he was too soft to do anything, and, after a moment, he lay back and rested his head on the pillows again.

He waited. In one part of him, he hoped that she would forget about the whole thing and that they could go to sleep. At the same time, he desperately wanted her to keep trying. He was afraid, as he was afraid every time they made love, that she would suddenly, with a swift, final gesture of dismissal, give up on him.

Vivian rose to her knees, bent over him, and took his penis into her mouth.

Chris closed his eyes and tried to relax. He saw random images, green mountains in the distance, a sky with cotton-puff clouds in it, a white-shingled house he could no longer place.

Then he saw the boy in the heat room—Robbie—his slim, muscular body gleaming with sweat. Chris approached him and took him into his arms, tenderly, firmly. Robbie resisted a little, but only to show Chris that he loved him too much for it to be an easy thing. Chris forced him down onto the stone floor. He pushed back Robbie's legs until his knees were beside his head and drove his cock up his ass. The boy cried out with pain and joy.

"Oh, that's *good*, darling," he heard Vivian say approvingly. "You're nice and hard."

19

ERIC DROVE the ball to Chris's backhand side, and, once again, Chris was a tiny fraction of a second too late.

"That's game," Eric called out happily. "It's five–three."

Chris shook his head ruefully. "Let's take a break," he suggested.

"What? When I'm smelling victory for the first time?"

"I don't feel so hot."

Chris went over to the bench and sat. Eric joined him, somewhat reluctantly, since he suspected this might be a ploy. These tennis dates had become a fairly regular thing between them— every other week or so, they would reserve a court in the park— and so far, for Eric, the games had been exercises in masochism. He was something of a tennis whiz in the publishing crowd, but with Chris he invariably went down to defeat by scores of six–one and six–two. Now, unexpectedly, miraculously, he was on the verge of sweet revenge, and he wasn't about to let himself get psyched out at the last moment.

"Go on, tell me," Eric said. "You have a bad cold or the flu. Ruin it for me."

Chris smiled. "No, I'm not sick. But I've got some junk in me. It makes me feel funny."

"What kind of junk?"

"Some pills Delphine has been giving me. Placidyl."

"Placidyl? What does *that* do?"

"Helps me go to sleep at night. And calms me down during the day."

"Do you need calming?"

Chris looked at him askance. "Have you noticed that things haven't been going too well for me lately?"

"You mean, because you haven't worked for a while?" Eric shrugged. "These dry spells happen. It's just part of the actor's life, isn't it?"

"Yeah, it is. Now, if I could only make Vivian understand that," Chris said wryly. "She seems to think there's something wrong with me—like I'm lazy or degenerate."

Eric heard the slight slurring of the syllables in "degenerate" —a remarkable speech lapse for Chris, who had an actor's precise diction—and realized that he was, indeed, in a mildly drugged state.

"What the hell am I supposed to do?" Chris went on. "*You* can do your writing every day, a painter can paint, but an actor between jobs is nothing. He's the next thing to dead—just waiting around for the phone to ring, for someone to ask him to come to life again."

"You'll get something big soon," Eric reassured him.

"That's what Delphine keeps telling me. But, I don't know, it won't be easy."

"Why should it be difficult now? You're an established actor. You're practically a star already."

"In the theater," Chris pointed out. "But I've turned my back on the theater."

"Completely?"

"Well, if I was offered a great part on Broadway, I'd have to think about it. But great roles don't come along very often. And I'm not doing the usual theater stuff any more—winter stock—regional theater—Off-Broadway—" With a crisp little gesture he concluded, "It's films or nothing now."

"Does the transition have to be so extreme?"

"Delphine says that, when the time comes to make a change, you should go all the way with it—not fudge it—not try to cling to the past." Chris paused, then with a touch of sadness added, "So, I've made a clean break. I don't see *any* of my old theater friends any more."

Eric was about to ask why he couldn't see them socially at least. Then it occurred to him that these "old theater friends" might all be gay. Instead, he asked, "Does Delphine give you career guidance, too?"

Chris didn't seem to know quite how to answer this. "I listen to her," he said. "After all, she knows what's best for me."

"Then has she told you that you'd be better off going out to the Coast? That's where the movie work is, isn't it?"

"Delphine thinks it would be better if I stayed here."

Eric didn't ask for Delphine's reason. But, unavoidably, he had the thought that she might not be willing to lose Chris as a patient.

"Anyway," Chris went on, "Vivian doesn't want to leave New York."

"If it were just job-hunting, you could go out alone—for a month or two."

"No, I can't be apart from Vivian," Chris said simply. "Not for a month. Not even for a few days."

"Are you so dependent on her?"

Chris reflected for a moment. "I need her," he replied. "We don't always get along, but I need to be around her. Whatever that means."

"It means you're happily married, I guess," Eric said lightly, with no real conviction.

"Yeah," Chris said, with a laugh. "Yeah, I guess that's it. That's what marriage is." He gave Eric a teasing, meaningful look. "You'll be finding out yourself soon enough."

"Maybe not *that* soon," Eric said uncomfortably. He didn't want to be reminded of Lucy at that point. Since his last session with Delphine, he had put off seeing Lucy two nights in a row. "So, tell me about married love," he said, quickly getting back to the main subject. "Is it all it's cracked up to be?"

Eric was being somewhat flippant, but Chris considered the question gravely. "It's different," he answered after a moment. "Different from what I expected it would be. There's tenderness," he said slowly, "there's exhilaration, even—and there's fear."

"Fear? What are you afraid of?"

"Nothing, really. Just that something might go wrong." His sensitive face, responding as if to a cue, shaded into a haunted, frightened expression. "Sometimes I lie awake at night, with Vivian sleeping beside me, and I feel that it's all so beautiful that something terrible has *got* to happen." He looked at Eric a bit self-consciously now, as if he realized he was being melodramatic. "Otherwise, everything's fine," he said, more cheerfully. "It's like I'm really living for the first time. Yeah, being married is just great!"

Perhaps it was the drug, throwing off his actor's timing, but Eric noticed that, even as Chris smiled brightly, his fearful expression lingered on.

"I would never have made the first move," Vivian insisted. "You know that. When I saw him coming toward me on the sidewalk that day, I pretended I didn't see him. I was going to walk right past him."

"Yes, you told me," Delphine said.

"*Ward* was the one who stopped and said hello. *He* was the one who suggested we go have a drink. *He* was the one who proposed we have lunch the next day. *He*—" Vivian broke off, as she realized she was protesting a little too much. She sat back and with a light shrug admitted, "I could have refused, of course. But that didn't seem very grown-up."

"What do you mean by 'grown-up'?"

"Well, after all this time you'd think we ought to be able to have a civilized friendship. And he was being so nice and charming—he was acting the way he did when I first met him. I mean, he seemed *really* glad to see me."

"For any particular reason, do you think?"

"He's lonely. And, though he didn't say it directly, I could tell"—with quiet satisfaction, she said it—"I don't think he's been getting along with his new wife."

Delphine nodded, as if it were only what she had expected. "You think Ward has missed you?"

"Yes, I know he has," she said emphatically. "He says he thinks about me all the time."

She paused and looked at Delphine uncertainly. Her therapist was giving her no clue as to how she was taking this. Delphine had once been very positive about Ward. But since the affair's end, since that night Ward had humiliated Vivian at her birthday dinner, Delphine had seemed to cease having any opinion about him at all.

"So, okay," Vivian went on, "we're seeing each other again. Is there anything wrong with that? If we get together now and then just to talk? It's harmless, isn't it?"

"Harmless, yes." Delphine smiled slightly. "Except now, you say, he wants to go to bed with you."

"Yes," she replied softly.

"But that's not really a problem, is it? All you have to do is say no."

Vivian looked away. "I don't know if I *want* to say no."

She had come out with it, finally, the disturbing truth that she hadn't been able to voice, even to Delphine—that she wanted Ward, had wanted him from the moment she had seen him again on the street. She had downplayed her renewed acquaintance with him in her last few therapy sessions, making it sound casual and unimportant. But now Ward himself had raised the issue. He had told her that he wanted to go back to their old relationship; though modified, of course, to allow for their present circumstances.

"Does Chris know you've been seeing Ward?"

"No, of course not."

"You've been keeping it from him?"

She shrugged. "I'd just rather he didn't find out."

"How do you and Ward communicate with each other?"

"I've called him at his office. And he phoned me at the apartment once."

"Wasn't that taking a chance?"

"Not really. There are certain times that Chris is almost always out of the apartment, when he's at the Actors' Studio or at the gym. Or," she added, "when he's here. I've told Ward those times."

"You make it sound as if you have a clandestine affair going already," Delphine commented.

"We've been careful," Vivian said. "We don't want to worry Chris."

Delphine thought for a moment. "Do you love Ward?"

"No."

"Do you love Chris?"

Vivian was a little surprised that she even had to ask. "Yes, you know I do," she said. "I adore him. But—" She let out her breath wearily. It was time to get to the point. "Love doesn't have much to do with it."

"What do you mean by that?"

"Well, I've told you about our sex life."

Delphine nodded. "You're sexually dissatisfied, is that it?"

"Dissatisfied? I don't know if that's the right word. I do have orgasms, that's not the problem."

"Then what *is* the problem?"

"It's not that Chris isn't an expert lover—in his own way. And he does try so hard to please me. Maybe that's it, he's always doing it for me rather than for himself. I mean," she went on unhappily, "all those delicate techniques—the oral stuff and so on—it's not *enough*. Sometimes I wish he'd just take me—brutally—gratify his own appetites, without giving a thought to me."

"That's the way Ward would take you?"

"Yes." Vivian paused, then more reflectively said, "I realize now that, for all my obsession with Ward, it basically came down to the sex. Maybe there was never much more than the sex. I was using him just as he was using me." She looked at her therapist inquiringly. "Does that mean I'm kinky? Sick? That I need a man who'll degrade me?"

"We don't have to pass a moral judgment on it," Delphine murmured. After a moment, she asked, "How would you feel after sex with Ward?"

"Soiled—and marvelous."

"Evidently, then, it's the kind of sex you need. It works for you."

Vivian gazed at her uncertainly. It had sounded as if there were a note of approval in Delphine's voice. "Are you saying I should start up with Ward again?"

Delphine smiled, almost to herself, as if she had detected Vivian's faint shock and was amused by it. "What would happen if you didn't give in to this need?" she asked. "What would happen to your marriage?"

"I don't know," Vivian replied. "I guess I'd just go on being frustrated. And things would get tenser between Chris and me."

"So, denying your need can only have a negative effect on

your marriage. And a negative effect on Chris."

"But it wouldn't be right, would it, if I slept with another man?"

"It's not a question of right or wrong. It's a question of fulfilling yourself as a woman, of being happy. If you are a fulfilled and happy woman, you'll be a better wife to Chris. And Chris will be happier."

Vivian was silent for a moment, as she thought this over. "If Chris ever found out," she said, "it would kill him."

"But there's no reason for him to find out."

"No," Vivian agreed, "not if we're careful."

The hour was up and there wasn't time to discuss it further. But as Vivian rose from the chair, she already felt lightened, almost giddy with relief. It hadn't been such a heavy problem after all. The answer seemed ridiculously obvious, now that Delphine had pointed it out to her.

Lingering at the door of the office, she gazed into Delphine's glowing gray eyes. She was suddenly overcome with gratitude, and she threw her arms around her therapist and hugged her. "Oh, Delphine, you're wonderful! What would I do without you?"

Delphine's lips were very close to her ear as she whispered, "It's common sense, darling. Whatever makes you happy is right. It's always right."

20

THE BULLETIN BOARD of the Actors' Studio was in the front office, right by the door, and it was the first thing that Chris glanced at as he came in off the street. As soon as he saw the name posted on it, he knew he couldn't stay.

There were four names, actually, printed in ink on the tacked-up sheet of paper, the names of the Studio members who would be doing scenes in class that morning; an actor and an actress in a scene from *The Seagull*, and two actresses in a scene from a play he had never heard of. But the top name was the one that caught his attention. Dale Murphy.

Murphy had just gotten into the Studio and the Chekhov would be his first scene there. He had been admitted to membership by special dispensation, without even having to audition. But, then, the Studio board was always quick to take in any suddenly hot actor—and Murphy was the hottest thing on Broadway, at that moment. He was starring in Noah Porterfield's new show, playing the role that had been originally tailored for Chris. The show was a smash, it was playing to near capacity, and the word was that Dale Murphy was a good bet for the "best actor" Tony award.

Chris had never seen Murphy's work. He hadn't seen him in Noah's show, and he couldn't bring himself to see him now, even in a simple scene for class. He smiled a vague hello at the members who were standing around the office, turned, and went out again.

It wasn't quite eleven and suddenly he had nothing to do. He walked at an easy pace along West Forty-fourth Street, turning up a block when he reached Eighth Avenue to avoid passing the theater where Noah's show was playing. One reminder in a morning was enough.

He decided against taking the subway—there was no hurry to get any place—and kept going across town until he reached Madison Avenue, where he caught an uptown bus. As the bus crept through the traffic, he concentrated on the street sights, trying to keep his thoughts away from Dale Murphy, Noah, and his screwed-up career. But it was useless; he was bugged all over again.

He hadn't taken a pill that morning, he realized. He would take one as soon as he got home. It would help a little anyway.

When Chris arrived at the apartment, it was a quarter to twelve. He called out Vivian's name and got no reply. She wasn't there. He was puzzled for a moment. She had told him she was having lunch with a girlfriend, but that wasn't until one. Well, maybe she had stepped out to do some shopping.

He went into the bedroom to check the answering machine. The red light was on, indicating that they had a message. He crossed to the machine and turned the switch to PLAY.

The voice on the tape was female, young, secretarial, and rather nervous. "This is Ward Kennan's office," it said, "and this message is for Mrs. Greene. Mr. Kennan has been called out of town today and he won't be able to keep his lunch date with you. He would like to change it to tomorrow. The same time, the same place—La Boule d'Or at one o'clock. If he doesn't hear from you, he'll assume this is confirmed. Thank you."

Chris heard the hang-up and then the dead air of the disconnected line.

He switched off the machine and stood there motionless. He felt nothing in particular; he didn't know if he *should* feel anything.

He tried to get his thoughts in order, to piece it out logically. Vivian was supposed to have lunch with Ward Kennan. All right, that in itself didn't mean much. It could be an innocent get-together. But she had lied to him. She had told him that she was having lunch with—who was it?—Tina Nevins. If it were innocent, would she have lied? She could have told him; he would have understood if she had wanted to see Kennan again for one time.

Was it just this one time? A chill went through him as it suddenly occurred to him that she might have been seeing Kennan all along. She had been going out a lot during the day lately, on vague errands and to have lunch with people. For all he knew, she had lied to him before, had been lying to him systematically.

He could ask her about it, but it wouldn't do any good. She might just lie to him again. No matter what she said, he still couldn't be sure.

Maybe it was still going on. Maybe it had never really stopped. Maybe they were both laughing at him—she and that pig, Kennan!

He could hear his pulse beating in his ears now, deafening him as it would in that moment of panic before he went out on stage. And, as sometimes happened in that moment, he disengaged from himself, floated off to a distance, observed the man standing in the wings, and wondered what he would do next.

Chris turned the answering machine back on. The red light was off now, since he had already played the message. He thought for a moment, then solved the problem. When he went out, he would phone his home number, listen to his recorded announcement, then hang up, as people often did, leaving a blank minute on the tape. That would turn the red light on again, and Vivian, when she returned, wouldn't know he had been there. She would play her message, erase it, and keep her newly scheduled lunch date.

La Boule d'Or—one o'clock.

He had a long afternoon of wandering the streets ahead of him. And an unbearable full day of waiting.

But then he would know.

"I think I'm going mad," Mandy said.

"Oh, don't be silly, darling," Vivian said, rather impatiently. She had promptly responded to Mandy's phone call, had dropped everything to take a cab to the Algonquin, and now she was in no mood for absurd, self-pitying statements. "You're the least likely candidate for a nervous breakdown I know."

"Okay, then, I'm sane," Mandy said. "*Life* has gotten crazy."

"That can happen," Vivian said.

Mandy smiled and took a thoughtful sip of her drink. She already seemed more relaxed, and Vivian feared that they might be settling in for a discussion of the meaning of it all. If Mandy had that in mind, she wanted to discourage it. She was in a hurry to go on to her lunch with Ward and she had no time for digressions. As it was, she was a little annoyed. She had wanted to look perfect for Ward, and Mandy had called her away in the middle of fixing herself up, so that her hair was still a bit untidy and her eyes weren't completely done. But Mandy had sounded very tense—without saying anything directly, she had let her know she was undergoing some new, painful, emotional crisis—and Vivian, dutiful friend that she was, had dashed out of the apartment with such haste that she hadn't even stopped to answer the phone, which had started ringing as she was going out the door.

"Why does life seem so crazy to you?" Vivian asked. "You've got your new company started—and things are going very well, aren't they?"

"With my work, you mean? It's never been more exciting. Though, of course," Mandy added, "I won't know how really well I'm doing until after we have our first show."

"When will that be?"

"In March. We're going early." She let out her breath nervously. "It will be a biggie."

"In what way?"

"Well, it won't be your ordinary fashion show. I've decided we have to introduce the Mandy line with a splash. Something spectacular that will put us on the map right away. So, I've hired Oliver Dussault."

"Who's he?"

"If you were in the rag trade, you'd know him. He has a p.r. firm and he specializes in creating fashion presentations. It's like theater with him—he does it with music, choreography, mixed media effects. Oliver took me to Elaine's last night," she went on, "and told me what he had in mind. He wants my show to be very special—classy, but a little more far-out than the others. It has to be an Event, he says, that everyone will talk about. He's going to use projections and wild lighting and that kind of thing." She paused, as her enthusiasm seemed to be momentarily dampened by a touch of trepidation. Then, with a wan smile, she concluded, "It will cost a lot of money, but it should be worth it."

"And this is why you think you're going insane?" Vivian was determined to get her to the point.

"No, of course it's not that," Mandy said. Her face darkened. "It's something that happened last night, while we were at Elaine's."

"What happened?"

A disturbed look came into Mandy's eyes and, once again, she seemed dazed and rather disoriented, as she had when Vivian had arrived. "Oliver and I were sitting by ourselves at a table," she began, "all caught up in talking about the show, planning it. And this man came over and said hello to me. I glanced up at him, without really looking at him too closely. He was a slim, handsome man, kind of elegant. He looked vaguely familiar, but I couldn't place him. He said it was good to see me again and he wished me the best of luck with my collection. I just said, 'Thank you,' and turned back to Oliver. The man went away, and I saw that Oliver had a funny expression on his face. I asked him, 'What's the matter?' He said, 'Don't you know who that was?' 'No,' I said, 'who was it?' 'That was your husband.' "

Vivian laughed with disbelief. "You mean, it was Jeff and you didn't recognize him?"

"Well, he's totally changed! He's lost about sixty pounds—he's shaved his mustache—he has his hair cut in a new way. But I was stunned, I couldn't believe it! I looked over at him—he was sitting at another table with some girl I'd never seen before—and I realized it *was* Jeff, looking *gorgeous*," she said emotionally, her eyes filling with tears. "I guess he must have been offended, because he pretended not to notice me any more. So I got up and left. I went home and cried all night."

Vivian looked at Mandy, who was slumped miserably over her drink now and couldn't think of anything to say. "It happens," she murmured soothingly. "People change. You shouldn't take it so hard."

"I *am* taking it hard. I've never been so shaken up by anything in my life! That I could live with a man for ten years, sleep in the same bed with him, and not even *know* him when I saw him! Isn't that crazy? Don't you think it's crazy?"

"Yes, it's crazy," Vivian agreed.

Almost immediately Mandy perked up. She sat up straight,

wiped away her tears, and took a swallow of her drink. It occurred to Vivian that Mandy probably hadn't called on her
because she had wanted any advice from her. She had simply
needed to tell her bizarre story to someone. And, now that she
had done so, she felt better.

"Are you going to tell Delphine about this?" Vivian asked.

Mandy looked away. "No. I don't want to."

"Why not?"

"She's confused me enough already."

Vivian was a little surprised by this negative reference to their
therapist, the suggestion of disloyalty. But she chose not to
comment on it. "Well," she said, "Delphine would have the
time to go over it with you. I'm afraid *I* don't right now,
darling. I have to leave."

"Of course, I understand," Mandy said. "Going back to fix
lunch for Chris?"

"No, he's at the Actors' Studio today. I'm meeting someone
for lunch."

"Anybody I know?"

Vivian hesitated. "No," she said, "it's no one you know."

Eric settled into the armchair, took the top off the ream box,
and looked down at Delphine's manuscript. The title leapt out
at him: HOW TO GET WELL. He gently dumped the manuscript onto his lap, put aside the box, and straightened the
stack of paper. It was a thin manuscript, not much more than
two hundred pages, and there was no need to divide it up into
sections for more comfortable handling; he could grasp the
whole of it as he read. He slipped off the title page and
started in.

The next page had a dedication on it: "This is for Sergius
Winter, M.D., my beloved analyst once, my dear friend
always."

Eric went on to the first page of the book. It began:

> We are born naked and afraid. As we grow, The Others clothe us with beliefs, in God, in the Nation, in the Family, in Good and Evil. These concepts are nothing more than that, flimsy garments woven by The Others to conceal the truth from us. That each one of us is alone in an empty, unfeeling universe. That we have only ourselves.
>
> You must accept this. Once you realize this truth you can be strong. You can be happy. You can Get Well.

A good, vigorous beginning, Eric thought. It presented a rather chilling view of human existence. And he didn't know how her brusque dismissal of God, Country and Motherhood would go down in the Bible Belt. But the opening did what it was supposed to do: it made the reader sit up.

But what was this business about "The Others"? To whom was she referring? It disturbed him. It had a faintly paranoid ring to it.

Eric read on. In this first section, Delphine gave her prescription for a healthy attitude toward life. Basically, she argued, no one cares about you but yourself. All other people will try to impose their ideas on you for their own selfish purposes. Only you can know what you want, what really will make you happy. A healthy person sets out to get what he wants, to satisfy his own desires. After stating this in no uncertain terms, she proceeded to soften it a bit by saying that such a healthy person then becomes a better friend, a better lover, a better parent or mate.

This brought her to the question of love.

> Harry Stack Sullivan defined love as having a greater concern for someone else's well-being than for your own. Sullivan was wrong. You cannot love anyone else if you do not love yourself first. Your main concern must be with your own happiness. Then, if you are

happy, you can include someone else in your happiness, share your happiness with another person. This is the only meaningful love between people.

As she went on, she became more specific. She gave hypothetical examples of "sick" and "healthy" behavior. In general, a person was sick if he frustrated himself by deferring to the values inculcated in him by his parents or taught him by the community. He was healthy if he did what he wanted to do, even if it went contrary to the beliefs of The Others.

She concluded the chapter by putting together some examples in a litany:

> If you're a businessman and want to be rich, but hold yourself back because you feel you should "give time to your family," then you're Not Well. If you singlemindedly pursue your goal, work day and night to make a fortune, then you're Getting Well.
>
> If you're a housewife who has always wanted to be a painter, but you have neglected your talent so that you can care for your husband and children, then you're Not Well. If you rent a studio, spend your days doing the work you love, and hire someone to look after your children, then you're Getting Well.
>
> If you want to rise in a company and your advancement is blocked by incompetent superiors, and you do nothing about it because you worry about "loyalty" and "team spirit," then you're Not Well. If you put forth your ideas, cut down the incompetents, and win your promotion, then you're Getting Well.

Eric paused in his reading, uneasy without quite knowing why. In her own way, she was presenting a fairly conventional doing-your-own-thing philosophy. But there was something wrong with the tone of it. Or perhaps something was missing.

What about values? Standards of behavior? If, in your heart

of hearts, you wanted to rape little children, and you did so, were you Getting Well? At what point did the pain you caused others outweigh the benefits of self-gratification? It was as if the question had never entered Delphine's head. Or, if it had, she was strangely indifferent to it.

And what about the meaning of life? He noticed that almost all of the examples she gave dealt with success—people who were striving for fame, power, or wealth—as if worldly success were the one unquestionable value. Had she no comfort to offer the humble, the ungifted, the losers?

The title of her next chapter, in a sense, answered this question. It said "You Are What You Think You Are."

The chapter began:

> You are a flicker of consciousness in the vastness of time, and you can only exist as you are conscious of yourself. The Others may impose their perceptions of you on your consciousness of self and alter it. But, finally, you are nothing more or less than what you see yourself to be.

After this metaphysical opening, with its grand invocation of eternity and nothingness, Delphine became specific again. If a soprano's voice sounded unpleasant to other people, she said, but was beautiful to her own ears, then she was, indeed, someone who sang beautifully. Her consciousness of the beauty of her voice was all that mattered. Beauty and ugliness otherwise were subjective judgments that had no basis in unknowable absolute reality. If a man thought of himself as a great lover, and some of his bed partners found his technique lacking, he was still the Casanova he imagined himself to be. His consciousness of himself defined what he was.

This brought her to the question of the distinction between heterosexuality and homosexuality. Your sexual orientation, she said, stems simply from your conception of yourself. In her practice, she had had success in curing patients of their homosexuality by helping them to look upon themselves in a new way.

> One of my patients, a well-known Broadway actor, due to the unfortunate circumstances of his early youth, had come to think of himself as a homosexual. I taught him to see himself as a normal heterosexual man, needing a woman, wanting the emotional security of marriage. He has since married a beautiful, loving woman and has found the happiness and peace that had eluded him for most of his life.

Eric was sure she was referring to Christopher Greene. And he thought of Chris now, as he was when they had last played tennis together, his movements listless, his timing gone, his speech slurred from the drugs he was taking. He remembered the look of fear that had come into his eyes when he had talked about his marriage. What kind of "happiness and peace" did Delphine think he had found?

He read on. Delphine elaborated on her theory for a few more pages, and then went in another direction with it.

Some people, she said, had strong conceptions of themselves, others had weaker ones, still others had virtually none at all. This was the basic distinction between the strong and the weak. The strong could stand alone, secure in knowing who they were. The weaker ones needed support in their conceptions of themselves, from psychotherapists or from the reinforcing institutions of society. The last, those who had no real sense of themselves, were beyond hope. They could not survive.

Suddenly, she turned personal.

> Let me give a melancholy example from my own life. My mother died young, and my father was left to raise two daughters, my sister, Ariane, who was the beautiful one, and I, who was the smart one. Natu-

rally, we vied for our father's love and attention. But it was an unequal competition. Our father, who taught Latin and Greek at a New England private school, took pride in my intellectual achievements and gave me most of his love.

Poor Ariane could not bear this. She came to believe that she was worthless, nothing as a human being. I tried to help her, tried to make her understand that she was a fine person who would always be valued for her beauty and the sweetness of her disposition. But it was useless.

Ariane died when she was sixteen. Meningitis was the physical cause. But, in reality, she lacked the will to survive because she had no conception of herself. She was weak. She could not live.

Eric puzzled over this strange non sequitur of a story with its disturbing overtones. He read it a second time, then lowered the manuscript.

This woman is insane, he thought wonderingly. She's completely insane!

21

CHRIS ORDERED a third cup of coffee and went on waiting. From where he was sitting, on the inside curve of the horseshoe-shaped counter of the luncheonette, he could look out the window and see the French restaurant across the street. It was an unpretentious little place with a painted red door and a sign that had the name in white on black letters: LA BOULE D'OR. He never let his gaze stray from the red door for more than a few seconds. Almost an hour before, Vivian had entered the restaurant, and, two minutes later, Ward Kennan had gone in. Soon they would come out. Or it would be soon, anyway, if they had more to do during a long lunch break than simply dine.

The waitress brought him his new cup of coffee and Chris sugared it, meticulously measuring out a spoon and a half, concentrating on the task to give his mind a momentary respite from his thoughts. He had made too much of this thing, he told himself, for the tenth or twentieth time. And, once again, he went through the plausible explanation. Vivian and Kennan had had an ugly break-up. Months had gone by without their seeing each other, and now Kennan, as a making-it-up gesture, had invited Vivian to lunch. It was nothing more than that. Vivian hadn't told him about it simply because she hadn't wanted to worry him.

He didn't know whether he believed this or not. He was arriving at no conclusions. He was just going ahead, doing what he had to do, acting out this particular scenario, carrying out his action. He had no idea what was about to happen. He could see no further into the future than this present moment, in which he was sipping coffee and staring out a luncheonette window.

Nor did he know what he would do if what he feared turned out to be true. There was nothing he *could* do, really. Not immediately anyway. He knew he wouldn't confront them. That pathetic kind of scene wasn't his style.

For that matter, he couldn't even retaliate against Kennan's network. He had already signed the contract for the TV movie—Chris bitterly regretted that he hadn't waited just three days more—and there was no getting out of it now. Not without a valid, act-of-God type reason. Not if he didn't want to be blackballed from ever working in television again.

If he killed Kennan, he thought grimly, that could be a way out. There must be something in the fine print about killing the East Coast head of programming.

Well, what the hell, he shouldn't be thinking this way. There was probably nothing to this thing at all.

Suddenly, Chris sat up straight. Vivian and Kennan were emerging from the restaurant. Kennan walked out almost to the curb, and Chris thought he might be about to hail a cab. But, instead, he turned, took Vivian's arm, and started toward Lexington Avenue.

Chris threw a couple of dollar bills onto the counter and hurried out. He paused in the entranceway of the luncheonette, careful not to make himself conspicuous, and peered across the street at his wife and Kennan. They were walking at an easy pace, leaning into each other slightly as they conversed. Kennan, in his light-gray tweed suit, looked even bulkier than he remembered. Vivian, in her navy-blue pants suit, seemed petite and almost childlike beside him.

Chris followed them, walking at the same speed. When Vivian and Kennan reached the corner, they turned down Lexington. Chris quickened his step now, crossed Lexington, and headed down the avenue on the opposite side from them.

This section of Lexington, in the East Forties, had had a toniness once. But it had slipped, as had most of midtown Manhattan, and now the hotels along this stretch catered to the less well-heeled commercial travelers and the more discreet ladies of the night. After a block and a half, Vivian and Kennan went into one of these hotels.

It happened abruptly, and Chris was unprepared for it. He stopped in the middle of the sidewalk, momentarily paralyzed. It was several seconds before he could breathe again. Then he felt a panic of indecision. What should he do now? Suddenly, without thinking, he ran across the street, straight through the moving traffic, ignoring the honking horns and the car that screeched to a halt just two feet away from him.

When he reached the far sidewalk, he joined the stream of pedestrians that was flowing by the hotel. He positioned himself next to a woman carrying shopping bags, hoping she would screen him if Vivian or Kennan happened to glance out the hotel entrance as he passed by.

When he came up to the entrance, he jerked his head around and looked in through the glass doors. Kennan was at the desk, registering. Vivian was standing off to one side, as if she wanted to divorce herself from the transaction.

Chris kept going. But his legs were suddenly weak under him, and, after a few steps, he faltered, came to a stop, and leaned against the stone facing of the hotel for support.

He stared down at the pavement dazedly, feeling sick to his stomach and a little foolish. He wished he hadn't done this now. It might have been better if he hadn't known.

He became aware that someone was looking at him. He glanced up and saw that a plump young woman with a broken-out complexion—a secretary on her lunch hour, perhaps—was avidly gazing at him as she approached. She had the slightly ga-ga smile of a fan recognizing him on the street.

He was on, he reminded himself. Even now, with his wife about to betray him on the other side of this wall, he was on.

Chris straightened up, smiled back at the girl vaguely, graciously, and quickly walked past her.

Vivian stared up at the mottled ceiling of the hotel room and wondered why she didn't feel better than she did. The sex had worked, as always. But the down had already started. Usually, it didn't happen until a couple of hours later.

Maybe it was because she hadn't been able to keep Chris out of her mind this time. She was uneasy about him. Suddenly, for no clear reason, he was behaving strangely. He had been distant to her all the previous evening and that morning; he had barely said a word to her. When she had left the apartment, he had seemed totally indifferent to her going. And yet, when she had turned back at the door, she had caught him looking at her steadily.

She supposed he was upset about signing for that TV movie. It was painful to his ego, she knew, that he had to take a job that was connected, even indirectly, with Ward.

But Chris had to be realistic. They both had to. You couldn't carry out a career, or a pleasant life, if you insisted on harboring grudges.

Beside her, on the bed, Ward lay in thoughtful silence, his hands behind his head. She imagined he was thinking business thoughts, looking ahead to whatever was waiting for him back at his office. She had, she estimated, five minutes left with him. She could calculate it with fair precision, since Ward, during his business day, timed everything down to the moment. He was in constant touch with his wristwatch, even when making love.

She thought of Chris and the TV movie again, and she was tempted to ask Ward the question that she had wanted to ask the last two or three times she had seen him. It would make no difference now. The contract was already signed.

"Ward," she asked, "did you have anything to do with Chris getting that movie?"

"No, it was the producer's idea." After a moment, he added, "I could only have had something to do with his *not* getting the movie."

"But you approved him."

"Yeah."

"Right away?"

"No. It was up in the air for a while."

"Until you started fucking me?"

"That's right."

"And then there was no problem?"

Ward turned his head toward her and smiled. "Let's say that, after that, I looked upon your household with a more sympathetic eye."

"You bastard!" Vivian said wearily, without anger. "Sex is always a negotiation with you, isn't it?"

"That's nothing new to *you*, is it?" His tone was dry and amused.

"I wasn't negotiating this time," she said. "I just wanted you."

"So you ended up doing your husband some good, without even meaning to. Why worry about it?" He removed his hands from behind his head, propped himself on one elbow, and looked at her curiously. "Do you feel cheapened?"

"Yes."

"Degraded?"

"Yes."

"Does it make you stop wanting me?"

She was silent for a moment, then quietly answered, "No."

Chris held the ruby-colored, tubular capsule between his fingertips for a moment, then popped it into his mouth. He downed it with water. It was his third Placidyl in six hours. He was overdoing it, he knew, he had better watch it. Well, it wasn't a usual day.

He left the bathroom, went out to the living room, and looked at the clock. It was ten past three; Vivian should be back any minute. He glanced around the room, and only then noticed that the Christmas cards on the mantelpiece had doubled. The day before, there had been four cards, the early birds. Now there were eight, standing in a row. He noticed also that Vivian had put out some fat red and green candles on the mantelpiece to go with the vases of holly. She had said they should have a Christmas tree, too, he remembered. We're a family now, she had said, and we should have a tree. Fine, Chris had said, let's have a tree. Just let me know when I should go out and get one.

That had been three weeks ago, and Vivian hadn't mentioned it again.

He went to the couch and stretched out full-length on it, resting his head on a throw pillow. The drug seemed to be taking effect already; the sweet relaxation was beginning to flow through him.

At the same time, the sense of unreality was sharpening, growing in him. It could be a side effect of the drug, he thought. Or it could be that life had actually, and inexplicably, gone out of kilter.

How else was he to think of it? Nothing made sense any more.

Only a week or so before, he had been awakened in the middle of the night by a light touch on his face. Through half-parted eyelids, he had seen that Vivian was bending over him, caressing his face tenderly, wonderingly. He had slipped back into sleep, feeling warmed and protected by her love.

Did she caress Kennan's face in the same way, when he dozed off after they had sex together? Did she brush her lips against his earlobe, ruffle his neck hair? Chris had thought these gestures existed only for him, were particular to her love for him. But perhaps they were just something she *did*, with any man.

He felt confused. He wanted to have an accurate view of Vivian, no matter what harsh truth it involved. But, even now, after what he had just discovered, he didn't know what she was—shallow, or phony, or so complex and ambiguous a creature he could never hope to understand her.

He heard a key turn in the lock, and he sat up quickly. Vivian came in, walked briskly through the entrance hall and into the living room, and greeted him with a bright smile. "Oh, what a day!" she moaned, mock-dramatic. "I went to Bonwit—I went to Bloomie's"—she had a cutesy habit of calling Bloomingdale's "Bloomie's," and it grated on him now—"and I just couldn't find it."

"Find what?" he asked.

"The right tablecloth—for when we have civilized company." She came over to him and looked down at him. "You just sitting here?"

"Yeah." His eyes were fixed on the crotch of her slacks. There was a small, round, wet stain, barely visible against the navy-blue. "We have plenty of tablecloths," he said.

"But the one I love—you know the one I mean?—with the checked pattern?—it's gotten ragged. We have to replace it."

"That's bullshit."

She looked at him perplexed. "Well, I'm not going to go on using it."

"That's bullshit," he repeated. "You weren't at Bonwit or

Bloomie's. You weren't looking for a tablecloth."

Her expression changed instantly. Her face went blank, and a wariness came into her eyes. In a careful, uninflected voice, she asked, "All right, where was I?"

"You were with that guy. I followed you from the restaurant to the hotel."

With an actor's eye, he studied her reaction. First, Vivian froze. Then she seemed to stand taller by an inch or two. Her face went hard, it took on a calm, and her gaze held steady on him. Pride, that was the way she was playing it. She was confronting him with unassailable pride, and dignity.

Her voice was very quiet as she said, "Now I suppose I have to defend myself?"

"You don't have to do anything," he said. "I'm just telling you I know."

"It has nothing to do with the way I feel about you."

Chris stared at her, astonished by the statement. "How can you say that?"

"Because it doesn't. It's just sex, that's all. It shouldn't affect us."

"You come back fresh from fucking another man and you say it shouldn't *affect* us?"

Her eyes flared with anger. "I'm not going to let you make me feel guilty!"

Her sharp, accusatory tone threw him for a moment, and he felt helpless to reply. His impulse was to apologize, explain that he wasn't trying to hurt her. Then the absurdity of it struck him. How had it gotten turned around, so that *he* was the wrongdoer? For Christ's sake, she *was* guilty!

Wearily, he said, "I'm just trying to understand."

"Trying to understand what?" He sensed something coiled and dangerous in her now. "Why I need to do this?"

Her use of the present tense chilled him. "Are you going to go on doing this?" he asked.

"Yes," she said defiantly, "if I want to."

"Why?" He asked it numbly, knowing he ought not to, but unable to stop himself. "Why do you have to do this?"

"Because sometimes I need a *man!*"

She knew what she had done the moment after she had said it. He could tell from the look of horror that came onto her face. She had killed it. With a half-dozen words, she had put an end to it. It could never be the same now.

Vivian stared at him for a few seconds. Then she bit her lip, ducked her head, and rushed out of the room.

Chris gazed blankly before him, at the mantelpiece with its cards, candles, and branches of holly, all the festive decor that meant a family together at Christmastime.

It was a joke. A goddamned, miserable joke.

22

THERE WAS a grand piano in Sergius Winter's living room, and on it there was a framed photograph of a young woman with a 1940s' hairdo. Without asking, Eric knew this was Dr. Winter's wife, and that she was long since dead. He looked at the photograph for a moment, and then turned back to Winter and politely asked, "Do you play the piano?"

"I used to play passably well," Winter replied, "when I was young. Then, for many years, I was forced to neglect it. But now that I've had to give up going to the clinic, I have some time for music again."

Winter spoke in the soft, slow way of someone who has been seriously ill and knows he must never excite himself. He sat very still in his chair, a thin, white-haired man in a cardigan sweater, frail and with the life delicate in him, so that it seemed that the icy wind that swept off Riverside Drive and in through the cracks of the windows might blow it out.

"If you would like a drink," Winter said, "please help your-self." He gestured toward the bar.

"Thanks, I think I will."

Eric crossed to the bar and poured himself some Scotch, which, in this peculiar situation, he felt he needed. There was no ice, and he didn't ask for it. He knew he was imposing on the old man as it was, and he wanted to put him out as little as possible. He returned with his glass and sat.

Winter watched him with a psychoanalyst's patience as he took a swallow of the whiskey. Then, when the conversation was ready to begin, he said, "So Delphine has dedicated her book to me. That's very thoughtful of her."

"Yes," Eric said. "And that, of course, is why I decided to come to see you."

Winter looked at him quizzically. "Because Delphine thinks so well of me?"

"Not simply that," Eric admitted. "In her dedication, she describes you, not only as her dear friend—but as her analyst."

"That was a long time ago, Mr. Bayliss."

"I realize that. But you must know her better than almost anyone else." He paused awkwardly. "And I feel I have to know her."

"As her patient?"

"No. As a friend of some of her other patients."

"You're concerned about them?"

Eric nodded. "I'm concerned."

Winter's gaze was calm and unsurprised, and, almost imper-ceptibly, his interest seemed to quicken. "Tell me what con-cerns you," he said.

Eric went on to describe, as succinctly as he could, the experi-ence that each one of them had had with Delphine. He told his own story in a few sentences, gave a little more time to Mandy, but concentrated mainly on Vivian and Christopher Greene.

Winter listened intently. When Eric was finished, he said, "I don't quite understand. I gather you disagree with Delphine's course of therapy in each of these cases. But do you expect *me* to comment on them?"

"I wanted to talk to you about them."

"Mr. Bayliss, surely you realize that it's improper for one doctor to criticize another doctor's work? Particularly when he has no connection with the patients involved?"

"Yes, I understand that, Dr. Winter. But I *would* like your opinion."

"I'm afraid my opinion wouldn't be of much help, since I don't know these other people. Perhaps," he added, "if you want to tell me more about *yourself*—"

"No," Eric said, "let's forget about me. I mean, my case isn't important. Delphine helped me kid myself that I was a writer, she confused me to the point where I quit my job, and she tried to turn me against the girl I love. But I'm a healthy-minded sort, I know now that I made some mistakes, and in the long run, I guess, no real harm has been done."

"I'm glad to hear that," Winter said with a slight smile.

"And Mandy Huber— Well, she had a good, working marriage, and Delphine broke it up. But Mandy isn't all that neurotic a person. In the end, things may turn out all right for her too." He paused, then asked, "But what about Christopher Greene?"

"What about him?" Winter echoed.

"He's the one who worries me. Maybe it's because I feel a little responsible."

"Responsible? Why?"

"Vivian's daughter came to me, just before Chris and Vivian got married, and pleaded with me to try to persuade them not to go through with it." He shrugged and said, "I stayed out of it."

"*Could* you have stopped it?"

"No. But at least I could have made an effort. Now Chris is starting to disintegrate before my eyes. He hasn't worked since last spring—he's all doped up on drugs—he's lost that quality of excitement he had, the youthful magnetism, and the poor guy keeps trying to convince himself he's happier than he's ever been."

"And you blame this on Delphine?"

"Yes," Eric said, "I blame it on her."

Winter thought for a moment. "I must admit," he said, "her course of therapy with this young man seems a little out of date. The more enlightened psychiatrists no longer deal with homosexuality as a disease. They think of it as an alternative life style. If a patient feels anxious with this life style, the therapist helps him adjust to it and be rid of his anxiety."

"Yes. And that would have been the sensible way to help Chris, right?" He looked at Winter questioningly. But the old man's expression remained carefully noncommittal. "Something has occurred to me, though," Eric went on. "I've remembered something that someone told me about Delphine. Someone who knows her pretty well and doesn't like her." He paused and tried to remember Jane Loring's words exactly. "She said that what Delphine wants is control over people. Pure, naked control—for its own sake."

Winter's mouth tightened. "Go on," he said quietly.

"Well, the surest way to gain control over someone is to help him live out his fantasy."

"This applies to Christopher Greene?"

"Yes. Because Chris didn't want to be homosexual. He wanted to be straight. He probably told himself that he really *had* been heterosexual all along, and it was only an accident that he'd been doing this other thing. So Delphine had nothing to gain by helping Chris to adjust to something he didn't think he wanted to be. But if she convinced him that he *was* as straight as he thought he was, pushed him into a marriage, and created a whole heterosexual self-image for him, she owned the guy."

Eric waited for Winter to make some comment. But the old man said nothing. He lowered his eyes and seemed to retreat into his thoughts. His pale face was drawn now, with a sick man's weariness, perhaps; or possibly it was something else, Eric thought, a deep sadness. At length, Winter looked up at him and asked, very gently, "Mr. Bayliss, why have you told me all this?"

"Because you know Delphine," Eric replied, "and you yourself are a psychotherapist." There was another, deeper reason, but he hesitated to mention it yet. "I want to understand more about this. And I want to find out if there is anything that can be done. I mean, doesn't your profession have some way of reviewing the work of its members? Disqualifying the ones who might be dangerous?"

"For gross misconduct, a doctor can be called up before the state board. For gross incompetence, a doctor can be sued. But are we discussing a malpractice situation here?" Winter asked. "Has a misdiagnosis led to a patient becoming paralyzed? Has a drug been given that has killed a patient?"

"No, of course not."

"Then there is very little that the psychiatric profession can do. You, as a layman, disagree with Delphine's recommendations in certain cases. You may be right, or, in the long run, she may prove to be right. This is a very gray area. There is no way we can be absolutely sure."

"But this is a science, isn't it? There must be some objective criteria."

"I'm afraid I must correct you, Mr. Bayliss," Winter said mildly. "Psychotherapy is not a science. It's an art. And an imperfect art, at best."

"There *is* a science of psychiatry, isn't there?"

"Oh yes, definitely. But, these days, it's mostly concerned with biochemistry. The majority of psychiatrists now believe that the causes of mental illness are physiogenic rather than psychogenic. So, the current research seeks to understand the delicate chemical balance of the brain, to isolate the substances that may be the key factors in mental disorders."

"But what about psychotherapy?" Eric asked. "It's important too, isn't it? And doesn't it have some scientific validity?"

Winter weighed the question for a moment. "Psychotherapy is of great importance, certainly," he answered, rather carefully, "and it is very necessary. There is valuable work being done in the area of supportive therapy, for instance, helping those who are dying, or those who have suffered the loss of a loved one. And therapy is needed for alcoholics, for drug addicts, for child abusers, for habitual criminals. In short, for any individual with a pattern of behavior that is destructive to himself or to others. In many of these cases, the intervention of a concerned, specially trained psychiatrist can help." He paused, then slowly repeated the second part of Eric's question. "But does verbal psychotherapy have scientific validity? You mean, I suppose, the way a shot of penicillin has scientific validity?"

"Yes," Eric said. "And I'm not talking about alcoholics and drug addicts. I'm asking about the kind of practice Delphine has. Or that you had before you started your clinic—when you were dealing with common, everyday neurotics."

Winter nodded. "They have done several major studies in the last quarter of a century. Each time, they have followed two groups of people that were identical except in one respect—the people in one group were in therapy, the people in the other group were not. What they found was that the neurotic symptoms of the individuals got better, stayed the same, or got worse in exactly the same proportion in both groups. They could not demonstrate, in any of these studies, that verbal psychotherapy has any curative value at all."

"But surely, in your own practice, you must have helped some people?"

"I would like to think I did," Winter replied. "And I'm sure Delphine has, too. But we should take this out of the medical context entirely," he went on. "Most people don't go to a therapist like Delphine because they have a disease that needs to be cured. Rather, they are people who are looking for guidance in life problems. In the old days, when the extended family was the basic social unit, such a person might have sought out his wise old grandfather for advice. Or he might have gone to his priest. But now the extended family has broken down and religious institutions have lost their hold. The belief in God itself has faded. It has been replaced, in most people's minds, by a belief in science. Just as the priest claimed to speak with the authority of God, the psychotherapist claims to speak with the authority of science." Winter paused, then with a faint smile said, "It's a questionable claim, certainly, but it may very well have a beneficial effect—since people need to believe in *something*. And, after all, the priest—and the wise old grandfather—usually gave sound advice. So, let us hope, does the psychotherapist."

"We're not talking about someone who's been giving good advice," Eric reminded him.

"Perhaps not. But how would you define good advice? When it comes to the problems of living, what seems to be good or bad advice depends on current social values. And a successful psychotherapist tends to express and reinforce the values of his society." After a moment, Winter asked, "What does Delphine say in her book?"

"She says that nobody cares about you but yourself. That you're the only one who knows what you really want. That you should try to get what you want, satisfy your own desires, and to hell with everybody else."

"What about feelings of guilt?"

"Guilt? She doesn't even consider it. Most of the hypothetical examples she gives are of people who want success. She says that, if you want riches and power, you should go after riches and power. Nothing else matters."

Winter nodded thoughtfully. "Very Adlerian," he commented.

"Adlerian?" Eric echoed uncertainly.

"Alfred Adler, as I'm sure you know, was Freud's first

apostate, the first disciple to turn against him. He rejected Freud's sexual theory and, instead, stressed the drive for power and the need for self-esteem. Adler's ideas—in a corrupted form, at least—have had a great vogue with New York therapists lately." He paused, then asked, "Does Delphine go into the question of how you should regard yourself?"

"Yes. It's the big thing with her. She says that if you learn to love yourself and think you're terrific, everything will work out fine."

"In other words, she's offering a therapy for selfish materialists—a rationale for narcissists." Winter smiled slightly. "As I said, a successful psychotherapist reflects the values of his society. Delphine's book could do very well."

"I imagine so." Eric was silent for a moment. It was time to get to it, he decided, time to ask the real question that was in his mind. "But there's something else that disturbs me, Dr. Winter. Something other than Delphine's intellectual approach."

"What is it?"

"As you've explained it, a psychotherapist invokes the authority of science to sanctify the current values of his society. And therefore he's likely to give very practical advice. But what if the psychotherapist is insane?"

"Insane?" Winter's face darkened. "Why do you ask that?"

"Well—" Eric felt very uncomfortable now, and he had difficulty in finding the proper words. "In my own field, I'm something of an expert. I mean, I'm an experienced reader, and I can detect the subtle nuances in a writer's work—the kind of things the average person might not catch. As I read through Delphine's book," he continued, "I got the sense of something deeply irrational about her. I began to suspect, in fact, that she wasn't in her right mind."

Winter's gaze was holding on him with a peculiar intensity. "Not in her right mind? What precisely do you mean by that?"

"It's hard to put my finger on it. It's something indefinable that comes across in her book. Dr. Winter, you were her analyst. Was she—or is she—mentally unbalanced?"

The life had gone out of Winter's face. It was a pale, uncommunicative mask. "I can't tell you that," he said softly. "I can't talk about her at all."

"But I have to know! Some people I care for have put their trust in her. If she's dangerous, I want to warn them."

Winter remained silent for a few moments. "I'm afraid you'll have to excuse me," he said finally. "I'm very tired. It's time for my nap."

Winter studied the notation on the cassette. It read: *Delphine Heywood—April 7—incident with sister*. He had searched through the several dozen tapes of Delphine that he had. He had kept them stored in his file cabinet, along with all of the other tapes that dated from that period of a few months when he had experimentally tape-recorded his sessions with his patients. As he remembered, Delphine had recounted at various times a number of incidents involving her sister. But this was the only tape that was specifically labeled as such. He knew it had to be the one he was looking for.

Winter crossed to the desk, switched on the desk lamp—it was getting dark in his study—and sat in the swivel chair. He opened a drawer, took out his tape recorder, set it on the desk before him, and inserted the tape in it. He pushed the PLAY button and heard the first few words of that long-ago session. Then he jumped ahead, hitting the FAST FORWARD button several times, until he found the section of the tape he wanted to listen to again.

". . . that I could *never* forgive her for," he heard Delphine say. "I could never forgive her for what she did on Daddy's birthday."

Winter leaned forward, resting his arms on the desk, and

listened closely. He heard himself ask, "Which birthday do you mean? When was this?"

"It was when I was fourteen and Ariane was twelve. By then, I was the real lady of the house. I did all the shopping, cooked all the meals. Ariane never did anything."

"Why didn't she?"

"Because she was lazy. All she ever did was look at movie magazines, try on clothes, and admire herself in the mirror. She was stuck up."

"Because she was pretty?"

"Because Daddy kept *telling* her she was pretty." He could hear the bitterness, a teenager's petulant bitterness, oddly coloring the mature woman's voice. "For his birthday, I was going to cook him a special dinner, roast beef, banana cream pie, all the things he liked the best. And I bought flowers and arranged them in vases all around the parlor. And I spent all day cleaning, so that Daddy would find the house spotless when he came home from the school.

"Ariane wouldn't lift her finger. She just stood around, making fun of me for working so hard. I got mad at her and told her she should help clean up, just so *she* would have done something to make Daddy happy. She got sulky, but then she picked up a dust mop and started dusting the surfaces in the parlor. She was clumsy and she knocked over the big vase with all the roses in it. It smashed to pieces on the floor.

"We were terrified, we didn't know what to do. It was Daddy's favorite vase. It had been in his family a long time. He had grown up with it and he loved it. Finally, we decided that we'd tell him it had fallen by itself. A gust of wind had blown through the house, the door had slammed shut, and it had fallen."

"So, what happened?"

"Daddy came home, and we showed him the pieces of the vase, and, as we expected, he was upset. I told him the story, just the way we'd worked it out. But Daddy started to get angry. He said it was a ridiculous story and I wasn't telling the truth. Suddenly, Ariane blurted out, 'Delphine broke it! *She* knocked it over!' Daddy looked at me stony-faced, as if he hated me. He said it was bad enough that I had broken the vase, but it was worse that I had lied to him. He didn't want to have dinner with us, he said. He told us to go to our rooms.

"We both went upstairs. I waited in the hallway until Ariane had gone into her room, then I went after her. She turned as I came in. I hit her in the face as hard as I could. She fell to the floor. I got on top of her and started strangling her. She tried to scream, but all that came out was a funny, choking sound. Her face turned purple and her eyes started to roll up into her head. That's when Daddy rushed in and pulled me off her." There was a brief silence. "In another minute, she would have been dead."

"But you didn't *intend* to kill her?"

"Yes. Yes, I did. I wanted to kill her."

"You just think you did. You would have stopped before it really happened."

"No, I wouldn't have. She was Daddy's pet. He couldn't see how bad she was. I could. And I knew what she had done to me. She deserved to be killed. I wish I *had* killed her."

Winter switched off the tape recorder. He was chilled now, as he had been then, by the emotionless calm in Delphine's voice. *She deserved to be killed. I wish I* had *killed her.* There had been no overtones in her voice, no suggestion of hidden conflict. It had had a purity, the frightening purity of her hatred.

He had approved her to be certified by the Institute. He had approved her to practice psychotherapy.

What had he done?

23

"First," Eric said, "let me give you back your book."

Delphine took the ream box from him. Her expression had turned grim. Amateur writer though she was she clearly knew the meaning of a returned manuscript. "You didn't care for it?"

"I found it very interesting," he said. "My professional opinion is that it has good commercial possibilities. My personal feeling is that I want no part of it."

Delphine regarded him calmly, as if she weren't surprised at all by his reaction. "It's not your kind of thing?"

"Not in the slightest."

With a light, indifferent shrug, she said, "Then I'll try elsewhere."

She crossed to her desk and put the ream box down on it with a crisp little bang, setting aside the matter with finality.

Then she returned and sat in her chair. "Let's begin," she said, as assured and professional as ever.

But Eric, this time, didn't sit in the patient's chair. He stood where he was and said, "We're not having a session today."

"We're not?"

"No. I just came here to return your manuscript. And to tell you that I won't be seeing you any more."

She looked up at him perplexed. "Can you explain?"

"I don't think I'm getting any good out of this."

He hadn't intended to put it so gently. But, unexpectedly, he found himself hesitating to hurt her feelings, wanting to soften the pain of rejection.

"It's too early to say that," Delphine said, in her reasonable tone. "We still have a long way to go."

It was her standard response, and he was not in the mood now for psychoanalytic clichés. He realized he would have to dispense with delicacy. "All right, I'll tell it to you straight," he said more firmly. "I think you've harmed me, you've tried to manipulate me, and I'm afraid of you."

She was expressionless for a moment. Then a sweet smile came onto her face. "Is this Eric speaking? Or is this Lucy speaking?"

"It's Eric speaking, goddamn it!" The playfulness of her tone had suddenly infuriated him. "Lucy is a sane, decent girl who happens to love me. You are a sick, irresponsible woman who doesn't give a shit for me!"

The violence of his outburst astonished him. But he was even more astonished by the fact that Delphine seemed completely untouched by it. It occurred to him that this might be a familiar situation for her, and that other patients before him might have lashed out at her in much the same way.

"There *was* a sick, irresponsible woman in your life," Delphine said, her voice meaningful. "But it wasn't me, was it, Eric?"

"No, it was my mother," he said curtly. "But why bring her up?"

"You know what's happening between us, don't you?"

He eyed her warily. "Transference? Is that what you mean?"

"Yes. You're projecting all the hostility you felt toward your mother onto me."

"Look, don't play your shrink games on me!" Her steady, luminous gaze was unsettling him now. "My mother was screwed up and domineering, but she *was* my mother. You are a stranger that I've been paying by the hour to help me. I'm not going to let *you* control me the way she did."

"So, what will you do?"

"As I said, I'm quitting this so-called therapy. I'm giving up my fantasy of being a writer. I'm asking for my job back at Galton and Hill. And I'm going to marry Lucy." Sarcastically, he asked, "Is that all right with you?"

"Yes, it is," she replied gently. "If this is what you want to do, do it."

"I will. From now on, I'm just going to be myself. I won't let you, or anyone else, influence me."

"Good," Delphine said.

"Okay, then." Eric had expected some resistance from her, and he felt awkward now that he found that he was getting none. "I guess there's nothing more to say. It's been interesting. Goodbye." He started toward the door.

"Eric—"

Reluctantly, he turned back. Delphine was sitting perfectly still and erect in her chair, gazing at him fixedly. In that moment, she seemed to him nothing so self-questioning as human flesh. Rather, she had the hard stolidity of a temple idol.

"You said that you didn't think you'd gotten any good from this." Her voice was flat, impersonal, with none of her professional warmth in it now. "But, a moment ago, you told me that, from now on, you were just going to be yourself. That you wouldn't let me, or anyone else, influence you. *That* is what you should have told your mother years ago. At last, you've been able to say it to *me*." Her face was softened, turned human again, by a quietly satisfied smile. "You're free now, Eric. You've gotten well."

It wasn't until Eric was out on the street that the oddity of it struck him. He was as convinced as ever that Delphine Heywood was dangerous. He was still determined to save his friends from her. But now he recognized the truth of what she had said.

In spite of everything, she had helped him. He was cured.

"I feel like she's cut off my balls!" Chris said anguishedly.

Delphine seemed distressed by the image. "You're exaggerating, don't you think?"

"Well, it's the way I feel. I mean, she starts screwing with another man—when I find out, she acts like she hasn't done anything wrong—and then she tells me she's going to go on screwing with this guy, if she wants to—" He threw up his hands helplessly. "And there's nothing I can do about it!"

"Nothing?"

"Not unless I leave her. And, if I don't, what am I supposed to do? Beat her up? Kill her? She knows I'd never hurt her. And she's taking advantage of it. She's made me look weak—feel weak—oh, she's cut off my balls, all right!" Uncomprehendingly, he asked, "Why is she doing this to me?"

"I don't imagine Vivian thinks she's doing anything to you at all," Delphine said. "You may not enter into it. She may be doing it entirely for herself."

"But we're *married*, for Christ's sake! Doesn't that mean you commit yourself? Give up being selfish? I've tried. I've tried to give her everything she wants. I've tried to please her—please her in bed, please her every other way. I haven't fooled around,

I've been faithful. And then she *hurts* me like this!" He felt the rage rising in him and he put his fist to his mouth to hold it back. "Oh, that cunt!" he moaned. "That miserable cunt!"

He was sobbing now and there was nothing he could do to stop it. He bit into his hand as the tears wet his face.

Delphine rose and came over to him. "Lie down for a while, Christopher," she said softly, taking him by the arm and helping him to his feet. "Lie down and relax. You'll feel better."

She led him over to the couch, then sat at one end of it herself. Blinded by tears, Chris felt for the leather, sank down onto it and lay back. His head came to rest on her lap. He closed his eyes and concentrated on the light touch of her hand, stroking his hair, the soothing warmth of her thighs.

He felt better and, at the same time, ashamed. He was like a little boy, he knew, who was feeling sorry for himself and had to be babied and comforted by his mother. He was almost thirty; he should be past this kind of thing.

He opened his eyes and looked up at her. "Delphine, will I ever be a man?"

"You're a man now, Christopher."

"If I were a man, Vivian wouldn't have done this."

"Don't be silly."

"That's what she said."

Delphine's hand paused in the midst of a caress. "She really said that?"

When he had told her the story, Chris had omitted this one detail. But he could no longer keep the pain of it to himself. He sat up, putting a few inches of distance between himself and his therapist, and without looking at her said, "It's the way she explained it." He voiced it with difficulty: "She said that sometimes she needs a *man*."

Delphine remained silent, as she pondered this for a while. "Christopher," she said finally, "there are other ways of asserting your manhood than through sex. Brute sex is merely the lowest, most primitive expression of masculinity. An artist, such as yourself, exists on a higher level. He asserts his manhood in his work. And very soon," she reminded him, her voice brightening, "you'll be working again."

"That TV movie? It's crap."

"But your talent is strong, of the first order, no matter what you appear in. And there will be other, finer movies after this one."

"You think so?"

"I'm sure of it."

She said it with such calm certainty that he could almost believe she had an inside line to the future. "Let's hope so," he murmured.

"It's unfortunate," Delphine went on, "that you've been out of work through these early months of your marriage. That has been the problem, I think. Not the sexual thing, but the fact that you've been unfulfilled in your career. This kind of dissatisfaction can affect both partners in a marriage equally." She paused, then asked, "Hasn't it affected Vivian?"

"Yeah, it's been tough on her, I guess."

"I don't think you should give up on the marriage yet. This little affair may be meaningless, simply an expression of Vivian's unhappiness with your situation. When your career is going well again, when you're happy, she'll be totally yours. She'll share your happiness with you."

"Maybe so." She made it sound plausible, the only sensible way of looking at it, and now he began to feel a little sheepish for having gotten hysterical in front of her. "You think I've made too big a thing of this?"

She smiled. "I think you may have overreacted."

"Yeah. Well, I didn't mean to cry like that."

"You should always let out your emotions."

"But I'm not usually a crybaby. Today's been different. I've felt tense, teetering on the edge of something, ever since I got up." After a moment, he said, "I'm out of pills."

Delphine's face darkened. "Already? When did I write the last prescription?"

He felt a twinge of anxiety. Maybe this time she wouldn't give him a prescription. "Oh, a few weeks ago," he replied casually.

"No," she said, "it was more recently. I remember now. It was just two weeks ago." She gazed at him thoughtfully, a bit disturbed. "You must have been taking five or six pills a day."

"Well, I've been going through hell, you know that," he said. "The pills have helped. Without them, I might have killed myself."

He had said it with no particular emphasis, simply as a figure of speech. But he sensed the sudden tensing in her.

"You don't mean that," she said.

"Yes, I do." He followed up on it now, with the quick cunning he had had as a child, when he would discover a key that would make his mother give him what he wanted. "Sometimes it seems to be the answer. I think that all I have to do is go out the window—and, in a couple of seconds, it's over. Nothing can hurt me any more."

"You must never talk like this again, Christopher." Delphine's voice was low and intense, her bright gaze was insistent. After a moment, she said, "I'll give you another prescription."

"Thanks, Delphine. It's only for a little while, until I get through this. I know I'm going to be fine." He reached out and shyly, gratefully, took her hand. "As long as I have you, everything will be all right."

PART FOUR

24

"DON'T LET Babe get to you," the stunt man said.

Chris, startled out of his thoughts, looked at the stunt man quickly. The two of them were alone at the foot of the pier, not paired at this spot for any particular reason, but simply standing around aimlessly, waiting for the next shot to be set up. The director, the crew, and Babe were all at the far end of the pier. The camera was in position and they looked almost ready to go.

"He isn't getting to me," Chris said.

"Babe always does this," the stunt man said.

Chris gazed at him curiously now. The stunt man, under his hip-length leather jacket, was dressed the same as Chris was under his sheepskin coat; a blue work shirt, blue jeans, a large-buckled belt. His hair had been cut, tinted, and curled to match Chris's hair. In another hour or so, as the climax of the fight scene, he would plunge off the pier in Chris's place. The water was midwinter icy, the undercurrent was reputedly tricky, but none of this seemed to concern the stunt man right now. Rather, he was regarding Chris with sympathy, worried that he might have been unduly upset by Earl Grayson's bad mouth.

"Have you worked with Babe before?" Chris asked.

"Yeah, I been in three or four of his pictures," the stunt man drawled. He had a Texas accent to go with his permanently sunburned look. Chris guessed that he might have been on some small-time rodeo circuit before he made the move to Hollywood. "Babe can get real mean with young guys like you."

Chris looked down the pier to where Earl Grayson, known to everyone in the industry as "Babe," was standing, talking with the director. Six foot four, studiously larger than life, he loomed over all those around him.

A couple of minutes before, Babe had swaggered up the pier and had joined them for a moment. "We'll be rehearsing the fight soon," he had told Chris. Then, with his world-famous, arrogant-amiable smile and a jerk of his head toward the stunt man, he had said, "Maybe you'd better have Sammy here give you some pointers on how not to get hurt. It'd be a shame if a pretty face like yours got busted up by accident."

Chris had merely smiled back at him. But now his cheeks tingled as he remembered it. "I don't think Babe cares for me," he said to the stunt man. "I gave him some notes on his acting."

The stunt man chuckled. "No, I don't suppose Babe would take to that. But that's not the reason he's been ridin' you. It's because you're too good."

"How can anyone tell?" Chris was genuinely perplexed. The unfamiliar, stop-and-go technique of filmmaking confused him, and he himself had no way of judging whether he was being terrible or competent.

"They've been watchin' the dailies in New York. You've been lookin' great—the a.d. told me. And Babe knows it. So he's tryin' to rattle you." The stunt man gave him a kindly smile. "Don't take it personal."

"I'll try not to."

Chris was pleased to hear that he was, in fact, doing well. And he would have liked to believe that that was all there was to it—an aging star's jealousy of a young actor's talent. But he knew there was something more. He had sensed Earl Grayson's antipathy to him from the first day they had started shooting in this Cape Ann fishing village, though Babe had always been careful to overlay his hostility with a comradely jovialness. But last night at the inn, for one moment at least, the ugliness had surfaced.

Babe's room was next to his, and, as usual, Chris had been kept awake by the boozy voices, the roars of laughter, coming through the wall. Babe held court in his room almost every night, breaking out the whiskey for his invited favorites. These affairs at their peak could be as noisy as a college beer bust.

Last night though, suddenly and inexplicably, everything had gone silent. Then Chris had heard whispers in the hallway, stealthy footsteps.

Curious, he got up, went to the door and looked out. Babe's guests—two supporting actors, the assistant director, and the assistant cameraman—were grouped around a closed door, farther down the hallway. The a.d. was standing on the assistant cameraman's shoulders, peeking through the old-fashioned transom above the door. He was smiling gleefully at whatever it was he was seeing. The others were suppressing giggles, like mischievous little boys.

Chris quickly put on his trousers, went out into the hallway, and looked into Babe's room.

Babe was half sitting, half reclining on the bed, a glass of whiskey clutched in his huge hand. Even in this New England inn, in a room decorated with framed prints of clipper ships, he emanated his movie persona. He was the strong silent cowboy, relaxing in the bunkhouse after a day on the trail.

"Come on in, Chris," Babe said genially.

Chris stepped into the room. "What's going on?" he asked,

gesturing toward the hallway.

"The script girl picked up a waitress down at the restaurant," Babe said. "The boys are watching the fun."

"But what are they doing?" Chris asked, rather stupidly. "You mean, the script girl is—?"

"Yeah, she's a dyke." Casually, Babe asked, "They got dykes down in New York, Chris?"

There seemed to be some sly innuendo intended. "There are a few," Chris replied.

Babe was silent for a moment. Then he asked, "Care for a drink?"

"No, thanks." It occurred to him that this was the first time he had been alone with Babe. He should take advantage of the opportunity, he realized, before the others returned. "But there's something I'd like to talk to you about."

"Sure." Babe waved his hand toward a chair. "Sit down."

Chris came further into the room, but didn't sit.

"What's on your mind?" Babe asked.

"You know, Babe," Chris began hesitantly, "when we do scenes together—well, it would be a big help to me if you would look at me."

Babe's face darkened. "I *do* look at you."

"You sort of look at me," Chris said, "but not really. You don't look me in the eye."

"It comes across fine to the camera."

"Maybe to the camera, but not to *me*. It's hard for me to work without eye contact."

Babe regarded him impassively for a moment. Then he stared at his glass morosely. "Well, I should have expected it," he said finally. "I should have known, if I agreed to do one of these cockamamie TV things, I'd get saddled with someone like *you*."

"Now, don't take offense, Babe," Chris said.

"I'm not offended. I just don't know what the hell to make of it." Babe had a mildness to his tone, but his mouth had tightened with repressed anger. "You know how long I've been working in movies, Chris? Thirty-four years! I've been getting star billing for thirty years. And in all that time nobody has *ever* complained that I don't look people in the eye!"

"Well, maybe I'm used to working a different way," Chris said uncomfortably.

"Because you're from the New—York—stage?" Babe stretched out the phrase, mocking it. "I've worked with stage actors before. Most of them weren't worth a bag of warm spit in front of the camera. But they kept their mouths shut. None of them tried to tell me how to do my job!" His voice was quivering with rage now. "But you're different, aren't you, Chris? Yeah, they told me all about you," he said meaningfully, a malicious gleam coming into his pale blue eyes. "You're different in a lot of ways."

"I'm sorry I brought this up," Chris muttered. "Let's forget about it."

"You'd *better* be sorry!" Babe roared. "Because you're not gonna be able to play your games with *me*. I'm not one of your fag New York producers!"

"See you in the morning," Chris said grimly. He turned and started for the door.

"Hey, don't go away mad!" Babe called after him, with sudden friendliness. Chris turned back. Babe was looking at him with the crinkly, good-guy smile that had made him beloved by millions. "I wish I could help you, son," he said softly. "I guess I just don't need to have my cock sucked."

No, Chris thought now, as he watched the a.d. separate from the group and start up the pier toward him, it wasn't just the work. Babe had made it personal. *Very* personal.

The a.d. stopped halfway up the pier. "Chris!" he called out. "We need you!"

Chris walked down the pier and joined the others.

The director, a brisk little man in a peacoat, said, "Okay, Chris, we're going to rehearse the fight now."

"I'm ready," Chris said.

"Have you done any staged fights before?" the director asked.

"Nothing elaborate," Chris replied. "Not movie-type fighting."

"All right," the director said, "I'll just block it out roughly. And then I'll let Babe show you the fine points. He's the expert." He turned to the star. "How many on-screen fights have you had now, Babe?" he asked deferentially. "Over a hundred?"

Babe smiled good-naturedly. "Who's been countin'?" In front of any gathering large enough to be thought of as an audience, Babe would drop his "g's" and grow subtly more twangy.

The director and crew chuckled, the director most audibly of all. Then the director went to the very end of the pier and, tentatively pantomiming the movements, described the action of the fight. He addressed Chris mainly, since, presumably, he had already worked it out with Babe. He specified what their positions should be at every stage of the fight in relation to the camera. Then he walked away, saying, "Okay, Babe, you can take it from here."

Babe removed his heavy plaid lumberman's jacket and tossed it aside. Chris took off his sheepskin coat, being careful not to wince from the bite of the near-freezing air. They faced each other, about five feet apart. Chris, who was reasonably tall, felt oddly dwarfed. Glancing down, he saw that the giant Babe had built-up heels on his shoes, giving him almost the height he would have had in cowboy boots.

"The first thing you should know," Babe said to him, "is that we're doin' this without sound. We'll give 'em a lot of movement on camera, and they'll put in all the bone-crunchin' sounds later. It's the sound that makes the people think they're seein' a real brawl. "Now," he went on, "you're throwin' the first punch. So aim a right at me. Try to miss my jaw by this much." Babe held up his thumb and finger, indicating a three-inch distance.

Chris set himself, then threw a rather sloppy, uncoordinated right that passed Babe's chin at the requested distance.

Babe automatically began his simulated recoil from the punch, but then stopped in the midst of it. "What the hell was that?" he asked, staring at Chris in amazement. "For Christ's sake, can't you even throw a punch?"

"I'm the shipyard owner's son," Chris said. "I've gone only to the best schools. I wouldn't know how to throw a punch properly."

"Don't give me that Method crap!" Babe said disgustedly. "This is a fight in a movie."

"It's between your character and my character. We have to be truthful."

Babe turned his head toward the director and gave him a "can-you-believe-this-guy?" look. But the director's expression was carefully noncommittal. For the time being, it was clear, he was staying out of it.

Babe let out his breath wearily and looked at Chris again. "Okay, then," he said, with the heavy patience of someone talking to a retardate, "accordin' to the script, you've been workin' on my crew for two or three months now. You've been learnin' the shipbuilding business from the ground up. You've been followin' us around, goin' to bars with us, watchin' us get into scrapes, watchin' us get into fights. You've been learnin' how to be a man. Maybe, by now, you even know how to throw a punch. All right?" He paused, but not quite long enough for Chris to answer. "Now, let's try it again."

Chris planted his feet a little more firmly and threw a straight right, putting all of his weight behind it, the way he had been taught at the athletic club in Racine. For safety's sake, he missed Babe's head by more than a foot.

Babe turned to the crew and threw up his hands in a broad

gesture of exasperation. "For cryin' out loud, it's like he's wavin' a lily at me!"

The crew laughed.

"It was a good punch," Chris said.

"Son," Babe said, turning back to him, "we can't spend all day teachin' you how to fight."

"It was a good punch,' Chris repeated, through clenched teeth.

"Okay, okay," Babe said impatiently, "let's go on to the next thing. When you hit me, I fall on my back. Then you throw yourself on me. What you're tryin' to do is pin me so you can smash me some more. But, before you can, I flip you."

"When I throw myself on you, how do I keep from hurting you?"

Babe did a little take. Then, turning to the crew, he asked loudly, "Did you hear that? This kid is afraid he's gonna hurt me!"

The crew chuckled appreciatively.

"You don't have to worry about me, son," Babe said to him with kindly condescension. "Just look out for yourself. Now, let's mark it."

They squared off again. Chris threw the straight right and Babe staggered backward and fell. With easy, slowed-down movements, Chris started to pounce on him. Babe's knees came up quickly and caught him in the chest. Chris felt himself turn in the air and then he came down on his back hard.

The wind was partially knocked out of him, but he managed to scramble to his feet at once. Babe had risen just as quickly.

"Now I hit you with a left," Babe said, throwing a round-house hook, "and you go back a step." Chris did so. "Then a right—" As the fist passed his chin, Chris went back another step. "—and a left." This time, Chris stood where he was. He was inches from the edge of the pier. "And here's where we cut to a long shot of Sammy goin' into the drink for you."

"You got that, Chris?" the director asked suddenly.

"Yeah, I think so," Chris replied.

"All right," the director said, "let's do it."

As they returned to their original positions, Babe said to him, more confidentially, in his off-screen accent, "Let's try not to screw it up. This picture is running overtime as it is. I want to get home to my old lady."

"I want to get home to my wife, too," Chris said.

Babe stopped and looked at him, with genuine surprise. "You got a wife?"

"Yeah, I've got a wife."

"Who fucks her for you?"

"Let's get set," the director said crisply.

Chris was looking down at the splintered wood of the pier. The harbor sounds had faded. He felt suspended in a cold, silent void. He raised his head and stared into Babe's eyes.

"Roll 'em."

The director's voice seemed very distant. Chris waited.

"Action."

Chris stepped forward and hit Babe in the mouth. The big man toppled backward and fell to the pier heavily.

Chris sprang onto him, pinning his shoulders with his knees. He had a brief image of Babe's stunned expression, of the blood welling up from his mouth and the smashed bridgework tilting at an angle. Then he drove his fist into his face.

He hit him again, and then again, and he had his fist raised to hit him still one more time when the arms seized him and pulled him away.

The cab stopped on the opposite side of the avenue from his building. Chris paid the driver, then clambered out, pulling his suitcase after him. The cab went on and he was alone on a Fifth Avenue that seemed as empty, dark, and still as the New England village he had just left behind him.

He gazed at his building, counting up the rows of windows

until he reached his apartment. The lights were on. Vivian was still up. Even as he looked, he saw her silhouette appear briefly on the curtains that were drawn over the bedroom window. She seemed to be wearing a robe.

Chris stood where he was. He didn't step off the curb, he didn't start across the street. Suddenly, he was unable to go forward, to carry out the last part of the homecoming pattern.

He wasn't prepared, he realized. He was returning a week early, unexpectedly, without even phoning first, and he had no good explanation for her.

The hard facts were clear enough, of course. He had put Babe Grayson in the hospital. The movie had been suspended. And he had been fired.

He could make a funny, colorful story out of it, try to amuse her with it. It *was* funny, he supposed—except for one thing. He had just wiped out his movie career. It was over even before it had started.

Chris looked up at the bedroom window again and a sudden, chilling throught came to him. What if she weren't alone? What if someone were in the bedroom with her?

It was ridiculous, he told himself. Of course, she was alone. The bad times were over. It was going to be better between Vivian and him. Delphine had promised it. *When your career is going well again,* she had said, *when you're happy, she'll be totally yours. She'll share your happiness with you.*

But all signals were off now. He had screwed up. How could he break it to Vivian that he had blown all of her hopes for him in one brief fit of anger?

So, then what? It was back to reality. But what reality? Lying around the apartment, an apartment he had never felt was really his, hiding away in the corners of it to escape her contempt?

He wasn't supposed to be there, he remembered. He wasn't supposed to be there for another week.

A cab was coming down the avenue. His hand went up, almost without his realizing it. The cab slowed.

For a moment, he was about to correct himself, wave the cab on. But he didn't. His hand remained still in the air.

The cab came to a stop in front of him. Chris opened the back door, threw his suitcase in, and climbed in after it. He sat back wearily and said, "Downtown."

"Where to, downtown?" the driver asked.

"Just downtown."

25

I⊤ WAS WARM in the dressing area behind the screens and the air was slightly sour with the combined nerves of all of them, the twenty models, Phyllis and her assistants, and herself. The canned rock music resonated deafeningly in the vaulted hotel ballroom and the quickly changing projections were spilling their kaleidoscopic colors through the screens onto them. But Mandy was aware of nothing for the moment but Trish Ludlow's pearl earrings. She moved in closer, bringing her head to within a foot of Trish's gorgeous, angular face, and focused on the earrings. "I'm not sure I like those," she muttered to herself.

On the prepared tape, another musical number suddenly came on, one even more ecstatic than its predecessor. It startled Mandy, and, distracted for a moment, she allowed herself to envision what the audience was seeing on the other side of the screens.

Mandy herself had seen it at the rehearsal for the first and only time—Oliver Dussault's creation, his opening for her fashion show. Slide projections flashed onto eight connected, side-by-side screens, eight different images projected simultaneously, the images changing in an irregular rhythm up and down the line; brightly colored fabric designs, angled segments of Mandy's outfits—a bit of skirt here, a bit of jacket there, Mandy's face, MANDY in huge letters, her face again, her name again. It seemed to her that her name or face popped up on one or the other of the screens forty or fifty times.

Mandy had felt embarrassed. But she hadn't said anything to Oliver. She knew there was nothing she could do about it. She had paid for it and she would have to go along with it.

She concentrated on the pearl earrings again. She had carefully accessorized each outfit several days before, but she wasn't beyond making last-minute changes, and she was beginning to think that one was called for now. Trish was wearing one of the simpler Mandy outfits, a striped blouse with a front-pleated gray skirt, and the pearls might be a little too much.

"No, they're wrong!" Mandy said suddenly. "Wrong!" She reached out to remove the offending earrings.

"If you say so, bubi," Trish murmured dreamily.

In these frantic last minutes before the models went out onto the runway, Mandy had been too concerned with the clothes and accessories to pay any attention to the people wearing them. But now, as she disengaged the earrings from Trish's earlobes, she noticed the odd, glazed look in the model's eyes. Trish's languid half-smile seemed peculiar too; it had a goofiness to it.

Mandy pocketed the earrings and went over to where Phyllis was counting, for a second time, the extralong, narrow shawls that were laid out on the big table.

"Is Trish stoned?" Mandy asked.

"I wouldn't doubt it," Phyllis replied.

"What's she on?"

"Meth, I believe."

"My God! Nobody told me she took drugs!"

"What *were* you told?"

"Oliver said she was deliciously trashy, and we should use her."

"She's trashy, all right," Phyllis said. "And she's a speed freak."

Mandy looked over at Trish, who was standing where she had left her. Horrified, she realized that some of her most exciting creations were about to go up for judgment before the big buyers and fashion editors, displayed on the gaunt figure of a model so spaced-out she hardly seemed to know where she was.

Well, maybe no harm would come of it, and anyway it was too late to do anything about it. The models were lining up to make their entrances. Trish drifted over and eased into her place in the line.

Phyllis took her position by the entrance to the runway. Everyone was still now, waiting for the light change. A few moments passed and then the music abruptly turned sensuous, the screens went dark and the lights came up on the runway. Phyllis signaled with her hand and the first model started out.

Mandy rushed to the peephole that was between two of the screens and peered through it. It gave her a clear view of the runway and that part of the audience sitting along its length on the far side. The model walked to the very end of the runway, moving swiftly in time to the music, a slack, cold smile on her lips, her arms swinging casually, her hips swaying invitingly, as if she were a high-priced prostitute cruising one of the more chic boulevards of the world. It was a deliberate effect; Oliver had coached all of the models in what he called the "hooker walk." Trashy sex was in this year, he had said.

The second model came out, just as the first one turned to walk back up the runway; and the show continued in this rhythm, a new model appearing every ten seconds or so. All of the girls walked in the same provocative way, and each had found her own discreetly brazen expression, but at least, Mandy noted thankfully, they were being restrained. As it was, the hooker thing was at variance with the numbers that were being displayed in the opening part of the show. They were the kind of things Mandy had designed at Huber Casuals, simple print dresses and blouse-and-skirt combinations; clothes for modest working girls, not professional seductresses. Still, so far, the show seemed to be going well. Several of the numbers, new variations on her old dependables, received light but sincere-sounding applause.

Then Trish came out and started down the runway, a vacant smile on her lips. With Trish, there was no restraint. She moved a little more slowly than the others, with the exhausted sensuality of a Times Square whore near the end of a hard Saturday night. Her hip swing was exaggerated and gamely challenging, and she paused at the end of the runway, swaying trancelike, to look down at the buyers in the front rows through half-closed eyelashes. The men visibly perked up.

An interesting performance, perhaps, but it certainly didn't do much for a striped blouse and a front-pleated gray skirt.

Mandy rushed over to the entrance and met Trish as she came off the runway. "Cool it, Trish!" she whispered sharply. "You're supposed to be selling my clothes, not your ass!"

"Fuck you, bubi," Trish said sweetly, and drifted on to make her change.

Mandy went back to the peephole. The models were coming out in her more adventurous numbers now—her strapless bloomers, her crepe-de-chine dress with flying ribbons, her thigh-high culottes with ballooning big sleeves. All of the models were now wearing Mandy shawls. This was the gimmick she had conceived for her show, the brilliant touch to cap her more imaginative creations—a twelve-foot-long, narrow, brightly colored shawl. Each model wore one of these shawls twined around her like an exotic snake, coiled about her neck, her arms, her waist and hips, the loose ends flapping.

It was a stunning effect, Mandy thought happily, as she saw it realized on the runway; mad but fun, a bit silly but stylish, the kind of thing she had never had the nerve to try until now. She peered at her models, parading in their crazy long shawls, and savored the kooky look of it.

Then she noticed that the audience had gone silent. The applause had stopped. She sensed a resistance in the stilled ballroom, a hostility, perhaps.

Mandy stepped back from the peephole, suddenly panicked. Glancing toward the runway entrance, she saw that Trish was about to go out again, wearing her very favorite design, a mid-thigh bubble dress of checked silk taffeta in candy colors. An assistant was wrapping one of the long shawls around her.

Mandy hurried over to Trish. "Don't slouch along out there," she whispered to her. "Move fast. Keep up the tempo."

Trish opened her mouth to say something, but she didn't have the chance. It was time for her entrance and she shot out onto the runway.

Mandy dashed back to the peephole. She saw that Trish was whipping down the runway rapidly, her legs flashing angrily under the bubble dress. Obviously, she had taken offense.

Mandy felt a sudden apprehension. For all the briskness of Trish's walk, there was a perilous instability to her, as if she were careening along a cliff's edge. It occurred to Mandy now that the reason Trish had moved so slowly before was that she was too stoned to be sure of her balance. The long shawl was coming undone around her, and, as Trish made her turn at the end of the runway, Mandy sensed the disaster about to happen. A moment later, it did. The loosened shawl tangled Trish's legs and she went down in an ungainly heap.

The audience laughed. Trish struggled to her feet, glared at the men in the seats by the runway, then thrust up her middle finger fiercely. The finger, Mandy noticed with a sick, sinking feeling, was aimed in the general direction of the buyer from Neiman-Marcus.

Mandy buried her face in her hands. Maybe it hadn't really happened, she thought dazedly. Maybe she had just imagined it.

But, when she lowered her hands, she saw Trish reappear in the dressing area, her hair disheveled. She angrily flung the shawl aside.

Mandy rushed over to her. "How could you *do* that?" she asked in anguish.

"Did you hear what that guy said to me?"

"I don't care who said what to you! You've ruined the whole thing!"

"What do you mean *I* ruined it?" Trish stared at her scornfully. "I didn't design this shit, bubi."

"How dare you?" Mandy gasped. "How dare you?"

But Trish was no longer there. She had brushed past her and was lost in the crowd of models who were changing for the finale.

Mandy sank into a chair and stared at the floor dully. She had done the best she could do. If people didn't appreciate it, that was *their* problem.

But she had never felt so terribly alone in her life.

At length, Mandy looked up again, and took in her breath with shock. She was surrounded by papier-mâché caricatures of her own face, grinning at her.

Then she realized what they were. Oliver had designed Mandy masks for the finale. Each model was carrying a likeness of her face, fastened on a stick. The masks hadn't been ready in time for the rehearsal. They were being used now for the first time.

Phyllis, tight-lipped, lined up the models by the runway entrance. The assistants rushed from girl to girl, adjusting the shawls. The models were holding up the masks, completely covering their faces with them, obliterating their identities. Mandy, glancing up and down the line, couldn't even tell which one of them was Trish. Each model was nothing now but a grotesque travesty of herself.

The music of the finale came on. Phyllis gave the signal, and the masked models, hips swinging, filed out onto the runway.

The finale music was the loudest, brassiest number of all. But it wasn't so loud that Mandy couldn't hear the first snicker in the audience. Or the snickers that followed.

Don't look! she told herself. Don't look!

But she had to. Fearfully, she rose, went to the peephole, and peeked out.

The models were milling about the runway in general disorder. The masks seemed to have confused them, deprived them of their bearings; the eyeholes, evidently, were too small for them to see through. But, elegant to the end, they strutted bravely and uncertainly, like so many blind beauties. Two of them bumped into each other and their shawls came undone and wilted like wet spaghetti around them.

Mandy had seen as much as she could bear. She turned away from the peephole, numb with humiliation.

Soon it would be over, she consoled herself. Then she would go back to her apartment and never come out again.

There was a reception in the lounge afterward—or there would have been if enough people had lingered.

But, when Mandy finally got up her courage to appear, she found about a dozen members of the audience standing by the long tables that were laden with bottles of champagne for a hundred. The only other people in the ballroom lounge were the members of her staff. All of the models had vanished. Oliver Dussault, not too surprisingly, hadn't stayed, either.

Those few buyers who had remained were the ones she had been most friendly with in the old days at Huber Casuals. They approached her now in the spirit of kindness and uttered the appropriate adjectives—"lovely"—"fascinating"—"exciting." But they mouthed them with the sweet, sad smiles of mourners at a funeral. Their respects paid, they, too, quickly vanished.

Nan Powell of *Women's Wear Daily* passed by Mandy on her way out. "Some people would call it an ego trip, darling," she said, barely breaking her step to purr it. "But I thought it was interesting—what you *tried* to do." And she walked on.

Mandy gazed after the departing fashion editor. At least old Nan was consistent, she thought bitterly. She clawed you when you were down just the same as when you were on top.

"Don't pay any attention to her," a familiar voice said behind her.

She turned. Jeff was standing there, looking shyly at her. He seemed to have appeared from nowhere.

"What are *you* doing here?" she asked, astonished.

"I crashed," he admitted with an apologetic smile.

"You mean, you saw the show?"

"I saw it."

"Then I suppose you're glad!" she said with sudden anger. "I fell on my ass! Doesn't that make you happy?"

"No, it doesn't make me happy," Jeff replied quietly. "I'm not happy at all." He paused, then said, "I felt like taking a punch at one or two of those guys who laughed."

"Why? Why should you care?"

"Because that was some of your best work up there."

There was no mistaking the sincerity of his praise, and she instantly melted with gratitude. "You really think so?"

"Two or three of the numbers were truly exciting conceptions," he said, "your finest ever." With a shrug, he added, "Of course, the presentation was faulty."

"Oh, brother, was it ever!" Ruefully, she said, "I really made a botch of it, didn't I?"

"All you needed was guidance," he said mildly. "That's all you've ever needed—a little guidance."

Mandy gazed at him silently for a moment. She still couldn't get used to his new look. But she realized now that, inside that slim, unfamiliar body, he was still the same patient, good-natured Jeff.

"So, how's the business?" she asked. She knew the answer already, but she had an urge to torture herself more by hearing it.

"Pretty good," he replied casually.

"*Pretty* good! They say you're having your best year ever."

"In gross sales, maybe." He shrugged. "But it hasn't been the same without you. Huber Casuals has gotten dull. What's the point of getting richer, if you become boring?"

"What about your new designer?" she asked, a bit acidly. "You don't find her too entertaining?"

"She's a good technician. But she isn't you."

"I didn't bore you, huh?"

"No, Mandy," he said, "that's one thing I can say. In all the years we were together, you never, for one moment, bored me."

He said it with a simple fervor that touched Mandy, and, unexpectedly, tears came to her eyes. But she fought back the emotion. She had to keep her cool with him. Too much had happened, after all.

"What about your private life?" she asked. "I hear it's been pretty exciting."

"Ridiculous, you mean," Jeff said with a wry little laugh. "I'm forty-seven years old. What's a man my age doing trying to be a swinger? No," he concluded, "there's nothing in it."

"I'm sorry to hear that," she said, not quite sincerely. "I thought, at least, *you* were having a good time."

He quickly picked up on her implication. "It hasn't been too great for you, either?"

She looked away unhappily. "Why talk about it? What's done is done."

"What's done can be undone," he said. "I mean, in business, for instance, nothing is eternal. Companies split—companies merge. The only thing that doesn't change is people. You and I, Mandy—we really don't change."

She met his gaze again. "You don't think so?"

"No, I don't." With a touch of uneasiness, he added, "Though maybe your shrink wouldn't agree."

"Don't mention her," she said darkly.

A slow, pleased smile came onto Jeff's face. "Okay," he said, "we won't. We've got too much else to discuss. Your new designs—and other things." With elaborate casualness, he asked, "Do you have time to go out for a drink with me now?"

He was the ageing little boy again of a dozen years before, trying to be worldly as he timidly asked her out, and Mandy couldn't help but smile.

"I have time," she said.

26

THERE WERE new drapes on the living room windows, Eric noticed, particularly handsome, expensive-looking ones. But he decided not to comment on them. He didn't want to raise, even as something unspoken, the question of where Vivian had gotten the money. He wasn't there to pry into her current love life. He had dropped by to talk about other things.

He lounged back in the armchair, took a sip of his Scotch, regarded her bare thigh for a moment—her housedress was split to her hipbone; he hadn't seen her wear anything quite so provocative since before her marriage—then, casually, as if simply making conversation, said, "I hear Mandy and Jeff have gotten back together."

"Yes, isn't it wonderful?" Vivian said brightly. "Jeff moved back in yesterday. Mandy called me this morning to tell me about it. She sounded ecstatic. She says she feels like a newly-wed."

"What happens with her business?"

"She's dissolving it. She's joining up with Jeff again at Huber Casuals."

"So, they're right back where they started," Eric commented.

"No, it's better now. Delphine says they needed this break-up." She paused, then recited carefully: " 'To purge and re-affirm the marriage.' "

"She told Mandy that?"

"She told *me* that. Mandy isn't seeing Delphine anymore."

"I should hope not," Eric murmured.

"Jeff insisted she stop going to her—as a condition of their getting back together, I guess. He's never really understood what Delphine has done for Mandy," she said, a bit sadly. "But it doesn't make any difference now, anyway. Mandy has gotten all she could from her."

"Sure," Eric said, "Delphine almost ruined Mandy's marriage, almost ruined her career. What more could she do for her?"

Vivian gazed at him coolly. "I know you feel hostile to Delphine. She told me how you turned against her," she said, with a touch of reproval, "after she guided you to your big break-through."

"Let's not talk about *that*," he said quickly.

Eric felt suddenly uneasy, not simply because he realized that Delphine had told Vivian more about his case than she had any right to, but also because it occurred to him now that this visit was badly timed. He had waited too long.

He had intended to have this heart-to-heart talk with her months before. As soon as he had seen the truth about Delphine, he had wanted to warn Vivian and Chris immediately. But then Chris had gone off to act in that TV movie, the one that had worked out so disastrously for him. Eric had decided to wait until he got back.

But Chris never had come home. He had simply disappeared. The marriage had abruptly ended. Vivian had been shattered, and Eric had known it wasn't the time to raise doubts in her mind about her psychotherapist. Vivian had needed her more than ever.

Then, also, despite his good intentions, his selfish concerns had prevailed and had pushed the matter aside. When he had gone back to Galton and Hill, he had found himself working harder than ever. It had been easy to forget about Vivian and Christopher Greene and their peculiar shrink. He had lost touch with the situation. Even at that moment he still didn't know what had happened to Chris.

Now, after a friendly phone call from Vivian, he was belatedly trying to fulfill his moral obligation. He had come there to try to reason with her about her therapist. But already he sensed it would be useless. Enough time had elapsed for Delphine to reprogram Vivian in such a way as to undercut anything Eric might say.

"You have every right to feel whatever you want about Delphine," Vivian said now. "But you should have been more perceptive about her book."

"Her book?" He was taken aback. "What does her book have to do with it?"

"She told me how you tried to discourage her. How you said you wanted no part of it."

"She's exaggerating. I simply said I wasn't interested."

"Well, you were wrong. I suppose you know it's going to be published?"

"Yes, I know."

Eric was aware, as the rest of the trade was, that *How to Get Well* was one of the upcoming hot titles. *Publishers Weekly* had already had a human-interest item on it, telling how one of Delphine's patients, a writer of get-rich-quick books, had shown the manuscript to his publisher, who had snapped it up instantly. Eric guessed that this must have happened immediately after he had turned the book down. The omens were good for *How to Get Well*. A large first printing had been announced.

The Psychology Today Book Club had selected it. An excerpt was going to appear in *McCall's*.

"I never said it wouldn't be commercially successful," Eric said. "Just that *I* didn't like it. Have you read it?"

"No, not yet," she replied. "But I'm looking forward to reading it. I'm sure it's very wise."

Eric was tempted to contradict this, but then thought better of it. "Never mind the book," he said. "We were talking about Mandy and Jeff."

"What about them?"

"I was struck by something you said—or that you quote Delphine as saying. That Mandy and Jeff needed to break up so that they could be happy together now. Well, that doesn't make sense to me. It's like saying you should hit yourself over the head with a hammer because it feels so good when you stop."

"Are you being witty?" she asked, rather acidly.

"No, I'm just pointing out that Delphine has it set up so that she never loses. She's right if the Hubers stay apart, she's right if they get back together. And what about *your* marriage?" he asked suddenly. "How does she explain that? Is it good that Chris and you have broken up? Does it mean you'll have a better marriage later?"

"No," Vivian said quietly, "Chris and I will never have any kind of marriage again."

The flat certainty in her tone stopped him for a moment. "How can you be so sure?"

"Because Chris has a problem—a problem I don't think he'll ever solve."

She left it unspecified. But her meaningful look conveyed that she assumed Eric knew the nature of the problem as well as she.

Eric simply nodded thoughtfully, then asked, "Where *is* Chris now, by the way?"

"I don't exactly know. I could find out, but I haven't tried to." She shrugged. "The main thing is he's gone back to his own world."

"The theater world?"

"The gay world."

She had actually uttered the word now. It made it easier for Eric to pursue the point he wanted to make.

"Tell me, Vivian, didn't you know Chris was gay when you married him?"

"No, I didn't. Oh, the issue had been raised about him often enough. But he seemed to love me as a man loves a woman. I felt sure he wasn't an out-and-out queer."

"But what about Delphine? Didn't *she* know?"

Vivian seemed to hesitate. Then quietly she said, "Yes, she knew."

"But she didn't tell you at the time?"

"No."

"So, haven't you called her down on this?" he asked. "She encouraged you to marry him, didn't she? Shouldn't she have told you he was homosexual?"

"We've talked about it," she said. "She explained that she didn't feel it would serve any good purpose. She had been helping Chris to change. She thought he'd made great progress. At the time, she hoped it would be all right."

"Okay, then, she was wrong." He pounced on the fact triumphantly. "Here is a case where Delphine Heywood was wrong."

"She wasn't necessarily wrong."

Eric looked at her perplexed. "But Chris left you, didn't he? He gave up on the marriage and went back to the gay world."

She looked away. "Maybe it wasn't his fault," she said softly.

He noticed the fleeting expression of anguish that passed across her face, and it occurred to him that he was making righteous, and possibly blundering, statements about a relationship he had never really understood. He said nothing further now.

At length, Vivian looked at him again and attempted a smile. "This is too painful for me to talk about, Eric."

"I'm sorry. Then we won't."

"I know you came here to denounce Delphine to me. I'd rather you didn't do that, either. What were you going to say? The same sort of thing Jane says? That she has an evil hold over me?"

"Something like that," he admitted.

"But why would she want power over me?" she asked reasonably. "I'm nobody. I'm not well-known like Chris and Mandy. I don't have an influential job like you. I don't even have the money to pay for my sessions, most of the time. Why should I be so important to her?"

"I don't know. But you are." He had never really thought about it before, but the odd truth of it struck him now. "You're more important to her than anyone else."

"That's preposterous," Vivian said. "Delphine is my friend and doctor, and all she's ever wanted to do is help me—as a friend and doctor."

They fell silent for a few moments. Eric had given up any hope of changing her mind about Delphine. But her last, enigmatic reference to Chris, with its vague suggestion of a hidden, painful guilt, had led him to suspect that the marriage, after all, might not be a closed issue.

Finally, Eric asked, "If, as you say, the break-up wasn't all Chris's fault, then don't you think you should try to see him?"

"I can't," Vivian said with an agitated shake of her head. "Whoever was to blame, he left me. Without speaking to me— without even saying goodbye—he was gone. It hurt me too much. I just can't see him now."

"But what if he still wants to make a go of it?"

"He could contact me."

"Maybe he's in some kind of emotional trouble. Maybe he needs your help."

"There's nothing *I* can do to help him." After a moment, she added, "Anyway, he has Delphine."

Eric stared at her. "He's still going to her?"

"Yes, of course." She seemed perplexed by his astonishment. "He needs her now more than ever."

"How can you know?" Chris asked helplessly. "It *felt* right with this guy. I mean, he wasn't just like anyone you would have sex with at the Baths."

"Why did he seem different?"

He couldn't see Delphine's face—she was sitting behind him as he lay on the couch—but he heard the skeptical dryness in her voice. It implied she didn't think there *could* be any difference.

"I don't know, you just sense it." He paused. His headache was excruciating and he was finding it hard to express himself clearly. The headache was the reason he was stretched out on the couch. Ordinarily, he might have refused when Delphine had suggested he lie down; he preferred eye contact with his therapist. But today he was grateful that she wasn't looking directly at his bruised, swollen face.

"I hoped we could have something more together than just the fun and games," Chris went on. "He was tough—even a little crude, I guess—but, underneath, he seemed to have a gentleness. You could tell he didn't have much education, but he talked sort of like a poet—the way he put words together. We had a *rapport*—or I thought we did anyway."

"So, after that night at the Baths, you arranged to meet him again," Delphine said, recapitulating what he had already told her. "You invited him to come see you at your hotel. And he did."

"Yeah. And I told you what happened." He said it curtly, trying to discourage her from retracking any further. He didn't want to have to go over it all again.

"You told me in a general way only," Delphine said. "Some of the details I'm not too clear about." She paused, then asked, "Did he attack you before or after you had sexual relations?"

"What difference does it make?"

"It could have some significance."

"After," he answered. "Right after."

"Had you been the active or passive partner?"

Chris almost winced with embarrassment. There had been a time when Delphine had been unwilling to hear any specifics at all about his gay lovemaking. Now she seemed to have an indecent curiosity about it.

"Passive," he murmured.

"Is it possible that he thought you expected him to hurt you?"

"Oh, for Christ's sake, Delphine," he protested, "this wasn't an s-and-m thing, if that's what you mean. He was just some hood who fucked me, beat me up and robbed me."

There was a silence behind him, and Chris immediately regretted his outburst. He was afraid he might have offended her.

"I'm not saying that you consciously intended this to happen," Delphine said finally in her low, patient voice. "But in your subconscious you may have wanted it. In my book," she went on, "I have a chapter in which I deal with the question of self-image. I point out that you are what you see yourself to be. Perhaps you've reached a stage where you see yourself to be a victim. And now you are impelled to fulfill that role."

His headache had gotten worse, his loosened tooth had started throbbing again, and a heavy depression was numbing his thoughts. But still, in the one clear corner of his mind, he noted the oddness of the irrelevant citing of her book. It was the second time she had referred to it that hour.

"I *was* a victim," he muttered, "but I didn't want to be one."

"Then why didn't you fight back?"

"I couldn't."

"Why not? You're young and strong—strong enough to beat up Earl Grayson. Why couldn't you handle this person?"

"I couldn't do anything," he said. "I was too drunk."

There was another silence. Apprehensive now, Chris waited. At length, he heard Delphine's voice again, quiet and cool. "You were drunk? You didn't mention that."

"I had a bottle in the room. You know, just to be sociable."

"You've been drinking lately?"

Chris hesitated before answering. He had avoided telling her about it, since he had known she would disapprove. But now he had let it slip. "More than I used to," he admitted.

"At the same time you've been taking the Placidyl?"

"The pills don't work any more. Not since you've reduced the prescription," he added, a bit accusingly.

"I *had* to do that, Christopher," she said gently. "To protect you. We don't want you becoming an addict, do we?"

"I'm not an addict," he said. "I'm just bugged, and I need something now and then—to relax. If the pills don't do the trick, then I have a drink."

"That can be dangerous, drinking while under the effect of Placidyl. How many pills do you have left?'

"I'm down to four. I'll need another prescription."

"It might be a good idea if you stopped taking the pills completely for a little while."

A pang of fear went through him. "I can't," he said quickly. "I'm not ready."

"If you insist on drinking, it's too risky. The drug and alcohol, taken together, can have a synergistic effect. It could kill you."

"I don't care!" Suddenly, his misery was something palpable, thrashing about within him. He tossed from side to side on the couch and cried out, "Oh, I hate myself so much! Sometimes I want to die!"

"No, you don't," she said softly.

"What's going to become of me?" he asked despairingly. "That thing that happened the other night—I don't understand! Am I turning into some pathetic old queen who gets picked on by rough trade?"

"Don't be silly. You're very young still."

"I'm old," he said. "I feel old." He closed his eyes wearily.

Something soft-textured was patting his forehead and cheeks. He had broken out into a sweat, he realized, and Delphine was dabbing at his face with a tissue. The tender solicitousness of it was comforting, calming.

"Now, listen to me, Christopher." Her voice was firm and at the same time hypnotically soothing. "You're unhappy now. But it will pass. Believe me, it will pass. This stage you're going through—this relapse into homosexual behavior—is only temporary. A necessary purgation. I think it best that you act out your compulsions for now. But a time will come when it will all be behind you—and you'll revert to your true self." She paused. "Then—who knows?—you may want to put your marriage back together."

Chris opened his eyes, a bit startled by the suddenness of the suggestion. It was the first time Delphine had even mentioned his marriage that session. "Would Vivian take me back?" he asked uncertainly.

"Yes. I'm sure she would."

He hesitated, then asked the question he had been afraid to ask until now. "Does she know about this? What I've been doing?"

"No."

"Good," he murmured.

After a moment, she asked, "Do you want to go back to her?"

"I can't."

"Do you still love her?"

"I love her, I guess. But, I don't know—I just want to be happy again."

"You'll be happy again," she assured him, "once you're working. And that should be very soon," she went on brightly. "What did you tell me last time? That you may be in one of Joseph Papp's shows? What was it? Something by Shaw?"

"*Candida*. They want me to play Marchbanks."

"You'd be a marvelous Marchbanks."

"But I have to audition first."

"Is there anything wrong with that?"

"It means they're not so sure of me. No one is these days."

"It shouldn't be any problem. I imagine you'll audition very well."

"I don't know," he said, "I can't seem to audition any more. My confidence is gone. I'm scared—scared from the moment I go in to the moment I go out." He paused. "You'll have to give me some more pills. I can't get through this without them."

"I told you, Christopher, I don't think it would be a good idea."

He sat up, swung his legs around and faced her. "Please, Delphine!" he said, gazing at her intensely.

As he took in her expression, he felt slightly surprised. He had expected to see her stern face or her pained, compassionate face. Instead, she had a pensive, almost calculating look. Rather than considering the issue at hand, she seemed to be thinking ahead to something else.

At length, casually, Delphine said, "I can understand your concern. Auditioning is frightening, isn't it?"

"Terrifying."

"Having to prove your worth to strangers in a few minutes," she went on thoughtfully, as if she were trying to imagine the experience. "I may have to face something like that myself soon."

"What do you mean?"

"Well, as I think I mentioned, part of my book is going to be published in *McCall's*. One or two of my more knowledgeable patients have suggested that I should try to go on television when that issue of the magazine comes out. It would be good advance publicity for my book—or so they say. I don't know how I feel about appearing on television, though." She smiled modestly, self-deprecatingly, as if the thought of such exposure seemed faintly ridiculous to her. "I can't see myself as a performer. But I suppose I owe it to my publishers to try to promote my book."

"Yeah, I guess so," he murmured, puzzled. Why on earth was she talking about her book now?

"Of course, I would need someone to arrange that sort of thing for me."

"Wouldn't your publishers do it for you?"

"Normally, I suppose they would. But they disagree with me on this." For an instant, her expression registered displeasure. "They don't think I should appear on television until my book is published. They say they don't want interest in it to peak too soon."

"Maybe they're right."

"Yes, maybe. If you're considering *only* my book. But I feel I have things to say beyond what I've put in the book." There was no pretense at shyness now; her tone was steely with self-confidence. "And I would like to be able to say them to more people than I can meet one-by-one in this office. Sometimes," she went on, a distant look coming into her eyes, "I've thought it would be nice if I could go on television, or on radio, every now and then—be a regular guest on—what are they called?—"

"Talk shows?"

"Talk shows, yes."

"You'd be good at it."

"I think so."

She fell silent, and Chris hoped that this line of conversation was at an end. It was something he didn't want to have to cope with now, the realization that even his psychotherapist secretly yearned for show business stardom.

But Delphine's gaze was intent on him and it was clear that

she wasn't about to drop the subject. "You're with a very big agency, aren't you?" she asked.

"Yes. William Morris."

"Do you think you could introduce me to someone there who might be able to help me?"

"I'm not sure I could," Chris said. "The only person I really know there is my own agent. Booking talk shows is another department."

"Oh. Then you can't do it." Her face went blank. Her eyes held on him coldly for a moment. Then she glanced at the clock. "Your hour is up."

"Already?" He was suddenly panicked. "But you haven't said whether you're going to give me the prescription."

"I told you my thoughts on the matter."

"Yeah, and I see your point. But can't you make an exception this one time?"

"Are you asking me as a doctor or as a friend?"

"As a friend."

"Friends help each other, Christopher," she said quietly.

He saw it now, hanging there. The trade-off. It had been stupid of him not to see it before.

"Yeah," he said after a moment. "About what you were asking, I think I *could* talk to Ira about it. He would probably refer me to someone else at the agency. Someone who specializes in talk shows. I should be able to get you an appointment."

Delphine smiled. "That would be nice. I'll write your prescription now," she said, rising. "For the full amount this time."

27

THE MAÎTRE DE told him Mr. Sherwin wasn't there yet, then led him to one of the banquette tables that were across from the bar. Eric hadn't been to the Russian Tea Room very often, but even so he knew that these tables by the entrance were for the select few. The fact that Christopher Greene's agent had one reserved for him indicated that he was a person of some stature in the entertainment world. Eric had imagined as much, anyway, but this bit of confirmation served to heighten his curiosity. Ira Sherwin hadn't explained over the phone why he wanted to see him. But, if he was a bigshot who didn't lunch lightly, it had to be something fairly urgent.

Eric kept his eye on the door and, after a couple of minutes had passed, Ira Sherwin appeared. He recognized him instantly as the long-faced, melancholy best man at Chris's wedding. The agent, of course, didn't know what Eric looked like. He checked with the maître de, had his table pointed out for him, then came over to Eric with his hand outstretched.

"Eric? I'm Ira Sherwin."

In the show business fashion, he was first-naming him at the moment of first meeting. Eric rose and, getting in the spirit of it, shook his hand and responded, "Glad to meet you, Ira."

Ira sat, signaled to a waitress in a Russian peasant dress, and ordered a vodka martini. Eric, to keep him company, ordered a spritzer. While they waited for their drinks, the agent small-talked about the two or three celebrities who were sitting near them in the row of banquette tables. A couple of tables away, on their left, a TV anchorman with a household face was chatting with a colleague. Next to them, on their right, a floozyish movie actress was dining with a youth half her age. Ira had a discreet but up to date piece of inside information to relay about each of them.

Their drinks arrived. Ira took a swallow of his martini, then, in a suddenly businesslike tone, asked, "Should we have something to eat first or should we get right to it?"

"Let's get to it," Eric replied. "I'm curious as to what this is all about."

"It's about Chris Greene."

"You said that on the phone. But you didn't tell me what the problem was. How is Chris these days?"

"He's in bad shape."

"Emotionally or physically?"

"Emotionally, he's a wreck. Physically too. He's really let himself go to hell."

"In what way? Is he drinking?"

"Yeah." Ira hesitated, then lowering his voice a bit, he said, "Worse than that. He's on drugs."

"Drugs! What is it? Heroin?"

"Not heroin," Ira said impatiently. "I don't know what it is. It's some junk that goddamned shrink of his gives him."

"Oh." Eric realized what he was talking about now. "I think I know what it is. It's called—Placidyl, or something like that. It's a strong tranquilizer—to calm him."

"Calm him!" Ira stared at him. "It's completely ruined him! He barely functions—he can't get work—"

"He can't get work because of the drug?" Eric had heard otherwise, and he ventured, "I'd thought maybe it was because of that incident with Earl Grayson."

"You know about that, huh?" The agent looked pained at the reminder. "No, it didn't help any when he punched out Babe. It will be a long time before Chris can work in any major movie. But that didn't affect his theater work. If he isn't getting stage jobs now it's because he's stoned all the time on that goddamned drug. Look, Eric," he went on, "do you know what it is to be a top-level stage actor? It's like being a major league athlete. You have to have super-energy, super-reflexes, your timing has to be absolutely perfect. If you lose just a little, if you go off even a fraction of a second, you're finished. You go back to the bush leagues. A couple of days ago, Chris had a big audition. It was for a part I thought sure he would get—that he *deserved* to get. Marchbanks in *Candida*. Afterward, they called me and told me what Chris was like when he read. They said that he dragged himself around the stage in a daze. His speech was slurred, he had no energy. He seemed like a zombie. They said I shouldn't send him out to read for anything any more, it was hurting his reputation too much." Ira paused, then said, "They're right. I won't submit him again. Not until he gets off the drug."

"Have you told him this?"

"Yeah. Yesterday."

"What did he say?"

"He said he didn't want to give up his pills. They helped him. Of course," Ira said, with a short, rueful laugh, "that's what any addict will tell you. Chris can't do it on his own," he declared flatly. "He's hooked. He needs professional care."

"Theoretically," Eric pointed out, "he *is* getting professional care."

"Yeah. That shrink! She's his dealer. She's the one who's feeding him the junk." Ira was starting to get agitated, but then he caught himself and, cocking his head as he looked at him, put it more delicately. "This Dr. Heywood is a problem, right?"

Eric nodded. "She's a problem."

"I've met her only once," Ira said. "Chris sent her in to see me."

"Why did she want to see you?"

"She has a book coming out and she wants to be placed on talk shows. I turned her over to someone at the agency who can handle that for her." He paused as he seemed to be recalling his meeting with Delphine. "She's a weird broad, all right," he said finally.

"If you thought she was so weird, why did you accommodate her?"

"As a favor to Chris. And we've got weirder clients than her," Ira said with a philosophical shrug. "But, back to yesterday," he went on, picking up the thread of what he had been saying. "When Chris said he couldn't give up the pills, I told him he *had* to. I said he should go into a hospital—like Riggs up in Massachusetts. In a place like that, he could get clean again."

"That was a very sensible suggestion."

"Sure, it was sensible. But he wouldn't buy it, not at first. I *pleaded* with him. I practically got down on my knees and cried!" He stopped and looked at Eric uncertainly. "Does that sound funny to you?" he asked with a touch of self-consciousness, as if he feared it might seem unprofessionally sentimental to confess to tears. "That I should take this so seriously?"

"No, it doesn't sound funny."

"Chris isn't just any client to me, you know. I *love* that kid. He's like one of my own sons. My wife and I have had him up to the country I don't know how many times. Now he's cut himself off from us, we don't see him any more. I can't just let him go down the drain like this!" Ira burst out emotionally. "So, yes, I pleaded with him." After a moment, he concluded, "And I think I finally got to him."

"He agreed to go to a hospital?"

"Not exactly. But he agreed to do it if his shrink said he should."

"She won't."

"That's what I told him. Then he said if I felt so strongly about it I should go see her and talk to her myself. And I said okay, I would. A little later, I got to thinking about it—and I phoned *you*."

"Why me?"

"Well, Chris has told me a little bit about you. He says you're a bright guy, you went to this shrink for a while, and you turned sour on her. So, okay, *I* can't figure out this Dr. Heywood. I wouldn't know how to get a bead on her. But *you* know her—and you probably know most of her tricks. Maybe if you came along with me, the two of us together could handle the situation."

Eric didn't say anything for a moment. At length, he murmured uncomfortably, "I was hoping I'd never have to see that woman again."

"I know it wouldn't be much fun for you. But this is an emergency," Ira said earnestly. "I'd appreciate it if you'd help me."

Eric thought about it further. But there really wasn't anything to debate. The issue was, quite simply, Chris's well-being. His own feelings didn't matter.

"Okay," he said, "if you think it will do any good, I'll go see her with you."

They had made a fatal mistake. Eric realized it when they were only five minutes into the conversation. They should have

specified in advance that Chris Greene wasn't to be present at
this meeting. As it was, Chris was there in the office with them.
Delphine had contrived it so that this whole scene would be
played for his benefit.

"I won't stand in the way, Christopher," Delphine said to
him now, with her sweet, reasonable smile. "If you wish to go
into a hospital, feel free to do so. I happen to think it's totally
unnecessary, but you won't find out until you try it, will you?"

"Well, if you don't think it's necessary—" Chris began
weakly, then broke off.

He seemed in a fog that afternoon. Then again, Eric thought,
it might be the way he was all the time. He hadn't seen Chris in
months, and he had already been struck by the marked change
in his appearance. As Chris sat, leaning forward slightly on the
edge of the couch, he seemed puny and helpless, like a sickly
little boy waiting for his fate to be decided by his elders. His
torso, once so athletically hard and strong, now seemed frail,
without muscle tone; it clearly had been some time since he had
been near a gym. The expression on his face was dully passive,
as if the will had drained out of him and he could be pushed in
any direction, according to whatever stronger force prevailed.

"It *is* necessary," Ira insisted. "Chris's career is finished if he
doesn't kick this addiction."

"Addiction?" Delphine smiled pleasantly at the agent. "I'm
afraid I must correct you, Ira. I have been prescribing a drug to
ease Christopher's tension. He has become habituated to the
use of it. That is not the same thing as being physically
addicted."

Ira said nothing, cowed for the moment. Eric understood his
insecurity; he couldn't help but feel a little uncomfortable himself. Sitting as they were, facing Delphine across a big desk,
seeing her against a backdrop of thick medical volumes, it was
easy to be intimidated by her air of superior knowledge.

Nevertheless, Eric spoke up challengingly. "Are you saying
that Placidyl can't be addictive?"

"Only rarely," she replied.

"I looked it up this morning," he said. "It's a sleeping pill. Why are you prescribing a sleeping pill as a tranquilizer?"

Delphine eyed him coolly. She had been constrained with him from the moment he had come into her office. Now her look was nakedly hostile. "It also serves to relieve anxiety," she said. "In some cases, I find it more effective than the conventional tranquilizers."

"And in the book it says that it *is* addictive," he persisted. "Physically and/or psychologically."

"If overused. I have prescribed it carefully. Christopher is not addicted." She looked over at Chris, who was gazing at them from the couch. "If you wanted to, Christopher, you could stop taking your pills, couldn't you?"

Chris's answer was a little slow in coming. "Yes," he said finally.

She turned back to them. "There, you see?" Her light gesture indicated that she felt the subject was closed.

"All right," Ira said suddenly. "But, addicted or not, Chris can't work when he's all doped up like this. I told you what happened the other day."

"That audition, you mean?" She looked at Chris again. "You told me about it, too, Christopher. How do *you* think it went?"

"Well, I don't know," Chris said uncertainly, "it felt *good*. I was into the part—I had a lot going inside me—"

"*You* may have felt good," Ira broke in. "But none of it came across to the people."

"Were you there, Ira?" Delphine asked with a smile.

"No. They told me over the phone later."

"But if you weren't there, you can't be absolutely sure, can you?" Eric noticed that Delphine remained softspoken and ingratiating with Ira. He remembered that she was now represented by his agency; he guessed that she was taking care not to offend him. "Isn't it possible," she went on, "that Christopher did, in fact, audition brilliantly? And that what you were told was merely an excuse for not hiring him? It could be they wanted to use a favorite of theirs instead."

"That's not the way it works," Ira snapped impatiently.

"No, perhaps not," Delphine said after a moment. "You know far more about show business than I do." There was a flattering deference in her tone. "It's your field of expertise. Just as psychotherapy is mine," she added pointedly.

She rose, went over to Chris, and put her hand lightly on his shoulder. "How do you feel, Christopher?" she asked gently. "Is it painful for you to hear us discuss you so openly?"

"I don't mind," he said.

She turned back to them, but her hand remained resting on his shoulder. "Christopher and I have been working through a long and demanding therapy—but a rewarding one, I think. We've opened some doors—crossed several bridges—but we still have a distance to go." She looked down at Chris, smiled, and ruffled his neck hair affectionately. "There's no way we could explain it to them, is there? All that we've worked out together?"

He smiled up at her, instantly responding to her caress. "No, I guess not," he said.

"It may seem confusing to you," she said to them, "mysterious, even. Christopher, I grant, is going through a very difficult period now. But in healing we sometimes have to break down before we can rebuild. I assure you, when our therapy is completed, Christopher will be a stronger, healthier, more fulfilled person than he was before."

Her left hand was lightly stroking his curls where they spilled over his collar. It was a delicate, almost imperceptible action, with a negligent tenderness to it, a casual possessiveness, as if she were absently petting a dog.

Eric couldn't bear it any longer. "For Christ's sake, Delphine, let go of him!" He was on his feet now, speaking with an intense anger he hadn't realized was in him. "What use is he to you now? Don't you ever let *anyone* go?"

Her hand froze on Chris's neck. "You are being very melo-dramatic, Eric." She said it calmly, but her gaze was fixed on him with a bright hatred that chilled him. "And you are con-fusing the issue with your paranoia."

Eric went over to the couch and, ignoring Delphine, spoke to Chris directly. "Chris, don't you want to get into good shape again? A short stay at this hospital couldn't hurt you. And it might make all the difference. Isn't it worth a try?"

Chris looked down at the floor and didn't reply.

"Why don't you answer?" Delphine asked him in her warm, cajoling tone. "Is it what you want? To go away to a hospital, far from here?"

After a moment, Chris looked up, not at Delphine, but at Eric. His sensitive face, more beautiful than ever in its gaunt-ness, had come alive with an expression of vague longing. "Sometimes I think I'd like to go away somewhere," he said softly, "to some place with trees and fresh air—just to rest for a while—to try to get some perspective on things."

"Then you should do it, Christopher," Delphine said. She removed her hand from him and stepped away.

With her touch gone, Chris seemed suddenly to grow panicked. His head jerked around and he stared at her fearfully. "But I'd come right back to you," he said.

"No, Christopher," she said, "that's not the way it works. You can't break off treatment halfway and then return to it at some later time. If we stop now, everything that we've accom-plished together would come undone. There would be no point in our seeing each other again. But, of course," she added, "that may be what you want—not to see me any more."

"No!" he blurted out. "That's not what I want!"

Delphine smiled, went to him again, stroked his hair, then drew him to her so that his cheek rested against her thigh, as a mother would who comforts her frightened child.

She looked at Eric and Ira, her expression quietly triumphant. "I think you have your answer, gentlemen."

28

He wondered why nobody helped him up. It wasn't a usual thing to be doing, after all, to be lying flat on his back on a sidewalk, with his head bleeding. Chris *thought* it was bleeding, anyway. He brought up his hand slowly and touched his scalp at the hairline. His fingertips made contact with a warm moistness.

Why didn't someone stop? It was broad daylight on West Eighth Street and there was no lack of people, but they all passed by him, curving their paths away from him slightly as they did so. His vision was even more blurred than it had been before he had walked into that thing, whatever it was, and, looking straight up, he saw dim, featureless masks where faces should have been.

Chris tried to focus, tried to figure out what had clobbered him, and after a moment, as his head cleared, he realized what it was—the low-hanging iron joint of a folded shop awning. His

vision was a little sharper now and he could make it out, suspended menacingly six feet above the sidewalk. Walking along
swiftly, blindly, he had bumped against it. Whoever owned that
shop should be more careful.

The legs continued to flash by, and now it dawned on him.
They thought he was a bum. All of these good people thought
that he, Christopher Greene, was some pathetic, dirty derelict
who had had an accident. They didn't want to get involved.

He sat up and then painfully struggled to his feet. The verti-
cal position started the blood flowing. He felt it trickling down
his forehead.

A boy and a girl, student types, were approaching. The boy
slowed down uncertainly, but the girl yanked at his arm, the
boy ducked his head, and they hurried on past him.

"What kind of town is this?" Chris screamed after them. "I
could die and you wouldn't care!"

He stood there dazedly, astonished at himself. Was that *he*
who had yelled? Like a crazy? He almost laughed as he realized
it. He was turning into a New York crazy, shouting in anger at
strangers.

The nausea hit him suddenly. He lurched over to a lamp
post, propped himself with one hand, and retched. No food
came up—he hadn't eaten all day—just the sour residue of the
gin he had drunk before leaving his room.

He couldn't be a very pretty picture, he knew. With an effort
of will, he straightened up and turned. A girl was standing there
looking at him. After a blank second or two, he recognized her.
It was Jane.

"Oh, hi, Jane," Chris said with feeble brightness.

"Are you all right?" she asked.

"Sure, I stand here this time every day and bleed."

It was a good joke, he thought, but Jane didn't even smile.

"I ran into that awning iron there," he explained, pointing in
the general direction of it.

"Let's go to a drugstore," she said, briskly taking charge of the situation. "I'll get a bandage for that."

"That won't be neces—" The word was like mush in his mouth, and it took him a moment to get it out distinctly. "—necessary. Have you got anything on you? A handkerchief? A Kleenex?"

Jane hesitated, then reached into the pocket of her jeans and came up with a crumpled ball of tissue. It looked like it had been used for some purpose already, but Chris took it from her and wiped the blood from his forehead.

Discarding the reddened ball of tissue into the gutter, he said, "There! Nothing to worry about. I'm as good as new."

Jane gazed at him somberly, her eyes concerned, and said nothing.

"What are *you* doing down here, Jane?" he asked.

"I live down here."

"No, you don't." He concentrated for a moment, then remembered. "You live on the West Side."

"I've moved. I'm on Barrow Street now. Do you live in the Village too?" she asked.

"Near it. I'm staying at the Chelsea."

Jane nodded gravely, as if making note of the fact.

"How's your mother?" Chris asked.

"She's fine." It was as much of an answer as she seemed willing to offer. After a moment, she said, "You don't look good, you know, Chris."

"Well, you're not seeing me at my best."

"Would you like my phone number? You can call me and we'll get together soon." She reached into the other pocket of her jeans and took out a pencil. "Do you have something to write on?"

"No, not a thing," he said quickly. "You can give it to me next time. I have to go now. I've got an appointment." He was vaguely aware of how absurd it sounded, but it didn't matter. He wanted to get away now, at all costs. "Nice seeing you." He took a step to go.

"May I call *you*?" Jane asked.

Chris turned and met her sorrowing gaze. "No. I'd rather you didn't do that," he said quietly. "Give my best to Vivian."

He hurried away down the street.

"Delphine," Vivian asked, "do dreams mean anything?"

"To Freud, they did," Delphine replied. "And to the ancient soothsayers." She said it rather negligently. It was clear that, as far as she herself was concerned, dreams were of no great importance. "Have you had a dream that you believe to be meaningful?"

"It's no one dream. It's all of them. He seems to be in almost every one of them."

"Who does?"

Vivian was a little surprised that she was asking. "Chris. We were talking about Chris, weren't we?"

"Yes, of course," Delphine murmured.

Vivian had sensed an indifference in her therapist, perhaps even an impatience, when they had discussed Chris during this hour. A couple of times she had seemed on the verge of changing the subject. And now there was the faintest hint of ennui in Delphine's tone, as she inquired, "Are these dreams of a sexual nature?"

"No, not usually. They're just the crazy sort of dreams you have. But Chris is always in them—not doing anything, he's just there. I mean," she went on, "there's a dream that's kept coming back all my life. I'm in a rowboat on a lake, rowing away madly, trying to get somewhere, and people in bathing suits are lounging on the shore, pointing at me and laughing."

Delphine smiled and nodded. "Yes, that's a very typical anxiety dream."

"But now when I dream it, Chris is in the boat with me—just looking at me, with that teasing grin of his."

Delphine thought for a moment. "After all," she said,

"you've had a traumatic experience with him. It shouldn't be too surprising that your subconscious is still dwelling on him."

"No, I guess not," Vivian said. "But when I left David, I didn't dream about him. I've *never* dreamed about him. Of course," she added, "David didn't leave any traces of himself behind. And I still have Chris's things."

"Which things?"

"Well, his pictures and his scrapbooks. His tennis rackets. And his clothes—his suits and sports outfits—he's never come for them, they're still there. In a way, it's like *he's* still there. I can feel his presence throughout the apartment."

"Do you have pictures of him around?"

"I've put them away, of course." She paused, then, a bit timidly—she knew Delphine would disapprove—admitted, "Last night, I took out some pictures and looked at them. Pictures of Chris by himself—pictures of both of us together. There's one shot I just love—of the two of us at the beach. We both look gloriously happy. And Chris—he's just wearing bikini swimming trunks—looks absolutely out of this world." Fervently, she whispered, "He was so beautiful!"

"*Was* beautiful?"

"*Is* beautiful," Vivian corrected herself. "I do that sometimes," she said after a moment. "I talk of him as if he were dead." Then it struck her, the chilling realization. "The dreams—I always dream about people I've loved who are dead. My father—a boy I loved a long time ago who was killed in a car accident—they've stayed in my dreams for years." She looked at Delphine fearfully. "Why do I think of Chris as dead?"

Delphine gazed at her steadily, with an almost preoccupied fixedness, and remained silent. Then suddenly she asked, "How do you like my dress?"

"What?" Vivian was startled.

"My new dress. How do you like it?" Delphine rose to show off the garment. "I bought it for my television appearance."

The abrupt diversion was jarring, and Vivian just stared at her, trying to adjust to it.

She had noticed immediately, when she had arrived, that Delphine looked different. And she had been more or less aware that her therapist was going to be on a television talk show that was being taped that afternoon. But, caught up in her emotional turmoil as she was, she had given little thought to it. Her own problems, after all, were the reason she was there.

Now, dutifully, she studied Delphine. Her hairdo, of course, was the most marked difference. Ordinarily she wore her hair drawn back and severe. But in the last day or so some hairdresser had redone it and had teased it out into an aureole that flatteringly framed her face. The dress itself was less of an improvement. It was a clinging print dress, with shades of bright blue and orange in a busy combination that had the effect of making Delphine look stouter. The neckline plunged, within modest bounds, and revealed the uppermost reaches of breasts that were well-rounded and milky-white.

"I like the cut of it," Vivian said. "You really have a very nice bosom. You shouldn't be afraid to show it."

Delphine smiled, girlishly pleased by the compliment. Then her eyes seemed to brighten and hold on her with a peculiar intentness.

Vivian felt a little uncomfortable now. "You haven't answered my question," she reminded her.

The therapist's expression returned to its professional set, and her smile was once again benign and enigmatic. "Let's sit on the couch," she said. "Let's talk this over as friends."

Vivian was puzzled as to why they needed to change their positioning at this point. But obediently she rose, crossed to the couch, and sat. Delphine sat beside her, took her hand, cradled it in her gentle grasp, and held it on her lap. Now that they were close together, Vivian noticed that, rather than smelling of her usual lemon soap scent, Delphine was casting off the fragrance of a musky perfume.

"You ask why do you think of Christopher as dead?" Delphine's voice was low and intense. "It's because he *is* dead." When Vivian gasped, she went on swiftly, "I don't mean he's *literally* dead. But, as far as you are concerned, as far as being any part of your life, he has ceased to exist. Do you understand that, Vivian?"

Vivian was silent for a moment. Then, softly, she said, "I don't want him to cease to exist."

"Why not?"

"I miss him."

"That's very understandable," Delphine said. "But you'll feel the loss for only a little while longer. After all, you can't go on forever yearning for the impossible."

"*Is* it impossible?"

A look of sadness came onto Delphine's face. "You've tried. We've both tried. I'm afraid that Christopher is hopelessly and irrevocably committed to his way of life."

Vivian looked down, fixing blankly on Delphine's hands, strong and sure as they enfolded her hand. Her therapist had told her already, more than once, that she had to give up on Chris. But with each passing week, it was getting harder for her to accept.

"Delphine," she began hesitantly, "you've told me that Chris has gone all the way—has turned completely gay. I haven't wanted to ask you too much about it—"

"I haven't wanted to tell you. Some of the things Christopher has told me I could never repeat to you."

"But one thing you haven't told me." She met Delphine's gaze. "Is he happy? Has it made him happy?"

Delphine considered the question. "More happy than before, I think," she said. "The struggle is over for him. He can find peace now, as he learns to accept himself as what he is."

"As a homosexual? I can't believe he really and truly is one."

"There is no really and truly for any of us. We are as we create ourselves. And we survive through compromises. Homosexuality is a compromise. But it can be a necessary compromise—if the alternative is a psychotic breakdown."

"I don't know," Vivian said wistfully. "When things were at their best, we were so happy. And Chris was everything a woman would want of a man—kind and gentle and loving. I won't find anyone like him again."

"Of course you will." Delphine squeezed her hand encouragingly. "You'll find someone who is all that and more."

"Well," she said with a little laugh, "I'm getting on. I may not have the pick of the crop any more."

"Don't be silly. You're still enormously desirable. And you remain beautiful—your skin—your eyes"—Delphine was taking her in with rapt absorption—"your hair. I love your hair, it's so dark and lustrous!" Almost to herself, she murmured, "My sister had hair like that."

"Your sister?" Vivian echoed. "I didn't know you had a sister."

"She's dead now. Something about you—your hair, the shape of your eyes—has always reminded me of her."

"Oh," Vivian said, a little uneasy.

"You'll find someone," Delphine went on, returning to the main point, "someone who is better for you than Christopher. You must go with the strong, Vivian," she said emphatically. "Christopher is weak, doomed to failure. He's not the person for you. You are naturally attracted to someone like Ward, who is strong, who has always been destined to succeed." She paused. Her glowing eyes were looking directly into Vivian's. "It may be why you have been drawn to *me*."

It was an unexpected idea, an unsettling one, and Vivian instinctively tried to remove her hand from her grasp. But Delphine wouldn't release it.

"I've never thought of you in those terms," Vivian said. "You're my doctor."

"Yes, I'm your doctor and you're my patient. But we've been more than that to each other, you know we have." There was an intimacy in Delphine's tone that suggested some longtime secret understanding between them. "We've been friends," she whispered. "Haven't I been your friend?"

Mesmerized by her bright gaze, Vivian could only murmur, "Yes. My best friend."

Delphine leaned forward and kissed her on the lips. Her mouth was surprisingly soft, and the kiss was gentle and hungry; it lingered with sexless passion.

Vivian froze for a few moments, not daring to react at all. Then she drew back, rose, and took a few steps away from the couch.

Delphine looked up at her calmly. "Did that upset you?"

"No. I just wasn't ready for it, that's all." Vivian smiled nervously, suddenly concerned, as she usually was with awkward lovers, that she might hurt Delphine's feelings. "It was nice."

"I thought so too," Delphine said, casually humorous. She stood up and smoothed out a wrinkle in her new dress. "I must cut our appointment short today. I have to prepare for my television show."

She was relaxed and businesslike, as if nothing unusual had happened. But then, almost as if it were an afterthought, she fixed her gaze on Vivian again and said, "You need to lean on someone strong. That's why you've been with me. That's why you *always* will be with me."

29

She waited for Jane to get to the point of her visit. Vivian knew this was no mere duty call. Jane gave her little enough time these days as it was, or, at least, no more than a parent could ordinarily expect of a nearly grown daughter who was living on her own. If she was there in the living room now, it was because she had something on her mind; something more, at any rate, than the latest books she had been reading, which was what they had been discussing for the past twenty minutes or so.

They came to a pause in the conversation. Jane, curled up on the couch, seemed to withdraw into her thoughts for a moment. Then suddenly she asked, "Did you see Delphine on TV last night?"

"No, as a matter of fact, I didn't," Vivian replied.

Jane's eyes widened with astonishment. "You didn't? I can't imagine you missing it."

"I had something else to do," Vivian lied. Actually, her previous day's experience with Delphine had left her too shaken to want to see her therapist again so soon, even on the screen of a television set. "Was she good?" she asked.

"She was terrific. She's a real star." Dryly, Jane added, "But we've always known that, haven't we, Mother?"

"What did she do? Just talk?"

"Yeah, she said her usual things. But it's the way she comes across on camera. Those eyes of hers! They must have given her a hundred close-ups. And she was pure charisma in every one of them." With a shrug, she concluded, "I guess she's going to be famous now."

"It's what Delphine has always wanted," Vivian said.

Jane looked at her askance, as if she didn't know what to make of this vaguely disrespectful comment. "You've noticed that?"

"Well, I mean, I don't think she wrote her book because she wanted people to ignore her. It's only natural to want recognition."

Vivian had defended her therapist automatically, from force of habit, but there was no real conviction in it now. She had been thinking about Delphine quite a lot in the last twenty-four hours, in a different way than she had before. And she had been thinking about Chris too, with increased sorrow, with sharpened guilt.

"I wonder if Chris saw her?" she mused aloud.

"He might have," Jane said. "They probably have television sets at the Chelsea."

"The Chelsea?" Vivian stared at her. "Is that where Chris is?"

"Yes."

"How do you know?"

"He told me. I ran into him the other day."

"Where?"

"On Eighth Street."

"How is he?" she asked eagerly.

"Not good," Jane replied.

The ominous note in her daughter's voice chilled her. A bit fearfully, she asked, "What was he doing?"

"When I saw him? Just wandering. He seemed to be drunk, or stoned, or both. He looked kind of dirty—and he was very thin, as if he doesn't eat much any more." She paused, then added, "And he was bleeding."

"Bleeding!"

"He'd hit his head against something. I tried to help him, but he wouldn't let me."

Jane was telling her all this very calmly, relating it dispassionately as she would any set of facts. And yet Vivian had difficulty accepting it. The details didn't fit into the picture she had of Chris as a healthy, well-adjusted gay. She realized that she had derived this other conception of him solely from what Delphine had told her. But, after all, it was only the day before that her therapist had informed her that Chris was happy, was finding peace in his new way of life.

"Are you making this up?" she asked.

A look of faint annoyance passed across Jane's face. "No, Mother, it's true. I wouldn't have come here to tell you lies about Chris."

Jane had all but let it out now, the real reason for her visit. "Is that why you're here?" Vivian asked. "To tell me this about Chris?"

"Yes. And, even though it may be none of my business, to let you know what I think."

"What *do* you think?"

"I think you should go see him. You know where he's staying now—the Chelsea. You're still his wife. I have a feeling he needs you very much."

Vivian looked away, too confused now to think of any reply. At length, she asked, "Did he mention me?"

"Yes."

"What did he say?"

"Nothing remarkable. Just the conventional things—'How's your mother?' and 'Give my best to Vivian.' But it was the way he said them—with sadness and tenderness. Chris is a very sweet guy."

"Yes," Vivian said, "I know."

"I think you should go see Chris right away," Jane repeated. "Something terrible is happening to him. Maybe you can help him before it's too late. You'll regret it always if you don't try."

Jane had made her point, perhaps more forcefully than she had intended to, and, somewhat uncomfortably, she excused herself and departed.

Vivian was left alone, to carry on the dialogue with herself, to try to come to an understanding of what she should do. But, before she could arrive at any decision, she knew she would have to make sense of a fact—a strong likelihood, anyway—that would have seemed unthinkable as recently as a few days before.

Delphine had lied to her.

If Chris could be found wandering down a street, his head bleeding, dirty and emaciated, in a drunken or drugged stupor, he wasn't happy, he hadn't found peace with himself, he wasn't someone who no longer needed her. Then why had Delphine kept this from her? Why had she told her the opposite? Had it been to spare her pain?

Perhaps. But then, she suddenly wondered, what had Delphine told Chris? Vivian had assumed that, since he had never contacted her, Chris was content in his new life. If, in fact, he was in such a bad way, wouldn't it have been Delphine's duty as a doctor to encourage him to attempt a reconciliation with his wife?

It was possible, she realized now, that Delphine was deliberately keeping Chris and her apart, just as once she had intentionally brought them together.

She didn't need to look far for a reason. She had only to

remember the hunger in Delphine's kiss, the lover's yearning in her eyes. She couldn't escape the fact now—for a full day she had been trying to learn to accept it—her therapist wanted her for herself.

She could feel no anger. If anything, she was moved. She had always sensed Delphine's loneliness, had always been disturbed by her unnatural isolation. If now Delphine wanted to reach out to her for some love, some shared tenderness, should she hate her for it? She remembered Delphine as she had been the day before, with her new dress, her new hairdo, confident and vibrant with her new success, and she realized that, after years of patiently and selflessly helping Vivian, her therapist had simply been claiming what she felt she rightfully had earned.

But then, Vivian wondered, had Delphine *always* felt this way about her? And did that mean that all of her therapy with Vivian had been influenced by it? When Delphine had encouraged and guided her in her relationship with Ward, had she simply been providing for her beloved? When that hadn't worked out, had she urged her into a marriage with Chris, the successful, rising actor, for the same reason? And when Chris's career had collapsed, had she steered her back into Ward's arms to make sure she would be properly taken care of? A sick uneasiness overcame Vivian as she asked herself these questions. She felt as if she had been slyly used, unwittingly made to participate in perverse acts. Delphine didn't seem so much a doctor now as a concerned, solicitous pimp.

She remembered the stricken look on Chris's face, that day he had confronted her about Ward, his look of anguish when she had contemptuously declared her independence of him, her right to seek elsewhere for her satisfaction if she found him inadequate. She had tried never to think back on that moment, but she remembered it now with shame, with the realization that she had destroyed it then and there, his frail belief in himself as a man. But it wasn't all her fault, she insisted to herself. She had only said what Delphine would have wanted her to say, what Delphine had taught her to think. She had accepted it as a sane, healthy attitude, not suspecting that her therapist might have hidden motives of her own.

She had trusted her. She had believed her. And now she knew that Delphine didn't always tell the truth. In that case, was it the truth when Delphine told her that Chris was hopelessly homosexual? Perhaps he hadn't changed, after all. Perhaps he was still, essentially, the tender, masculine lover she had married, the caring, passionate male of their most beautiful nights together.

She didn't know. She couldn't know unless she sought out Chris and ascertained the truth for herself. But she did know that Ward Kennan had become repugnant to her, that she could no longer bear the idea of letting him touch her. And she knew that she had never been so happy as when she had been happiest with Chris.

Perhaps it wasn't too late to find that happiness again.

"When are you going, Chris?" the man asked, in his whispery, insinuating voice.

Chris was trapped against the bar, wedged between the man and his larger, rough trade friend. But he paid no attention to them. He was peering up at the nude figure, made of some rubbery material, that was suspended from the ceiling. It was a boy hanging from a crossbar, his wrists bound to it with leather manacles. A heavy, leather confining mask enclosed his entire head. His erect, swollen penis was encircled by a leather thong. The painted features within the mask were contorted with pain and despair.

Chris felt himself floating up toward the boy. Light with gin and beer, primed to his lid with pills, it was easy; no trick at all. He hung from the ceiling in front of the boy and looked into his staring, tortured eyes.

"When are you going?" the man asked again.

Chris glanced at him now, taking in the main details of him. Thinning, silky, blond hair, pale-blue eyes, drooping yellow mustache, a shaved chest exposed by a half-unbuttoned sports shirt, an insistent smile. Nothing really out of the ordinary, but Chris almost shuddered. He realized that he knew this man from somewhere, from one of his recent blacked-out nights, and the residue of the lost memory had a bitterness to it.

"When am I going where?" Chris asked.

"Out to the Coast."

"Soon."

"You said soon last time."

"What last time?"

"Last time you were here."

"I've never been here before."

"Yes, you have," the man said softly, pleasantly. "You've been here before."

Chris gazed past the man's friend, a weightlifter type in a sleeveless leather shirt, with broad, bronzed shoulders that partly blocked his view, waited for the crowded room to come into focus, then studied it. It didn't look too different from the other hole-in-the-wall gay bars that lined the waterfront at the foot of Christopher Street. You could only tell it was S and M by the master-slave club posters that were on the wall above the Evel Knievel and Elton John pinball machines. The largest poster proclaimed the club's name—BERLIN—and depicted a pack of leather boys lounging in front of some Third Reich official palace. And, of course, among the men in the bar, there were a half-dozen or so characters, most of them fiercely bearded, who were dressed up in their leather outfits, black motorcycle caps, leather vests, iron-studded leather bracelets, and tight jeans with keys bunched on key rings hanging from either pocket, left pockets for masters, right pockets for slaves.

Had he ever been here before? He looked up at the hanging, naked boy again. He dimly recognized that angelic, agonized figure. He had thought he had known it from a dream. But no, he realized now, he had seen it in this place, during some lost night, some night that had been erased by pills and alcohol.

He drained his can of beer—it mixed sourly with the gin in his stomach, but it couldn't be helped; the place had no liquor license—then looked at the yellow-mustached man again. "Do I know you?"

"Of course, you do," the man replied. "I'm Martin. And this is Frank."

Frank, he was sure, was new to him. Olive skin, oily, black curls, hawk nose. For the past few minutes, Frank, with insolent carelessness, had been pressing his body against him. One moment his hip would be against Chris's crotch; he would be giving him the feel of his bulging penis the next. But all the time his bored eyes were directed elsewhere. He didn't seem to be really listening to the conversation.

"Who's going to be in the movie with you?" Martin asked.

"Liza Minnelli," Chris replied.

"You said Jacqueline Bisset last time."

"Maybe it's both of them," he muttered. With dull annoyance, he realized that the jukebox, at that moment, was playing Liza Minnelli's rendition of "New York, New York." It was too obvious where he had come up with the name, to substantiate a story he didn't even remember telling. "Why are you bothering me?" he asked Martin now. "Why don't you leave me alone?"

"I don't want to leave you alone," Martin said, his voice hushed and intense. "I'm one of your great admirers, Chris. From when you used to be on the stage."

"I'm *still* on the stage."

"You haven't been for a long time, Chris."

"I get offers. Joe Papp asked me to do *Candida.*"

"The title role?" Martin inquired innocently.

"Marchbanks," Chris said, ignoring the bitchiness.

"So, what happened?"

"The billing wasn't right. I told Papp to go fuck himself."

Martin made no comment on this. He turned to his friend and said, "I adored this boy, Frank."

Frank, now that he was addressed, looked at Martin with the ghost of a smile, polite in its blankness. It was the uncomplicated response of a horse turning its head on hearing a sound. Chris found it strangely appealing, and he felt a beginning prickle of excitement in his loins.

"After I first saw him in a play," Martin continued, "I went home and jerked off, thinking about him. He was the most beautiful creature I'd ever seen."

"Why are you talking about me like I'm dead?" Chris asked.

"You're not dead," Martin said with smiling earnestness. "You're nostalgia. We don't have to go home to watch TV for our camp nostalgia, Frank," he said to his friend. "We have it here in living color."

Chris recognized it now, the goading nip of the loser. "What are you? An actor?"

"I *was* an actor once. But I couldn't get jobs. I wasn't big, like you were."

"I'm still big," Chris said under his breath.

"If you're big," Martin asked reasonably, "why aren't you out in Hollywood?"

Chris paused a moment before answering. "My wife doesn't want to leave New York."

"You don't have a wife, Chris."

"Yes, I do. We're living apart right now. But we'll get it straightened out."

"You don't have a wife."

"I have a wife," Chris insisted, with anger now. "Why don't you believe me?"

"Because you don't have a wife, any more than you have a movie out on the Coast—or that Joe Papp wants you for anything. That's all in Nowhere Land, Chris. Otherwise," Martin asked, "why would you be *here*?"

"I'm here because"—Chris licked his lips, then uttered the

words slowly—"it appeals to my sense of the theatrical."

"That's not it, Chris. You were up high, way above the rest of us, and you fell far, far down. And now you're here. You know why you've come here, don't you, Chris?"

"Why?"

"To be punished."

Chris leaned his head back and closed his eyes. He was aware of nothing for the moment but the pressure of Frank's hips, pinning him against the bar aggressively now, imposing his animal strength on his helplessness. He felt weak with excitement, giddy with the sense of honeyed danger.

He half opened his eyes and saw the hanging boy above him, crying out with the pain of his leather crucifixion.

"Yeah," he murmured to himself, "maybe I've got it coming to me."

After one ring, there was no answer. It wasn't too late to hang up, and Vivian, very slowly, started to do so. She heard the second ring at a distance. Then, as she was about to rest the receiver on the cradle, a faint, unfamiliar voice spoke out of it. "Hello?"

She quickly raised the receiver to her ear. "Is Chris there?" she asked.

"Yes. But he's busy now." It was a man's voice, cooingly soft, speaking barely above a whisper. "Who's this?"

"His wife."

There was a silence at the other end of the line.

Vivian felt a sick apprehension. Then she tried to reason it away. The man had said Chris was busy. That could mean they were working on a project, something for the Actors' Studio. It was near midnight, but she knew that Chris sometimes rehearsed scenes for class at the oddest hours.

The voice spoke up again. "May he call you back?"

"I'm downstairs in the lobby," she said.

"You are?" There was surprise in the voice. "You are?" it asked again, this time with excitement and a note of delight.

"Who are *you?*" Vivian asked. "What's going on?"

"We're working out something with Chris," the voice said carefully.

"Working out what? A scene?"

"Yes. A scene."

"Well, maybe I shouldn't interrupt you. I can come by some other time."

"No, don't go away." The voice was very cordial now. "Come on up."

"All right. Thank you." She hung up.

Vivian stood for a moment by the house phone, uncertain, uneasy. She was sorry that she had called now. But she had announced herself, she had said she was coming up. There was no backing out of it.

The elevator doors were only a few feet away. Vivian went over and pushed the button. As she waited for the elevator to descend, she glanced around the rear of the Chelsea lobby uneasily, at the night clerk reading his paperback behind the protective glass that shielded the desk, at the contemporary paintings, Abstract Expressionist and Pop Art, that took up almost every foot of wall space. With a twinge of panic, she realized that she was totally unprepared for this. She was plunging ahead into it, even though, just ten minutes before, she had had no clear intention of doing it at all.

She had simply gone to a movie—though perhaps it had been no accident that she had chosen one that was not far from the Chelsea. She could barely remember the film now. She had meant to escape her thoughts, to find distraction on the screen, but, instead, she had spent two hours in air-conditioned darkness, thinking of little else but Chris, and Delphine, and what Jane had told her that day.

Afterward, rather than taking a cab home, she had started walking uptown toward Twenty-third Street. She had been curious to see the hotel; she had wanted to get a close look at where Chris was staying. When she had gotten there, she had stood on the opposite side of the street, staring up at the red brick facade of the building, with its old-fashioned, cast-iron, floral balconies, wondering if Chris was on the other side of any of the lit windows. Then, impulsively, not quite knowing why she was doing it, she had crossed the street and had gone into the lobby.

The elevator arrived. Vivian stepped into it and pressed the button for the eighth floor. As the elevator rose, she felt a quickening of excitement within her. Her fears vanished and suddenly she was sure that she was doing the proper thing, that it was going to work out. The ascent seemed agonizingly slow. She couldn't bear their separation lasting even these final, protracted seconds. She wanted to be in Chris's arms at that very moment, saying the words that would make everything right again. *Forgive me, darling. Delphine told me lies about you. But now I understand. Let's go home and start over.*

But Chris wasn't alone, she remembered. She wouldn't be able to say anything so direct, so personal. In the presence of others, she would have to keep cool, mask this as a mere social call. Perhaps it was just as well. There had been too much pain, too much misunderstanding, for there to be any swift, easy reconciliation. It would be better if they took it slowly, at first, with cautious, restrained steps.

Still, when the elevator let her out on the eighth floor, she started running down the corridor. Then she stopped and put her hand to her hair. What did she look like? She hadn't freshened her makeup, she hadn't combed her hair. Oh, God, what difference did it make?

She walked on another few steps, stopped again, and checked the number on a door. It was one digit off. She went on to the next door. It was the right number.

She knocked on the door. Almost instantly, it opened. A man with a yellow mustache was standing there, smiling at her with manic glee. He stepped back and, with a grand flourish of his arm, wordlessly invited her in. Vivian entered the room, then froze.

Two naked men were on the bed. One, muscular and bronzed, was kneeling over the other, a deathly-white, frail figure crouched on all fours. The kneeling man was thrusting his arm up the other one's anus. The man on all fours was Chris. His glistening face was turned toward Vivian. His eyes were closed, his mouth was hanging open, and he seemed barely conscious. But then the other man withdrew his arm a few inches, sank it deeper into him, and Chris moaned.

Vivian screamed and ran out.

30

ERIC KNOCKED on the door. He waited, but there was no sound from within the hotel room. He knocked again. Another few seconds passed, then he heard footsteps approaching the door. It opened, and Chris looked out at him.

"Oh, hi, Eric. Come on in." He said it remotely, almost bewilderedly, as if Eric, rather than being there at his request, had been the last person in the world he had expected to see.

Eric stepped into the room, then looked at Chris more closely. It hadn't been that long since he had seen him at Delphine's office, and yet in the brief interim he had changed startlingly. He was completely wasted now; his bones seemed to have no flesh left on them. All of the muscles of his face were taut, freezing his expression in a mask of perpetual agony. It was cool in the room, but he was sweating through his shirt; the armpits were soaked, damp patches were forming on the front.

"Did I take you away from your work?" Chris asked.

"No, I'm through for the day. It's almost six."

"Is it?" Chris squinted at the clock that was across the room on the dresser. "Oh yes," he murmured, as if he could see the time. Actually, the clock had stopped at eleven-thirty. "Sit down," he said, vaguely waving his hand toward the armchair.

Eric sat. He glanced around the room and found nothing of Chris in it. It looked exactly as it must the hour before he moved in, as it would the moment after he was gone. There wasn't even a book by the bed or a coat thrown over a chair. A nearly-empty gin bottle on the dresser and the stopped clock were the only tokens of his presence there.

"Would you like a drink?" Chris asked.

"No, thanks," Eric said. He gazed at Chris patiently, waiting for him to clarify the meaning of his phone call that afternoon. He had told Eric it was an emergency, had pleaded with him to come see him, but he hadn't explained the reason for it.

Chris had remained on his feet, neither standing still nor walking, but, hunch-shouldered, shifting about restlessly in one spot, turning at one oblique angle to Eric and then at another. At length, he asked, "How's the job going?"

"Fine," Eric replied. "I couldn't be happier."

"And how's Lucy?"

"She's fine too. We're getting married next month," he added.

Chris smiled, a fleeting but genuine smile. "Good. I'm glad to hear that." Then he looked away and, the bright moment past, his face set in a still deeper agony than before. It was as if the few seconds of small talk had left him spent.

"Chris," Eric asked finally, "why did you want to see me? You said it was important."

"Yeah," Chris muttered. "Yeah, it's important." He stared at Eric and with sudden intensity said, "You're going to have to talk to Delphine."

"Me? Why?"

"She won't talk to *me*. Not any more!"

"I don't understand. Aren't you still her patient?"

"Yes. But when I call, she cuts me short—she hangs up— she—" He broke off, his mouth opening and closing helplessly, as if he were momentarily unable to form words. His whole body was trembling now.

Eric gazed at him. "Chris, what's the matter?"

"Don't you see what's happening to me?" Chris asked, in a thin, strangled voice. "Don't you see what's happening?"

"Are you sick?"

"I'm out of pills!" Chris cried out, in anguish. He was shaking so violently he could no longer stand, and he sank onto the bed. Propping himself with one hand, he repeated it, quietly now, exhausted. "I'm out of pills. I took my last one yesterday."

Eric understood now, and he was angry at himself for not having recognized the drug withdrawal symptoms sooner. He rose, went to the bed, sat beside Chris, and put his arm around him. "Just take it easy, Chris," he said. "You'll feel better in a little while."

"No, I won't," Chris said hopelessly. "Not unless I get my pills."

His body, within the curve of Eric's arm, was rigid, but the shaking had stopped and he was breathing regularly again. Eric withdrew his arm and sat back. "Tell me what happened," he said. "Did Delphine just cut you off the pills?"

"I don't think she meant to," Chris said after a moment. "But she went away—on a publicity tour for her book."

"Oh yes." Delphine's book, he knew, was being heavily promoted, and with success. Less than a month after publication, *How to Get Well* was already on the best-seller charts. "How long was she gone?"

"A couple of weeks."

"And what was the problem? You didn't have enough pills to last you?"

"Just barely enough. But I wasn't worried. I knew I'd be seeing her as soon as she got back. I *thought* I would, anyway."

"And you *didn't* see her?"

"Well, because her schedule was changed, she hadn't made any appointments. I was supposed to call her. I did, and she said she couldn't see me that day. I called again the next day, and it was the same thing—she was too busy, she couldn't see me. I asked her if I could come by just to get a prescription. She said no—she didn't seem to want to be bothered. This morning, I called her and *begged* her to let me have some more pills. She said I should learn to do without them—and hung up." His eyes were wide with incomprehension and hurt. "She said it so coldly! I've never heard her sound like that before."

Eric was trying to keep his face expressionless, so as not to reveal his shock. "You know, Chris," he said reasonably, "she has a point. You *should* learn to do without the pills."

"I know," Chris said impatiently, miserably, "but I'm not ready yet. I mean, Ira and you are right—I realize that now. I should go to a hospital and get clean. But not *now*. Not *this* time."

"You can't stick it out?"

"The physical part, maybe. But not what goes on in my head. The pills kept it all down. Now it's coming up—everything!" He was shaking again. "I can't stand *thinking* about those things!" He leaned forward and put his head in his clenched hands, pressing his fists against his temples, as if he wanted to force back whatever disturbing images were in his mind. At length, without looking up, he said, "You're going to have to talk to Delphine. Tell her I need her, more than ever. She can't just turn her back on me!" He was silent for a moment. Then he murmured, "Maybe I didn't say it right to her over the phone." He straightened up and gazed at him appealingly. "*You* tell her, Eric. *You* make her understand."

"I could try. But, Chris," he persisted gently, "if you can hang on for just a couple of days, you'll have kicked this. You won't need the pills then. You might not even need Delphine. If you get through this, you'll be all right."

"*If* I get through it," Chris said softly.

Eric was chilled by what he saw in Chris's eyes. Terror, and something else beyond—a terminal despair.

"I'll call her right away," he said.

Eric couldn't doubt the urgency of the situation now, and he sensed that there was no time to be lost. But he didn't want to make the phone call in front of Chris. He stayed a minute longer, then left and took a cab home.

As soon as he got back to his apartment, he looked up Delphine's number in his address book and dialed it. After two rings, he heard her voice. "Hello?"

"Delphine? This is Eric Bayliss."

There was the slightest of pauses. Then, coolly, she said, "Yes, Eric. What can I do for you?"

"I'm not calling for myself. I'm calling for Chris Greene."

"Christopher? Yes." She was waiting for him to go on.

"He's in pretty bad shape. He's on the verge of a complete breakdown—or maybe something worse. I think you'd better go see him."

"I'm afraid that isn't possible right now. I'm busy."

"If it's an appointment with a patient, cancel it. This is an emergency."

"I'm not seeing a patient," she explained. "I'm about to go to station WMCA. To be on a radio program."

"A radio program?" he echoed.

"Yes, a talk show. It's in connection with my book." There was a touch of complacence in her voice, and a hint of rubbing it in with the man who had rejected her best-seller. "I can't skip it, Eric. It would be too upsetting to my publisher."

"Delphine," he said slowly, deliberately, "I don't think you understand the situation. Chris is going through severe drug withdrawal. And he is in a deep depression."

"I understand that situation very well. In another twenty-four hours, he'll start to feel better."

"I don't think he's going to make it!"

"Eric, please," Delphine said with weary patience. "I assume you have just seen Christopher, and as a layman, you of course are distressed. But, believe me, whatever a drug addict says in the throes of withdrawal is not to be taken seriously."

"Will you at least let him come see you? Why have you turned him away?"

"I'm extremely busy these days. My little book has found favor with the public," she said demurely, "and I can't possibly make time for all the people who want to see me now."

"But Chris is one of your regular patients!"

"Eric, you don't seem to understand what I'm telling you." Her voice was cold and precise. "I've done all I can for Christopher. There's nothing more I can do for him. It's time for him to see another doctor."

There was a click and the line went dead.

He was freezing again. Ten minutes before, he had been burning up. Chris curled more tightly in the fetal position and waited for the chill to pass, as it had a dozen times already. Then, he knew, the fever heat would come back, and once again he would break out in a sweat.

This has to end, he told himself. *Sooner or later, it has to end.*

Delphine would come soon. She would take care of him, make him well. If she wouldn't let him have his pills, then she would give him another kind of pill, or a shot of something, to get rid of the hot and cold flashes, the sharp craving in the pit of his stomach, the headache that was like a steel clamp crushing his forehead.

The thought made him feel a little better. He uncurled and sat up on the bed. He rubbed his forearms to warm them. He worked his mouth a bit, trying to get some saliva flowing to wash out the putrid taste.

He felt a gust of wind, and, looking to one side, he saw that the French doors that led out to the balcony were half open. Had he been out there? he wondered. He had no distinct memory of what he had done since Eric had left, and for all he knew he *might* have gone out on the balcony. The idea of it filled him with fear, and he averted his gaze from the angled glass doors.

The phone rang. Chris stared at the black instrument apprehensively. Then he reached over and picked up the receiver. "Hello?"

"Chris, I've talked with Delphine." It was Eric, and his voice was solemn.

"Yes? What did she say?"

"She says she's too busy to see you right now."

Chris felt no real surprise. He realized that, in some part of him, he had known all along that this would be her answer. "When *can* I see her?"

"She was vague about it."

"Oh. She doesn't want to see me at all?"

"I didn't say that," Eric said quickly. "But, Chris, I don't think we should wait. I'll find another doctor for you."

"I don't want another doctor."

"You don't?" He heard the uncertainty in Eric's voice. "Not even to give you a prescription?"

"No. I don't need the pills now."

There was a silence. Then Eric said, "I'm coming over there."

"No, Eric, you really don't have to. I appreciate your trying to help me. But there's nothing more you can do."

"I'll just keep you company."

"Thanks, but I think I'll rest for a while. Don't worry. It's going to be all right now."

He hung up.

Chris stared at the wall and felt almost at peace. It was so simple, now that he could see himself as Delphine saw him, clearly, without illusion, and could admit the truth. He wasn't much of a person. He had no real value. He wasn't worth bothering with. It was comforting to accept this at last.

It's going to be all right now.

He rose and glanced about the room absently, trying to think if there were any final things he should do.

Should he write a letter? It was customary. But to whom? His mother and father? He hadn't written to them since Christmas, and he didn't know what he could say to them now.

Vivian?

He convulsed suddenly with shame. Damn it, he wasn't going to think about her! It meant remembering that scream, and wondering all over again.

He put his hands to his eyes, trying to shut it out, but it came back to him, nevertheless, and he experienced the degradation of it, as he had so many times before, heard the woman's shrill scream again.

They had told him it was Vivian. But they could have been lying, torturing him in still another way.

He couldn't know. He didn't want to know. He would never know now.

All right, he would put her out of his mind. No more humiliating thoughts. He had to concentrate now. He had to concentrate on playing his action cleanly, with style.

Chris went over to the mirror, picked up his comb and passed it through his hair. He might as well try to look presentable. But, after two or three strokes, he gave up—he was too badly in need of a haircut; the curls were hopelessly tangled. He stared at his face—it was pale, paler even than in the moment after taking off his makeup—then caught the glint of silver in the bushy sideburn. How odd, he thought, that he would notice his first gray hair *now*.

He crossed to the glass doors, opened them wide, and went out onto the balcony. He hesitated only a moment, then put one foot up on the cast-iron, floral railing. Gripping the top bar with both hands, he swung his other foot up and squatted on the railing, monkeylike. He waited a few seconds, then slowly, very carefully, holding his arms out for equilibrium, straightened to a standing position.

The roar of the traffic, eight stories below, was rising up to him, but he didn't let it mar the moment. He didn't let it distract him as he exulted in his athlete's sense of balance.

"It's going to be all right now," he said.

With a sweeping glance, Chris took in the copper-gray evening sky. Then he stepped into air.

31

VIVIAN LOOKED over at the bald, well-dressed man who was alone by the coffin, lost in his thoughts. She didn't have to ask who he was. She knew it was Noah Porterfield. He had entered a minute before and, without glancing at any of the fourteen or fifteen people gathered in the flower-bedecked room, had gone directly to the coffin. He stood by the upper end of it now, looking down intently, as if he could see through the gleaming oak to the smashed face beneath.

Jane tugged at her sleeve. "Mandy and Jeff are here," she whispered.

Vivian turned and looked through the open doorway. The Hubers were signing their names in the guest book that rested on a stand beside the funeral parlor elevator. They came on into the room. Mandy, seeing Vivian, approached her with arms outstretched, eyes shining. "Oh, Vivian!" She embraced her with wordless sympathy.

"Thank you for coming, darling," Vivian murmured as they separated.

Jeff, with stiff formality, had shaken hands with Jane. He turned back to Vivian and said, "When we read about it in the paper, we just couldn't believe it."

"If there's anything we can do—" Mandy said.

"There's nothing," Vivian said. "But thank you."

They were uncomfortably silent for a moment, as if they all felt somewhat trapped in the situation, required as they were to mouth the hackneyed but necessary phrases, the verbal formulas that were the only things that could safely be said at a time like this.

"Will the funeral be here in the chapel?" Mandy asked. "The paper didn't say."

"No," Vivian replied. "Chris's parents are arriving tomorrow. They're taking him back to Wisconsin."

Mandy nodded and didn't pursue it. Vivian knew that there was nothing to be said after her awkward admission, that she wouldn't be burying her own husband, that he was to be taken back by the parents she had never met, that, even though she was going through all of the motions now, she wasn't truly a widow any more than she had been truly a wife.

Perhaps the Hubers were thinking nothing of the sort. Still, Vivian didn't want to discuss it any further. "Eric and Lucy were asking about you," she said to them. "Why don't you go over and say hello?"

"All right," Mandy said readily. And Jeff and she started away.

Vivian looked across the room at Noah Porterfield again. He remained as she had last seen him, head declined, standing motionless by the coffin.

"Who's that man?" Jane asked.

"Someone who knew Chris," Vivian replied. "An old friend of his."

Had he been more than that? She had never asked Chris.
Well, it didn't matter now.

Noah Porterfield turned away from the coffin, went over to
Ira Sherwin and exchanged a few words with him, then quickly
left. He had come and gone without speaking to her.

Vivian glanced around at the mourners in the room, checking
the guests from habit, feeling an incongruous touch of hostess's
anxiety. She knew only half of the people there. The ones who
were unfamiliar to her, the gentle young men, seemed
genuinely grief-stricken, and each had offered his condolences
to her in the most delicate way.

Eric and Lucy were talking with the Hubers. But now Eric
left the group and came over to her.

"Vivian," he said, "there's something I have to tell you. It's
been on my mind. I want you to know."

"What is it?" she asked.

Eric looked at Jane. Her daughter walked away a few steps,
leaving them alone.

"I told you I saw Chris that last day," Eric began.

"Yes. And you were on your way to see him a second time."
She knew that Eric had been just two minutes too late, that he
had arrived as the crowd was starting to gather around the body
on the sidewalk. It was too horrible to think about, now or ever,
and in a low voice she said, "Let's not go through that again,
Eric."

"There's one thing I didn't tell you." Eric's expression was
grim, and he seemed to have some difficulty getting his words
out. "I phoned Chris—just before it happened. I sensed what
he was about to do. I should have called the police, and I
didn't. I've been blaming myself ever since."

"You couldn't be sure, could you?"

"No, I couldn't be sure."

"Then don't blame yourself, Eric," she said gently. "Please,
don't. I don't think any one of us is to blame."

Eric tried to smile, but the disturbed look had not gone from his eyes. "Okay," he said. "Just wanted to let you know." He turned quickly and walked away.

Jane came back to her. "What was the matter?" she asked.

"Nothing," Vivian said. "Eric is just feeling badly. We all are."

They were silent for a moment. Then Jane said, "It's getting late, Mother, and I think everyone's here who's going to come."

"Yes, I suppose so." But Vivian glanced quickly at the empty doorway, as she had several times already that evening, uneasily responding to an imagined, limping footstep.

Jane seemed to read her thought. "*She* won't come," she said.

"I hope not," Vivian said.

It was their only reference to Delphine. Vivian had tried to keep her out of her mind. But, a few minutes later when they were in the cab on their way home, she started thinking about her again.

She hadn't really expected her to appear. She had known, as Jane had, that Delphine would be too shy at the last, would defer to death. Still, she had a feeling that she would be hearing from her very soon, that, before the night was over, she would reach out once again to assert her claim on her.

Delphine seemed to have grown unsure of her. Perhaps she feared that Vivian might be about to end their relationship. Vivian had considered it, but had gone on seeing her. It was because, after what she had glimpsed at the Chelsea that night, she had been forced to admit that Delphine was right. And she had understood that if her therapist had concealed part of the truth from her, it had been only to spare her feelings.

Anyway, she had felt that she still needed Delphine. She had put nine years into it, nine years of sharing her most intimate thoughts with her, her most painful emotions. It all couldn't be canceled in a moment.

But she could no longer feel the same way about her. And

she had been finding excuses to go to her less frequently. Since Delphine had returned from her book tour, Vivian had seen her only once.

So Delphine had taken to phoning her, inexplicably, compulsively. It was as if their roles had reversed and her therapist was now the insecure one, calling for instant reassurance over the wire.

Her last phone call had been the day before, less than twenty-four hours after Chris's death. Vivian had been in a daze, and she couldn't remember much of the conversation now.

"Christopher was too weak to live." She remembered Delphine saying that. "No matter what we did, he would have ended this way. There's no point in brooding over it. We should try to forget him."

Vivian must have said something angry, because the next thing she remembered Delphine saying was, "I understand. I understand your hostility." Her voice had been cooing and desperate at the same time. "When you come in, we'll talk this over. We'll work it out."

What did she think she could say to her? Vivian wondered now.

Delphine had been right. But what kind of right was it? How right is a therapist whose patient ends up in a coffin?

When they got back to the apartment, Vivian went directly to her bedroom. She turned on only one light, the little lamp on the writing table. She sat down on the bed and gazed at the framed photograph that was standing at the near end of the writing table, the photograph of Chris and her at the beach—their happiest moment together. She had slipped it into a frame that morning, had placed it there, and had taken all of the other photographs in the room and had put them away. From now on, she wanted to see just this one picture.

She fixed on the image of the smiling young man in swimming trunks, unearthly in his beauty. What had she known of him? What had Delphine or anyone else known of him? He had had a mystery about him, a mystery that perhaps he himself had never fathomed. It would be a mystery forever now.

It was best that way.

The phone rang. Vivian looked at the instrument by her bed. The second ring was cut off as Jane, in the living room, answered.

A minute passed, then Jane came into the bedroom. "It's Delphine. Do you want to talk to her?"

"No," Vivian said.

Jane left.

Vivian lay back on the bed. She could feel the loneliness creeping into the room with her. The loneliness she had feared for so long. It was there. It was settling in to stay.

Jane returned. "Delphine wants to know if you'll be coming for your appointment tomorrow."

"No."

Jane looked at her silently for a moment. "Shall I tell her you won't be seeing her again?"

"Yes, darling. Tell her that."

Jane nodded and went out.

So many years left, she thought. So many years to go before it ended. But it could be managed. It wasn't impossible to live them with some meaning, or, at least, grace.

She would have to find the strength in herself.

"Christopher Greene?" Delphine looked at Winter quizzically. "Why should you care, Sergius? Did you know him?"

"No, I didn't," Winter said. "But when I read about his death in the newspaper, I remembered I had heard he was your patient."

"So you've come all the way over here to—commiserate with me?"

"I've come because I'm concerned."

"But why?" Delphine's smile was incredulous. "You and I are both doctors, Sergius, and we know that these tragedies are unavoidable. If a patient has terminal cancer, you do your best. But there's no sense in brooding about it afterward."

"Was this young man such a hopeless case?"

"Yes, I'm afraid he was. I had hope for him once. But I helped him in every way I could, and still—" She shrugged sadly.

"How did you help him?"

"I gave him insight into himself."

"Does insight lead a young man to throw himself to his death?"

"If he can't bear what he sees, yes." Her gaze met his, unwavering. She seemed serene, free of any doubts, beyond criticism. "Perhaps it's for the best that way."

The doorbell rang.

"Excuse me," Delpine said. She rose and left the office.

Winter stared at the drawn curtains that perpetually hid the garden and suddenly felt very tired. The trip across town might have been too much for him. Or perhaps he was oppressed by her office, an office that, in all of its furnishings, duplicated his own almost exactly; a compliment once, a mockery now. He was having difficulty breathing and the leather arm of the chair had gone cold under his hand. It was the patient's chair—Delphine had led him to it when he came in—and it seemed clammy with the desperation of all of the people who had sat in it. Winter slowly, painfully, rose to his feet and stepped away from the chair.

He didn't have much time, he realized. He had delayed too long without getting to the point, and now a patient had arrived and he had only a minute or two left. Well, perhaps it made no difference. He had little hope of convincing Delphine. He would say what he had to say. But it would be not so much for her sake, he knew, as to ease his own conscience.

Delphine returned. "A new patient," she said. "She's here for the first time. Lovely girl. From a quite wealthy family. She's having some problems in her marriage."

"Well, I won't keep you any longer." He went to her and took her hand. It was soft, warm, without any tension in it. He held her hand and made no move to go.

She looked at him questioningly, with a faint, uncertain smile. "Aren't you going to tell me?" she asked. "The real reason you came here?"

"The reason? A whim. Something I wish you would do."

"What?"

He sensed the childlike expectance in her—after all the years that had gone by, it was still there—the expectance of the daughter-patient waiting for her father-doctor to utter the possibly magic, possibly transfiguring words. In that moment, he could almost hope that he might actually reach her.

"Delphine," Winter began, "I'm quite alone now. I no longer have my work. Nor do I have very much time left. I would like to devote what time does remain to me to those few people I care for." He paused, then said, "I wish I could see *you* more often."

Delphine's eyes moistened. "You want me to visit you?" she asked softly. "Yes, of course, Sergius. Whenever I can."

"I don't mean now and then. I would like to see you regularly. Then we could talk together. The way we used to."

A moment passed, then her face hardened and she drew her hand away from his. "You want me to go back into therapy?"

"Not therapy as such. We'd just be two old friends, talking over things."

Delphine stared at him with astonishment and hurt. "But I've gotten well!"

"I think there are some problems we haven't resolved."

She eyed him warily, apprehensively. Then a knowing smile came onto her face. "I see what you're doing," she said. "You're projecting onto me. You poor old man, you're projecting *your* sickness, *your* weakness, *your* fear onto me! You're jealous, isn't that so, Sergius? Jealous of my strength? My health?"

"Is this health? Passing away your life in this dark, lonely office?"

"Health is people knowing who I am, recognizing me when I go out because they've seen me on television. Health is a million people reading my book. Health is the three hundred and fifty thousand dollars—*three hundred and fifty thousand,* Sergius—that I've made from this one book so far. Health is people from all over the country wanting to come to me. Health is being in demand—people needing me, loving me!"

"And what about you, Delphine? Do *you* love anyone?"

A look of pain fleeted across her face. "I've learned one can function without that," she said quietly.

"Then there's nothing more I can say," Winter said, and started out of the office.

He walked down the hallway slowly, with Delphine's limping footstep just behind him. As he passed the living room, he looked in at the young woman who was sitting on the mauve sofa. She was blond, very pretty, with the poignant, clouded face of a troubled angel.

"I'll be with you in a moment, dear," he heard Delphine say.

The girl nodded and tried to smile. She gazed out at Delphine with awe in her eyes, and hope, and fear.

Winter went on to the front door, then turned and faced Delphine.

"I won't be seeing you again, Sergius," she said.

"Perhaps not. But, remember, you can come and talk with me any time you want."

"I'll remember. But it's a matter of time. I'm just too busy these days."

With a half-turn of her head, Delphine glanced back at the

living room, and her whole being seemed to incline toward the waiting girl, impatiently, almost hungrily. Then she fixed her glowing, ecstatic eyes on Winter again and, her voice soft with sorrow, said, "There are so many people who need help! So many people!"

Mel Arrighi is the author of seven previously published novels, among them *Turkish White*, *The Hatchet Man*, and *Daddy Pig*. Also a dramatist, he has had two plays produced in New York and has written for television. He lives in New York City.